KAY BURLEY

First Ladies

HARPER

Harper
An imprint of HarperCollins*Publishers*
77–85 Fulham Palace Road,
Hammersmith, London W6 8JB

www.harpercollins.co.uk

A Paperback Original 2011
1

A catalogue record for this book
is available from the British Library

ISBN 978 0 00 736460 2

Set in Sabon by Palimpsest Book Production Limited,
Falkirk, Stirlingshire

Printed and bound in Great Britain by
Clays Ltd, St Ives plc

Mixed Sources
Product group from well-managed
forests and other controlled sources
www.fsc.org Cert no. SW-COC-001806
© 1996 Forest Stewardship Council

*To mum and dad
I miss you every day*

Acknowledgements

My heartfelt and continuing thanks to Kathy Lette, whose coaxing cajoling and belief in me has been immeasurable. Tasmina Perry who inspired me, with her own work. I want to be you when I grow up. Sarah Ritherdon, my wonderful editor, whose tough love saved the day. Caroline Michel, an agent who every author dreams of. Luigi Bonomi who made me smile, when I wanted to tear my hair out.

Damian McBride and George Pascoe-Watson, without whose insight into the corridors of power this book would not have been possible. Lord Mandelson, the so called Prince of Darkness, who's a softy really. Thank you for your kind words. Bertie Ahern, the former Taoiseach, for his guidance on Irish politics. And Gary Honeyford, a valued colleague, who made time to gently correct my schoolgirl mistakes. Claire Irvin and Victoria White who allowed me to cause havoc among their editorial teams at *She* and *Company* magazines.

Lord Archer, your words of wisdom were priceless. Nicola Ibison and Sophie Turner-Laing, who inspired me when I didn't believe. Kath Hinton who taught me the healing qualities of champagne and shopping, especially together.

Camilla Tew, Hannah Tallett and Ruth Gold, thank you ladies for having the patience to read my scribblings and offer sensible adjustments.

Thanks to Ants, Amanda, Peter, Jean, Penny, Nikki, Tessa, Dawn, Jacquie, Carol, Maria, Kate, Ellie, Amy, Jane, Phil, Deborah and Alan who all tolerated me being a rubbish friend, as I struggled with this writing lark. Especially Robert and Meribeth Parker, who sometimes refused to take no for an answer and dragged me away from my computer to feed me.

Thanks also to those who didn't want to be mentioned by name but whose guidance and insight are on every page.

Most of all, thank you to my raison d'être, my precious son Alexander whose loyalty and support swell me with pride.

1

'Tell me, have you met the Prime Minister before?'

It was a question that Valerie Jenson, the Prime Minister's wife, had asked her guests a thousand times. She was hosting a Christmas lunch at Chequers, the Buckinghamshire weekend home gifted to the nation by the Lee family at the end of the First World War. Since then it had been a place to relax for the serving leader and now an absolute must-have invite for all of London's 21st century media glitterati. They were certainly gathering in abundance to belatedly celebrate a landslide second term for Julian Jenson.

Valerie, a tall, slim, beautiful, 40-something sipped from her water glass. Dressed in McQueen couture, she was looking particularly stunning, even by her own high stand-ards. The first lady mingled with her guests, feigning interest at the responses to her stock question about meeting the PM. She had little curiosity about those who had gathered there. Scanning the Great Hall she vaguely recognised the editor of *The Times*, the political editor of the *Sun*, that chap who had compiled the top 100 most influential names in media for the *Guardian* and so many others she simply didn't care to know either.

Oh, how she hated the press. Why on earth couldn't her husband have invited David and Victoria Beckham instead, or Lorraine Kelly or Nancy Dell'Olio just as Tony and Cherie Blair had done during the Cool Britannia era? No, their guest lists had to be so turgid and dull.

In Valerie's view the most influential figure ever to have walked through the elegant oak front door of Chequers was her grandmother Betty. The 92-year-old was beside herself with excitement when invited to spend the weekend in one of the 10 bedrooms at the country retreat.

'Oh, our Valerie, you've done very well for yourself, love,' was Betty's first response as she walked into the French chateau-style home nestled in a fold of the Chiltern Hills. That seal of approval had guaranteed the 1,000-acre estate would always have a special place in Valerie's heart.

As she reflected on those happier times, Valerie allowed her mind to drift to a life before politics. She had been a successful businesswoman whose no-nonsense approach had struck fear in any member of the board who foolishly thought her Chanel LBD and killer heels meant she could be easily dismissed as frivolous.

Valerie was a grafter who had tirelessly and persistently hauled herself up the ranks to become managing director of non-fiction at First Stop publishing. Sporting biographies had been her speciality and the deal to sign Frank Lampard from under the noses of the bigger publishing houses was legendary. But the arrival of two babies and the demands of her work-aholic husband who was completely focused on achieving the highest political office meant something had to give. Hopes of becoming chief executive at First Stop, a real possibility after the Lampard deal, faded. Instead they gave way to the high profile, but for her far less inspiring role of 'first lady', which meant swapping Civvy Street for Downing Street.

Valerie couldn't deny that she had found the initial

transition tough and as the years passed she was becoming increasingly frustrated. Julian was frequently away on business and the children had both recently been sent to boarding school. Alone, but trying very hard not to feel unloved, Valerie was living what she considered a neglected existence trapped inside a media goldfish bowl. Every smile, grimace or wardrobe faux pas was minutely analysed, even by the broadsheet press who frankly should know better.

Valerie continued to meander through the familiar, grand reception room. It had previously played host to such esteemed company as Indira Gandhi and Nelson Mandela but this afternoon was filling up with TV bosses and Fleet Street's finest.

Her glass half full, Valerie sauntered among the throng, a gentle smile reassuring her apprehensive guests. None of them realised she was half cut so early in the day. She had promised herself she'd stay away from the booze but succumbing to a tiny little shot or two of vodka was making the time-filling much less tiresome. Still, she wished Julian would hurry up and join the gathering.

He was as usual on the phone, this time to Washington. The already tense situation in Afghanistan was escalating and both leaders were anxious to avoid announcing the need for more troops just before Christmas. It was not a challenge the PM really wanted to think about right now, but it helped that the US president, the most powerful woman in the world, was always keen to break off from government business to chat and heap praise on his broad, handsome shoulders.

There was no doubt that Julian was a ladies' man but Valerie had always been safe in the knowledge that despite his occasional wandering eye he was at heart only ever this lady's man. She loved him as intensely as when they'd first met.

Realising she may have to keep the pre-lunch small talk

rolling for some time yet Valerie took another reassuring sip from her glass. She preferred gin but Ben had suggested that odourless vodka would need less explanation. He was an oppressive bully but either tipple did the trick for her, so no matter.

Ben Watson was her husband's uber spin doctor and widely credited for Julian Jenson's overwhelming re-election victory. Valerie had tried very hard indeed to like Ben but had failed miserably. As he caught her eye she returned nothing more than a watery smile. Ben was anxious that Valerie's history of heavy drinking should not become a problem. The staff had been warned, no top ups for the first lady, no matter what, and he was reasonably confident she would be no trouble today.

This Christmas buffet lunch was a big deal for Julian Jenson and nothing could go wrong. It had been meticulously planned as a political springboard to launch his next five years in office. Ben had personally drawn up the guest list of heavy hitters, with only one or two adjustments by the PM. The lunch was also a belated thank you to those whose support the Party had enjoyed during the marathon six-week general election campaign. Support the Prime Minister would need to rely on in varying degrees throughout the life of the next Parliament. Lunch simply had to pass without incident.

Ben scanned the room and noticing a well-known Fleet Street editor arrive with his wife and beautiful daughter, he strode across to greet them warmly. The paper's support during the campaign had been key, especially the deft handling of that little mix up involving the home secretary. That escort girl posing provocatively for photographs on the ledge of his duck house could have been tricky. To make matters worse she had woken several of his elderly neighbours from their slumber by squealing with excitement while swimming naked in the freshly cleaned moat. Alarmingly, one of the Sundays had photographs and an interview with a disgruntled resident, but a timely chat with the friendly editor had ensured an obliging spoiler in his rival paper. Ben was relieved and suitably appreciative of the help. That was exactly the sort of valuable support that would guarantee the editor exclusive news of the latest government reshuffle planned for the following week. Ben couldn't count how many times he had warned the PM that the home secretary was a bloody liability. There was absolutely no doubt that he would be first out in the 'job swap' as he called it, when they were back in Downing Street tomorrow.

Valerie shuddered involuntarily as she watched Ben working his black magic by the door. Fixing a smile in place she walked towards the magnificent fireplace where two women she half recognised were nursing their wine glasses. They were admiring *The Lion and the Mouse,* a painting originally by Rubens but retouched by a 'relaxed' Churchill one evening when he felt the mouse too small for the expanse of canvas.

Finishing his conversation with the editor and his family, Ben Watson moved on to a TV executive he needed a brief but private chat with. It took only a couple of minutes for the tête-à-tête to reach a successful conclusion. Conversation over, he checked his watch again before glancing around the room, keen to keep an eye on Valerie until Julian made his entrance.

Ben noticed the perfect storm brewing just a moment too late.

He had warned Julian that inviting those two was a monumental mistake but the PM was still flushed with success at another five years in office. The country loved him, world leaders loved him, his family loved him. He was King of the World and could do no wrong. So, despite Ben's insistence,

Julian hadn't been prepared to listen and the invites had been posted.

Now all the strategy, the planning, the clever tricks and double spin over the last four years and particularly in the last few days of the general election campaign was about to come crashing down.

Ben stood motionless, paralysed at the realisation that even his superior talent could not prevent the calamity. He watched from the other side of the Great Hall as a meeting that would undoubtedly crucify the Prime Minister unfolded. There was nothing to be done. Valerie spoke first.

'So, tell me ladies, when have you met the Prime Minister before?'

July

2

Cabinet Office Briefing Room (COBRA), five months earlier

Julian Jenson slammed his hand onto the highly polished burr-walnut table.

'Bloody Germans, don't they know there's a war on?' he bellowed in the thankfully soundproofed room.

Shoving back his brown leather chair, he glared at the director of special forces. Julian's temper was once again getting the better of him. Publicly he was always the suave, sophisticated PM with a cheery smile and a relaxed manner but on days like this he was finding it increasingly difficult to control himself. Ben had had a gentle word a couple of times about shouting at the staff. Personally, he didn't give a monkey's but hadn't wanted them talking to the press, not after that nonsense with Brown and the bullying helpline. If necessary, he could spin it into pre-election tension, but he'd rather not have to.

Looking around at the roll call of familiar faces seated at the table, Julian was reminded that the situation in Afghanistan was dire. The heads of MI5 and MI6 were there as were the defence secretary and the foreign secretary, who

9

despite the benefit of expensive air-conditioning in the war room was still sweating profusely, leaving dark, wet patches on his hand-tailored navy blue Turnbull and Asser shirt.

The men and woman had been urgently summoned by Julian to the fortified, windowless bunker that is the Cabinet Office Briefing Room or COBRA where the British government meets to coordinate its response in times of emergency. In the past, such meetings had taken place in Room A, hence the acronym. Recently the meetings had moved to Room F. However COBRF didn't have the same ring to it, so COBRA it remained. The only item on the agenda was very much an emergency and the atmosphere was heavy.

The special forces director stood behind the high-tech lectern with its built-in computer screen bringing him the very latest developments from Helmand Province. An extremely volatile hostage situation involving several Britons was ongoing. The PM's loud interruption was not welcome and ignoring it the director continued with his briefing.

'As you are aware, Prime Minister, an elite team of my men had been part of a NATO mission to liberate four journalists, two of them British, the two others German women. I'm afraid the mission has not been successful. Three people have been killed, four others taken captive by the Taliban. It is of significant concern to me that there are British service personnel among them.'

The foreign secretary was attempting to use a monogrammed handkerchief to wipe away sweat from his brow but with little effect. Leaning forward, he spoke via a microphone from his seated position at the table.

'Prime Minister, we believe the Taliban has asked for a substantial reward for the safe return of the journalists. It has further demanded that Germany and Britain immediately remove all their troops from Afghan soil.'

So far the hostage crisis was being kept under the radar

by both governments. A news blackout meant the public was unaware that Britons and Germans were being held hostage. Enormous plasma screens around the walls of the bunker confirmed the blackout. The TVs were tuned to the country's 24-hour news stations which were speculating ad infinitum about an early general election. It clearly illustrated that the channels had no better news to bring their viewers. For now the crisis was still a secret, giving COBRA valuable time to discuss and plan. The foreign secretary continued.

'There has been no further update today on the fate of the British service personnel or the civilians. As the SF director has already said this is of significant concern. At this stage we are unclear what action, if any, the German chancellor plans to take.'

'Bollocks,' shouted Julian. He jabbed his finger towards a screen where the TV anchor was informing viewers of breaking news from Berlin. The volume was increased and the room fell silent.

'We're just hearing here at Sky News centre that Germany could start withdrawing its troops from Afghanistan soon. We're not sure what has prompted the German chancellor's decision or of time lines at this stage. We believe it would involve closing the Faizabad base in Northern Afghanistan and removing about 500 soldiers. The move is expected to come in for heavy criticism from the United States. The president had been expected to ask for more troops from Berlin. We're not yet aware of the British government's reaction to the news,' continued the TV anchor before the sound was muted.

'Oh yes we are,' growled Julian and reiterated his earlier statement.

'Don't the Germans know there's a bloody war on?'

Clenching his fists he turned determinedly back to the lectern, a signal for the director to continue his briefing.

'What's the plan?'

'Well sir, our highly trained negotiators are being briefed as we speak. We are aware that the Taliban demand is not acceptable to our government and we are acting within that parameter. We are also formulating a liberation mission, but that of course would need your approval. I suggest a continued news blackout for 48 hours while plans progress.'

'Done,' agreed Julian, already marching towards the blast-proof, steel-reinforced door. He was keen to leave the room before his short fuse burned out. Stopping abruptly he turned to make a final point.

'We need to get our people out of there as quickly and safely as possible. I am sure you remember Sierra Leone well, Director? That's the happy conclusion I am looking for here. I want no more mistakes on this mission. Do I make myself clear?'

Operation Barras had been a successful SAS and SBS rescue mission carried out in the African jungle. Royal Irish Rangers, working on a UN peace-keeping mission had been taken hostage by ruthless and heavily armed thugs. All the special forces had worked supremely well together and the hostages returned home safely from the war torn country.

'Indeed so sir, we are working towards the same outcome on this occasion,' concluded the director, his confident tone disguising an uneasy concern.

Julian nodded curtly and headed off with Ben along the series of anonymous corridors which led back to Downing Street. As they emerged into the daylight inside Number 10, Ben was the first to speak.

'You know what, boss? You should visit our boys pronto. This German bollocks will cause a wobble in the polls and we don't want that so close to an election, now do we? I can just read the bloody headlines now: *Bring Our Boys Home. Why Are We There? PM Puts Our Troops In Unnecessary Danger.*

It's A War We Can't Win. I suggest you go instead of heading to Chequers. Tell you what, let's take the defence secretary with us as well. She can announce that her son is set to join the Armed Forces when he finishes his full-time education.'

Ben was warming to his theme and had little concern about the ramifications.

Julian laughed at Ben's ridiculous suggestion.

'But Judith's son is studying the sciences, Ben, and plans to go on to Bristol University. He wants to be a surgeon.'

'Not as much as his mother wants to remain in government,' responded his ever-scheming right hand man with a wry smile. Julian never ceased to be amazed at his spin doctor's Machiavellian streak but it was a discussion for another time as the pair walked along the plush carpeted corridor towards his office.

'OK, I agree we should go to Helmand and we can . . .' but his train of thought was interrupted by an incoming text message on his mobile.

Call vanessa URGENT.

Vanessa Lewis was his personal lawyer. She rarely contacted the PM during office hours. It must be important. He looked up at the Downing Street grid which mapped out his schedule for the day and saw he had a 10 minute window.

'Have to take this, Ben. Tell Judith we're going by the end of the week, leave the announcement about her son for me to raise with her, please. I'll be back in a few minutes.'

Leaving Ben glued to his phone to make the necessary plans, Julian headed towards his private office and closed the door. He dialled Vanessa on a pay-as-you go mobile, the most effective way to make a secure call. He assumed her text meant she had important confidential information to impart.

'Hi Vanessa darling, what's up?'

The lawyer was used to her client's over familiar tone and really rather liked it.

'Hello Julian, I expect you have already seen page 22 of *The Times* today. I thought it may be of interest given your present predicament.'

Vanessa was referring to Julian's domestic dilemma. The Jenson marriage which had once been a happy union, built on solid foundations of love and respect, had slowly disintegrated into two individuals who shared little more than parenting duties.

Gradually, Julian had become frustrated with Valerie and his attentions were now very much focused on another. She was a rather foxy, glossy magazine editor by the name of Sally Simpson. Valerie was resisting any change, but Julian was determined. 'Of course I love you, but not in that way' had become his nocturnal mantra as a more and more distressed Valerie tried to convince him his enthusiasm could be reignited. But Julian believed that the passion with his wife was long gone and it was now only Sally who aroused his interest. Originally, he had hoped to continue in a lame marriage while nurturing a delicious but discreet relationship with Sally. Those hopes were no longer realistic, not least because of a worrying increase in Valerie's drinking.

Of course that wasn't the only reason. Desire played its part. Sally was smart, sassy and occasionally ever so slightly tempestuous. Their soirees were a welcome distraction as the charade of his marriage staggered on.

Fading beauty maybe, but always deliciously raunchy, there was nothing she wouldn't try. In fact, she had a rather persuasive way of illustrating to 'JJ', as she called him, what he would be missing on the nights he reluctantly returned to the marital bed. Sally was adventurous, insatiable and always thrilled to see him. It was temptation beyond endurance and with the children now safely away at school, Julian

14

had for the first time begun thinking the unthinkable: a divorce.

Vanessa Lewis was the best divorce lawyer in the business. She had handled both high profile royalty and celebrity break-ups with a deftness that only a few could muster. She was also very choosy about her cases, politely but firmly rejecting requests from several very well known would-be clients if she considered their behaviour somewhat crass, especially when they had seemed desperate to play out their break-ups in the full glare of publicity.

Julian was slightly piqued by the query about his morning reading. Did she really need to bother him with a newspaper review?

'No darling, I haven't seen the article you're referring to quite yet, tad busy running the country. Is it really this urgent to call during the day?'

The silence from the other end of the line spoke volumes. Suitably chastised, Julian reached over to the pile of papers still sitting untouched on his desk and turned to the indicated page.

Stop Giving Ex-Wives These Undeserved Millions, Urges Expert In Family Law read the headline. It was accompanied by a photograph of Heather Mills who had received £24m after a three-year marriage to Sir Paul McCartney.

Vanessa was very aware that one of the major stumbling blocks to Julian divorcing Valerie had been the Jenson fortune. Old money and an ancestral pile must stay within the family. His father would articulate the same view more eloquently when Julian eventually plucked up the courage to broach the matter with him. Fine to party with show-girls but keep your hand on your wallet and the old girl happy had always been his watchwords. The family motto – 'Never Surrender' – came to mind as Julian skimmed through the story.

'Most interesting, but I have been married to Valerie for almost 20 years. How will this help me?'

'Well, Prime Minister,' Vanessa's formality suggesting the clock was running on her £800 an hour plus uplift fees, 'the reason for my rude interruption during office hours is that today I find myself lunching with Bruce MacDonald from the Family Division of the High Court. As you may well know, he is an expert in all matters matrimonial.

'After luncheon, Bruce is heading up to St Andrew's for a few days R&R with several of his learned colleagues. I am sure that during their well-earned break they may well find themselves comfortably ensconced at the 19th. While there they will no doubt want to discuss the increasing injustices of a wife of however many years' marriage, receiving half of her husband's assets without any parliamentary legislation to that effect.

'Indeed my learned friend may be keen to further increase his already impressive profile by subsequently taking to task some of my own colleagues. I refer to those representing spouses whose demands on a husband's fortunes could be considered by any right-minded person to be unreasonable.

'While you would no doubt accept that Valerie should most certainly be entitled to significant funds, the Jenson inheritance was quite obviously not built up during the course of the marriage. A claim against half of those funds could therefore be reasonably contested.

'I assume I have your permission to broach the subject with Bruce, Prime Minister?'

Julian was only a second behind Vanessa's razor sharp brain.

'You're brilliant.'

'And reassuringly expensive,' concluded Vanessa before replacing the receiver without another word.

Julian laughed. That was exactly the sort of conversation

16

that could hold the key to setting him free from these chafing matrimonial handcuffs and he felt his mood now lighten considerably. Julian swung his feet off the desk, threw *The Times* back onto the newspaper pile and headed for the lift to take him up to the Downing Street flat. He was optimistic that Valerie's Valium should have worn off by this time of the morning.

Entering the mirrored elevator Julian admired his matinee idol reflection as he waited the few moments it would take to reach the third floor. The pressure of high political office had taken little toll on his handsome face. With a rigorous exercise regime and bespoke Jermyn Street suits, he cut a dashing figure as he strode through the corridors of power at the Palace of Westminster. Confident, powerful and privileged, Julian Jenson feared little apart from the ire of his father which he went to great lengths to avoid.

As the lift doors creaked open he bounded up the last few thickly carpeted stairs to the family's apartment, a determined spring in his step, a potentially much more rosy future ahead of him.

3

'Hello darling, goodness, you look so handsome this morning. Are you having a lovely day?'

Valerie was still in her pyjamas and watching Jeremy Kyle baiting his guests on an old portable TV in the kitchen. Frustrated at the scene, Julian ran his manicured fingers through the hair above his ear and scoffed. How could it have come to this? Here he was perfectly groomed in a Gieves and Hawkes tailored suit accompanied by an Hermès tie, a gift from Sally, while walking tall in the finest Church's shoes. Significant government business of the day had already been tackled. In comparison, Valerie, a once sultry, curvaceous beauty who had made his pulse race whenever he even thought of her was sitting cross legged on a chair still wearing crumpled M&S nightwear, the remnants of breakfast around her mouth and no sign of a plan to dress any time soon.

'We have to talk. It's important,' began Julian sternly.

'If it's about Germany pulling out of Afghanistan darling, I know. What on earth are we going to do? They can be so unreliable, can't they? Have you had an opportunity to speak to the president yet, what does she think?'

Valerie was doing her best to avoid Julian's glare. She had

18

learned that the best way to deal with her increasingly judgmental husband was to play the role of 'wifey'. No challenges, no confrontation, no grey matter, just acquiescence at all times.

'It's not about Afghanistan.' He remained stone-faced.

'Oh, isn't it darling?' she replied breezily while unsuccessfully trying to push bed-head hair away from her still bleary brown eyes. She reached forward and selected another piece of toast from the rack her mother had bought them as a wedding gift from John Lewis, before surreptitiously half turning to watch the TV again.

'What else is happening in the world?'

'It's not about politics or what's happening in the news, Valerie. It's about us. I want to talk about us.' Julian involuntarily straightened the knot on his expensive tie before continuing.

'I want a divorce. Do you understand me Valerie, I want a divorce. Your behaviour has become intolerable and no longer constitutes what I consider to be a proper marriage.'

He had been rehearsing the phrase, prepped by Vanessa, in the lift on the way up to the flat and had delivered it with the confidence of a House of Commons dispatch box speech.

Jeremy Kyle was about to open a DNA result in front of a hushed studio audience. The burglar who had just been released from a two-year jail sentence wanted to know if it was possible for him to be the father of the month-old baby his wife was cradling. Valerie gasped loudly. Julian was unsure whether her reaction was in response to Jeremy Kyle's bombshell announcement or his own, but nevertheless pressed on.

'We can't continue to live our lives like this. I am deeply unhappy as I'm sure you are. We merely exist together and I don't intend to spend the rest of my life with a woman who has little interest in anything other than daytime TV. Our marriage is over, Valerie. We should end it now before any further heartache is caused to either of us.'

Julian was aware that his tone was rather too forceful. Strangely he was also finding the soliloquy more challenging than he had expected. He had once loved Valerie more than anyone else in the world, but standing here in the Number 10 kitchen, that seemed a lifetime ago and there must be an end to it.

Once her raison d'être, Valerie now tried very hard to avoid any unnecessary communication with her husband, increasingly fearful of what he might do or say next. In her darker moments she had perhaps realised that this day may come. Life with Julian was hollow. No love, no friendship, no passion, just co-existence. Yes, she had feared a show-down, but hadn't considered how she would react.

To make matters worse she was still feeling a little fuzzy from her bedtime medication. Reluctant to continue with the conversation but realising the choice was not hers, she reached for the battered old remote control, banged it on the side of the table to make sure it would work and pointed it at the TV. The kitchen fell quiet.

Aware of her husband's glare, Valerie continued to watch the set, willing the white dot not to disappear from the centre of the screen. Eventually though it did and taking a sip of tea, she very slowly turned to look up at the angry face of a man who had been her lover, her confidant and her best friend for so many years, now little more than a stranger.

A thousand thoughts flooded into her confused mind. The conversation had caught her off guard and she was faintly aware that she couldn't feel her legs. The room was starting to spin and as she reached for a sip of water she noticed the glass was shaking in her hand.

Julian continued to stand silently, impassive, still waiting for a response. Valerie tried very hard to stay calm, but was beginning to feel nauseous. She gripped the sides of the Formica table, unsuccessfully attempting to fight off the panic and clear her blurry head. She pulled her knees up to her chest and wrapped her shaking arms tightly around them.

Without any further warning, the first tears began to fall, soaking into her well-worn pyjamas. The relentless demands of political life had created an intolerable gilded cage for Valerie in which she felt trapped. Her energy had been sapped away a long time ago, she now merely existed with no identity beyond that of Julian's wife. But she had accepted the confines of that fur-lined rut and despite everything she still loved her husband.

Her first instinct was to fling her arms around him but feared she may not be able to stand. Instead she remained seated and eventually found the strength to speak.

'Don't talk like this, darling. I love you so very, very much. Whatever has happened, whatever has brought us to this, I know that we can work it out together. My life, my whole life is you and the children. Think about our beautiful children?'

Julian hated to see his once strong, focused, elegant wife sitting broken in front of him but he had steeled himself for an emotional confrontation and would not be deflected.

'What about the children, Valerie? What sort of mother would be half cut for most of the day, then unconscious on sleeping pills at night?'

Valerie rocked in her chair, surprised at the venom in Julian's voice, realising this really was the long anticipated marriage showdown. Nevertheless, floppy not stroppy, was the best way forward with her judgmental husband.

'I know darling, I know, but it's because at the moment I'm finding life very difficult to cope with. You're travelling so often and now the children are away at school. I feel so lonely sometimes. That's why I drink. It dulls the sadness, and the pills, well they help me sleep, darling. But, I can stop, really I can. I just need to know that you still love me and we can start afresh, start again. I love you so much.'

A subtle bleep from Julian's mobile interrupted the

confrontation. Irritated still further he dug the phone from the pocket of his tailored suit. It was a text message from Sally:

Have you told her yet? x

Always immaculate timing my love, thought Julian as he dropped the phone back into his pocket and turned again to face his distraught wife.

'Well, I can no longer accept that this is the sum of our life together. I want a divorce. It's over, Valerie. I no longer love you.'

And there it was, five words that struck the fatal blow. I No Longer Love You.

Valerie lowered her head and remained still, save for the tears dripping off the end of her nose. She felt desperation overwhelm her. Without her husband's love there was no light or shade, just grey.

A tap at the door announced the untimely arrival of Ben. He had been eavesdropping outside in the hallway and waiting for the conversation to conclude. Seemingly oblivious to Valerie's pain he wandered into the kitchen nonchalantly and selected a slice of toast from the rack. Smothering it with butter he plonked himself down at the table. Valerie was shocked at the crassness even by Ben's standards and turned away. He didn't mind, the dislike was entirely mutual. She considered him a snake in the grass and he thought Valerie an old soak and millstone to any potential general election campaign.

To further increase the embarrassment, Ben began whistling 'Always look on the bright side of life' out of tune to himself while munching contentedly on his stolen breakfast. Valerie wiped her nose and wondered how long this odious little man would linger at her kitchen table. Eventually he spoke.

'You're needed back in COBRA, PM.'

Without another word the two men left.

Valerie remained seated, still unable to move. Once again tears began to fall, splashing onto the newspaper lying open on the table in front of her. Her husband had failed to notice that while watching TV she had also been reading Page 22 of *The Times*. She may be rudderless, but lacking intelligence, certainly not. Julian's plans were completely transparent to the woman who had spent more than 20 years at his side. She understood that her husband was choosing to ask for a divorce now because he thought there was a chance he could jettison her without undue financial or material damage.

Some politicians are inspired by a need for social justice. Some have a desire for individual greatness while still helping those less able. Julian's principal incentive was without doubt to further improve his personal and financial standing on the international stage when he finally stepped down as British PM. The direction of their lives over the last few months meant he had no intention of sharing that with Valerie.

Those were the stark facts and she started to tremble as the ramifications of what had just happened began to crystallise. By trying to be all things to everyone she had lost sight of who she was. She simply couldn't allow this.

Looking around her at the basic kitchen Valerie cursed, not for the first time, at the limitations of living within the confines of the public purse. She had accepted long ago that her taste would have to be tempered as long as they lived in Downing Street. She had tried to convince Julian that they could fund a refurbishment of the kitchen out of their own pockets, but Ben had as usual vetoed her suggestions.

Pushing her hands down onto the chipped table and pressing her bare feet on the linoleum floor, Valerie slowly straightened her spine, closed her eyes for a moment and breathed deeply.

She began to focus on the inner strength that had taken her, despite all the odds, to Oxford and then marching onwards, smashing through the glass ceiling at First Stop publishing. Deep inside she knew there was still that steel core that had given her the strength to support her husband as he climbed the slippery pole of UK politics. That had allowed her to graciously relinquish her grip at First Stop, safe in the knowledge she could return in due course.

She tried desperately to reach it but it was still just beyond her grasp, for now.

Valerie stretched for the remote control and flicked back to Jeremy Kyle. The ad break had just ended and he was finally about to reveal the much anticipated results.

'The DNA results show that Shane is not your son,' he told the jailbird.

'I want a divorce.'

'Not you too,' whispered a washed-out Valerie. 'Not you too.'

As the audience bayed and the host said goodbye to his viewers for another day yet another commercial break began, this time with a promotion for *Where There's Muck There's Brass*, a new cash in the attic reality show starring the latest TV sweetheart, Jimmy Phillips.

Valerie once again flicked off the set and feeling more in control of her legs she stood and padded through to the sitting room and opened the drinks cabinet. Pouring herself a significant gin and tonic, she took a rather un-ladylike gulp before curling up contentedly on one of the sofas. Patiently, Valerie waited for the alcohol to transport her to a more tranquil place where she could recapture happier times with Julian.

Valerie Mitchell had met her future husband on the very first day of her three-year history course at Corpus Christi College, Oxford. Her parents had driven her all the way from Lancashire in their ageing Ford Mondeo. Her dad, Frank, had been a bit worried about the temperature gauge as they trundled down the M6 in the slow lane at exactly 56 mph, the precise speed for optimum fuel efficiency. He had insisted on pulling in at Keele services for half an hour just to be on the safe side.

'Best to let the engine cool down a little bit, love,' suggested her father as he reversed precisely into a parking space and switched off the ignition. As they settled down, her mother Sheila produced an ageing but still functional tartan decorated thermos flask from her cavernous shopping bag. Balancing it on the dashboard she reached into the bag again. This time she produced a Tupperware box crammed with freshly made sandwiches.

'Would you like a nice butty and a lovely cup of tea to calm those butterflies, our Valerie? I know I'm going to.'

Sheila had insisted on making the 300-mile round trip journey to keep her husband company. 'We've got corned beef or cheese.'

'No, I'm fine thanks, Mum,' smiled Valerie. She was content to sit in the back seat and look out at the motorway traffic as it zoomed by their stationary vehicle. So many people with so many places to go while the Mitchell family sat patiently waiting for a radiator needle to indicate all was well with the car engine.

'We could go inside and have a cuppa in the service station if you want, Mum?'

'Oh no our Valerie, it's much too expensive. Anyway, there's no need, I've got some of your favourite Jammy Dodgers in my bag.'

As Frank took off his driving gloves and reached for a sandwich, Valerie knew they'd be there for at least half an hour. She settled herself further into the slightly frayed back seat and watched bemused as her father did his best to tune in the antiquated car radio. He was searching hopelessly for the cricket scores on long wave.

Three further stops, several games of I Spy and car snooker and many, many hours later the ancient Mondeo finally arrived at Corpus Christi College, Oxford. Frank, with the help of his wife's map-reading skills and a well-thumbed copy of the RAC's *Road Atlas of Great Britain*, pulled up outside their daughter's new home. Noticing a parking space just next to the quadrangle, he made full use of the wing and rear view mirrors, easing the steering column precisely through his leather gloved hands to reverse perfectly into the spot. Frank came to a complete stop and applied the handbrake before switching off the engine.

The silence within the car was overwhelming. It was the first time any of the Mitchell family had secured a place at such a prestigious university and no one knew quite what to say. Her nervous parents were trying hard to hide their anxieties and Valerie in particular was very unsure about what university life held for her. Oxbridge was certainly an achievement. Her headmistress had tried to prepare her for the cultural and academic challenges ahead but Valerie still felt as timid as a re-homed kitten as she peered past the porter's lodge and into the quadrangle beyond.

'Love, it's very grand, isn't it?' said her mother. She was subconsciously trying to slide just a little lower in the passenger seat but found herself restricted by her tightly fastened belt.

'I am so proud of you, love,' added her father. 'Imagine our Valerie coming to Oxford to study, Sheila. Who would have thought it, eh?'

They turned together and smiled reassuringly at Valerie who was staring wide-eyed at the majestic 16th century architecture that would become familiar scenery over the next three years. Looking at her watch, Valerie realised her parents would have to start on their journey to Lancashire soon if they hoped to make it back that day. Taking a deep breath she reached for the car handle and opened the door to her future.

Unfortunately, she hadn't seen the cyclist coming and caught him square in the handle bars, knocking him off balance and sending him crashing to the ground.

Julian Jenson noticed the car door opening a moment too

late. He was thrown clean over the bars and landed face first onto the unforgiving tarmac. The stinging sensation that promised deep grazes or worse reached his brain only a moment or two before Frank Mitchell was by his side. Frank was a trained first aider and immediately took control.

'Don't move, lad. Where does it hurt? Sheila, get the first aid kit from the glove box, will you love?'

Frank slipped off his car coat and placed it carefully under Julian's head. Valerie couldn't help but think that her father's reaction was perhaps a little over the top for a strapping bloke who after all had only fallen off his bike. Still she knew better than to challenge her father when it came to first aid. He had been so proud of his St John's Ambulance course success. His laminated certificate took pride of place on the kitchen wall, enhanced by the most expensive frame Sheila could find in John Lewis.

'Can you hear me, lad? Tell me, where does it hurt?' pressed Frank who was checking Julian's pulse before considering the recovery position.

The initial shock was quickly wearing off for Julian and he began trying to disentangle himself from the jigsaw puzzle of metal which was preventing him from standing.

'No, no don't move, lad. Try to stay calm. I'm here, you'll be fine,' continued Frank, his tone relaxed, reassuring and very, very northern.

Julian was by now completely aware of the increasingly comedic situation. His embarrassment at not being able to safely negotiate a sleepy Oxford lane grew even more acute as he noticed the bemused student crowd that had gathered around them. He was not prepared to lie prostrate in the middle of the road outside Corpus Christi for a moment longer. Moving to sit up, Julian caught his first glance of Valerie, half concerned, half laughing at his dilemma. Slim, tall, her mini dress accentuating legs that went all the way up to the maker's label. He was immediately smitten by her teenage beauty.

Valerie was oblivious to his interest. She had never really been aware of her appearance. Always more concerned about her studies, boyfriends were unimportant to the straight A student. It had been left to her brother Monty, named by his patriotic father after the D-Day commander, to attract the opposite sex. Their mother trod a well-worn path to the hall phone as night after night young ladies would call in the hope of speaking to the most sought after boy in school.

But Valerie's own blossoming beauty was certainly not lost on Julian. Smiling broadly while politely extricating himself from Frank's concerned grasp, he offered his hand.

'Hello, my name's Julian.'

'Valerie Mitchell and these are my parents Sheila and Frank.'

Valerie was already charmed by this very handsome undergraduate who had manners to match.

'I'm really very sorry about knocking you off your bike, I hope you're OK?'

Frank was concerned about concussion and was about to speak but Sheila, noticing the chemistry between her daughter and this dashing young man, touched her husband's arm. A smile and 25 years together meant no further communication was necessary. Frank went to collect Valerie's suitcase from the boot while Sheila started to search earnestly for nothing in particular from the glove box.

'Have you just arrived? Perhaps I could help you with your things and show you to your room?'

Valerie nodded acceptance and Julian raised his arm to guide the way. He was still slightly flushed from the drama but no longer concerned about his grazed limbs or bruised pride.

The fond long-ago memories faded, interrupted by the phone on the table next to the over-stuffed sofa. Valerie picked up the receiver to be greeted by the welcome voice of her brother Monty.

'Hiyah sis, how are you doing? Can we meet up later?'

Monty Mitchell was a supreme cricketer and the nation's newest sporting hero. He'd called while driving his plush new Aston Martin to Lord's to play in the second test of The Ashes Series. Superstition meant he always rang his big sister before he reached the ground. Other match day rituals included putting his left pad on first, eating half a Double Decker and keeping a lucky bottle top in his pocket. The last one had become more difficult after the Kiwis were caught doing the same. Their ball-tampering motive had been somewhat different to his lucky omen reasons.

Valerie was always happy to hear from her baby brother and she was determined that he shouldn't pick up on her desperately stressful morning. Ten years her junior, she considered herself a mother figure to him.

'Hi love, all set for today?'

'Yeah, thanks. I'm on speaker phone sis, Julia is with me in the car. I'm dropping her off at Harrods, she has a wedding dress fitting.'

His stunning blonde girlfriend wiggled excitedly in the hand-trimmed soft leather seat of her fiancé's DB9 while lovingly caressing her platinum set, emerald cut, Cartier engagement ring. She had wanted five carats but Monty had guided her towards a less 'ostentatious' stone. A pouting Julia had no problem with showy but Monty had been insistent.

Celeb magazine was paying for the reception and honeymoon of their October wedding. In exchange the magazine would secure exclusive access of the couple on their big day along with their family and friends, including of course the country's dashingly handsome Prime Minister. But the magazine's generosity did not extend to wedding rings and Julia's expensive taste was making quite a dent in Monty's finances.

Valerie disliked Julia, though her little brother would never know. It was the ease with which the self-absorbed 22-year-old wriggled her size zero frame into the role of free-spending cricketing WAG that was so difficult for her to stomach. Valerie was also deeply unsure of Julia's loyalty to her brother.

Their parents had always had a loving marriage. She couldn't remember even a crossed word between the couple who still sat holding hands together on the sofa watching *Coronation Street* or *Strictly Come Dancing*. Problems with her marriage would be hard for them to cope with but romantic challenges for Monty too would push them too far. Valerie shook her head, she was being silly. Monty's nuptials were right on track and she was wrong to project her own insecurities onto his wedding plans.

'Not sure if you fancy it, but you and Julian can come to watch us thrash the Aussies for the afternoon session. I've organised a couple of seats for you in the ECB box if you want, sis. Please will you come, be great to see you?'

'Oh, I do hope so, love. Julian is snowed under at the moment, but we'll try to come along for an hour or so sometime after lunch if we possibly can.'

Valerie knew that while her husband had that very morning steadfastly insisted on a divorce, he would not pass on an opportunity to bask in the reflected glory of his brother-in-law's cricketing success at Lord's. He would also be very unlikely to turn down a refreshing ale or two after the game as a guest of the MCC. Valerie meanwhile would be expected to wait patiently elsewhere in the ground meekly abiding by the ridiculous 'no ladies' rule in the Long Room.

'That'd be great. I hope so. Really look forward to seeing you later, sis. Love ya loads.'

Valerie blew her brother a telephone kiss before ending the call, draining her drink and headed a little unsteadily towards the shower.

4

Celeb magazine

Across town Sally Simpson stood next to the glass-topped desk in her corner office on the executive floor of *Celeb* magazine. She was admiring her reflection in a floor-to-ceiling art deco, bevelled-edge mirror, bought as a birthday gift by her Prime Minister lover. Sally had popped in to John Frieda for a quick blow dry on the way to work and was very pleased with her new Cheryl Cole style extensions. Lester was right, brunette did suit her skin tone much better than blonde. She would have to change a significant amount of her wardrobe as a result of course but the new season Prada was just perfect for her tiny frame. She'd ask the magazine's marketing team to ring the designer's press office later in the day.

Ballsy and brusque, Sally had now been the editor of *Celeb* for the past three years. As with all professional challenges throughout her career she had been stratospherically successful in taking the magazine from a lacklustre publication to the biggest selling weekly glossy.

A once timid child, educated by nuns, she was the only daughter of elderly Irish parents who had insisted she complete her full time education with a course in medicine at Trinity College, Dublin. But the role of tending the sick held little importance for Sally who was more interested in sharpening a pencil than a scalpel and she began a life-long love of journalism while editing the university magazine.

Many suitors had tried to ensnare the carefree beauty over the years but she did not concern herself with those who lacked the intoxicating combination of power and money. Sally had almost succumbed in her 30s when she found herself single and pregnant, but after a nanosecond of contemplation she kept the child and junked the bloke.

All of that had been 'BJ' – Before Julian, the Adonis who was the man of her dreams.

Sally moved a little closer to the mirror for closer scrutiny of a little off the peg two piece she'd picked up on her way in. She stroked her cheek. The little bit of filler last week had seen off those pesky lines around her nose for another six months. That together with her regular gym, sweat and no beers routine guaranteed that although north of 50 she still had the body any 30-year-old would die for. Yes, Sally was very pleased indeed with herself and the ultra-confident editor was sure her life was about to become a whole lot sweeter.

Her staff had also been delighted at the magazine's rise to the top step of the podium but still knew to tread carefully around the mercurial boss. She certainly didn't suffer fools gladly, a fact that her ever cautious deputy was only too aware of as she walked in with the layouts for this week's magazine. Sally had gambled that Julian would finally be as good as his word and ask for a divorce. It would be the perfect opportunity to openly criticise her oblivious love rival in this week's edition.

'How's it looking?' she asked Maria, who was this morning dressed head-to-toe in Armani Black Label.

Sally was very aware that her deputy, while loyal for now, was completely focused on taking over the top job just as soon as she possibly could. She reminded Sally of herself 30 years ago and the wise old hack knew exactly how to outflank any attempted coup.

Looking down at the proofs as they were spread out on her desk, Sally was trying her best to concentrate while finding it hard to take the smile off her face. With rumours rife of a possible general election before the autumn, politics was a hot topic in the newspapers. She knew Julian hadn't yet decided on a date and that only served to fuel speculation.

Sally was fascinated by the subject but accepted that political policy was a dry topic for her readers. *Celeb*'s demographic was much more interested in sporting celebrities and pop stars than politicians. They really couldn't care less about a general election for now. But, Sally was a woman on a mission, she wanted to be first lady and that meant Julian had to win the election. So, Sally had dreamed up a popular angle to elevate Julian's profile in her magazine but with a very personal twist.

Celeb was carrying six pages on the summer fashion faux pas of the Prime Minister's wife.

'*Valerieeek!*' screamed the headline. It was a story ghost written by one of her team but with the by-line of this season's top supermodel. Accompanying the words were a series of unflattering photographs of Valerie, taken from various awkward angles.

'NFU' were sometimes offered by photographers, but usually rejected by discerning picture editors as 'not for us' images. Sally had demanded as many as her team could track down.

'Seriously sweetie, I want to know what you think?'

Maria thought the spread was unfair and unkind but knew her boss well enough not to comment negatively.

'I think it's very marketable, Sal. Should put on 10,000 copies this week at least. Want to do a TV ad to go with it?'

Sally knew from Julian's complaints that Valerie was becoming increasingly boozy and brittle. Now with today's divorce body blow, a TV campaign would perhaps be too much for her to take. Looking down at the photographs again, she hesitated for just a moment. Was this really necessary? Running a photo spread like this was bullying in its ugliest form.

A single mum for most of her son's life, Sally had seen firsthand the impact harassment had had on her teenage boy, Sean. A bright, lively child at junior school, he had become withdrawn when he moved up to secondary school. His teachers could offer no reason for the change but the stark difference in her son was a continuing challenge for both of them. Sean spent hours in his room playing violent computer games, unwilling or unable to communicate with his mother.

Sally reached down to smooth out the creases of her skin-tight suit. Was it really appropriate to further ridicule an already vulnerable Valerie with a TV ad campaign as well?

'Yes please, Maria. Can you bid for the slot in the *Coronation Street* ad break? They had 10 million viewers last night.'

Maria nodded, hurriedly collecting up the proofs and trying to leave as quickly as possible, keen not to betray her distaste at her boss's vitriol. She needn't have worried. Sally was completely unaware of her deputy's view, much too wrapped up in the morning events and JJ's text. Wandering over to the window and looking out over the Thames, Sally sighed.

IT'S DONE was all the simple message from Julian had said, but she knew that now finally, finally she could plan their future together. The road had been long and the journey often challenging but after more broken promises than a political party manifesto, Julian Jenson was ready to divorce his wife, Valerie, for her, Sally Simpson.

As she gazed out at the pleasure boats taking foreign tourists on expensive excursions up the river, Sally began to reminisce about how she had first met the Prime Minister.

She laughed out loud as she remembered straddling a urinal at the upmarket Saatchi Gallery on London's Kings Road. Not for her the polite but lengthy line for the ladies.

Julian had nipped out of the tedious function and escaped into a lavatory cubicle to text a lover, well away from the prying eyes of Ben Watson. Joy of text over he'd slid open the bolt on the cubicle door and was momentarily shocked at the sight of Sally with her Prada calf length dress hitched up high. She was mid-pee while also feverishly tapping away on her BlackBerry advising the office about a late page change in that week's issue of *Celeb*. Sally was startled at the unexpected appearance of the Prime Minister, but quickly in control.

'Prime Minister, how lovely not to have seen you this evening, especially in such embarrassing circumstances.'

Julian grinned widely at her chutzpah, nodded his head in understanding and turned to leave.

'But it would be equally charming to meet you in a more appropriate setting,' added Sally, rather too briskly.

Julian kept his back to the woman who he was sure he recognised but couldn't quite place, giving her time to wriggle from her unladylike podium, while he took the opportunity to surreptitiously glance at another incoming text.

'What a simply charming idea. Should we touch base via my communications director, Ben?'

Julian was aware of the sound of Sally's Jimmy Choos clipping across the tiled floor announcing her arrival at the washbasins. He turned to her but this time he was met by a scowl. Sally was furious at the very suggestion she should communicate through a third party. Especially one she had sacked.

Her previous incarnation had been in regional newspapers. She'd been one of several young women journalists brought in by a Birmingham newspaper editor to brush aside the dusty remnants of the Old Boys' Club and provide more female friendly content for readers. Ben Watson was the paper's all-powerful chief reporter who hadn't taken too kindly to the flighty bit of skirt moving in on his patch. Sally considered Ben a sexist, Machiavellian bigot who she nicknamed Gollum, an unflattering tag that stuck. Nevertheless, he was a supreme journalist and his regular, if questionably obtained political exclusives, kept his by-line high in the paper.

But Sally was a patient woman, certain that the over-confident hack would err. His fatal mistake had come after holding court at one of his regular liquid lunches. Foolishly stumbling back to the office in a pugilistic mood he had swung an inebriated fist at a rival. It was something that might not have been considered out of place before the arrival of the new tranche of females. Sally snatched the opportunity and alerted the boss who called them into his office. Despite Ben's protests the editor couldn't lose face in front of Sally and he fired him on the spot. A furious drunken lunge at her had guaranteed he left without any financial recompense, while a triumphant Sally continued to make her way up the newspaper ladder.

After a period in the journalistic wilderness, Ben opted for a poacher turned gatekeeper role and a new career in politics. He had quickly become the brains and confidant of rising star Julian Jenson and subsequent ubiquitous spin doctor when Julian became Prime Minister.

Eight years later, Ben still hated Sally Simpson and the emotion was entirely mutual. Furiously rinsing her hands at the mention of his name, Sally washed away the awkward meeting. Sensing her displeasure but unsure what had prompted it, Julian was keen to make amends but also equally keen to leave. The inappropriateness of the meeting, in a white-tiled urinal in one of London's swankiest venues, would not read well if a journalist wandered in.

'I must return to my hosts, but perhaps if you gave me your card, we could reconvene at a more appropriate location?'

Sally was not to be placated so easily though. Did he not even know who she was?

'Well, Prime Minister, my diary is pretty full but why don't I ask one of my writing team on *Celeb* to get in touch with your Press Office. I'm sure there must be something we could do with you mid-term.'

Of course, she's the editor of that rather successful glossy mag, thought Julian. He knew that he recognised the gorgeous creature from somewhere. Her photograph was in the diary columns all the time. Wow, she looked pretty foxy in the flesh.

'Here's a better idea. Why not find space in your diary for a light lunch out at Chequers, say the Sunday after next? Always better to be interviewed by the editor, guaranteed a much bigger spread in the magazine.'

Sally and Julian both smiled and with a slight nod of acceptance she succumbed, offering her card before heading back to the party.

Bullying, that's what Sally would interview the Prime Minister about. *Celeb* had launched a campaign against bullying in the work place and it was building up some serious traction with readers. The campaign had been Maria's idea. The irony was lost on Sally. An authored piece by Julian Jenson would add significant weight.

A week or so and a couple of flirtatious texts later and plans were made for the interview. On the day itself Julian had duly dispatched his family from Chequers to varying parts of the UK. He had a light lunch all planned and greeted Sally warmly at the door before guiding her through to the Hawtrey Room.

Sally was as excited as a teenager on a first date. She'd taken forever choosing what to wear before settling on a new season Prada with high neck and knee length hem. Nothing too risqué, especially for lunch. She couldn't remember having felt so nervous, ridiculous given she was perfectly comfortable in the presence of pop stars or royalty.

Julian Jenson's magnetism was legendary but she had always dismissed it as silly girls being intoxicated by celebrity and had passed on every Downing Street invite to an appreciative member of her team instead.

Now here she was alone with him and completely spellbound by this charmer who oozed power and charisma. What to say? She felt a spark between them and was unusually lost for words. As always, Julian was in control.

'Something to start?'

Sally was immediately flirtatious and gambled with an inquisitive: 'Depends how you would like to finish?'

'Simultaneously,' had been Julian's razor sharp response and Sally was smitten.

That had been two years ago and the relationship had flourished, without the need for Ben's involvement. She knew from her sources that Gollum was furious and determined to get rid of her. But Sally was in no way concerned. She still knew where all the bodies were buried and while the paper had hushed up the reason for his departure at the time, she was confident that Julian would certainly not take kindly to being told his spin doctor had tried to hit a woman. Gollum could cause her no harm without self-destructing too.

For now though it was a different foe who was very much in Sally's sights and as she wandered back to her desk, she began to ponder editorial content about Valerie for next week's magazine.

5

COBRA

As his lover plotted the very public destruction of her rival, Julian found himself back in COBRA much sooner than anticipated. A ridiculous schoolgirl gaffe by the defence secretary had put the lives of the hostages in Afghanistan at risk. An immediate reconvene had been requested by the director of special forces.

Leaving 10 Downing Street by the front door, the defence secretary had ignored the waiting press shouting the obligatory questions from behind the barriers at the other side of the street. Deep in thought at the fate of the hostages, she'd headed back to her own department. Unfortunately, long lenses trained on the paperwork in her right hand had captured the 'TOP SECRET' heading. It hadn't taken journalists long to enlarge the images and realise her elementary mistake.

Government Plans Dramatic Rescue Of British Hostages From Taliban Camp, had been the headline on *The Times'* website within minutes of her error. Until that point only a handful of people had known of the hostage situation. Now the entire world was aware of what was happening and swift action was paramount. The mood in the room was tense.

'You're a stupid fucking bint,' yelled Ben as Judith walked into COBRA.

'Don't you ever read the papers? Long lenses, top secret documents and the most famous street in the world . . . what's wrong with this fucking picture? It's not fucking where's fucking Wally. It's people's lives we're talking about here.

'What the fuck is wrong with you? You know it happened to Mandelson and he's smart. It happened to Caroline Flint, and let's face it sister, she has better legs than you, but surprise, surprise the lenses were still trained on the paper-work rather than the pins.

'I'm going to buy you a fucking briefcase for Christmas. You're going to need it for carrying your useless applications to the job shop.'

Judith reddened and slunk across to her seat. No one else spoke for a moment. Ben's tongue-lashing was plainly over the top but everyone realised the magnitude of the mistake and the possible human cost. Eventually the silence was broken by the clipped delivery of the director of special forces.

'Prime Minister, if I may update you on the latest developments.

'We now believe there to be two strongholds which need to be penetrated. The enemy has demanded a reward of £10 million for the safe return of all Britons. Further, they require all British troops be removed from Afghan soil within a period of three months.

'We have provided the Taliban leader with a satellite phone to better communicate further requests to us.'

'Should we offer him a selection of iced cup cakes and an ironed copy of the *Sunday Times* too?' interrupted a sarcastic Ben who was monitoring the TV screens broadcasting what they knew about the hostage situation.

Despite frantically trying to call as many heads of news channels as he could think of to plead they maintain the news blackout, he was already too late. The immediacy of 24-hour coverage meant the defence secretary's gaffe had been broadcast even before he could reach for his BlackBerry. In addition, online websites detailed every aspect of the story. It would be all over tomorrow's papers too. The 48 hours grace period to help put a rescue plan together had been blown out of the water.

The director ignored Ben's sarcasm and continued.

'The use of the satellite phone has allowed us to pinpoint the exact position of the Taliban leader and the hostages. As a result we have put in place an observation team. They have a series of parabolic microphones with them which will further allow us to monitor discussions in the camp. It would seem the spirits among the Taliban are high, especially after the expectation that the German government is set to comply with their demands.'

Ben leaned across to whisper to Julian and the room fell silent again for several moments. Eventually the PM nodded at the SF director to continue with his briefing.

'We propose, Prime Minister, the use of Chinook helicopters carrying RAF Special Forces along with a combined SAS/SBS fire team. Stealth will be impossible. Maximum speed and firepower is our preferred option, offering the enemy little time to react and kill the hostages.'

With that the director closed his file and returned to his hushed audience at the COBRA table. Almost imperceptibly he turned his chair slightly away from the defence secretary as he sat down.

'What is the maximum risk of casualties?' asked Julian.

'Well sir, we hope that it would be extremely limited. The mission is of course dangerous for everyone taking part including all those on the ground. However, we are hopeful of a successful conclusion, with the liberation of all the hostages and without any military loss of life.'

Julian paused and closed his eyes. The room was now completely silent save for the hum of the over-worked air-conditioning system. His options were limited. What to do? A failed mission would mean the loss of many lives but there was no other option, no alternative. He opened his eyes again and spoke resolutely.

'Yes, I am happy to give my authority to this mission. God's speed.'

'Very good, sir.'

Ben and Julian remained seated as the other attendees filed out to start their work.

'So, my suggestion?' pressed Ben, clearly quite pleased with himself.

'The official visit to Thailand is tomorrow until Monday, boss. By then the rescue mission will have been completed, one way or another. Obviously, we're hoping successfully. Anyway, what do you think of the idea of a stopover in Helmand on our way back to the UK? We can be there just long enough to pick up the freed hostages and then return to Heathrow. All hail the conquering hero. An election winner in the bag.'

Julian pondered the plan and pushed to the back of his mind a less positive outcome. Ben could read the tension on Julian's face and changed the subject.

'So, it's all over with the Mrs then?'

Julian winced at his spin doctor's bluntness. The resolution to leave Valerie had been a pivotal moment in his life. He didn't want to dwell on the morning's events and the pain he was causing his wife. Although he'd been hard on Valerie in the kitchen, it was still a very tough decision. He was now trying to block out the hurt and the repercussions, not yet prepared to face up to the devastating impact it would have on the children. Julian stood to leave and the two men walked the well-worn path back to Number 10 in silence.

The light-hearted delivery of Ben's question about Valerie had a very serious underlying point. He knew the sniff of a Downing Street marriage scandal would have a major impact on Julian's political career, unless carefully managed. His planning and plotting of the PM's meteoric rise from the backbenches had been fraught with challenges and he wasn't about to allow the small matter of a divorce to blow him off course.

Ben already had the germ of a press campaign in mind, but needed to be absolutely sure that separation was on the cards before he embarked on the dark art of spin of which he was an undisputed grand master. Arriving back at Number 10 within minutes, Ben suggested a quick stroll round the garden. He needed more time with his boss in private.

They still had some time before the Macmillan Cancer Nurses reception in the White Room so Julian nodded his agreement. As they walked out into the sunshine, both men took a moment to enjoy the heat. It was turning into a barbecue summer, despite Met Office predictions of a washout. Ben leaned down to pick some mint from the herb patch and rubbed it between his fingers. It released a smell that reminded him of Pimms, his long-suffering wife Gayle's favourite tipple. He smiled at the thought of his three young boys. They'd be playing football in the playground at school about now.

Continuing to stroll in relative privacy with Julian, he noticed his boss was playing anxiously with the signet ring on his little finger, a symbol of his lineage. Ben had tried to get him to ditch it saying it made him look like a toff at the dispatch box. Julian who had already dropped the second part of his double barreled name to make him more user friendly on the way to being elected, had stood firm on the family signet ring.

'You know that I'll take care of things, don't you, boss? We have so many favours to pull in from our Fleet Street mates. It'll be pretty straightforward to keep things under wraps until at least after the election. Then another successful vote in the bag and the great British public will have five years to fall out of love with Valerie and in love with Sally if that's what you really want.'

The spin doctor paused for his boss to say no it wasn't what he wanted and he was ditching Sally too, but Julian remained silent. Oh well, a dream for another day thought Ben. He had no intention of making the transition easy for Sally, but now was not the time to kick up dust.

'Don't worry, I have everything under control, honestly. Give Sally a call and I'll make small talk with the nurses for five minutes.'

Julian smiled appreciatively at his gatekeeper and reaching for his mobile, turned to take another lap of the garden alone.

'Hello darling, sorry I haven't called before now, we have a serious situation developing in Afghanistan, but I did it, I told her, it's you and me now.'

Sally squealed with delight at confirmation of the news. She had been perched on the edge of the leather sofa in her office when Julian called. Her tight suit made it impossible for her to relax any further into the sumptuous seat. The waiting was over. There had been so many shattered dreams over the last two years she had begun to lose heart. Now, finally, the long, lonely nights yearning for him to be with her punctuated by the snatched, exquisite evenings of laughter and lovemaking would meld into a lifetime together.

There had been so much heartache in the past. The carefree days of her late 20s had given way to the challenges of raising a child alone. It had been more of a trial than she could ever have expected and dark moods had been in danger of overwhelming her. On occasion Sally had bitterly regretted turning away from Sean's father and had considered returning to him. Then Julian had burst into her life and brought excitement, happiness and affection. For the first time in her life, she had allowed herself to fall in love.

Sally had so many things to say to him, but it could all wait. Instead she pressed the phone closer to her cheek and whispered into the receiver, 'I love you.'

Julian was strolling across the lawn and smiled at one of the parks' gardeners planting salad leaves into pots in a corner of the walled garden. Aware he now had an audience he spoke more quietly.

'Thank you darling, remember though, we can't break cover until after the election, but I simply have to spend time with you before then. Come to Thailand with me on the official visit. We'll say you're doing a feature about how hard our PM works,' added Julian, pleased at his own ability to spin illicit sex into a magazine spread. Ben would be proud of him.

'Anyway, I'll see you later darling. Bye.'

Dropping the phone back into his pocket, Julian bounded up the metal staircase to the terrace and through the open French doors back into Number 10. Sally's smile wilted into a pout as she replayed the conversation in her mind.

'Why didn't he tell me he loved me too?'

Stung by what she considered Julian's insensitivity, she wandered back to her desk computer and took another look at the photographs of Valerie. She had certainly been caught in the most unflattering of poses. Sally used her mouse to search through the images that even she had initially rejected as too unkind to publish. She paused at one of the first lady sat at a nursery school table with three-year-olds, her dress falling awkwardly and revealing unflattering underwear.

'Right, that's in as well now,' she spat spitefully. Buoyed by bitchiness, Sally gathered up her Dior bag and sunglasses and headed for a spot of retail therapy in preparation for her trip to the Far East.

6

Thailand

'It's over, Prime Minister, it is OVER.'

Ben had disturbed his breathless boss in the very early hours with the news that the siege in Afghanistan had ended. Julian gently eased himself away from under Sally's glistening body writhing seductively above him and focused instead on his spin doctor's mobile phone call.

'Successfully?' asked Julian as he swung his legs from the bed and headed for the bathroom of the luxurious hotel in Bangkok.

'Successfully,' replied Ben.

'There's a call coming through from the director of special forces in 30 minutes to a secure line at the Embassy. See you in 10 in the hotel lobby.'

'Be right there.'

Admiring his tanned, muscular frame in the bathroom mirror, Julian smiled with relief and not for the first time considered his good fortune. The last four years had seen him blossom from a tentative, hesitant politician into a bright star on the world stage. Today, a smile and a handshake from Julian Jenson could iron out many a potential diplomatic row, as it had done here in Thailand as well.

The two countries were very old friends who had helped each other through numerous challenges in the past. Occasionally they'd quarrelled over issues of national pride and recently the relationship had been struggling through a sticky trade patch. That was before the arrival of the enchanting British PM with his Savile Row suits, hand made shoes and winning smile. Add to that an expensively educated and suitably deferential diplomatic team and any local differences were easily smoothed over.

Now the military operation had also ended successfully and Julian was relieved to finally be free of the stress that had dominated the last couple of days. He had always been confident Anglo-Thai relations could be easily improved but the hourly updates on the critical situation in Afghanistan had been much more worrying, the outcome by no means certain.

Ben's warning that any loss of life would play very badly in the polls had irritated Julian who insisted they should be more concerned about saving lives than counting votes. Ben had relied that enough support at the election would allow them to continue in their efforts to rebuild Afghanistan and bring the troops home. In the end both men could be content with the triumphant conclusion.

Julian was distracted as his lover strolled into the bathroom, naked. He thought her figure sensational for a woman in her mid-40s. He had no idea she had already reached another milestone and Sally went to great lengths to make sure he never would. In their two years together Julian had constantly lavished her with gifts and adoration. She was mischievous and magical, she had the brains and a body that had made him want to throw everything away and start a new life with her.

But, the look on Sally's face now suggested there was perhaps one person not completely satisfied with the morning's business so far. Glancing at his watch and realising there was just enough time to change that, he lifted her into his arms.

'I'm so sorry, darling. Where were we?'

Ben sat in the foyer of the Conrad Hotel waiting impatiently for the PM who was no doubt satisfying his stupid bitch floozy who really shouldn't be here anyway. He was furious that Julian insisted she make the journey with them to the Far East. Now Valerie was effectively toast, Ben's master plan had been to gently ease Sally out of the picture too. He hadn't reckoned that his nemesis would move quite so quickly into Valerie's shoes.

Until now Julian had done little without Ben's guidance and the supremely powerful spin doctor was determined not to relinquish his influence to a woman who had him sacked. OK, he'd taken a swing at her but it would be his word against hers if she ever tried to use it against him with Julian. He certainly wasn't about to allow Sally to start taking control of Julian's life, conveniently pushing him onto the scrapheap, not again.

Ben clenched his fists and his blood pressure began to rise as he remembered his time in the jobless wilderness with a then pregnant wife and child to support. Struggling to compose himself, he focused instead on the events of the previous evening and his night out with the London press pack.

He'd been on a fact-finding tour of the more choice sections of Bangkok nightlife with some of the usual suspects. Ben was used to being surrounded by sycophantic hacks vying for his attention. An invite to party with 'Gollum' was seldom rejected by those who saw it as a key to face-time with the Prime Minister. Ben's motives were rather different. Foreign trips like this never failed to provide him with enough ammo to keep almost anything out of the papers when necessary.

Walking down the street together in search of a decent watering hole, the other boys had noticed Erica first as she entered a non-descript bar. Initially, everyone had thought the leggy, scantily clad beauty was of the fairer sex. As she turned in the doorway, only the most intoxicated would have made any further mistake. Ben had joined in the laddish jokes and insults while making a mental note of the address.

After an over-priced dinner and a few more drinks, the pack had moved on to visit the Asia Hotel. There they commented rowdily on a drag performance before politely being asked to leave. Ben had secretly found it fascinating but was careful not to register his enjoyment other than bloke-ish backslapping and the odd guffaw as the drunken group headed back to the team hotel.

Earlier in the evening he'd organised for Sally to be escorted up to the office on the cordoned off prime-ministerial floor. Her cover, for the benefit of security personnel, was to check a few facts for her article. When the coast was clear, she was discreetly invited by Julian into the connecting bedroom suite. They were still entertaining themselves there as the group arrived back.

Downstairs and as the press pack began to retire, Ben spent a few minutes loitering in the lobby. He waited just long enough to take a discreet note of which political correspondents were choosing to spend the night in a bedroom other than their own. A shorthand record of those drunkenly tucked up with others they shouldn't be and Ben retraced his steps back downtown to the large yellow house with no number on the door. Venturing nervously inside he ordered a Jack and Coke before finding a red Dralon-covered booth where he could see the other customers in the bar without being seen. Ben was initially shocked when he realised it was a totally over the top go-go boy club. He had seen television footage of anything-goes Bangkok nightlife and had even indulged in the odd internet foray, but coming face to face with the reality was still an eye-opener. Considering it too much for a straight guy, Ben was about to leave when he noticed Erica arrive at the bar.

A tall, dark haired beauty, her long, long legs were soon intertwined with a middle-aged overweight consort, who appeared totally enraptured by Erica's flawless skin and delicately tattooed eyebrows. She was wearing little more than a bikini top which revealed far too much of her pert breasts. A skin-tight, thigh skimming skirt was complemented with Satan-red, four-inch heels and completed the lady boy look. From his cautious viewing point Ben was very much admiring the scenery and found himself spellbound as Erica leaned forward and whispered suggestively in the tourist's ear. It took only a few minutes before the obviously aroused man with a strong American accent was paying the extortionate bar bill and heading off with his prize to a nearby hotel.

Content to be a spectator, Ben chuckled at the punter's gullibility, fascinated at how others chose to enjoy their downtime. Settling into the booth, Ben was starting to unwind. Another drag performance began, his second of the night but the first he could enjoy without inhibitions. Ben ordered another drink and began to relax with his mate Jack Daniels.

As the performance ended he drained his glass and looked at his watch, 2.30 am, time to call it a night. He absentmindedly reached for his BlackBerry which he always kept beside him to unobtrusively monitor calls and emails. As he did so his hand brushed against something much softer than the sharp lines of the phone.

'Hi,' whispered Erica. 'Fancy a drink?'

She'd noticed the short, bald gringo watching her earlier while she sat at the bar. To be honest, she really didn't fancy it much but business was slow and she was still $2,000 short for her final operation. His Rolex suggested there was cash in his wallet. Men like this one never carried credit cards in gay bars. Cash couldn't be traced back home.

A quick fumble here in the booth, then they'd wander through to the stall in the bathroom. Looking at him it would be over in 30 seconds and she could be off with the wallet before he had his trousers back up. He would never report it to the police.

'I was just leaving,' stuttered Ben. 'Really, just leaving. Time to go.'

'Oh no, please don't go just yet,' pressed Erica, sliding a little closer to Ben as she signalled to the barman.

'Another JD and coke please, José.'

'I noticed you watching me earlier, you know. Is there anything I can do for you?'

'No, no, no,' said a flustered Ben. 'This is not really my scene. I'm not gay.'

Erica giggled at Ben's embarrassment and allowed her hand to rest on his inner thigh. The tension in Ben's muscles started easing as he felt his interest grow.

'I'm sure you're not. I'm sure you're not,' she soothed and moved just a little closer still.

'Sex and sexuality come without guilt here in Thailand. We are happy to enjoy love with both men and women. We make no moral judgments, we just like to have fun. Interesting, no?'

Erica had practised the short speech taught to her by a bisexual language professor for many months. It was now honed to perfection. But Ben was less than convinced and moving Erica's hand away he grabbed his BlackBerry and threw some dollars on the table to pay for the drinks.

'Really, I have to go.'

'Well, if you must, but if you are ever here again perhaps we could grab something to eat,' teased Erica coquettishly. 'My English is limited and I would love to try some.'

'OK, yeah, that would be great. I'm a really good teacher,' spluttered Ben as he fled, knocking over an empty chair in his rush for the door.

Still shaking with tiredness and confusion, he had arrived back at the Conrad Hotel just a few minutes before the call from London came informing him that the siege was over.

7

British Embassy, Bangkok

'Very many congratulations and my heartfelt thanks to everyone involved.'

Julian was speaking on a secure conference link to COBRA in London from the comfortable surroundings of the British Embassy in Bangkok. The director of special forces along with the heads of MI5 and MI6 had gathered there to pass on the excellent news.

'Thank you, Prime Minister. Our team did a first class job and the mission was completed successfully without any loss of life. A magnificent result.'

Ben nodded his agreement while making the mental calculation that there was just enough time to brief some of his favoured hacks for tomorrow's papers. He hastily scribbled on a notepad in front of Julian: 'Details'.

Standing to pace the ornate room, Julian conveyed his spin doctor's request while Ben scribbled bullet point notes.

'Well, sir, the assault began before dawn. There was little movement reported in the camp and our plan was to capture the enemy off guard by hitting them fast and hard. My men entered the compound with the aid of ropes lowered from Chinooks. The enemy was quickly located and while it is fair to say they were disorganised they were nevertheless completely fearless. After some 30 minutes of concentrated resistance they were eventually and effectively neutralised. All the hostages were being held together and were liberated. They were then taken back to Camp Bastion without further injury or incident. One of the females has suffered significant unpleasantness at the hands of her captors and is receiving appropriate medical attention.'

Julian winced, understanding that the diplomatic language used by the director veiled a sinister sexual assault on one of the German women.

'Once again Director, I would ask you to please pass on my appreciation to everyone involved in bringing the operation to a successful conclusion. Well done.'

Julian was just about to end the call when Ben began frantically scribbling again. Julian paused to read the note and then spoke once more to London.

'As an indication of my gratitude, Director, I would very much appreciate the chance to visit Camp Bastion. I would like to take the opportunity to personally thank our brave men and women for risking their lives. I will ask my aide to organise a slight detour as I return from Thailand to the UK.

'I am also happy to offer the hostages the comfort of returning to London aboard my official flight.'

'Fucking opportunistic politicians' mouthed the director to those gathered 6,000 miles away underground in a Whitehall bunker, but responded audibly with, 'Very good, Prime Minister.'

Even before the conversation had ended, Ben was already texting the political editors of *The Times*, *Sun* and *Telegraph*, summoning them to an off-the-record briefing in the lobby of the Conrad Hotel. That would give them just enough time for the story to make it into their papers' final editions. The added bonus for Ben was to stiff the other political editors who hadn't played ball on helping to bury the home secretary duck house gaffe. The first they would know about the end of the siege was when it was splashed across the front pages of their rivals. That would leave them with some serious explaining to do back in London.

'This is going to be sensational press. I can see tomorrow's headlines now: *"FREE. We've Got 'Em."*'

'I'll tell you what boss, we need to seriously think about calling that election when we get back. It's in the fucking bag.'

August

8

Downing Street

Isla McGovern first met the Prime Minister while she was perched uncomfortably on a silver TV camera equipment box opposite Number 10. At the time she was cringing at the memory of bad sex with her ex-boss. It had reminded her of being slobbered on by an overzealous Labrador as he bounced around with over-excited eyes and a wet nose.

She had been staked outside the most famous front door in the world for the last two weeks, though it felt more like an eternity. A newcomer to *Have a Nice Day UK*, the country's most watched breakfast show, she was far too pretty to receive kindness from any envious female producer. As a result, here she was on the graveyard shift for the 13th consecutive night with only a mildly flirtatious cameraman for company. Isla was bored stiff and a seriously unhappy camper.

It was 4.30 am and in the gloomy shadows of Downing Street she pulled her new, brightly coloured Karen Millen coat a little tighter around her too thin shoulders and allowed herself to feel very deflated indeed. Even the police officer usually posted on the step of the renowned front door had been given a break during the hours of darkness. He was no doubt drinking builder's tea with his buddies in the security centre. Isla meanwhile was freezing her bits off without a prayer of ever being on TV. What on earth was she doing here?

She'd swapped her killer whale status in North East news for that of a minnow in the piranha infested waters of London telly in the hope of achieving current affairs fame and Reality TV fortune.

Her CV was limited, boasting only an average degree from journalism college and a short stint as a reporter on regional TV. But Isla's unique selling point was that she was an absolute stunner unlike some others on her course who sadly had been gifted with a great face for radio. Her Twiggy-style bobbed blonde hair framed an alabaster, impish face that presented without a flaw. Striking green eyes offered a clue to her Irish ancestry and confirmation to the more observant that the collars and cuffs couldn't possibly match. If there was perhaps one chink in her armour, it was her dress sense. Isla had no clue what worked together and was far too new at the TV game for any station to have provided her with the services of a much-needed stylist.

Nevertheless, it was of no real surprise to anyone that she had strolled into her first job in Newcastle. Without question she had the X factor and was already making a cute little mark there when she was spotted by Michael Grifton. The head of news at *Have a Nice Day UK* had embarked on one of his regular nationwide trawls to search out new talent, or Totty Touting as his deputy referred to it, when he first saw Isla.

She was lightning quick to take up his offer of bright lights, big city, but it hadn't taken long for her great expectations to crash and burn. She was discovering the hard way that pretty girls whose looks play well with men who should know better couldn't flutter their eyelids as effectively with female decision makers.

'You must be freezing, pet. That coat will never keep you warm on overnights, even if it is erm, a very striking colour. Never mind, it won't be long now till the shift change. You OK?'

Bob was a wise old cameraman who had been in television since Adam was a boy and had seen many youngsters come and go. Some of them made it, but most of them didn't. He didn't hold out much hope for this one either. He didn't usually do overnights but was building up some overtime cash to celebrate his 40th wedding anniversary in style with his lovely lady wife.

'Yeah, I'm fine thanks, Bob. I was out for a big lunch today. Think I might have caught a bit of wine flu!' shivered Isla.

Bob thought from her intonation that might have been a joke but wasn't really sure. Instead he returned to his roll-up and Isla returned to her misery as she hunched her shoulders against the cold. There really was nothing glamorous about London life and politics, it was just show business for ugly people. The Prime Minister lives in a mid terrace that wouldn't be worth much up north and she was surrounded by dull, dull colleagues. What on earth was she thinking, giving up *Northumbria Tonight* for this?

The move to London had been a complete mistake and it was time to head home again. Confident that the editor she'd slept with as an insurance policy just before leaving *Northumbria Tonight* would look favourably on her return, Isla began to scheme. Luckily, she'd also saved those suggestive text messages from that bloke high up in the sports department, safely transferred from her phone and on to her home computer.

There was of course the niggling issue of that old bag presenter Christine Solomon continuing to squeeze her not insignificant backside into what should rightly be Isla's own anchor seat. That wasn't a major concern, though. Christine was ancient and must be due for yet another face-lift soon. Isla put her at maybe even as old as 40. The month or so off air that Christine would take for her surgery to settle would give Isla the chance to step in and shine.

Isla looked at her watch again. Another hour and a half before the on air reporter would take over the Downing Street position and she could head home to bed. To pass the time, she began mapping her triumphant return up the A1 and absent-mindedly scrolled through her mobile in search of her former news editor's number. As she did so, the huge, high gloss black door swung open for the umpteenth time that night. Isla, who remembered reading somewhere that it was changed from a dark green colour during the First World War but still had a wonky zero, in tribute to the badly fitted digit on the original door, didn't flinch. She had grown accustomed to a cleaner arriving for his early morning shift or, as was more likely, an on-duty press officer striding over importantly across the threshold. Ever since the rumours of an imminent general election first began to swirl a month or so ago, the press team had also had to work overnights.

Just then, Bob grabbed his camera and Isla instinctively spun around to face the door.

'Go on pet, now or never,' whispered Bob.

But instead of rising to the challenge, the young girl sat paralysed with fear as none other than Julian Jenson stood smiling in front of her.

Unable to sleep, Julian had been pacing the corridors of Downing Street for hours. He stopped as he always did to admire the portrait of his heroine Margaret Thatcher placed towards the top of the Grand Staircase rebuilt by William

Kent in the 18th century. Black-and-white photographs and engravings of previous leaders also lined the walls all the way up the staircase. Only Winston Churchill had the honour of his picture appearing twice. The images were rearranged slightly when necessary to make space for a portrait of the departing incumbent. Julian didn't plan to be sitting for his photograph any time soon, quietly confident of victory when he finally called the next election.

He had meandered through into the ostentatious Pillared Room, where he hosted the US president for the first time. He was hopeful Monty and the other England cricketers would soon be celebrating their Ashes victory there too. Julian stopped to smile at the portrait of Queen Elizabeth I over the fireplace remembering how his heroine Maggie had controversially had it replaced by a portrait of William Pitt during her dynasty. 'That's my girl,' laughed Julian as his mind turned again to thoughts of an election.

He'd been dithering for weeks about going to the country early and had up to another year in office if he chose, but holding on to the bitter end meant his power would undoubtedly be diluted. Those bastards in the cabinet, already sharpening their samurai swords would wield them mercilessly. The successful outcome to the Afghanistan siege had bought him time but also further focused his mind. Ben thought now was the optimum moment to allow the people their voice. Julian still wasn't sure.

Having paced to the far wall of the White Room where Edward Heath had kept his grand piano, Julian retraced his steps back to the wrought iron staircase.

Sitting a couple of steps down and gazing up at Maggie's photo Julian contemplated his options. Ben's words of warning came to mind: 'Remember boss, how dithering cost Brown?'

Of course, he was right. Unsure of whether to call an early

election, Gordon Brown had finally and belatedly decided against it. The opposition had a field day, creating *'The One and Only Bottler Brown, Zero Strength'* beer bottles and hurriedly issuing them to titillated journalists. There was still one behind the Stranger's Bar overlooking the terrace at the House of Commons. Julian smiled wryly at the damage a spin doctor could do.

He stood and peered through the bomb-proof, lace-curtain draped window and into the half light of Downing Street below. That's where it all ended for Maggie, he thought, casting his mind back to the images of a tearful Margaret Thatcher leaving Number 10 in the back of her government car for the very last time. She had misjudged the party mood and they'd knifed her.

Julian was distracted by the pretty little thing with her sharp blonde bob and strangely mismatched burnt orange coat brightening up the other side of the road. Tenacious journalists had been camped outside Downing Street for weeks in anticipation of an election, though their numbers had dwindled of late. Was the country losing interest? If he waited much longer would voters tire of the speculation? Even worse, by the time he did finally announce a date would they be so bored they wouldn't even bother to turn out to vote?

In that moment Julian Jenson made his decision. That was it – he would call a snap election. No more dithering, choice made. He glanced at his Cartier, 4.30 am. Ben wouldn't be up yet, Sally was away for a weekend with her son and there was no one else he could trust so he began to make his own plans.

He decided on a news conference in the Rose Garden to make the announcement. Tony Blair often invited the press into the garden for monthly news conferences when the weather was fine. It had also been the perfect romantic setting for the Dave and Nick love-in, with their his and his podia. Hadn't John Major made a back me or sack me speech there too? There was probably still one of his father's handmade gnomes nestling somewhere among the plants. Of course, a Rose Garden news conference, that's exactly what he would do. Brilliant idea, but who to tell?

With no Ben Watson to advise caution or calculation, Julian was acting on impulse. Ignoring the warning sirens blaring in his head, he bounded down the stairs.

Nodding brusquely at a surprised custodian who had dashed to open the famous door, Julian was across the street before he had time to consider the wisdom of his actions. Now standing directly in front of the startled journalist, he was completely stunned by the exquisite creature. Even after a night without sleep and a reddening nose from the cold, the young reporter was astonishingly pretty. Julian instantly forgot the mantra of all public figures, especially Gordon Brown: *You're never alone with a microphone.*

'Hey, I'm Julian, the Prime Minister. How ya doin'? You must be freezing out here? A gorgeous little thing like you should be tucked up warm in bed at this time of night.'

Julian had tried to sound the right side of flirtatious but failed miserably. That should have been enough. He should have turned on his heel and run as fast as he could back to the safety of Number 10. But completely smitten by this pretty little thing standing in front of him in the half-light, he stupidly pressed on.

'You know what, I now have the answer to that rather intriguing question you all keep on asking. Why not pop into the Rose Garden later and I'll tell you all about it.'

Bob the cameraman couldn't believe what he was hearing. He had covered countless political stories in the past and had interviewed Prime Ministers as far back as Harold Wilson, but never in the middle of the night without the aid of a spin doctor before. What was Julian Jenson thinking? Bob realised it must be a ridiculous attempt at flirting with young Isla. He stood rock steady and kept on recording.

Despite the lust and pumping adrenaline, Julian noticed the red light on the top of Bob's camera just in time and stopped abruptly. He began to panic. What on earth was he doing making small talk with a cute, wide-eyed journalist in the dark? Every fibre was now screaming at him to dash back and hide behind the glossy front door. But he was being recorded and Julian knew what he had just said would be broadcast ad infinitum unless he could offer something more newsworthy. His brain was racing. What to say, what could he say?

Isla was looking up at the Prime Minister completely smitten. She had never seen him in person before and he was so much more handsome than he appeared on TV. He was almost a foot taller than her and so muscular he could probably lift her with one arm. For a moment, she couldn't remember if he was married, not that that really mattered.

The arch seducer detected her interest but reluctantly accepted now wasn't the time to act on it. Gathering his thoughts, Julian finally spoke again.

'I really do hope you are not too cold standing out here, night after night? I assume you must be from breakfast television. *HND*, is it? Well, I would like your viewers to be the first to know that I am planning to ask Her Majesty to dissolve Parliament. I will go further and tell you that I plan to call the next election for 3rd October. I will hold a news conference in the Rose Garden later today to further outline my intentions.'

Isla still sat motionless on her camera case throne. Bob kicked her hard in the shins while continuing to record every word. He hadn't been voted cameraman of the year two years running for nothing. Granted that was 20 years ago but Bob was safe in the knowledge he still had what it took to deliver the goods and he was right.

Shaken into action, Isla jumped to her feet.

'Are you telling *Have a Nice Day UK* viewers that you are calling an early election, Prime Minister?' she blurted.

But it was too late. Julian had come to his senses and was already half way across the street and soon disappeared back inside Number 10, the door slamming shut behind him.

'Got it,' said Bob, matter-of-factly.

'Get on to the news desk, tell 'em he's confirmed it to us exclusive and to release it to the Press Association with a 6 am embargo. Make sure they email to confirm they'll credit us, if they don't fuck 'em and give it to Reuters instead. I'll feed it up from the wall box here and they should have it back at the Ingest Suite within a few minutes. Are you up to doing a piece to camera, pet?'

Isla's head was spinning, unable to comprehend what had just happened. Five minutes earlier this old boy had been rolling a fag while she stared dejectedly at the crowd barrier they were both sitting behind. Then this Piers Brosnan look-alike had appeared from nowhere and Bob had become a staccato news machine, firing a volley of instructions in her direction.

'But we didn't get anything on tape, no one is going to believe us,' said Isla.

Bob paused and handed her a pair of headphones attached to his camera. He replayed the audio from the PM that he'd recorded. Isla squealed with delight and threw her arms in his direction, but Bob was already connecting to the wall box and preparing to feed the footage back to the studios, his roll-up still hanging from his lower lip.

Meanwhile, across the street, Julian was panicking. No longer concerned about the hour, he galloped up the stairs to his office to call his spin doctor.

65

Ben Watson had been completely awake long before his mobile phone rang. Jetlagged, he had been unable to sleep and was replaying the brush with Erica. 'OK, yeah, that would be great. I'm a really good teacher.'

Ben was acutely embarrassed by his comment but was equally dismissive of the encounter. He'd been a stupid idiot who was blind drunk. Pissed out of his head and a daft bastard but definitely not interested in lady boys. He reassured himself by reaching out in the darkness to stroke his wife's feminine curves. Involuntarily he recoiled as he touched Gayle. If she hadn't succumbed to creeping obesity after each of their three children, then he wouldn't be plagued by such ridiculous thoughts. When it came down to it, Ben Watson knew there was no way he preferred men to women. His fantasy was a beautiful human form.

Visualising the perfection of Erica in his mind, Ben tentatively reached out to Gayle again. Sliding closer behind her he dispensed with any necessity for foreplay and satisfied himself quickly before moving away contentedly. It was then that the phone rang. As he answered it, Gayle quietly succumbed to muffled sobbing as she mourned the death of passion with her husband.

Ben listened with growing exasperation as a clearly flustered Julian confessed to his nocturnal nonsense.

9

Michael Grifton was right up to his double chin in doggy doo. It was 5.40 am and the head of news at *Have a Nice Day UK* knew he was sitting on the biggest exclusive the channel had ever had.

But as he slammed down the desk phone to Ben Watson he also realised that running the Prime Minister's off guard quote would cost him his marriage, his house and eventually his job. Jean had been more than tolerant throughout their 30 years together. She had turned her face away at numerous dalliances, but that junior reporter becoming pregnant had been an infidelity too far. One more public embarrassment for Mrs G and he was toast. As a result, his night-time and indeed occasional afternoon proclivities had become much more discreet.

Tracey Partington meant nothing to Michael, but the legs and the promise of easy sex had been too much of a temptation at the Labour Party Spring Conference in Blackpool. Tracey had a reputation for being a two pot screamer and Michael wanted a piece of the action. He was hopeful that a couple of glasses of Chardonnay at the bar of the Imperial Hotel followed

67

by the promise of a bottle of chilled Veuve Cliquout champagne in his suite would do the trick. As usual his 'play your cards right and I'll make you a star' luck was in.

He could just about remember heading for the lift with Tracey a few steps behind. Confident they had made it without being spotted he'd drunkenly lunged towards her, pushing a stubby-fingered hand down her low cut top as the lift doors slowly closed. A little too slowly, for Ben Watson had captured the stolen image on his camera phone as an insurance policy. That policy had just reached maturity.

Michael was furious with himself. Touting for totty in front of Gollum, what was he thinking? He clenched both fists so hard that his dirty nails dug into his palms. The gnarled Bic ballpoint he had been doodling with shattered into a dozen plastic splinters all over his untidy desk.

Certainly it had been an impressive trick by Tracey as she deftly knotted a cherry stalk with nothing more than the aid of her rather flexible tongue. The impromptu floor show had received impressed sighs from her male audience at the bar. Michael knew he was in for a great blow job if only he could coax her upstairs. Of course that had been easy with the promise of a reporting attachment on *Have a Nice Day UK*.

As he reminisced about the exhausting night with Tracey, Michael once more felt the uncontrollable stirrings of passion in his shiny polyester trousers. The memory quickly faded with a brisk knock at the door and the stark realisation that his infidelity could now result in financial meltdown, unless he capitulated to Ben Watson's impossible demands.

'Come in,' barked Michael.

As the door swung open he was instantly aware of frenzied newsroom activity. His programme editor, Carole Smith, stood glaring at him.

'We are 15 minutes away from the credits, Mike.'

Carole spoke calmly and concisely, used to briefing presenters in their earpiece as they broadcast live to the nation. She had become adept at using only the precise number of syllables necessary to convey the importance of what needed to be said. Carole was using that skill to practised effect now and Michael realised he needed to make a decision and fast.

'Time and titles wait for no man. As we speak, the presenters are being briefed on the exclusive by my new deputy, Jilly. You've not met her yet. Sid's across everything and is ready to go. Suzie is of course still in make-up. Her questions are being written onto autocue without any of those pesky big words that might trip her up. Are we going with it, Mike?'

The head of news squirmed in his seat and said nothing. Irritated by his lack of response, Carole continued in a lower, more precise tone.

'What am I telling the team about the biggest exclusive this TV station has ever known? Are we going with it or not, Mike?'

Michael closed his eyes. Carole had seen the tape feed coming in and knew exactly what the Prime Minister had said. The channel had the exclusive news that there was to be an early general election. It was the story that everyone wanted. Not only that, but they also had footage of the Prime Minister flirting with one of *HND*'s newest recruits in the middle of the night. It confirmed the growing rumours about Julian Jenson's lothario reputation. It was dynamite, but broadcast it and Ben Watson would make sure his marriage was over. If he didn't broadcast it, his career was over. Michael didn't know what to do and looked pleadingly at Carole.

Confused, she leaned against the door and eased it half shut. 'Make it quick, Mikey.'

Carole knew that her boss didn't like being called Mike and hated being called Mikey but it was her way of focusing his mind on what was happening outside the office. There was not only excitement in the newsroom but also the studio gallery. Belinda, the director, would already be rehearsing the opening scripts. Add to that the exhilaration of every one of her correspondents who had been woken from their beds at an ungodly hour and rushed to a myriad of locations. They were all ready to break the bombshell story that every other news organisation wanted. This was big.

'Ben Watson has a photograph,' he began hesitantly.

Carole rolled her eyes, glanced at her watch and saw there were eight minutes to go before the start of the programme. She shook her head and shut the door fully.

'No, Mikey tell me this isn't happening.'

'If we run the tape, he's going to email it to Mrs G and it's all over,' whimpered Michael.

Carole couldn't believe what she was hearing.

'Was it Tracey part-legs? Is that why she had that screen test after the party conference? Oh MIKEY, when will you ever learn to keep it in your pants?'

Carole was livid, but with the clock ticking, she knew that now was not the time for recriminations. There was another tap at the door. This time it was Jilly.

'Sorry to bother you guys, but I thought you'd like to know the chief exec has just walked into the studio gallery. He's heard about the early election exclusive and I thought one of you might want to be in the hot seat when we go to air.'

'What? How could he possibly know about this story?' blurted out Michael irritably.

He seemed to be the only person in the newsroom who was not aware that Barry Fritzenburg was increasingly enjoying the monosyllabic, but in many other ways hugely enjoyable company of Suzie Angel, the channel's pretty TV presenter. Jilly turned away and tried to stifle a giggle. Scowling, Carole corrected her before turning back to Michael. Any sympathy for a pathetic old hack had melted

70

away with the arrival of the chief exec and the realisation that her job could now also be on the line. Still, his desperately pleading eyes screamed out to her.

Although the newsroom was buzzing, only Carole and Michael from the editorial team had so far seen the tape feed with the Prime Minister's comments in full. Carole had been tipped off earlier in the morning by her old mate Bob, the cameraman, who was concerned at too many staff seeing the interview before it went to air. He'd known many exclusives ruined by rivals being alerted before transmission. Determined it wouldn't happen this time, the tape had been given immediately to the programme editor.

Carole was torn. Julian Jenson looked like a complete plank overtly flirting with a pretty young journalist outside Downing Street in the dark. It would certainly make great telly. On the other hand she was a big fan of Mrs G, a gentle older woman who had shown Carole nothing but kindness and support as she climbed the slippery pole of TV news. It was a tough job being a lesbian in a testosterone-fuelled newsroom. If she ran the tape in full that snake in the grass Ben Watson would undoubtedly carry out his threat and Mrs G would be made to pay for her husband's indiscretion.

Carole looked up at the wall clock – it was five minutes to the hour.

'Michael, in the gallery, now. Jilly, brief Sid. Tell him to whip it up a bit. He'll know the patter. Tell him to say stuff like: "If you're just tuning in we have startling news about the next election," and all that bollocks. Tell him not to give the date away yet though. All our rivals will be watching and they'll try to steal it as their own exclusive by 7 o'clock.'

Jilly hurriedly scribbled down Carole's suggestions before asking: 'What about Suzie?'

Carole had no time for pleasantries and the present audience didn't necessitate it anyway.

'Make sure droopy drawers doesn't say a word. Let her smile and look lovingly at Sid but don't let her say a word. I'll be there in two minutes. I'm just nipping down to Edit Four. The chief exec might ask why we're not running the grab from the PM at the top of the show. If he does, tell him, oh, tell him we want to build up the suspense until after the first break.'

Jilly raised an eyebrow but it was wasted on Carole. She was already sprinting down the corridor causing a moment of shock in a newsroom that had never seen the unflappable programme editor as much as walk briskly before. Jilly ran the opposite way towards the studio gallery. Michael moved dejectedly in the same direction as Jilly, wondering if he would still have a bed to sleep in that night. His thoughts momentarily turned to Isla whose exclusive had caused all the fuss. She had shown talent by securing the exclusive. See, he knew he was right to hire her. Although he was confident she would be a valuable asset to the company, Michael now found himself wondering whether he would ever be able to taste the forbidden fruit of that beautiful Newcastle lass.

Shaking the thought from his mind, Michael heard the familiar music accompanying the opening titles of *Have a Nice Day UK* as he descended the spiral staircase to the gallery. Pushing open the heavy, soundproof door he was met by the gaze of a bleary-eyed but nonetheless totally judgmental Barry Fritzenburg.

'Evening Michael,' greeted Barry, not a trace of irony in his tone.

Michael offered nothing more than a weak smile in return. Untroubled by Fritz's sarcasm at his late arrival, Michael knew his entire future now depended on Carole's next move and walked over to stand behind Jilly. She was briefing Sid through his earpiece via a useful little button on a panel in the gallery. Sid and Suzie were welcoming the early bird nation to their eternal summer with the help of a bright yellow sofa, a basket of pastries and a jug of freshly squeezed orange juice strategically placed on the low coffee table.

Sid, handsome, charming, mid-30s and every housewife's fantasy was a regular ratings winner. He'd recently been joined by Suzie, a stunning blonde with perfectly trimmed hair, immaculately coiffed all the way down to her Sonia Rykiel dresses. The initially speculative pairing had seen audience figures increase by 15% in the last six months. Together they were ratings gold dust.

'Hi everyone.' Sid was talking to camera and had his warm, friendly 'trust me I'm a TV presenter' smile in place as usual, but was injecting just a little bit of extra pace into his delivery this morning.

'We start this morning's programme with some startling news everyone. *Have a Nice Day UK* has an exclusive about the date of the next election. The Prime Minister has been speaking only to us about his plans to go to the country.'

Weary journalists on the early shift in newsrooms around the country were immediately intrigued. Normally they would have been watching all the breakfast shows on a quad split screen with the sound down, but the banner across the bottom of the *HND* broadcast had demanded their undivided attention. *Exclusive: PM announces date of next election.*

Carole was watching the output from an edit suite as she looked again at Julian Jenson's comments. What an idiot he was. No wonder Ben Watson had been straight on the phone to Michael. Glancing at the news wires on yet another screen in front of her, Carole saw their exclusive being reported by the Press Association, attributing the story to *HND* as agreed, but also giving the date. Shit, in all the drama with Michael she'd forgotten *HND*'s press office had briefed PA.

She urgently reached forward to an electronic panel in the edit suite and buzzed through to Jilly in the gallery. Her voice, as always, was calm but just a little too loud on the speaker.

'Change of plan, get Sid to announce the date now. Tell him we'll hear exclusively from the Prime Minister in just a few minutes but the date for the next general election is 3rd October.'

Michael felt a strange tightness in his chest. In the semi-darkness of the control room he suddenly found it impossible to breathe and was sure he was having a heart attack. What was Carole doing? That was it, his life was over.

In the artificial brightness of the studio, Sid who could also hear Carole's instruction was already half way through repeating the sentence, before Jilly had time to speak.

'Well everyone, I can tell you that the Prime Minister has told us exclusively that the date of the next election will be 3rd October. We'll be hearing from him very shortly indeed.'

Barry was suitably impressed by his senior anchor's quick thinking delivery. But, looking up at the bank of flickering monitors covering one wall of the gallery he noticed from Suzie's glorious camera close-up that she was starting to pout.

'Give Suzie something to say,' barked Barry.

Carole had explicitly told Jilly not to allow Suzie to say a thing and she looked pleadingly up at Michael who seemed to be gripping tightly onto the back of her seat for some reason. He appeared a little pale but nevertheless managed a nod of acceptance at the chief exec's instruction and Jilly leaned forward into her microphone, pressing the key to Suzie's earpiece.

'Could you possibly ask viewers to email in with their thoughts?' she whispered tentatively.

Barry was happy to see a smile instantly appear on Suzie's beautiful face and waited for her to speak.

'Could you possibly ask viewers to email in with their thoughts?'

She had repeated every word of Jilly's request verbatim. Shocked sniggers in the gallery were only subdued by the presence of the chief exec. Not missing a beat, Sid stepped in to catch the clanger.

'Of course I can, Suzie. Great idea. As Suzie was just suggesting everyone, why not email us with your views on our exclusive news this hour. That is that the Prime Minister is to call an election for 3rd October. You could Twitter if you prefer or perhaps text. Usual details, bottom of the screen. We'd be delighted to hear from you. Wouldn't we, Suzie?'

'Yes,' nodded his pleased co-presenter, blissfully unaware of her blunder.

In the gallery, Barry nodded his appreciation at Sid's deft handling of a potentially embarrassing moment. That's why they paid him the big bucks and Sid was certainly earning them this morning. Michael was relieved his senior anchor was on form but was more concerned about starting to fade from pale to blue and tried to breathe as normally as possible.

Belinda was about to take a commercial break when the heavy gallery door flung open and Carole burst in.

'Don't take the ad break, Belinda, we're staying on air. Cue up the tape.'

Michael let out an audible whimper and started to hyper-ventilate. Once again he tried to steady himself on the back of the producer's chair but almost fell over as Jilly, massively relieved at the arrival of Carole, leaped from the seat. Carole half laughed at her boss as she slid into position and began to brief Sid.

'Hey Sid, it's me, cross to Isla outside Number 10, then I can fill you in while she's talking.'

But Sid only half understood his programme editor's instruction. Thankfully Belinda who knew her presenters inside out noticed a moment of confusion in his eyes. She immediately cut away from the anchor and to library pictures of the PM during his recent visit to Afghanistan. Sid's microphone was still live but he took the opportunity to mouth silently to Carole via Camera 2.

'Who?'

She instantly realised her mistake. Isla was new to the station and had never been on air before. Sid couldn't be expected to know who she was.

'Sorry, big guy. *Is-la Mc-Gov-ern*. New girl. Her exclusive. Outside Number 10. All the details. Live.'

Belinda took natural sound from the library tape of Julian Jenson chatting to soldiers in Helmand, giving Sid the chance to jot down the instruction and gather his thoughts.

In the meantime Carole pressed a different button and spoke to his co-presenter in her ear. A tricky task, as Jilly had discovered, but Carole was more used to spoon-feeding.

'Suzie, listen to me: "If you are just tuning our way . . . we have some exclusive news . . . about the next election."'

As the library pictures of the PM ended with him boarding a jet back to London, accompanied by the freed hostages and pixellated faces of special forces personnel, Belinda cut back to Sid and Suzie in vision. Suzie spoke first.

'If you are just tuning our way, we have some exclusive news about the next election.'

'That's right, Suzie, *Have a Nice Day UK* has the date for when we'll all be going to the polling station and it's sooner than any of us was expecting. Let's cross to Downing Street right now and hear from our political correspondent, Isla McGovern. She has all the details on this exclusive news.

'Morning, Isla, great exclusive. What more can you tell us?'

Isla had never done a live broadcast before, though she had practised dozens of times in a mirror in her tiny north London flat. Taking a deep breath, she knew this was her moment to shine.

Michael Grifton paused from trying to breathe and rehearsing his pleading apology to Mrs G to will on his protégé. Carole was too busy to listen to a word of what Isla had to say, confident Belinda would catch her if she fell.

'Sid, I need you to link into the sound grab from the PM. Announcing date. Exclusive. News conference later. Rose Garden. Pad it out.'

As Isla ended with, '. . . then I pressed the Prime Minister if he could tell *Have a Nice Day UK* viewers anything more about calling an early election. Sid, he refused to say more and headed back into Downing Street.'

She concluded cleanly with: '. . . back to you both in the studio.' A line she had rehearsed a hundred times before.

Suzie picked up with her equally well rehearsed: 'Thank you. Sid.'

'Thanks, Suzie. OK everyone, as promised we do have that exclusive interview with the Prime Minister for you now. We're learning that there will be a news conference in the Rose Garden at Number 10 sometime later on today. Of course, our cameras will be there for you. This is certainly going to be a very big story throughout the day, but for now let's hear it in the PM's own words.'

'Roll tape,' said Belinda, the director, and the vision mixer cut to pictures of Julian Jenson outside Downing Street in the middle of the night talking to a TV crew. Michael Grifton let out another whimper and was afraid he might cry.

Over the breakfast table at Number 10, Julian and Ben Watson held their breath. There it was, the PM, like a complete numpty talking to a pretty journalist outside Number 10 in the pitch dark.

'If my quote is broadcast in full, it would indeed be unfortunate.'

'No shit Sherlock,' said Ben, his thumb hovering over the send button on his BlackBerry. An email with attachment was only moments away from Jean Grifton's inbox.

'I really do hope you are not too cold standing out here night after night? I assume you must be from breakfast television. *HND*, is it? Well, I would like your viewers to be the first to know that I am planning to ask Her Majesty to dissolve Parliament. I will go further and tell you that I plan to call the next election for 3rd October. I will hold a news conference in the Rose Garden later today to further outline my intentions.'

That was it. No more. The film ended with Julian heading back across the dimly lit road to Number 10 and Belinda cut back to the studio as the door swung shut.

'Wow. There we have it, ladies and gentleman. The Prime Minister confirming to us exclusively here on *Have a Nice Day UK* that he will call the general election for 3rd October,' informed Sid.

'Let's take a break,' smiled Suzie.

As Belinda finally took a delayed commercial break, an excited buzz broke out among the technical team in the gallery.

'I love you,' Michael whispered to his programme editor.

'You owe me,' snapped back Carole, throwing the original tape into his hands as she headed into the studio to praise her presenters and make sure they had their breakfast order taken care of.

Those watching the programme in Downing Street had a very different reaction.

'You lucky bastard,' joked Ben as he winked at a mightily relieved Julian who was flicking on the kettle for a celebratory cuppa.

'Black coffee, no sugar for me, boss. Now then, I have a plan so cunning we can put a tail on it and call it a weasel. Want to hear it, Baldrick?'

Julian made the coffee as Ben had a quick channel-hop to see what the other news outlets were saying.

Isla though was less happy with what she had just seen.

'Why are they only showing that? He said much more than that,' wailed the young reporter. She'd been listening to Julian's words via a portable TV while still sitting on the same silver camera box where she had first met the Prime Minister.

'What about when he was being all flirtatious? It was obvious he was coming on to me, Bob? Surely that's good telly, isn't it? We've never seen the Prime Minister like that before, have we? Why didn't they use more? They need to run all of it. I'm going to call the gallery.'

Isla dug into her handbag and rummaged for her mobile.

'Leave it, love,' warned her wise old cameraman.

Bob was aware of exactly what had happened. He could sense Carole's hand at work and knew the Downing Street spin machine would have been on full cycle.

'It's fine as it is. Take your bow, pet, and just leave it.'

Isla was angry and confused. What was he talking about? This was her big chance, her big break. Of course she wasn't going to 'leave it'. Silly old fool, what did he know anyway?

She was in the process of seriously contemplating quite a significant sulk when the glossy black door opened once again. This time it was a man she didn't recognise with a cup of black coffee in his hand, striding across the street towards her. Perhaps he was one of the press office team. What did he want? She needed to talk to the gallery and was in no mood for interruptions. Looking towards the security checkpoint at the end of Downing Street Isla could see other news organizations making their way through. Maybe this press office bloke was about to make a more general announcement.

But Ben had no intention whatsoever of raising his head above the press parapet. His mission was purely damage limitation and he needed to move quickly before the other hungry hacks pounced on their carrion. Nodding acknowledgement at Bob, he spoke directly to Isla.

'Get your gear love, move your arse, inside, now.'

Despite the explicit instruction, Isla stood wide-eyed at this ugly little man's rudeness. It was Bob who once again came to the rescue of the young girl.

'Grab the tripod, pet. I'll bring the camera and the lights. Looks like you've only gone and nailed yourself another exclusive.'

Moments later Isla found herself stood in the entrance hall of Number 10 being barked at again by this very, very rude man.

'Right, listen. Set up in the Cabinet Room, the PM will be down in 10 minutes. You've got 5 minutes with him. He'll tell you how he planned this as an *HND* exclusive all along. He wanted to instil some urgency into proceedings and to get on with the election as soon as possible. He understands the concerns of the British public and wants a mandate for another 5 years to push through his policies on education and Afghanistan. Got it?'

Isla was reeling. What on earth was happening? She'd already spoken to the Prime Minister today. Now this short bald-headed chap was telling her there was to be a second interview, this time inside Downing Street. Why? She looked across at Bob for guidance. He urgently nodded acceptance at the offer.

'Excellent, thank you. Just one question, erm, what's the Cabinet Room?'

Ben rolled his eyes as Bob grabbed Isla's sleeve, half dragging her down the corridor while at the same time phoning Carole in the gallery to inform her of yet another exclusive coming her way before the end of the show.

10

Thames riverside apartment

'Darling, he's called a general election,' shouted Jimmy Phillips
to his new husband, Charles, who was busy showering away
their lovemaking.

Jimmy was watching TV in the bedroom of the new
waterside apartment that they'd moved into just last week.
It was a glorious location. Glass-fronted glamour with a clear
view of Chelsea Bridge. But it hadn't come cheap and Jimmy
needed almost every penny of his new celebrity salary to
secure the deal.

Still, the astronomical rent was of no real concern to him.
The celebrity auctioneer's own currency was equally high. The
sensational viewing figures for his new prime time show *Where
There's Muck There's Brass* had taken the number one slot for
the channel last night. It was the second highest watched
programme on any station so far this year, almost as big as *The
X Factor*, his agent had said when he phoned with the news.

Jimmy had celebrated in appropriate style with his new
husband, before flicking onto breakfast TV while he waited
for the newly purchased retro Teas-made to do his bidding.

'Darling, the Prime Minister has called an election, quickly come see,' said Jimmy again, this time a little more loudly.

'Darling, can you hear me?'

But it was no use. Once Charles was in the shower, flossing and shampooing and goodness knows what else, he would be there for some time. Jimmy reached instead for his cuppa and reclining onto black silk pillowcases listened to Julian Jenson tell the nation his plans.

As he watched, he was momentarily reminded of the Prime Minister's well-known spin doctor. Their paths had crossed years ago when Ben Watson was a reporter on the *Birmingham Evening Mail*. Jimmy had been a struggling antiques dealer, or if he was honest, a scrap trader. The two young men worked together when Jimmy helped out with props for an article on *'Is There Hidden Loot In Your Loft?'*

The photo-shoot later developed into an impromptu party. That was a long time ago and Jimmy hadn't seen the young reporter since. He'd heard Ben had gone into political journalism. Goodness, how grand he'd become.

Charles wandered back into the bedroom, a tiny towel barely covering the biggest manhood Jimmy had ever enjoyed.

'Darling, guess what, the Prime Minister has called an early election for 3rd October. Isn't that a surprise? I think it's probably because the Afghan siege ended so well.'

'Really, that's interesting. Anyway, what are you doing for lunch today?'

Jimmy realised there was little point in pursuing political discussion with his partner whose notable qualities lay elsewhere. Instead he headed for his turn in the shower.

11

Downing Street

Julian and Ben were once again in the kitchen of the Downing Street flat, this time watching his Cabinet Room interview with Isla playing out on breakfast TV. The timings had been tight and Ben was unsure whether the interview could be recorded and then transmitted before *Have a Nice Day UK* went off air at 9.25 am. Its impact would be useless by tomorrow. It absolutely had to be broadcast today.

In the studio gallery, Carole was also doubtful and had a taped interview with Lewis Hamilton lined up just in case. As the clock ticked past 9.15 am, Ben had jumped in to cut the interview short and Bob immediately whipped the tape out of his camera and dashed across the street. A quick bit of technical wizardry and the tape could be played out live from the wall box outside Number 10 with literally seconds to spare.

Ben and Julian had raced up to the flat to watch the interview. Both were relieved and delighted. The spin doctor's brilliant idea for a more stage managed interview had taken some of the sting out of Julian's earlier knee-jerk decision.

Instead of a PM who acted on impulse, the hastily arranged sit-down had portrayed his boss as serious and dignified at the Cabinet Room table. Julian appeared calm, composed and determined to move ahead with an election for the greater good of the British people.

As the interview ended, the happy, smiling *HND* presenters said goodbye until tomorrow. They were replaced by yet another promo for *Where There's Muck There's Brass* and Ben switched off the set.

'Fucking hell boss, we only just got away with it, you daft bastard. What were you thinking of padding out in the middle of the night to talk to bloody reporters?'

Before Julian could reply, Ben was interrupted by his mobile. The phone hadn't stopped ringing since the 6 am exclusive on *HND*. Journalists, cabinet members and special advisors were all furious. Why hadn't they been told first? Julian though cared little about their anger. He was delighted that his spin doctor had dug him out of the mire and with the heat off, his attention was elsewhere.

Julian had been totally smitten by the young reporter. Breathtakingly attractive, she had a mischievous sparkle in her eyes that had completely captivated him. As he sat mentally undressing her at the Cabinet Table, Julian had briefly forgotten all about his impending divorce or future life with Sally. All he could think about was having endless fun with this playful kitten.

'Isla McGovern, that's her name. I would very much like to get to know her better. I think she could quite easily become my new favourite. Absolutely breathtaking, isn't she?'

Ben shook his head. Julian was one of the most powerful men in the world, with a sharp intellect. Family money provided financial security that most of the population could never dream of. Handsome, smooth and considered, he had a natural charm that won over even the most judgmental opposition. But the suave, elegant Prime Minister had an Achilles' heel and that was beautiful women. Here he was, once again behaving like a love-struck teenager. Would he ever learn?

'Yeah, she's as cute as a hamster in a tea cup. Totally worth screwing your whole career for I would say. No question at all.

'Anyway boss, just as a sidebar, now that you've called this election, should we perhaps run through a few quick ideas about what the fuck we plan to do next?'

Julian offered a playful army salute and both men pulled their chairs closer to the table. As they set about their task, a timid, fully-dressed Valerie crept into the kitchen and made her way tentatively towards the kettle. She was desperate for a morning cuppa and was also quite keen to know how Ben planned to fix the mess that Julian had rather foolishly created.

Ever since her husband's request for a divorce she had been hesitant to be in the same room as Julian and Ben. But Valerie also had absolutely no intention whatsoever of melting away into a footnote in Downing Street history without a very good attempt at saving her marriage first.

Although she was the only one who wanted to make it work, Valerie was still desperate to try to rebuild the trust and connection she once had with her husband. She had taken her vows seriously 20 years ago and she still wanted to honour them. Bad times didn't have to mean divorce, whatever Julian had said. She just needed to convince him that communication and honesty between them could help restore what they once had.

Valerie accepted that her excessive drinking was a major factor in the disintegration of the relationship and had been trying very hard to turn her back on the bottle. She wanted Julian to be able to depend on her again and had settled on a course of no confrontation, no altercation, no conflict while she regained her strength and formulated a plan. Part of that plan was to keep a low profile, sleeping in Jessica's room while her daughter was away at school and pottering around the flat only after Julian had left for the day. This morning though he had returned unexpectedly and with that snake in the grass spin doctor in tow. She had dawdled as long as she could, tidying Jessica's room while watching her husband behaving rather irrationally on breakfast television. See, he did need her after all.

As she entered the room neither man even bothered to look up from the scribbled notes and plethora of post-its already spreading out over the table. Health, Education, Armed Forces, Pensioners. All headings with growing lists beneath them.

As Valerie busied herself with inconsequential breakfast activities, she listened intently to the two men firing staccato comments at each other.

'With Parliament in recess, the backbenchers will be furious with me when they come back to London. What do I need to do to placate them?' asked Julian starting to appreciate the magnitude of his impromptu announcement.

He'd realised calling an election without telling the party first was a political no-no. He was now rather hoping his spin doctor was more aware of the niceties of the parliamentary system and had a solution.

'OK, so given the general election date has already been announced, albeit a little prematurely by your good self, we can go ahead and ask the Queen to dissolve Parliament as of today.

'The party is going to be pretty pissed, so what we need is for you to be as high profile as possible over the next six weeks and they'll soon get over it when you win again with another landslide.

'Just don't leave your lapel mic on,' warned Ben.

Valerie smiled wryly at Ben's Bigot-gate reference, as she gingerly lifted a breakfast bowl from one of the antiquated cupboards, careful not to make any annoying crockery noises. She was keen not to disturb the scheming breakfast interlopers as she crept over to the fridge. Her thoughts were coming together and she was feeling more and more confident that her marriage could begin again but not quite yet. Low profile at all times until she was ready to break cover. That was the plan.

Valerie had spent many hours walking around the extensive grounds of Chequers contemplating how they could have reached the point where Julian was considering divorce. When she returned to town, the country yomps had been replaced by strolls around the half acre Downing Street garden. They were followed by long nights sitting alone in the third floor flat while a gin bottle called to her from the drinks cabinet at the other side of the room.

Valerie's stoic attempts at not drinking had been spasmodic. At first, the thought of getting through the day or even worse, the lonely nights, without a drink, had proved temptation beyond endurance. Astute enough to know that her reliance on alcohol was her way of self-medicating for depression, she had tried new distractions to lift her mood. She read and took regular exercise including swimming in the Chequers pool whenever she was in the country. She'd also taken on more charity work. She'd even turned to helping Julia choose table centres for her wedding. It was on the face of it a dull, uninteresting task, but the by-product of making her brother very happy had made it worthwhile. Slowly, she had begun to recreate the old Valerie. One that she hoped Julian would fall in love with again.

The alternative was unbearable. Her parents would be devastated, her brother would want to seek revenge and her so-called friends would be more anxious about the Chequers invites drying up rather than how she would cope alone. In her darker moments, Valerie had feared there was little hope of a way back into her husband's affections, but she was still determined to try.

Even when Julian returned home, victorious from Afghanistan, he had all but ignored her. He'd claimed late night sittings at the House of Commons for his frequent absences. She didn't believe him but had been reluctant to check with the Chief Whip for fear of what the answer might be. However bleak the prognosis, Valerie was not prepared to accept defeat and had decided that her marriage repair strategy must be one of out of sight, out of mind until Julian came to his senses, which he must surely do. In the meantime, she was determined not to fuel her husband's frustration or fury, even if that meant she must accept being ignored. It had worked. Julian had not confronted her on any level for several days now.

Now fate had dealt her what she considered a well-deserved break. Valerie was secretly delighted at her husband's decision to call an election, even if he had gone about it in a rather ham-fisted way. She knew there would be no further talk of separation during the campaign. Julian may well be the nation's sweetheart, more popular than Simon Cowell, but coordinating divorce papers with the date for a vote was a political non-starter.

Turning to watch the two men plotting around the kitchen table, Valerie realised this was her moment, the one that could save her marriage. She needed to show Julian she wasn't a millstone but an integral part of his life and she had a plan. She breathed deeply and leaned against the sink to steady herself before beginning breezily.

'Morning boys, saw the news on breakfast telly, goodness we're going to be busy for the next six weeks, aren't we?'

The inclusive 'we' made both men wince but they knew she was right. Whatever their thoughts about Valerie, she was going nowhere for now. Still, neither wanted to offer her the courtesy of a response, so both simply ignored her and carried on scribbling furiously.

Valerie was initially deflated by their lack of reaction but having decided this was the start of the fight back into her husband's affections, she dug deep and tried again. This time she aimed her comments at her husband.

'I know you're going to have a very, very busy day today, not least because you have to go to see the Queen to ask her to dissolve Parliament. Anyway, I wondered, darling, if by any chance you might also be able to squeeze in coming to the Oval to see Monty play today?'

Ben scoffed at the crassness of her suggestion and turned to address Valerie directly. 'Oh, it's you. Thought you were being kept in a cupboard? Tad busy here princess, push off, there's a good girl.'

Waving his hand at her dismissively, Ben scowled and returned to his scribbling.

Valerie was rocked, not only by Ben's rudeness but by Julian's reluctance to chastise him for it. She momentarily considered defeat, but it was now or never and so she pressed on.

'I know, it's just a silly thought, especially when you are so busy. It's just that you did miss one of the Tests while you were away working so hard in Afghanistan resolving that terrible siege. Anyway, Monty tells me today is a really important day for the team.'

Both men stopped writing and looked up. Ben wondered what the mad bint was talking about now. She was driving him nuts. Noticing that she finally had their complete attention, Valerie paused. Her heart was beating so hard, she thought it would burst, but she was determined not to rush the punch line. It was a technique she had often taught her authors at First Stop publishing. Once you've got 'em hooked, there's no rush to land 'em. Valerie methodically dunked her teabag and opened the fridge door to retrieve milk for her Earl Grey. Drinking it white was a northern habit she couldn't get out of. Eventually picking up her cup, Valerie continued.

'Anyway, if England wins today, Monty says we recover The Ashes. I think lots of famous people are going to be there. Sir David Frost is definitely going, so is Sir Richard Branson. I believe Sir John Major and that rather handsome Ross Kemp will also be there. I heard Russell Crowe is going too and that witty chap, what's his name, erm, Stephen Fry, that's it. He'll probably tweet about it too, he has so many followers on Twitter.

'Monty says he's reserved places for us in the ECB box if we like, we just need to let him know. Anyway, it was just a thought. I can see you're busy, so I'll let you both get on.'

As Valerie left the kitchen, Ben and Julian turned to each other open-mouthed.

'Fucking genius, boss. Seriously, how better way to start off an election campaign than a photo op of you shaking the hands of the victorious England boys moments after they've screwed the Aussies? Bring it on.'

As Ben reached for his phone, Valerie was just outside the kitchen door trying to steady herself by leaning against the wall. It had been three days since her last drink and she was unsure if the trembling was down to alcohol withdrawal symptoms or perhaps because of what had just happened. Slowly regaining control, she allowed herself to consider that the fluttering in her stomach could be a result of the look her husband had just given her. Was she mistaken or was it a half smile of approval?

12

An hour later and the road outside Number 10 was crammed full of frenzied journalists representing news organizations from around the world. There was much pushing and shoving for a coveted position directly opposite the shiny black door. Still more journalists were arriving by the minute, with some chancing their arm and endeavouring to claim phantom designated spots. But late-comers were to be disappointed. Attempts at a pecking order were futile on a day like this when editors wanted the best possible shots of Julian Jenson when he emerged. That meant a premium spot and many had been there since 6.30 am to secure them.

Inside, space was also at a premium around the Cabinet Room table where the political temperature had reached boiling point. Ministers, party officials and financiers were all furious they hadn't been consulted before the general election was announced. Many were straining at the leash to vent their fury at the PM. Under intense pressure, Julian had his most charming smile in place while attempting to remain calm against the tsunami of frustration, but he could feel his temper starting to bubble just below the surface. Meanwhile in an adjoining room, Ben was also feeling the heat. He was with the PM's speech writer huddled around a laptop. They were striving for the correct form of words to ease Julian out of a potential constitutional crisis while also rallying the troops for the campaign ahead.

Valerie, feeling buoyed by her earlier kitchen sink performance, had somehow managed to wrestle away her craving for a congratulatory drink. She had instead turned to reassuring her husband's close protection that she had every confidence they could put the necessary security checks in place for an impromptu trip to the Oval after lunch. Job done, she was ready to initiate the second part of her fight back and made her way down to the ground floor to speak to Ben.

Initially shocked by the madness of political activity that greeted her, Valerie fought off the temptation to run back to the tranquillity of the flat. Today wasn't the day for shrinking violets. She pressed on, smiling at familiar faces and making small talk with custodians as she went in search of Ben. Eventually she found him among a growing number huddled around a computer screen and strolled rather anxiously towards him.

'May I please have a very quick word, Ben?'

Ben was in no mood for disturbances. He gestured towards his computer where a sea of words was drifting towards some semblance of a speech.

'What Valerie? No Valerie. For fuck's sake, what is it that you want now? Can't you see I'm busy or does it look like I'm doing a fucking Sudoku here?

'No, it doesn't, does it princess? That's because I'm not. In fact, what I'm doing is trying to save your husband's career.'

He dismissed her as he had done earlier with a wave of his hand and turned his attention back to the screen. David Cameron might have thought speaking without notes was a crowd pleaser, but Ben Watson wasn't about to allow his man to talk without a well-crafted security blanket. He carried on typing. Time was tight and this had to be finished.

A few moments later Ben paused and looked up as he considered the best way to phrase the middle part of the speech. He was furious to see Valerie still standing a few feet away, staring at him.

'Oh, what, what, what? Just push off princess, will you? There must be something on daytime TV you can watch.'

But the foot soldier had gone too far this time. Suddenly aware of the increasing disquiet of others, less content than Julian had been at the way he'd spoken to Valerie, the harassed spin doctor reluctantly altered his tone.

Looking a little more closely at her, Ben was struck by how Valerie had made a surprisingly good effort with her appearance. Her hair and make-up were immaculate and she was dressed beautifully in a stunning McQueen summer dress. He fleetingly thought he would have chosen a slightly darker lipstick shade, before shoving away the very idea.

'Sorry to be snappy, Valerie, but can't it wait? I'm totally up against it here.'

'Well Ben, I'm terribly sorry to disturb you. I can see you are very busy. It won't take a moment, I promise. It's just to give you a quick update really.

'I've spoken to security and Monty and everything is in order for later. I'm ready to go to the cricket whenever Julian is free but it does appear that may be a while away. Anyway, with everyone so busy, I wondered if you might be able to make use of another pair of hands?'

'Nope,' said Ben and turned back to the laptop.

But, Valerie was regaining her strength by the moment and was not to be deterred by this odious little man's unacceptable behaviour. She pressed on.

'Hmmm, well I did have a little thought that might be of some use. Tell me what you think, Ben.

'I wondered if I might be gainfully employed popping outside to talk to the press. I noticed there are lots and lots of them out there. I could go and have a quick chat. Wouldn't be any trouble, if you'd like me to?'

Ben stopped typing abruptly to consider what Valerie had just said, his anger instantly giving way to grudging admiration. He had to hand it to her, two genius strokes in one morning. What had happened to this girl? She was on fire. A loyal wife offering public support for her hard working husband was always a winner. Ever since Sarah Brown's address to party conference, the press had loved a good supportive spouse story. The big question was whether Valerie could pull it off. The old Valerie certainly would have had no trouble. She could command the attention of any audience. But Valerie, the drunk, had been blowing in the wind for months now. Was it worth the risk?

He looked her up and down. She looked and sounded sober and had definitely scrubbed up well today. SamCam had cornered the market in Oxford Street chic, but Valerie's look had always been more aspirational than attainable. He didn't want her looking too High Street. He immediately recognised the dress as designer. The heels, unquestionably Jimmy Choo. Good. Yes, this just might work. What was the downside? If she crashed and burned, it would make it even easier to dump her after the election. If she did well, then it could only reflect well on her husband and come to think of it, brilliantly on him too, since he would undoubtedly be credited with the idea. What was there to lose?

Ben softened his tone further and standing, walked the few steps to join Valerie before guiding her away from flapping ears.

'Are you sure, Valerie? Life's been a bit tough for you over the last few weeks. The press can be vicious if they sense any sign of weakness. Have you thought about what you might say?'

'Well, I haven't really thought about it until now to be honest, Ben,' lied Valerie, dropping her shoulder ever so slightly to ensure Gollum's clammy hand slipped away. She continued to walk towards the door of Number 10.

'I suppose I'll just chat as though I'm talking to my mum. I'll say how Julian has been agonising over calling an election for weeks. He really wants to do the right thing by the British public and wants a further mandate to push through his plans on social reform. Something like that anyway.'

Not quite the impact of Sarah Brown's 'he's my hero', thought Ben but it was still a risk worth taking. He nodded his consent. Valerie smiled back and turned again towards the door.

'It'll be fine, don't worry. Sorry to have interrupted, I'll let you get back to the speech writing.'

As Ben went in search of Julian, Valerie paused just for a moment in the entrance hall, her bravado suddenly slipping away. Had she over-stretched herself? Was this reincarnation too soon? What if Ben's concerns were valid and she couldn't think of anything to say? What if the press was hostile towards her? Would they be disappointed it was her and not Julian?

A thousand questions flooded into her mind and she faltered. She wanted to kick off her shoes and run as fast she could back to the flat and grab the gin bottle instead. But if her marriage was to have any hope of a second chance, now was the time to face her fears and reach for that inner core. This was her moment to shine.

Valerie stood firm. A second to breathe, a final check in the mirror, a constituency smile fixed in place and she nodded politely to the custodian.

As the door swung open she was met by a blizzard of flash photography. It was matched a moment later by shocked gasps as the waiting press realised it was the Prime Minister's wife who was standing in front of them. Alone.

13

Sally Simpson sashayed into the boardroom where she had called a brainstorming lunch meeting with her team. She was walking on air. The acerbic photo spread on Valerie's fashion faux pas had sold well and there had been great coverage in the national media. All the press had obligingly credited the piece back to *Celeb*, guaranteeing free publicity for the magazine. Her publisher was very happy indeed.

Valerie had been seen as a smart, confident woman popular with the papers for far too long thought Sally. Now that she was having a wobble, it was the perfect time to knock her off her smug perch and she knew exactly how to make that happen. Sally was not prepared to risk Valerie recovering from her present melancholy. She knew the first lady was fundamentally a tough cookie and had triumphed over much adversity on the way to the nation's affections. That had to stop. Valerie had to go. There was also the small matter of making sure her lover was re-elected which was the purpose of today's working lunch.

Sally's team, all keen, energetic 20-somethings were sitting around the oval, American oak table. Fashion was their business and all knew what worked on whatever budget. BlackBerrys were placed to one side and notebooks to the ready as the editor entered. Her girls had learned to first judge the mood of their mercurial boss before deciding on how to behave. They were relieved to see that their editor, who had been in an extraordinarily good mood for a couple of weeks now, was again at ease. Immediately, all were keen to attract her attention with their newspaper cuttings and editorial thoughts for the week ahead.

Sally smiled warmly at the enthusiastic but slightly anxious sea of faces. She well remembered her clamber up the editorial ladder. Her parents had been furious that she'd turned her back on an 'appropriate vocation' and chosen the rather unseemly profession of journalism instead. On entering the workplace she was acutely disappointed that her time on the university magazine counted for little in the real world. Initially ridiculed by judgmental hacks, when she did finally manage to secure a job on a local newspaper, Sally quickly learned that vicious humour was her key to inclusion. It was a skill her parents abhorred, driving them further and further away until they eventually became estranged. It was of considerable regret to Sally that they had still never met her son, Sean.

'Hello ladies, great sales last week, well done to everyone involved, really superb. Champagne at Soho House tonight for everyone who can make it after work.

'We can't afford to rest on our laurels though. The next question is how are we going to replicate those figures this week, now that the PM has called an early election?

'Make no mistake, it's going to be tough. I'm told by people much cleverer than me that politics doesn't sell. That said, who would have thought the Vatican could ever be box office until Dan Brown came along?'

A ripple of laughter lapped round the table.

'Anyway ladies, ideas please on what we can do to make politics sexy enough to sell to our readers next week?'

No one spoke, aware that Sally's question was rhetorical until she had offered her own thoughts first. She obligingly pressed on with the charade.

'No one? OK, I'll go first then. The problem for politicians is: who do they aim their campaign at in order to keep the attention of the great British public? In the past we've had stereotypes including Worcester Woman, Motorway Man, even Pebbledash People.'

Sally was momentarily surprised at the vacant looks. Clearly most of the youngsters had no idea what she was talking about, no appreciation of the importance of targeted demographics. They wouldn't have remembered Tony Blair apparently spotting a man polishing his Ford Mondeo and identifying him as the kind of 30-something, middle-income homeowner, whom Labour needed to win over from the Tories. Julian had done the same with the Bacardi Breezer target group. She paused, indulging herself for a moment with the thought of her handsome, caring, intelligent, witty, attentive, sexy lover who would soon be hers for all time. Reluctantly relinquishing the image, she was once more back in the room and determined to do what she could to help Julian win again.

'Cybermums, that's who we need to focus on. They're the key, the holy grail for the politicians and for our circulation. They're internet savvy and they don't need a coffee morning to stay in touch with each other. They know what issues might affect their kids and they're not afraid to ask the tough questions. I think the PM is planning a web chat with them next week.'

Sally was sure cybermums hadn't even registered on Julian's radar but she was rarely wrong on public mood and would suggest it to him later. He would wrinkle his nose and pat her bottom at her cleverness. Ben would sulk because it hadn't been his suggestion and try to scupper it but he would just have to do as he was told and once again *Celeb* would be ahead of the curve.

'So, ladies, I suggest a photo spread of charming children with gorgeous mums. No ugly babies, just cute as a button, please. Maria, let's take an ad out on mums.net to promote it.'

Those around the table scribbled furiously, aware that Sally was right on the money as usual. Long may her good mood continue.

'Any thoughts on a headline, Sally?' asked her deputy. She was dressed in an outfit so unforgiving that even the smallest morsel from the lunch platter would have burst her zip.

'Oh, something like: Net our votes if you want to win . . .'

Maria jotted down her suggestion. That sorted, Sally moved quickly on to what she really wanted to appear in next week's magazine.

'OK everybody, so cake.'

She could hear their loud gasps reverberate almost across the Thames. Most of those gathered were little more than a size zero and probably hadn't tasted cake since their 10th birthday. Glancing at the hardly touched lunch tray with just the odd empty grape stalk squeezing up past the uneaten sandwiches Sally involuntarily shook her head. Kate Moss had a lot to answer for with her ridiculous public mantra '*Nothing tastes as good as skinny feels.*' Sally had managed to keep her trim figure by gym work and sex, one she preferred much more than the other, but together they had the desired effect. With the ubiquitous queue for the bathroom after lunch, Sally was sure many of her girls chose a more disagreeable third way that had plagued the lives of many in the fashion business for decades. She pressed on.

'I want to talk to you about celebration cakes. We all know about birthday, wedding and anniversary cakes, well let me tell you they're just passé now, darlings. This season is all about

99

a different kind of celebration. I've had an email from a confectioner who is making divorce cakes. Can you believe it?'

In fact Sally's recollection was only a half-truth. She had been surfing for a fitting gift to send anonymously to Valerie to 'commiserate' with her marriage break-up after it was made public. Sally had squealed with delight when she discovered divorce cakes. She'd loved every second of scrolling through the numerous options. They'd ranged from a bride dragging her husband out with the rubbish through to a cake divided in half with the divorcing couple pointing revolvers at each other. Eventually after an amusing evening of much deliberation and at least half a bottle of Rioja, she had settled on her chosen creation. The bride was being shoved off the top tier by her beaming husband while his mistress shimmied deftly up the other side. How apt. The cake was duly ordered and would be delivered as soon as appropriate.

But as always with Sally, private victory was never enough. Her newspaper days had taught her that public humiliation was an essential part of being one of the gang. Initially ignored and ridiculed by those who felt threatened by the posh bird from Ireland, she had gone to great lengths to be included in the nightly trips to the pub even if it meant always being singled out as the figure of fun by the news editor. She'd lost count of the number of occasions she'd fought back tears of despair and willingly succumbed to insults with meek acceptance.

As her career flourished, Sally had incorporated that learned behaviour into the way she dealt with her own peers and staff, unaware she was turning into the bully she had once feared.

Now it was Valerie's turn and Sally wanted everyone to witness her crippling embarrassment. It was Valerie who was the posh bird outsider now. She was the one who would cry herself to sleep all alone, night after night.

Grinning like a Cheshire cat at her vicious plan, Maria's polite cough made Sally aware that her audience was starting to shift uneasily at her demeanour. She checked herself and continued.

'Anyway, I've researched it and the cake designs are sensational.'

Maria sensed disbelief among the young girls. They were all dreaming of a happy-ever-after marriage at some stage in the near future and hadn't even contemplated divorce, let alone considered celebrating it. As usual she braced herself to ask the question everyone else was thinking.

'Sally, do you think some of our readers might find a divorce cake a bit crass and perhaps even insensitive? Divorce can be very painful for those involved.'

Sally's smile immediately slipped.

'Nonsense Maria, we need a bit of humour in divorce. Get Arthur Edwards to shoot it for us. He's a brilliant photographer.'

Maria was about to try a different approach when she was distracted by a large group of staff in the open plan office next to the boardroom. They were crowded around a TV set. Unable to see what had caught their attention and with Sally's permission she flicked on the plasma screen.

Valerie Jenson was standing outside Downing Street alone with over-excited reporters screaming questions at her. Flashbulbs illuminated every angle of her fragile frame. The boardroom audience was as inquisitive as their office colleagues. Why on earth was Valerie Jenson standing on her own? Where was her rather dashing husband?

Sally could hardly contain her delight. It was finally happening and so publicly too. Desperate that everyone present witness her rival's very public demise she turned up the sound and stood to smirk.

'Ladies and gentlemen, thank you so much for coming. I

apologise you have all been kept waiting for such a long time and I am desperately sorry that my husband is not standing next to me today.'

Valerie paused and Sally sighed contentedly.

'As you know, my husband has this morning called a general election for 3rd October. He is presently preparing for a visit to the Palace to ask Her Majesty's gracious permission for the dissolution of parliament.

'Why has he done this? Well, I think it is reasonable to say that throughout the last four years in office my husband has worked tirelessly to do what he thinks is right for the British people. He is a good, honest, decent man who has the nation's needs at the heart of his government and that is why he has called this general election. The last few weeks he has slept little in his tireless efforts to bring about a successful end to the Afghan siege.

'It has been a huge challenge, not least for the hostages, their families and our brave armed forces, but also for us as a family.

'The role as Prime Minister can take a heavy toll on family life. With that in mind, ladies and gentlemen, everyone at home, I wanted to take this opportunity to speak to you on a very personal level.'

Valerie brushed a stray hair from her forehead only to be blinded by another wall of flashbulbs. Here it comes, thought Sally. A quick look around the boardroom confirmed everyone was riveted. Valerie was about to crumble in front of the staff. Could life get any sweeter?

'When the burden sometimes seemed too great I know that the love Julian has for his family, myself and our two beautiful children, has always given him the strength to do what he thinks is right. He is determined to press on with his agenda for social reform and feels he needs another five years in order to be able to achieve that.

'I hope with my hand on my heart that you, the British public, will show the same unwavering loyalty to Julian as he has shown me throughout our 20 years together. Make no mistake, he is a wonderful man and I love him with all my heart.'

Sally was speechless. This couldn't be happening. She rocked on her heels and momentarily collapsed into a steel and leather chair behind her before leaping back to her feet. Fighting to stifle an anguished scream, she stormed out of the boardroom.

'That was a brilliant idea, Ben – doting wife, solid family man – the voters will love it. You're a genius.'

Julian had been watching his wife on TV from the privacy of his office after Ben had rushed into the Cabinet Room to alert him to the plan. Julian had been less than sure that the appearance was a good idea, but Valerie had pulled it off. He found himself surprised by positive thoughts towards her.

Ben was happy to take the credit for the publicity stunt. After all Valerie had asked his opinion first.

'Aw shucks boss, thanks. He's a wonderful man and I love him with all my heart. Whitney Houston couldn't have sung it with more conviction.'

Julian put his right hand to his chest and was about to continue when his mobile rang. It was Sally calling. Hesitating for a moment, Julian was unsure what he would say to his undoubtedly livid mistress. The ringtone, 'Walking on Sunshine', went into a second loop and, panicking, Julian dropped the call. Switching the phone to silent, he hastily dispensed with it into a desk drawer and headed towards the car and the Palace.

14

Two weeks later . . .

The Pillared Room

Julian was feeling even more nervous than during his audience with the Queen to discuss his lack of election etiquette. He knew he really shouldn't be hosting the victorious England squad in Downing Street during a campaign but it was too good an electioneering opportunity to miss. Ben had appeased the opposition angst by inviting shadow sports ministers. That had smoothed over any potential protocol problems.

There had been much resting on the final Test, both on and off the pitch. England needed to win the game to recover The Ashes trophy and Julian knew a victory would instil a feel-good factor in the country ahead of the election. The players had not disappointed, now it was his turn.

'I know I speak for everyone in the country when I say how proud I am of the whole team. After years of one-sided encounters with Australia, you won back the cherished urn in the most unforgettable fashion. I have to say my nerves were being shredded as I watched those last few overs at the

Oval. It came down to the wire but you boys showed steely calm and determination. That spirit was appropriately rewarded with victory.

'I will try not to be biased, but Monty's run out on the final ball was nothing less than superb. He was, in my opinion, deservedly the Man of the Series. Of course cricket is not just about one player and I want you all to know how proud we are of your achievements. Bad luck Australia.'

Applause and cheering greeted Julian's speech and the players returned to their beers. But with a pooled TV camera invited into Downing Street to meet with the victorious team, his publicity savvy spin doctor had coached Julian with more. As the applause subsided he took his cue.

'With you all here, I wonder if we might also use the occasion to raise a glass to the future nuptials of Monty and his delightful fiancée Julia. As you know, their wedding is planned for 5th October, two days after the general election. Let's hope we have a double reason to celebrate that week.'

Relaxed players raised their glasses and roared approval.

'That's it, work it, old son,' smirked Ben, leaning against a pillar towards the back of the room.

'Finally, I just wanted to add that I hope Monty and Julia can be as happy and content in their future lives together as Valerie and I are in ours. We all look forward to serving the country in our different ways for years to come. Ladies and gentlemen, please raise your glasses to Monty and Julia.'

As applause and cheers filled the room, Valerie squeezed Monty's arm. She was so proud of him she could burst.

'Thanks for throwing the party, sis. We're all chuffed to be here, especially Julia. You know, I really hope that we can be as happy as you and Julian obviously are.'

Valerie smiled up at her strapping baby brother. Everything was going to be OK, wasn't it? Julian had definitely softened towards her since her 'wonderful man' speech. Surely, what he had just said meant he had changed his mind about a divorce? As Valerie took a sip of her sparkling water, she pushed away the sneaking suspicion that he was playing to the camera.

HND had been the only camera invited to the reception on the condition they share the pictures of the celebrating England team with other TV channels. Not surprisingly, Julian had asked Ben to make sure it was Isla who was wandering among the VIP guests with her handheld furry microphone, accompanied by her cameraman, Bob. She'd been meticulously briefed by the sports guys back at the office. It was just as well as cricket was a game she didn't understand. Her dad had tried to help with 'when you're out, you're in and when you're in, you're out'. Whatever that meant.

First politics and now sport, two topics Isla didn't have the first clue about. She had come to London to make her mark in light entertainment and had meticulously researched the name of every soap, pop and film star, in readiness for her big break. For now she was trying hard to make her way in current affairs and cricket was today's challenge.

Stumbling across the victorious captain Isla flicked through her notepad, desperately searching for the pre-prepared questions.

'Hi Monty, what was your best innings of the series and how do you respond to reports that the Aussies this year were a much weaker team than in previous years?'

Isla nodded sagely and feigned comprehension as she waited for Monty's lips to stop mouthing what may as well have been a foreign language. Looking down at her notes again, she continued.

'Really, and what chance do you think England has of retaining The Ashes when you face the Aussies again on their home turf?'

Monty was well aware that Isla didn't have the first clue about what she was asking. He also didn't like her. He wasn't sure why, there was just something about this girl that made him feel uneasy.

'And what about the tour to South Africa, will it be the same team?'

Monty said he hoped so with perhaps the opportunity for one or two new players to shine. Finishing that answer, he smiled politely and moved away. Bob picked up Monty's hostility and took that as their cue to leave. They had enough in the can anyway.

'That'll do, pet. Let's get out of here.'

Isla was relieved and thankful for Bob's intervention. Dropping her notebook back into her oversized Accessorize bag she turned to leave and walked straight into the immaculately presented Julian. Isla thought he looked gobsmackingly gorgeous and felt her heart flutter.

'We're making a habit of this, Prime Minister,' joked Bob who knew exactly what Julian Jenson was up to.

He'd seen the Prime Minister keeping an eye on Isla throughout the reception and had no doubt he would make an approach before they left. Why else would *HND* suddenly be receiving so much access to the leader? Bob swung his camera onto his shoulder and shoved Isla, who was still carrying the microphone in her hand, in front of Julian. The wily old boy was not risking a dumbstruck junior reporter for a second time and asked the question himself.

'Anything to say to *HND* viewers, PM?'

Bob was of course right in his assessment of Julian's interest in Isla. He had watched, captivated, as Isla wandered wide-eyed through the throng. Her silk, sleeveless cocktail dress, bought by her mum from Debenhams, while completely inappropriate for the lunchtime event, clung seductively to her nubile curves. Julian hadn't been able to stop thinking

107

about her since the day he had called the election. Why this particular pretty little thing had such an impact on him, Julian had no idea but he absolutely had to speak to her again before she left today.

Ben was keeping a close eye on Julian and noticing the camera already rolling he strode smartly over to his love-struck boss. Ben was worried he was about to make another complete tit of himself with Isla, and stood right behind Bob and directly in Julian's eye-line.

'Don't be a fuckwit,' he mouthed and Julian immediately came to his senses.

'Yes, I do have a word or two for your viewers. I want to say how delighted and proud I am of our victorious England cricket team. To recover The Ashes against such strong opposition is a sensational achievement. I'm sure I speak for all of your viewers when I offer whole-hearted congratulations to every single member of the team. Bring on the tour of South Africa, that's what I say.'

Isla and Bob both smiled. Bob had been aware of the dark forces of Gollum lurking over his left shoulder and could instantly pick up the change in the PM's demeanour. From flirty and familiar he was now focused and formal, very much back on a tight leash.

Isla meanwhile was delighted that she could head back to the office with yet another PM interview in her pocket. The political editor who had decided it wasn't worth coming along to the reception, not that he'd been asked, had scoffed when she gingerly sought his advice on whether Julian Jenson might say something on camera.

'To you, dearie? I wouldn't have thought so for a moment. You've had your 15 minutes of fame. Don't milk it, there's a good girl.'

His disparaging words were still ringing in her ears as she gathered up the microphone cables for Bob. Ha, let's see who laughs last. Thank goodness she hadn't succumbed and headed back to the North East. Her election exclusive had lifted her overnight from obscurity to the lofty heights of daytime reporter. She was keen to rise much further and already had her sights on Suzie's presenting job, but she was content to bide her time for the moment.

Checking that the camera equipment was safely packed away and his boss could no longer make a nationwide idiot of himself, Ben wandered off. He was keen to chat to the rather impressive spin bowler whose athletic prowess had been most striking throughout the series.

With Ben busy, Julian was once again allowing his hormones to rule his body parts and gallantly escorted Isla towards the stairway. Bob trailed a couple of steps behind but still very much in earshot.

'Great interview again Isla, thanks. Your organisation really needs someone incisive like you on the campaign trail. It's going to be a long six weeks and a young, energetic reporter with, shall we say a potential feel for politics is definitely what's needed. We'll sort out the necessary accreditation so you can join us on the road. I'll get Ben to speak to your head of news.'

Isla was unsure what the invite meant but looking up at Julian's beaming face, assumed she should be flattered by the offer. If she had a choice she would rather be sitting on the sofa next to Sid than on a bus next to Bob, but there was no doubt that the PM was hot and spending time in his company might be fun. She couldn't yet put her finger on why she felt so attracted to him but he was just so . . . powerful.

Realising he was waiting for a response, Isla replied: 'Thank you, Prime Minister. That's great. Can I just ask, who's Ben?'

Bob wondered if there was any hope for this girl.

September

15

Harrow on the Hill

Dominic Jenson had no fear. His top hat in place, silver cane held loosely in his left hand and his coat tails flowing in the autumn breeze, he strode determinedly over Harrow on the Hill. Dominic was a Harrow School monitor, or prefect, to mere mortals, and the son of the incumbent Prime Minister. The reflected glory of his father's role offered him a discreet level of privilege among well-heeled peers. Sadly, he didn't deal with that celebrity status with any degree of good grace.

'Did you know that they filmed scenes from the Spice Girls movie, *Spice World*, on those steps, just there?' offered Henry as they walked briskly over the pedestrian crossing opposite chapel.

The two boys were heading down the hill towards their boarding house, Elmfield, to change from Sunday best to more relaxed attire.

'Yes Henry, I did know that. You tell me every single time we walk by,' replied Dominic.

'Yes, but did you know Richard Briers was in it too?' pressed Henry.

'Yes I did.'

'As was Michael Barrymore and rather strangely Elvis Costello too, can you believe it?'

Henry's predilection for spouting pointless trivia was in danger of receiving a more negative response from Dominic. As they headed down Grove Hill, Henry twittered on.

'This was the scene of the first ever fatal road accident in the UK, resulting in the death of the driver. Did you know that, Dom?'

Dominic was no longer listening. Today was potentially quite a tricky day for the 18-year-old whose nonchalant yet superior air had made him unpopular with both masters and pupils alike. His haughty behaviour was causing numerous issues with fags who he felt should frankly better know their place. A ridiculous accusation of bullying, after that light-hearted dunking of the new boy in the masters' bathroom, was just not on. That little twerp would pay for his loose tongue when this latest misunderstanding had blown over.

'Is your mother coming today?' chattered on Henry as they reached Elmfield and headed inside.

'Unfortunately so,' shrugged Dominic. He loved his mother more than anyone else in the world but knew today's family lunch planned for the brasserie on the Hill was going to be tricky. She abhorred bullying and had badgered his father constantly until he agreed to include tackling it as one of the major planks of his schools reform. She was totally furious with him about the little mix-up with the fag.

'Lucky you, no one here for me this weekend. Might have to go for a jog round the track or maybe even a swim,' sulked Henry.

'Come to lunch.'

Dominic was delighted. His mother would be too embarrassed to chastise him in front of another pupil.

'Yes, excellent, come to lunch. Hurry up Henry, get changed or we'll be late.'

Four hundred yards away his mother was squirming uncomfortably at a rear table in Cafe Cafe. Sipping her iced tap water, she was wondering how best to tackle her son about his appalling behaviour. Valerie really wanted a stiff gin, but looking across the table at her mother, she knew that would be a bad idea.

'Thanks for coming, Mum. I've no idea what's got in to Dom at the moment. His headmaster is seriously considering excluding him for two weeks and with this being his exam year that could cause all sorts of problems.'

'Oh, now don't you worry, our Valerie. He's just being a lad. Too much energy, that's the only trouble, love. All we need is to get rid of some of it on the playing field like we did with our Monty. We'll have a nice chat over our dinner and everything'll get sorted before you know it.'

Valerie smiled meekly at her mother who always had her 'dinner' at lunchtime and 'tea' at dinnertime. Just one of those north/south language challenges like napkin and serviette she thought as she reached for hers from the table. But Valerie knew that her mother would be absolutely appalled if she had any idea of the accusations being levelled against her favourite grandchild. Sheila had raised her own children to show respect to others. Valerie was too embarrassed to confide in her mother the seriously unpleasant bullying claims she'd been told of by the headmaster.

Julian was also furious at his son's antics and had originally planned to come along today to read him the riot act. He had reassured Valerie how he well remembered the unpleasantness of Marlborough bullies and was not about to tolerate it from his own son. Unfortunately with the election only a month away, his time was not his own and he'd had to reluctantly cry off from the family lunch at the very last moment. Instead he'd headed into Downing Street to prepare for a three day visit to the North West and potentially a quick curtain call across the Irish Sea to Dublin where he was almost as popular as the Taoiseach. There was a problem brewing with an Irish bank that could have serious financial ramifications for British taxpayers, not what he needed ahead of a general election.

'Unleashing the forces of hell' on his chancellor was not on this Prime Minister's agenda. He wanted him on side during the campaign and so the issue had to be carefully managed. With so much to do and so little time to do it in, something had to give. Extremely grudgingly, he'd told his wife it would have to be the family lunch.

Valerie was frustrated that she would have to deal with the showdown alone but her disappointment was tempered by how her life with Julian had exponentially improved over the last few weeks. He had certainly seemed much more attentive ever since her impromptu chat with the press outside Downing Street. Talk of divorce had dissolved with Parliament.

As Valerie waited impatiently for their errant son to arrive she wondered what might happen after the election. Surely the increasing affection Julian had shown over the last couple of weeks could only flourish? They had hit a very rough patch that could have derailed less robust relationships, but she felt increasingly confident that their fundamental love for each other would be strong enough to survive the challenge. Her husband had been truly sorry not to be able to support her in what would undoubtedly be a challenging couple of hours with Dominic. She completely understood the demands of the election had to come first.

Valerie would perhaps have been less understanding if she had known the real reason for her husband's last minute change of plan, his continuing infidelity with Sally Simpson and a tryst in the Hampstead safe house.

As Dominic strolled in, the staff at Cafe Cafe took a collective gasp.

'Not him, not when we're this busy,' whispered Abi, one of the waitresses.

Dominic was oblivious but Valerie noticed their reaction and wanted to cry.

'Hi Mummy, hi Granny Sheila. How wonderful that you have come all the way to the dump on the hump to see me.'

'Hello love. Now then our Dominic, that's no way to talk about the school that your mum and dad are paying so much of their hard earned money to send you to.'

Henry's stifled snigger at Sheila's flattened vowels quickly became a yelp as Dominic deliberately pushed the back of the chair into his friend's ribs. Pulling it away from the table, he sat down next to his grandmother.

'Granny, I was teasing. This is the best school ever. Did you know seven previous Prime Ministers were educated at Harrow including Churchill?'

Sheila smiled at her teenage grandson, her chest swelling with pride at his cleverness. Valerie was not as easily won over, seething at Dominic for having brought a distraction to lunch in the shape of Henry. This would make the conversation all the more difficult but with the threat of temporary exclusion hanging over her elder child, he would not be wriggling off the hook this time.

Ignoring his mother's glare and concentrating on his grandmother, Dominic was warming to his theme.

'And you know what else, Granny Sheila, the poet Lord Byron was once involved in a plot to blow up the headmaster. Truly, you'll never guess what he did. OK, Granny should I tell you? Well, this is what happened. He laid a trail of gunpowder through passages in the house and then he tried to ignite it. Can you believe it, the beastly things those old Harrovians used to get up to?'

Dominic was relieved that Henry's pointless trivia had finally paid off. Valerie watched her mother lap up Dominic's nonsense knowing full well that the battle lines were being drawn by this suave, well-educated teenager who would now be able to count on his grandmother's support in any show-down. He has the silver tongue of his father, thought Valerie.

16

Hampstead, North London

At that exact moment, Julian was expertly using his silver tongue to offer intense gratification to Sally as he held on firmly to her taut, tanned thighs, tightly gripped around his handsome face. Lithe and muscular, he effortlessly lifted her from the bed and onto his broad shoulders. Sally felt all the excitement and exhilaration of a fairground ride as he continued to offer intense pleasure before she was finally sated and he lowered her gently back onto the round bed. Julian flopped contentedly beside her.

Sally was in heaven. How could she have doubted how much he loved her? He was magnificent in every way. The glow quickly passed though and was replaced by the question that had been niggling incessantly at the back of her mind. Why hadn't Julian contacted her for nearly two weeks? She couldn't understand why a man who had so recently pledged forever togetherness had dropped off the radar for a whole fortnight. It was no good, she needed answers.

Leaning over the edge of the bed Sally slipped her pedicured toes into Louboutin heels and stood naked in front of him.

As he panted with contentment, Sally put one hand on her hip and couldn't resist a half-pout.

'You really are a very bad boy, JJ, for causing me so much heartache.'

It was the first time the couple had managed to squeeze in some stolen pleasure since Valerie's speech on the steps of Downing Street. Sally's fury at the 'I love him with all my heart' delivery had given way to simmering unease and then frantic phone calls as she tried desperately to contact her lover. Julian had finally phoned. Her initial anger was followed by cautious acceptance of his economical excuse. That had now been rewarded by this afternoon tryst in the glorious surroundings of a stunning Hampstead home as the guests of a loyal friend.

Over the last two years they'd relied heavily on the open availability of the private residence with generous hospitality that also included regular dinner party invites. Even the security services didn't know that the only two invitees were in the bedroom rather than the dining room of the otherwise empty though well-lit house.

The generosity and discretion of the billionaire rugby club chairman had provided them with complete privacy to conduct their occasionally noisy love affair, well away from public scrutiny.

'Seriously, JJ, I was very upset. Why didn't you call?'

Wrinkling his nose to feign acceptance of his bad behaviour, Julian was instead admiring the view. Brains and a body to die for, it wasn't difficult to appreciate Sally's appeal. She was bright, with the sort of agile mind that had offered both good counsel and lofty disdain of political foes. 'At 20 we worry what others think of us, by 40 we shouldn't care' had been her watchwords to him and they'd served him well in dealing with irksome cabinet members. Intelligent and amusing, she was his rock, perhaps even his soulmate. A little more mature than previous lovers, she still scored easy victory over youngsters who were nubile but silent in the bedroom. Sally knew what she wanted and was always deliciously adventurous.

'Oh JJ, are you ever going to leave her? I've been so patient with you but it's just not fair anymore.'

Julian sighed, frustrated by her tone. If it was going to continue to be one of those conversations he may as well have gone to lunch with the family instead.

'Darling, of course we'll be together, but I can't have a messy divorce right in the middle of an election campaign now can I? I'm planning for our long term future together my love, you know I am.'

Sally immediately brightened, stupidly buoyed by a few choice words. After Valerie's Oscar performance outside Number 10 she had started to doubt if she would ever become the next Mrs Jenson. Her ultimate dream was to be lady of the manor with a rock on her finger so big she would struggle to lift her arm. Once Julian's father had passed over, the Herefordshire estate would fall to JJ and she would become not only the country's first lady but Lady Sally too. Until then, despite her uncharacteristic neediness, she would simply have to exercise patience.

Keen to keep Julian's attention until his libido caught up with hers, she turned on her pin heels and glided seductively away from the bed and towards the chaise longue. But the runway strut was wasted on Julian who was scrutinising his text messages rather than her derrière. Nothing from that little poppet Isla, despite making doubly sure Ben gave her his mobile number. How disappointing, he thought, quickly stuffing the phone under the duvet. Sally was none the wiser as she turned to face him again.

'Hungry?'

Julian lay back on the crisp, Egyptian-cotton sheets and

looked across the Osborne and Little decorated bedroom towards Sally who was draped against the leopard print chaise longue. She was absolutely magnificent and yet he was surprised to find himself wondering for the first time if he was making the right choice. Sure, the sex was fantastic and her quick wit and sharp mind kept him on his toes, but was that really enough to want to spend the rest of his life with her? He knew how to deal with a boisterous opposition leader who nurtured ridiculous hopes of unseating him in the election. He also had no concerns about offering the whisky and revolver to those less-than-loyal cabinet colleagues as soon as the public vote had been cast, undoubtedly in his favour. It was women, or more precisely lovers, Julian couldn't handle.

Sally hadn't been the only one, but she had been the Special One. She ticked every box and for the last two years he had shown little interest in other women, including his wife. But now for some reason Isla was sparking his interest and that could prove a problem with the ever suspicious Sally. Julian could never understand why all women weren't as reasonable as his mother.

Lady Agatha Jenson-Fitzsimmons had always been content with her lot. She was satisfied to spend her life subservient to his father while always ignoring the indisputable knowledge that Lord Jenson was a philanderer. Regular overnight sojourns to his London club were not spoken about and in return never caused embarrassment. As a result, Lord and Lady Jenson-Fitzsimmons had a perfectly functional and satisfactory marriage. Why couldn't Julian find a woman like that? Sally's raison d'être was certainly very different to that of his mother.

Julian gazed absent-mindedly at the magnificent crystal flutes they'd been sipping Dom Perignon from, delicately finished with platinum 18-carat white and rose gold. The glasses were stunning, but he began to wonder if like the champagne, the sparkle was starting to fade in this relationship. Sally was feisty, powerful and yes, dangerous. Stealing time with a journalist was a risky pastime for a Prime Minister and there would be considerable downsides to ditching Sally. He would certainly have to say goodbye to the positive press coverage she provided. Flattering photographs and warm words in *Celeb* magazine were almost always picked up by the newspapers and other glossy magazines. That had definitely helped with his popularity in the past and would be absolutely essential leading up to the election. Sally would crucify him if she was rejected and the press would have a field day.

As Julian looked towards his lover posing seductively on the chaise longue, the autumn sunshine seemed to catch her beautifully lifted face in not quite the most flattering light.

All things considered, would it be better to stay with boring, dependable, docile Valerie and develop a clandestine relationship with the mouth-watering Isla instead?

Sally sensed his disquiet and was having none of it. She reached across and picked up a remote control from the Lord Linley Trompe l'Oeil coffee table. She selected Smokey Robinson's *Sexual Healing* on the Bang and Olufsen sound system, the music they had first made love to.

Pressing play and reclining gently on the sofa, Sally parted her legs just enough to once again arouse Julian's insatiable interest in sex. All negative thoughts towards his lover faded as he threw back the duvet, careful not to reveal the mobile secreted there and eagerly joined her.

As Sally was again writhing with pleasure, Valerie continued to squirm uncomfortably at the family lunch across town. Everyone had finished their Sunday roast and Dominic had stalled for quite long enough.

'Henry, I hear that your knowledge of Harrow is legendary.

I wonder if you might put it to excellent use and be good enough to escort Dominic's grandmother on a short tour of the Hill? We'll wait here and catch up on a couple of things.'

'Oh yes Mrs Jenson, I'd be delighted.'

'Should we say about half an hour, mum?'

Henry who had failed to catch the pleading look from his school friend stood and offered Sheila his arm.

'Perhaps you'd like to see where Lord Byron's illegitimate daughter Allegra is buried? May I call you granny, Sheila?'

Sheila nodded willing acceptance and together they headed for a stroll towards St Mary's church. Finally outmanoeuvred by his mother, Dominic accepted defeat and remained seated. His mother took a sip from her cup before reuniting it with its saucer.

'So young man, I'm listening?'

17

Manchester

Julia and Monty's wedding plans were well in hand. They had a meeting scheduled with the editor of *Celeb* in the morning when they were due to sign contracts and would head down to London from Manchester tomorrow. There was an early train they could catch save putting unnecessary miles on the Aston, thought Monty. With everything under control tonight the cricketer had a free pass for his stag night with the England boys. Julia was with her mother, choosing flowers for the bridesmaids, and had arranged to meet her fiancé at Manchester Piccadilly station first thing.

Initially, the Home Counties cricketers had been keen to make the stag party a weekend celebration and head off for some Spanish sun but the Lancashire lads were less enthusiastic. After some deliberation Monty had decided on the bright lights and balmy weather of Manchester. A rather stiff but important looking chap with a striped orange and lemon tie, described by some as the colour of blood and vomit, had counselled against any shenanigans. What on earth his stag night had to do with the MCC, Monty hadn't the first idea, but it was a completely unnecessary warning to him anyway. He was a true athlete with no real interest in alcohol and had only reluctantly agreed to party with the boys. His best man, Charlie, a premiership footballer, had insisted on him celebrating his last few days of 'freedom'.

After The Ashes success Monty was much more keen to spend time with his beautiful fiancée than drink over-priced booze surrounded by groupies in an upmarket North West nightclub, but Charlie had been adamant, so here they were, cocooned by glass and mirrors while sitting on zebra print leather bar stools. There were benefits, the young women were certainly beautiful, though the appearance of some left Monty baffled. How could such scantily clad local girls look like they'd spent a fortnight in the Barbados sun when he knew for a fact it had been raining in Manchester for a month?

As a particularly attractive blonde cruised by, Monty was momentarily distracted by her suggestive smile and impressive assets until his mother's voice jolted him back: 'Don't go looking for mince when you've steak at home, young man.'

Monty had first met Julia on a blind date organised by Charlie. He'd arranged drinks at a bar in Richmond, a swanky area of south west London. Monty hadn't been keen but Charlie reassured him he wouldn't be disappointed. Arriving outside the trendy bar and glancing through the floor-to-ceiling window he could see Julia was already inside. One glimpse and he was immediately smitten. She looked drop dead gorgeous in a lime green satin mini dress and thigh length suede boots. Even from that distance he could see that she had the most beautiful deep blue eyes he wanted to swim in.

The couple clicked from that very first night and had spent every available moment in each other's company since. Julia was everything Monty had ever wanted in a woman and his proposal, within a year of their first meeting, was eagerly accepted. Their wedding on 5th October was now just around the corner.

'What you smiling at, mate?'

It was Charlie, who was surrounded by a bevy of stunning brunettes in the cordoned off VIP section of the bar.

'Julia. Just wondering what she might be up to.'

'Mate, don't be daft, have you seen what's around us tonight and they're all completely up for it. We're safe in here while those paps with their pesky long lenses are stuck outside in the cold. You have the rest of your life to be nagged at by Julia. Tonight, we party my man.

'Remember though, if you're not in bed by midnight . . . try a different girl!'

Charlie turned away from his friend to pay a little more attention to a young lady who was gently caressing his inner thigh. Her sole intention was to guarantee she would be the one the celebrity footballer wanted to call tomorrow. Telephone numbers exchanged and Charlie was back.

'Where was I? Oh yeah, women. Where would we be without them? Just a little word of warning though mate, if they're drinking spirits, best to give them a wide berth. Buying women Bombay Sapphire is like putting petrol in a diesel car. They're both guaranteed to break down by the end of the night.'

Charlie laughed at his own joke and raising his champagne glass turned back to his growing crowd of admirers. Monty shook his head at his best friend's brazenness. Charlie's problem was that he lacked the love of a good woman. What he needed was a Julia.

The two young men had been inseparable since school where they had both exhibited supremely able sporting ability. Their PE teacher swiftly identified very different athletic skills and had predicted great things for each of them. He had coached and cajoled them and the pair had trained hard, at first representing their house, their school and subsequently their county. Now, in their prime, they both had the honour of representing their country, equally fine ambassadors for football and cricket.

Off the field though, their lives couldn't be more different. Monty was content to be a one-woman man, happiest at home playing backgammon with his fiancée. Charlie meanwhile preferred to play the field. His wealth, celebrity and chiselled jaw guaranteed him a warm reception wherever he swaggered. A cocky wide boy who easily charmed the birds from their pants, observers often mistook Charlie for an East End barrow boy rather than a Burnley Comprehensive lad. Tonight was no exception. He was again thigh deep in attention, this time from a rather forward girl asking for a 'sloe comfortable screw against the wall.' Charlie had assumed that was a cocktail but was happy to oblige either way.

Looking at all the interest surrounding his friend, Monty knew that although he was already bored Charlie would have no intention of leaving any time soon. So grudgingly nursing his ludicrously priced champagne, he turned to make small talk with some of the other cricket boys who were lapping up the cupboard love.

'Is it always like this?' asked Phil, one of the younger players in the England squad. He had only made 12th man for The Ashes Series but was hoping for better things in the upcoming tour of South Africa.

Monty had been impressed with the youngster's attitude at the training ground and had high hopes the spin bowler would be included by the England selectors. Tall, handsome, with a flop of curly blonde locks, Phil was proving almost as popular as Charlie with the ladies, but certainly less able to cope with all the attention.

'I can't believe it Monty, there are girls everywhere and they keep giving me their phone numbers. It's fantastic, I don't know what to do.'

Monty smiled at Phil's naivety and put his arm around the youngster's shoulder.

'Always remember what yer mum told you. Keep yer 'and on yer ha'penny.'

Monty was a mummy's boy and was proud of it. She had always been his touchstone and had supported him throughout his fledgling cricketing career. Every Sunday night right through the winter she would drive him to the Lancashire Academy for the indoor training that honed his technique. His dad often had to work but Sheila attended every school and county youth game. She'd sit for hours in her fold-away chair armed with a flask of tea, the Sunday papers and heaps of praise for when he came off the pitch, regardless of how he'd played. If she was bored, she never showed it, unlike Monty who hated being in the outfield and was always frustrated waiting for his turn to bowl. But, Sheila would have none of it and drilled into him the importance of sporting etiquette. *Nobody likes a glory boy. Just do as you're told and wait your turn our Monty.*

'How's your Valerie?' It was Phil again who had bored of talking to beautiful but slightly vacant potential conquests.

'Yeah, she's alright, thanks. This election bollocks is taking its toll on her I think. Julian is away a lot and what with the kids at those posh schools, I think she's a bit lonely to be honest. I'm going to go and see her next week, make sure she's OK ahead of the wedding.

'Anyway, look at the time will ya. I don't know about Charlie, but I've had it with this place. Me and a couple of the lads fancy a quick pint at the Beech Tree if you want to come?'

Phil nodded his acceptance and the cricketers turned to leave. Charlie noticed the others starting to make a move through the heaving mass of Sunday night revellers. He promised he'd call several hopeful young ladies before reluctantly saying his goodbyes and sauntering over to join his friends. A trail of keen would-be conquests, unwilling to give up quite so easily, followed on behind. As the sporting group reached the exit they paused, waiting for minders, brought in by *Celeb* magazine to protect their investment, to move around them. Monty's wedding was big news and with the event itself strictly invitation only, the paparazzi outside the nightclub were desperate for any pictures they could snap ahead of the big day.

A nod from the minders and the group moved cautiously outside. They were immediately greeted by the obligatory blitz of flashbulbs and shouts. 'Monty, Charlie, this way, this way.' The heaving scrum quickly disintegrated into mayhem as photographers and revellers alike jostled to catch a glimpse of the sporting superstars. Even Monty was shocked by the sheer numbers outside the club and was keen to reach the safety of his vehicle as quickly as possible. Where had all these people come from?

With heads down, the athletes moved warily towards their chauffeur-driven Range Rovers, still being followed by the group of young ladies hoping to hitch a ride to a better life.

'We need to move Monty buddy, this is getting out of hand.' It was the cricketer's minder who had put a protective arm around his shoulder, almost lifting the six-footer off his feet as he guided Monty towards the car. Monty was relieved to be in such capable hands as he was steered expertly through the melee. Charlie was in a similar position just ahead of him but Phil was caught like a rabbit in the headlights and disorientated by the shouting and flashlights was becoming separated from the group.

'Phil, Phil, this way mate, come on, this way.'

Monty reached out and managed to grab the young player before starting to drag him through the crowd. With some brute force Monty was able to push Phil ahead, sandwiching the young player between himself and Charlie.

'Keep going mate, don't stop, just keep your head down and follow Charlie.'

Monty was trying his best not to panic but as the ambush intensified the mood turned ugly and club bouncers began to wade in just as the sports group reached the waiting vehicles. The first Range Rover had been allocated for the groom and best man and Charlie jumped inside. Monty was just a few steps behind and bundled Phil in ahead of him. The driver had his two passengers and pumped with adrenaline put his foot down, unaware that the cricket legend wasn't in the car yet.

Monty was unsure what was happening. The cacophony surrounding him had ended abruptly. Events suddenly began to slow to a crawl. All he could hear were muffled, cotton wool voices that appeared to be talking to someone else a very long way away. He could just about make out blurred, distorted faces too, one seemed to have a hand stretched towards him but it was completely beyond his reach. Could it be Phil? It looked like Phil. He wasn't really sure. As he looked again the faces became more blurred and the voices began to slow still further. Strangely though that didn't seem to matter anymore. Monty could feel himself tiring. He stopped trying to listen to what the voices were saying. Were they talking to him? He wasn't sure. He didn't care. He was becoming very sleepy. Very sleepy. Eventually he felt the open car door ricochet against the side of his temple. There was no pain, no anxiety as his powerful, athletic frame slowly crumpled and folded. He felt himself heading towards a very calm, relaxed, quiet place. Everything seemed peaceful. He was warm and unconcerned.

Monty was already unconscious before the shocked crowd realised he was trapped beneath the vehicle.

18

Downing Street

'Julian, it's Ben, where's the Mrs?'

The Prime Minister had been heading out of the Downing Street flat when he paused to answer the sitting room phone. He was on his way to Liverpool for a political rally at Albert Dock. The trip to the North West would also include a planned visit to Liverpool Football Club where he was due to meet the sports minister. That had been Ben's idea. He'd counselled that it was essential to include official as well as party business during an election campaign. That way the travel bill would be met by the public rather than the party purse. Julian was unhappy with what he considered such inappropriate financing especially after the MPs' expenses scandal. On top of that, this interruption so early in the morning was most unwelcome. Safe to say he was irritated with his spin doctor today and curt in his response.

'She's still asleep. I'm on my way down, Ben. See you in the car in a second.'

'Stay there boss, I'm on my way up. Wake her.'

'Ben, it's 5 am. I'd rather leave her sleeping if it's all the same to you, matey.'

Julian was becoming more and more frustrated by the increasing intrusion into his limited down time. He felt his life over the last month was no longer his own and he was exhausted. The campaign trail was taking a massive toll, zigzagging around the country and pressing the flesh 24/7. He'd told Ben that a six-week lead up to a general election would be just too long. The last thing he wanted was to head up to the North West for a rally. Now, yet another interruption. What on earth could be so important that he needed to disturb Valerie too?

'I really don't think . . .'

'Trust me boss, get her up now.'

Frustrated, Julian dropped the receiver back into its cradle and walked towards the bedroom to wake his wife. Julian had found it difficult to resist when Valerie had tentatively suggested they once again share the same bed. He hadn't wanted any more confrontation and was prepared to maintain an air of rapprochement until after the election when he would finally have to make a choice about the future romantic course of his life. There were other nocturnal benefits too for the insatiable sex lover.

Ben was hurrying up to the flat, having been tipped off by one of the night team on the *Sun* about Monty's accident. He'd immediately rung the hospital for more details. It looked bad. Apparently as the Range Rover had tried to drive away Monty had been knocked unconscious by the open rear door. His left leg had taken the full weight of the rear axle and he had a broken femur. Several eyewitnesses had fainted at the sight of the jagged bone penetrating his skin. His minders had only limited first aid knowledge but were soon supported by ambulance paramedics. Despite their best efforts it had proved very difficult to stabilise the cricketer who was losing a lot of blood and he was rushed to hospital. The ECB had already sent one of its top medics up to the Manchester Royal Infirmary. There they had been given the bad news that apart from a complex fracture of the left femur, a potentially life-threatening injury in itself, he had also suffered severe trauma to his head. Plans were being put in place to transfer him down to a specialist hospital.

As Ben arrived at the door to the flat he wondered whether Sheila and Frank Mitchell were already aware of their son's accident. They certainly weren't at the hospital. Either way Valerie would be the best person to speak to them.

Greeted after the first knock by a bleary-eyed Valerie and her grumpy husband, it was Valerie who remembered her manners first.

'Morning Ben, bit early, come in though, what's the matter?'

Walking through to the sitting room, Valerie flopped onto a ghastly cream sofa joined a moment later by her husband. Tucking her red, painted toes underneath her she tried to maintain her modesty while at the same time wearing rather revealing satin bed wear. The well-worn M&S pyjamas had been assigned to the bin as her husband's interest in her had once again begun to grow. Julian put his arm around his wife and pulled her closer to him. Valerie had been heartened by his increasing affection over the last couple of weeks, but to show such warmth in front of Ben was indeed unexpected.

'Valerie . . .' as Ben spoke, she was immediately alarmed. Never had she known such a kind tone from this man who had formaldehyde running through his veins and she instantly jumped to her feet.

'What on earth has happened?'

Unsure of what he was about to say she waved her arms frantically, beckoning him to rush to the point. What could possibly have happened?

'It's Monty, he has been involved in an accident.'

134

She was wide awake now. What had happened to her little brother?

'Tell me now and tell me everything, Ben. Where is he?'

Julian stood and walked over to his wife, taking her in his arms ahead of the bad news that was undoubtedly coming.

'He was hit by a car while leaving a nightclub in Manchester. He was taken to a hospital in the city and I can assure you, Valerie, he has been receiving the best medical care ever since.'

'Yes, but how is he, Ben?' Valerie broke free from Julian's embrace, little interest in his attempts to comfort her and desperate to learn more about her brother's condition.

'He's in intensive care and isn't conscious at the moment. He suffered severe head and leg injuries. The doctors are in the process of carrying out tests. They're doing all they can.'

'Is he going to die?'

Adrenaline was starting to take over and Valerie momentarily leaned her head against her husband's chest to steady herself as her legs began to buckle. Julian held her a little tighter and gently stroked her hair.

'The medical team have asked me to reassure you that they are doing absolutely everything they can.'

Valerie was shocked by Ben's response. Did that mean her brother was going to die? What were they doing to help him? Was it enough? Was he in the best place? Should he be somewhere else where he could receive better treatment? How long would it take for her to travel to Manchester and be with him? Her parents would be devastated. She needed to be with them.

'Where are Mum and Dad, do they know?'

'I don't know, Valerie. I have only just heard the news. They aren't at the hospital yet. There are no family members with him at the moment. The ECB was trying to track down Julia but she wasn't at home.'

Valerie immediately pulled away from Julian and ran barefoot towards the bedroom, closing the door behind her. She wanted to make the phone call to her parents in private. Julian took the hint and slumped back onto the sofa with his head in his hands, lost in thought.

Ben took a seat at the other side of the sitting room allowing his boss a little space to absorb what had happened. Julian's face carried genuine concern for his brother-in-law's well-being. Ben was also anxious about the no-nonsense Lancashire lad. He was a handsome charmer who was a good ambassador for the sport and for Julian. This accident was a terrible blow.

But Ben couldn't stop himself from considering a more positive spin. Surely the accident would mean that the wedding would no longer go ahead as planned. That would completely screw up Sally's big exclusive.

Ben checked himself and looked over at his boss. He could see that Julian was deep in thought. Still, now was the time to deal with another pressing matter while Valerie was out of the room.

'Valerie will want to come up in the helicopter with us, boss. It would be much quicker than driving. We could sort out being collected from John Lennon Airport straight down the East Lancashire road. She'd be at Monty's bedside soonest.'

Ben paused before adding: 'But we're full. What do you want to do?'

'Bump somebody then.'

Stupid bloody question, thought Julian. He was on his feet and pacing the floor of the sitting room while Valerie broke the news to her devastated parents in private. Should he go in to be with her or should he wait?

'I agree, boss. I was just wondering who would be the best person to get rid of to make room. Perhaps Isla?'

Julian spun around to face Ben, the point suddenly dawning on him. In all of the early morning drama he had completely forgotten that this was the long awaited trip Isla was to be on. He had planned to use it to woo the impressionable youngster before making a calculated move on her sometime within the next couple of weeks. Sally was caught up in London, planning the coverage of Monty's wedding. Valerie was busy settling Jessica back at school. There was also that all-important meeting with Dominic's headmaster. This overnight trip had been the perfect time to concentrate on seducing the impish Isla.

'Fuck.'

'It would appear not. Or at least not tonight, Prime Minister.'

Ben was also frustrated. He had spent the last couple of days meticulously planning for Isla to travel with the PM's party. The trip was organised under the premise that *HND* viewers would be given exclusive 'day in the life' access to Julian. The helicopter ride was part of the overall plan to impress the young reporter.

Julian was about to speak again when the bedroom door opened and Valerie dashed back into the sitting room. Looking at his boss, Ben raised an eyebrow. He wished he'd had a small wager on her first words.

'I'll come with you in the helicopter. It'll be quicker.'

An immediate left hook thought Ben, the boss would have no choice but to throw in the towel. Julian paused for a moment, aware of his obligations. He was truly sorry about the accident and of course he wanted Valerie to be with her brother as soon as she possibly could but he was also desperately keen to be able to carry on with his tryst if at all possible. What could he say?

'Hmm, of course darling, but you need some time to organise yourself, talk to the children and so on. Let me arrange a driver to take you up to Manchester in an hour or so when you're ready. He can take you straight to the hospital and then go to collect your parents. He'll be on standby wherever you need to go, much better than being without a car.'

Valerie looked aghast at her husband. Was this the same man who had been stroking her hair and offering comfort and support in bucket loads just a few moments ago? Had he lost his mind?

'Monty is in a drug induced coma, Mum and Dad are in shock, Julian. His fiancée is finally on her way to the hospital though goodness knows where she's been until now. I will telephone the children on the way. I need to be there right now. Let's go.'

Ben leaned back in his sofa, he was staying well out of this domestic. Julian was on the ropes and would have no choice but to concede defeat. Quite rightly too in his spin doctor's opinion. Isla could keep.

Julian was less happy to accept that outcome and tried a different tack.

'Darling, darling I know you need to be there right now but I'm only thinking of what's best for you and Monty. There will be photographers everywhere, we need to give Ben a couple of hours to organise things.'

Ben glared at his boss. Wanker, do your own dirty work. Valerie wasn't prepared to accept this ridiculous nonsense for a moment longer.

'That's exactly why we need to be there as soon as possible. Mum and Dad will not be able to cope with the press. They need me NOW.'

There it was, a clean blow to the conscience. He was on the canvas and wasn't getting up again.

Standing in the doorway, Ralph Lauren jeans and an Aquascutum roll top sweater pulled over her night dress,

Valerie glared at her husband. What on earth could he be thinking? It must be the shock. She was clutching a Joseph overnight bag stuffed with as many things as she thought she might need and could just about reach while on the bedside phone to her father. Her other hand was on her hip.

'I'm waiting, Julian. Now, let's go.'

And the moral bout was over. Victory was Valerie's. Even Ben had been surprised at Julian's heartlessness.

What would happen at the other end was for him to organise between now and landing in Liverpool. But one thing was certain – Isla wouldn't be travelling up with the official party.

19

Isla was squirming excitedly in the passenger seat of the crew car on her way to Battersea helidrome with Bob when she received a text from Ben.

Change of plan, no room at the inn. C u in liverpool.

She'd been up early, too excited to sleep at the prospect of travelling in a helicopter with the Prime Minister as part of an official tour. Her mum had counselled her to wear a warm coat because she'd heard it could be cold flying in a helicopter. Isla had laughed at the suggestion and gone for a Bolero jacket and ra-ra skirt instead, along with fingerless lace gloves from Coast just in case it was a little chilly. She was certainly all dressed up but did she now find herself with nowhere to go? Did the text mean that the trip was being cancelled? Isla handed her mobile to a rather grumbly cameraman.

'What does this mean then, Bobbie?'

Bob wasn't really in the best of moods this morning. He hadn't been due on shift for the next few days and had promised his lovely wife he would treat her to a few days away at their villa in northern France. He'd been packing when Carole phoned. She needed a big favour. Would he baby-sit Isla? A trip with the PM was no biggie for Bob but he knew the daft lass from Newcastle could very easily find herself in trouble if left to her own devices. Carole was of the same mind.

A brief chat with his eternally understanding Mrs and she had obligingly agreed to visit her sister in Sunderland instead. Bob had felt rather less obliging when his alarm woke him at 4 am. Putting on a suit and tie hadn't improved his mood either but he was a stickler for respect and always dressed appropriately when travelling with the PM.

Bob had been calculating arrival times at various locations for the day's shoot when Isla handed him the phone. Glancing at the screen he had a quick read through the text from the spin doctor. He shrugged, his confusion apparent, and leaned across to switch on the radio just in time to catch the news headlines. Monty's accident was leading the bulletin and without missing a beat Bob immediately turned the car around and set the Sat Nav for Manchester Royal Infirmary.

'Ring Gollum and tell him you want a line for the top of the 6 o'clock bulletin. He's on the back foot, pet, after bumping us, he'll give you something. Make the call.'

Isla nodded and scrolled through her BlackBerry to find Ben's number. He'd playfully written it on her forehead after that embarrassing moment with the PM in Downing Street when she hadn't known who he was. Or at least he said that it had been done in fun. She was about to call, but stopped herself, hesitant to rock the boat any further. She was still reeling from yet another tongue lashing from Stephen James, the political editor at *HND*, who was livid at her continued access to the PM. Only yesterday he had stormed into Michael Grifton's office complaining bitterly at Isla's 'day in the life' trip to Liverpool. Given that the trip wasn't happening now, she would much rather accept defeat and go back to the office.

'Go on pet, tick tock, tick tock, not got all morning. We're on air soon, ring Gollum, find out what's happening. You can do a live with Sid into the top of the show either on the phone or we can pull over and do it in vision if the story's big enough. We've got the kit in the back.'

Isla still sat motionless in the front seat of the Volvo estate, phone in hand, seen-it-all-before old boy beside her, mountains of camera gear in the caged boot. She was potentially across yet another massive *HND* exclusive access story when suddenly and inexplicably she began to cry.

'Oh shit, not now,' sighed Bob under his breath. He needed to get them up to the North West quicker than a Chinook could fly there from the capital and now he had a bloody sniveller on his hands. He'd been in this position so many times before. The pressure becoming too much for young journalists who, until that point, thought they knew it all but would then crack.

Swinging the Volvo estate into the nearest drive-thru he lowered the window and ordered his trusty first aid kit of a hot chocolate with a sprinkly, iced donut for Isla and a black coffee for him. Given the size of the lass, all those calories in one go would probably kill her, but it was a risk he would have to take to keep Isla stable while he contacted Carole.

'Get that down you pet, you'll feel a lot better before you know it.'

As Isla blew her nose and tentatively nibbled on her unhealthy breakfast, Bob surreptitiously texted the programme editor:

Got a sniveller. Sitting on biggie. Call soonest.

Within moments of him pressing send Isla's phone rang. The distressed youngster, whose mascara was running in rivulets down her pretty little face, looked at the flashing screen on her mobile. Who could want to talk to her at this time in the morning? It must be Ben.

'Oh Bobbie, it's Carole ringing. What should I do?'

'Best answer it, pet.'

Reaching for his Rizlas from the glove box, Bob opened the driver's door and headed for a walk around the fast food car park, leaving the two women to talk in private about snakes on the TV ladder.

20

Muswell Hill, London

Sally was running late as usual and had no time for distractions like a teenage son who wouldn't get out of bed. Dashing down the stairs she caught a quick glimpse of herself in the hall mirror and was as usual pleased with what she saw. Today she'd chosen a Stella McCartney trouser suit from her cavernous wardrobe, a new purchase to complement her darker hair. Sally wasn't really keen on wearing trousers, preferring to parade her pins whenever possible, but not this morning. She had to concede that bride-to-be Julia Cavan had even better legs and she certainly wasn't prepared to be embarrassed by the younger woman. So, power trouser suit it was.

Today was the day she was due to sign off on the Monty and Julia wedding-of-the-year spread, the biggest and most costly deal *Celeb* had ever done. In fact, the price tag had been significantly more than the magazine had originally wanted to pay. Monty's agent was certainly a shrewd negotiating cookie and had pushed for a sharp price. That had led to a few anxious negotiations with a significant hiccup or two only resolved by a last minute bit of love-bombing of the happy couple. Eventually, all issues settled, the deal was done. It included a belated at home engagement shoot, the wedding itself, honeymoon pictures and first baby shots. All in the bag. Sally's publisher was very happy indeed and was due to join them for a celebratory breakfast in the boardroom at 9 am. Normally, it would be a quick chat in the editor's office with the client's agent, a final look over the paperwork and two signatures. But Sally had been very keen Julia and Monty should come in personally to the *Celeb* building even though it had been Monty's stag party the night before. That in itself had been a bone of contention with Sally trying hard to include pictures from the night as part of the deal but Monty had drawn the line, so *Celeb* had to be content with minders protecting their investment instead. He'd better have made that train. She wanted them both there on the pretext that it would be a great fillip for her hard working staff to meet the celebrity couple. In fact, her ulterior motive was to subtly flirt with Monty, as indeed she did with every man she met for the first time. Sally then hoped that the next time Monty met up with his brother-in-law her name would be mentioned fondly in conversation.

If she was being completely honest, the wedding deal price was too high and she would have passed if it hadn't been for the Julian connection. Sally was increasingly concerned that he was becoming a little distant from her. They had met at the safe house only twice since he'd called the election and this wedding deal would mean she could be front and centre in his thoughts again.

To that end, she'd insisted that the wedding shoot must be overseen by the editor. There was too much at stake to leave it to a deputy. In truth, it was also the only way she would be invited to the big day and she already had the perfect 'look at me not the bride' outfit lined up. Smiling at her cunning, Sally checked her eye make-up in the mirror and not quite content with her work applied a little more Estée Lauder from her grey quad palette.

Looking at her Rolex she saw that it was already 8 am. She was late, late, late. Sally shouted up to Sean for the umpteenth time to get out of bed and ready for school. Dashing through to the kitchen she barked instructions at the housekeeper before dismissing her with a wave of her Elizabeth Gage ring-encrusted fingers and rushed towards the front door. Darting down her driveway, Sally clambered into the rear seat of the waiting Mercedes S class.

At that same moment Sean turned over and went back to sleep.

'Morning, Tom. Late, sorry, let's go.'

Her smartly presented driver had been Sally's rock for the last 10 years. He'd seen her through many of life's challenges and was the only man, apart from Julian, she could trust implicitly. He'd been with her since her newspaper days and she'd insisted he come with her to *Celeb* as part of the package. Tom knew almost everything about Sally. Late night journeys home after celebrity dinners or meetings with the publisher had elicited numerous heart to hearts with Sally divulging many closely-guarded secrets. He knew her foibles and idio-syncrasies, had counselled about the estrangement from her parents and the guilt she carried as a single mother. But even Tom didn't know about Julian though he had his suspicions. Sally had found it hard not to discuss the ups and downs of her relationship with the Prime Minister but knew discretion was the only hope of landing Julian for good.

Tom was aware of the many challenges Sally had faced in the early days of her career and was there to gently chastise when she bullied or shouted at her own staff in the same way now. He was also there to pick up the pieces when she occasionally crumpled. Sally adored him and treated him as a surrogate father, showering him with problems and gifts in equal quantities.

Settling into her seat, she was straight on her phone to Maria to finalise plans for the reception.

'Seatbelt.'

Sally scowled at Tom who knew she hated wearing a belt. She had often complained that it crumpled her clothes, but she reluctantly clicked it into place as Maria answered the phone.

'Morning Maria, big day today. Have you started chilling the Cristal? Julia likes the pink stuff, so bloody pretentious if you ask me. She'll probably want to use her own hairdresser for the wedding shoot too! Anyway, she can have whatever she wants today. The publisher will be there and we don't need any tantrums from our little WAG.'

Maria had a moment of panic. Her boss had obviously not yet heard the news. Oh bugger, should she incur Sally's wrath by being the one to burst her bubble or could she possibly dodge the bullet and allow her to find out in some other way?

'Erm, how's Sean?'

'He's fine, Maria. Are you listening to me? Is the champagne chilling and what breakfast choices did we go with? Julia eats next to nothing but Monty will probably want a full English after last night's party.'

Sally made a mental note to call her son and make sure he was ready for school as soon as she had finished speaking to her deputy who was quite clearly not grasping the magnitude of today's meeting.

'Did you see *HND* at all this morning, Sally? Suzie's on holiday, they were trying out someone called Tracey Partington, I think. She wasn't very good.'

Maria was desperately fishing to see if Sally had seen the news but her boss was losing patience.

'Maria, are you going out of your tiny mind? This is the biggest day *Celeb* has ever had and you're talking about the holiday rota of breakfast television presenters. Chill the bloody champagne, you stupid cow.'

Tom looked at Sally through the rear view mirror and raised an eyebrow. It was enough to calm his passenger.

'Sally, I think you need to ask Tom to put *HND* on in the car right now. Seriously, it's quite important that you catch the news headlines. We can talk again when you get to the office. Bye.'

Sally shook her head in disbelief. What was wrong with her deputy this morning? Dialling Sean's mobile she leaned forward to speak to Tom.

'Maria wants me to watch *HND*. As if I don't have enough to do today. Flick it on Tom, will you please?'

As she waited for her son to answer his phone Sally allowed herself a contented smile, thrilled at the prospect of the day ahead. Doing the deal on a sensational wedding spread with the country's top sporting superstar and his beautiful fiancée was a brilliant coup. Better still she was going to be there with Julian, well maybe not quite with him, but as good as. Whatever Maria was prattling on about in the news, it wouldn't spoil her day. Sean's mobile diverted to voicemail and she was about to try again when Sid's handsome face appeared in her HD TV monitor. He was looking particularly cute this morning thought Sally.

'We really should do something with him, Tom. Remind me to talk to Maria about an at home piece with Sid when we get to the office.'

Tom nodded but said nothing. He had seen the news and knew what was coming next.

'Morning everyone, if you're just tuning our way we want to update you on the terrible breaking news overnight. I'm sorry to have to tell you all that the England cricket star

148

Monty Mitchell is critically ill in hospital. It follows a freak accident outside a Manchester nightclub. His fiancée Julia Cavan is by his bedside. We believe Monty's brother-in-law, the Prime Minister, and his wife, Valerie, are on their way to the Manchester Royal Infirmary right now. His parents have just arrived there. The whole family is gathering to be with Monty in his hour of need. Thank goodness he'll be surrounded by those who love him most and they will all have each other for support at this incredibly difficult time.

'Our election correspondent Isla McGovern was due to be filming with the PM today and she joins us now.'

Belinda, the director, cut to Isla who was live somewhere nondescript halfway up the motorway. Carole's gentle words had worked wonders as they always did. Having made the call to Ben, Isla was once again making the most of her excellent contacts.

'Morning Sid, morning Tracey, morning everyone. The latest I'm hearing is that Monty is really not very well at all. In fact I can tell you exclusively that our cricketing hero is on life support. He was knocked unconscious by an open car door outside the nightclub. He fell under the vehicle and his left leg is broken in three places. He also sustained very serious head injuries and is in a drug-induced coma while doctors carry out tests. I can also tell you exclusively that his wedding, just three weeks away, is being postponed.'

As Isla spoke, the ticker at the bottom of the TV screen was underlining the breaking news for viewers: *Monty Mitchell critical on life support in hospital. Celebrity wedding postponed. PM and wife by his bedside soon.*

Sally was in total shock. She sat motionless, stunned, not knowing what to do, what to think. This couldn't be happening. She gripped the armrest and tried to compose herself. She was unsure of what she was feeling. Was her disbelief the result of the wedding being postponed, maybe even cancelled? Perhaps a little, but no, she was certain that wasn't it. There were plenty of clauses in the contract to safeguard *Celeb*'s money. The lawyers would make sure Monty's agent initialled the contract until the cricketer was able to hold a pen again. She also had the safety net of a holiday special with Wayne and Coleen in her back pocket which just needed cash and staff thrown at it. No problem.

No, sitting quietly in the back seat of her chauffeured car she realised her trauma wasn't connected to the deal, the magazine or Monty's injury. Sally knew it was much more personal. A sudden hollow feeling had settled into her solar plexus. Until a couple of hours ago, she had been an integral part of the lives of the PM and his family. She was holding wedding day purse strings. She was providing Julian with first-class media coverage well away from Ben's clammy claws. She was systematically destroying her rival in the pages of her successful magazine. She was in control.

Now, in a crisis, the family was gathering together to share love, comfort and support. Her involvement in their lives was no longer important. Instead they had turned to each other for strength. She, Sally Simpson, was completely superfluous.

Sally began to cry.

Looking through his rear view mirror, Tom, like Bob, had seen it all before. Turning the car around he headed for his own sure-fire cure for his passenger's occasional meltdowns, a Claridge's champagne breakfast.

21

Los Angeles

Jimmy Phillips' agent Tommy Gold had flown out to Los Angeles to meet up with his most lucrative client. He was keen to make sure the face-lift Jimmy had undergone looked more like he'd enjoyed the benefit of a good holiday than endured the work of a good surgeon. Scrutinising his client's face, he was reasonably pleased with the result but it was still very obvious that it was the knife and not the sun that had done the business.

'You look absolutely fabulous darling, but another couple of weeks' rest will totally do the trick.'

Jimmy was fast becoming the sweetheart of British television. Whenever viewers switched on their sets, they were bombarded with promos or programmes, featuring the celebrity auctioneer and antiques dealer. The channel saw ratings soar whenever the cheeky chappy was on the box. Negotiations were already well advanced for a *Where There's Muck There's Brass* Christmas Day special. Filming was due to start in late October, giving Jimmy's surgery another month or so to settle.

151

Charles, Jimmy's partner, had been totally against the aesthetic work and had pleaded that botox would be much less intrusive while equally effective. His mother had been having regular jabs for years and she looked great. On the flight over from London to LA the two men had quarrelled bitterly about the impending procedure. But Jimmy was not to be dissuaded and had already tracked down the top surgeon in the United States. With only a tiny amount of trepidation he'd undergone the rhinoplasty and face-lift in Beverly Hills.

Looking at himself in the mirror of his 10th floor Veranda Suite at the Beverly Wilshire, Jimmy was very happy and relieved with the results. Stroking his forefinger down the bridge of his new nose, he thought it looked great. He had been confident he was ready to introduce his new face to loyal viewers, but trusted his agent's judgment implicitly. Tommy had dragged him from humble beginnings to one of the most recognisable faces in the UK and hopefully America was next. Whatever Tommy said that's what Jimmy would do.

They'd first met at an auction Jimmy was hosting in the Midlands. Tommy had been impressed by the likely lad's ability to woo his audience. Even back then Jimmy had a talent for whipping up enthusiasm. He'd managed to raise more than £10,000 for a pair of gravy boats that had lain forgotten in their owner's pantry for decades. After the auction ended, Tommy, a top TV agent for almost 25 years, had introduced himself and convinced Jimmy of his own undoubted star quality.

In fairness, the auctioneer hadn't been much to look at back then. Overweight frumpiness was exacerbated by his ill-fitting cheap suit. His hair was unkempt and his teeth were like gravestones, but he had the X factor. There was also, rather unfortunately, a slight issue with skeletons in the closet. A brief period behind bars in his youth after a 'misunderstanding' with an escort could easily have blighted Jimmy's future plans but he reckoned without the supreme skills of Tommy. Counselling Jimmy to change his surname, his address and his attitude, together they hatched a story for the kiss-and-tell newspaper article that would inevitably come sometime in Jimmy's future. And anyway, Tommy's philosophy had been tell-tales only crept up from under the floorboards to haunt the famous. If it happened they'd both have already made a fortune.

Five years later and they were certainly well on their way to those big bucks. Even so, Tommy thought a suite at the Beverly Wilshire, complete with its own private marble and wrought iron stairway entrance, would be making an unnecessary dent in Jimmy's finances. Still, it was none of his concern. His 20% was safe with Harry at Coutts.

'Seriously darling, you look absolutely fabulous. The surgeon has done a sensational job, but really no need to rush back to the UK. The weather's horrible anyway. So much balmier out here.'

If Tommy was completely honest he was desperate to have Jimmy back in the UK as soon as possible. There was some profitable corporate work they could squeeze in before filming started again and he was in talks with Tesco about an advertising deal. But Tommy was equally keen not to rush it. He didn't want Jimmy's nose job scaring the horses.

'OK, well if you're sure Tommy, we're happy to stay out here for a little longer. I know, let's all go to Las Vegas instead?'

He was becoming bored rigid padding around the suite all day keeping his new face out of the sun. Charles was also starting to become fractious and homesick. He had quickly tired of solo trips to Disneyland and Universal Studios and there were only so many times he could find celeb spotting on Rodeo Drive interesting, especially if he was doing it alone. His eyes lit up at the thought of glitzy shows and gambling and he dashed over to give Jimmy a huge hug.

Tommy was less keen. He had no interest in gambling, it was a mug's game and he didn't really approve of his client's weakness for roulette either. Still, it was his cash and he could put it all on black if he chose to.

'That's a great idea, but you'll have to count me out. I have some more business here in LA, then I need to head back to London to sign off on the Christmas deal.'

Charles had no such concerns and squeezed Jimmy's newly stretched cheek.

'Darling, darling, darling, please can we go to the Hard Rock Hotel? I want to stay in the Paradise Tower. Remember that was where we had our first . . .'

'Anyway boys, time for me to go.'

Tommy was a well fed family man with a passion for Arsenal and a love of Savile Row suits and Thomas Pink shirts. Although very fond of his client, he was completely heterosexual and drew the line at learning about his client's bedroom proclivities.

Jimmy nodded his understanding.

'You start packing darling and I'll show Tommy out.'

Strolling back up the staircase Jimmy put his arm around his agent's shoulder.

'Sorry about that. No offence. Anyway we'll see you back in London by 2nd October. Julian Jenson will no doubt need my vote and we're both unbelievably excited about Julia and Monty's wedding on the Saturday. We've already chosen matching Italian white suits. Charles saw them in GQ magazine. I was a little worried we would look like gangsters so we've gone for multi-coloured cravats rather than string black ties.

'Tell me what you think about our wedding gift idea. We were contemplating a solid gold cherub carrying a Swarovksi crystal wand with their names carved into the torso. It's a variation on the place settings for Simon Cowell's 50th. What do you think, too ostentatious?'

154

'Shit.' In his haste to leave the lovebirds to it, Tommy had forgotten to tell his client the second most important reason for visiting.

Closing the front door he walked back down into the suite with Jimmy. Sombre-faced, he sat down with the newlyweds before breaking the news about Monty's accident and the postponement of the wedding.

22

Downing Street

Ben was furious with the party workers gathered around the Cabinet Room table. They were trying to come up with some fresh ideas for the election campaign. So far without success.

'For fuck's sake, you're all two bit numb nuts.'

They still had three weeks before voting day. Now was the time when so many previous elections had been won and lost and Ben wanted some clever ideas. Looking around the table none were forthcoming. He had been initially unsure if party workers should be allowed to sit around the Cabinet Room table. There may well be some ridiculous antiquated rule that only allowed ministers to sit there. So, he made sure that those who needed to know were aware that the room was being used in its other, less formal capacity, as a library today.

'If Obama can come up with a fucking three word slogan what won him the election, surely we can. Come on, I'm looking for ideas.'

'Well, all right,' shouted one wag recounting the catch phrase that irrevocably damaged Neil Kinnock's hopes of being PM. Everyone groaned. Political watchers had always felt the phrase, used during a 10,000 strong rally at the Sheffield Arena, as well as Kinnock's 'un-prime-ministerial' performance, had cost the Labour leader the 1992 election. It had been an embarrassing memory ever since.

'Not fucking funny Justin, get out.'

As the disgruntled party volunteer slunk towards the door the rest of the room fell silent, everyone instantly wary of Ben's cold eye. The polls were not as good as they should have been and he was in no mood for humour. He needed positive ideas from those gathered. Julian was as usual delayed so Ben had taken the opportunity to sit in the Prime Minister's chair, the only one around the 40 feet boat-shaped table with arm rests. The table had been designed by Tory Prime Minister Harold Macmillan to allow him to clearly see everyone seated. Ben was using the plain view to spot any further smart-assed waggery.

'OK people, this is the deal, I need 10 slogans from each of you by close of play today. Also smart ideas for a party political broadcast please, ladies and gentlemen, if it's not too much fucking trouble?'

Everyone groaned.

'I know, I know, they're stilted and dull but as you are all aware it offers us direct access to the voters without any sceptical hack putting their spin on our policy. Labour used Eddie Izzard in one of theirs and managed to really appeal to the young voter. That's what we need.

'Anyway, the good news is we've just signed up a big name Hollywood director to film it for us so I'm not letting you leave this room today until you come up with some ideas. There's no such thing as a free lunch especially in the Cabinet Room, sorry library. Now get your thinking caps on.

'Justin, get your arse back in here and no more lip or next time you're out the front door.'

As Justin returned to his seat, Ben checked the timepiece that Labour Premier Harold Wilson had positioned directly opposite the PM's chair. He'd had it put there to save him having to turn to look up at the wall clock behind him. 11 o'clock, an hour's brain storming was in order.

'See you at 12 and nobody sit in my chair.'

'Isn't it the Prime Minister's chair?' suggested an over-confident party worker from the far end of the room.

Ben had already stood and had his back to whoever had dared to question him so instead he threw a wooden drinks coaster and a handful of pencils in that general direction. Scowling, he headed towards the soundproof doors leaving eager young minds to save the election.

Meeting Julian in the corridor, Ben could see for the first time just how much the campaign was beginning to take its toll on his boss. Still affable and well presented, there was nevertheless an air of world-weary sadness about him. Hardly surprising, given the amount of political pressure that was being heaped on him at the moment. Ben suggested one of their increasingly frequent strolls around the walled garden. There they could speak without fear of eavesdroppers.

'I've left the children coming up with campaign slogans, boss. Should be a while.'

'Not, "well, all right"?' offered Julian with a thin smile.

'Already done that gag, boss, and frankly it wasn't funny the first time either.'

Ben fell easily into step with Julian and they both walked towards the back door of Downing Street.

'Lovely day, fancy a stroll around Horse Guards, boss?'

With no answer forthcoming, Ben turned towards the Prime Minister and was startled to see him distraught. Immediately taking his arm, a little for support but more to get him out of the building before anyone noticed, Ben walked quickly, tugging Julian along beside him.

158

Making it as far as the terrace, Ben gestured for Julian to sit overlooking the garden, his back to the building, shielding him from prying eyes. Ben sat down opposite. He had never seen his boss break down before. Neither man spoke for a long time. OK, the polls weren't great but there was still a long way to go. The Leaders' Debates would turn everything around again in Julian's favour. They'd been preparing for every possible curve ball and with his film star features he was born to appear on TV. Women loved him, men wanted to be him. He would once again be the nation's darling.

But for some reason the man, who to the outside world had everything, was crumbling. Ben felt the urge to hug him, but realised that it would be completely inappropriate and instead sat quietly waiting for Julian to compose himself.

Could it be domestic issues that were troubling him? The fuss over Dominic and the threat of exclusion for bullying? Ben didn't think so. Valerie had been to the school several times over the last month and Dominic, while on his final warning from the headmaster, had been allowed to continue with his studies.

So what else? One of the papers had been sniffing around about alleged marriage difficulties despite Valerie's speech. He was sure Sally, with her Fleet Street contacts, probably had something to do with that. Only one newspaper had been interested in the story so far. He'd soon resolved that by reminding the political reporter involved of who she had mistakenly shared a bed with in Thailand. Would she risk a fleeting front-page story for long-term marriage difficulty? No, Ben was sure that issue had gone away, at least until after the election.

Monty was still in hospital, but he was off the danger list and he had the best medical care money couldn't buy, thanks to the NHS.

159

So what could it be? Ben wasn't sure but he did know he needed to fix it. He poured them both a glass of water, sat back and waited. Finally Julian spoke.

'Tell me what to do, Ben.'

Hmm, thought his gatekeeper, might need a bit more of a clue than that Mr Prime Minister, sir. He tilted his head and waited patiently to hear more.

'Women, Ben, women. They pull you in every direction until they leave you spinning out of control.'

Ben was flabbergasted and just about managed to resist the knee-jerk temptation to stand up and leave. Here he was busting a gut running an election campaign and all Julian was worried about was getting his end away as per bloody usual. Sensing his spin doctor's disapproval, Julian leaned forward and put his head in his hands.

'Sit up.' Ben barked the instruction, concerned that one of the nearby campaign team could quite easily be looking through the bomb-proof curtains of the Cabinet Room. He didn't need them picking up on the PM's despair and was annoyed with himself for not having suggested they chat in Julian's private office instead. He was most keen to move off the terrace immediately.

'Want to have a beer later, boss, when there are less people around?'

But Julian wasn't listening. He needed to talk and his spin doctor was the only person he could discuss his emotional issues with. The floodgates began to open.

'I thought Valerie and I had turned a corner Ben, I really did. OK, so we weren't newlyweds anymore but we'd been getting on an awful lot better. She'd stopped drinking and had so much more energy. I thought her speech outside Downing Street was top drawer and she'd started to look really quite stunning.

'At the same time I felt the relationship with Sally, once

so passionate and all-consuming was reaching a natural end. Perhaps it was nothing more than a meaningless fling after all, even if the sex was sensational.'

Ben took that as a cue to leave the conversation right there and stood.

'That's more info than I need boss, thanks. Anyway, kids to corral.' Julian ignored him, determined to continue with his lover's lament and Ben reluctantly sat down again.

'I've been agonising over what is the right thing to do. I wasn't sure if I wanted to make it work with Valerie but I felt I wanted to end things with Sally.'

Despite Julian's sombre mood, Ben could no longer take the heart to heart seriously. Did Julian think he was completely stupid?

'Now then, I spy with my little eye something beginning with . . . Isla.'

'OK Ben, it's true she is a pleasant distraction and I have thought about that, but if all I was interested in was spending fun time with that slip of a girl, then why do I still feel so melancholy?'

Ben slumped back in his wicker sofa and feigned concern. Pondering options for a moment he offered one reason for his boss's dark mood.

'Hmm, maybe cos we're in the middle of a knackering election campaign and if you don't win you could find yourself as Ladies' Fashions manager at John Lewis in Oxford Street instead of one of the most powerful men in the world? Perhaps that's it, what do you think?'

Julian didn't laugh. Ben didn't care. He wanted to be anywhere but here right now. There was important election work to be done. Those kids were probably crayoning ladybirds on the Cabinet Room wallpaper by now.

'No Ben, the election is not why I am buckling. I'm buck-ling because of women and the intolerable strain they are putting me under. I feel I can no longer cope and I don't know what to do.

'Valerie is struggling with Monty's injury. It has hit her very badly. She wants to be up in the North West offering support to her mother and father. But she also says she wants to help me by being involved with the election and she really can't be everywhere. The prognosis for Monty is not good you know, Ben. The specialists are suggesting that he could be in a wheelchair for a very long time. The whole family is taking it really hard.

'To be totally frank, I'm afraid Valerie is slipping back into her old ways. The doctor has prescribed happy pills and Valium which have certainly changed her mood, but not in a good way and anyway, I don't think that's the answer. I also think she has started drinking again. In fact, I'm sure she has and I just can't handle the inevitable depression that will follow. I don't know what the answer is, Ben, but I honestly don't feel that I can be married to her for the rest of my life.'

Ben shook his head, not with any sympathy for Julian's predicament but for purely selfish reasons. They'd already agreed that any talk of divorce would be put on hold until after the election next month and here was Julian again, banging on about it. As if he didn't have enough to deal with. Ben's brain clicked into spin doctor mode as he considered the worst case scenario of a domestic break up before 3rd October, but Julian hadn't finished.

'I have thought long and hard about my future happiness, Ben. Despite a wobble or two over the summer I have decided that I really do love Sally very much indeed.'

Ben nearly fell off his chair. He'd thought from the way the conversation was going she was about to be replaced with potential Lover Mark II. The one with the sleeker lines, less miles on the clock and an all round smoother ride. He couldn't keep up with Julian's fickle frame of mind.

'Are you really sure, boss? What about Isla, she obviously floats your boat. Have a paddle with her after the election, eh?'

Ben hoped the reference to the young reporter would provoke a smile. It didn't. He tried again.

'Seriously, I saw the way she looked at you when she was here to cover The Ashes celebration party. She was acting like a smitten teen on her first date and to be honest so were you, boss. One hand in your pocket, working the room, trying to look nonchalant but stealing glances in her direction whenever you could. I nearly suggested you get a room.'

Julian did finally manage a wry smile of acknowledgement. He had to admit he was rather taken by the young TV reporter with the beautiful body and the captivating smile.

'She's certainly stunning but I don't know, Ben. I fear she is less interested in me and more interested in what I can offer her.'

How was that different to Sally's motives, thought Ben. That madam was definitely only here for De Beers. But Julian was probably right, that was Isla's motivation too, ice cold in the pursuit of her own interests, namely bagging a rich powerful bloke. However, for now she would no doubt be content with unparalleled access during the election campaign and that suited Ben just perfectly. He needed a tame TV reporter to spin positive stories during the campaign and if Isla also provided the added bonus of elbowing out Sally then so much the better. She would be much easier to manipulate.

'I think Isla is a sweetheart, boss, a pussycat. Someone you should seriously think about spending a little more time with after polling day.'

Julian pondered on Ben's words and as he gained strength from the conversation his resolve returned.

'Lovely thought Ben, but after much soul searching I have

decided that Sally is the one for me. I have ignored her far too much over the last few weeks and I have to admit that absence really does make the heart grow fonder. She is a magnificent woman who deals with challenging, potentially sticky issues with real toughness, but she can also be so gentle and soft at the same time.'

'Fucking hell, you make her sound like washing up liquid. Sorry to say that out loud, but come on boss, really.'

Ben was now completely exasperated by the heart to heart. He could see much more time and effort would be needed to see off super bitch and time was something he really didn't have at the moment. Julian though was just getting into his stride.

'She is relaxed and charming with her staff, a doting mother and an all round fabulous woman. I really can't imagine my future life without her.'

That was it, Ben really had heard enough this time.

'Talk to the hand, boss. I don't have time for this.'

He stood again but Julian had one more bombshell.

'Thanks for listening, Ben. There really is no one else I can talk to about this but finally saying out loud some of the stuff that has been flooding around my head has definitely helped. Once the election is over I am seriously considering asking Sally to marry me.'

Ben flipped.

'Fabulous news boss, I'll bake a cake.'

Briskly walking back inside, he stopped at the doorway, unable to resist one more cheap jibe.

'Just one thing to remember, first wives want a stable marriage, second wives prefer a marriage with stables. Pay your money and take your choice.'

23

Lancashire

Sitting on the couch in her parents' front room, Valerie wondered if there was a God, why he had forsaken them. Monty had just been released from hospital and was sitting opposite her in his wheelchair, shock and grief etched on his tear-stained face. He was holding a piece of folded A5 note-paper that had been waiting for him in an embossed Smythson envelope on his parents' sideboard.

Valerie had only just arrived from London and hadn't even had time to take off her Aquascutum winter coat before being guided into the room by her distraught mother. Rarely had Valerie seen Sheila this upset. She hadn't been due to travel up from London until the weekend but had received an urgent call from her mother. What on earth could have happened? As Valerie walked in and dropped her overnight bag next to the door, Frank was pacing in front of the smokeless coal fire. Not knowing what to say, he turned away and busied himself with the scuttle, putting more coal on the fire. It was Sheila who finally broke the silence.

'Don't you worry, our Monty. She'll find out soon enough

that the grass isn't always greener. Sometimes it turns out to be Astroturf, son.'

Monty said nothing and looked into the fire. Valerie was keen to be alone with her brother.

'Tell you what Mum, why don't you put a brew on and Dad, can you see if we have any Jammy Dodgers?'

Given a cuppa was the cure to all ills in the Mitchell house she knew they would readily act on her instruction. With their parents in the kitchen Valerie darted across to wrap her arms tightly around her brother's once muscular frame and hugged him close. All Valerie had been told by her mother on the phone was that Monty had received even more bad news. Could she come up to visit as soon as possible, which of course she had done as quickly as Julian could organise a driver.

As she rocked her brother in her arms, he began to cry. She held him close for a long time and whispered soothing reassurances. 'I'm here love, I'm here, let it all out. I'm here. Don't you worry, our Monty, I'm here now. Let it all out, love.'

As Monty's tears eventually subsided, Valerie gently moved away and looked pityingly on a young man who until recently had had it all. A beautiful fiancée, a loving family and a glittering career. His sporting values had been held up as an example to the nation. Life had been rosy for Monty Mitchell and now this. Surely he couldn't cope with much more heartache.

'I don't understand, our Valerie. I don't understand why this has happened. I don't want to live without her.'

He held out the note and she took it from him.

Darling Monty,
I am so sorry but I can't continue to live this lie. I really believed that I did love you. I wanted to be your wife, have your children and spend the rest of my life with you. But that was before I found Charlie.

I'm sorry but I'm calling off our engagement. Charlie says that because you are best mates this will be particularly hard for you. We're both sorry. We thought it was only fair for you to hear it from us first before you see the photo shoot we have done for this week's Sunday Sun. It's very tasteful and I only said good things about you. I hope you can forgive me.

Jx

PS I am keeping the ring as I'm sure you wouldn't want it back.

Valerie screwed up the note in disgust and threw it into the fire. She had so many questions she wanted to ask her baby brother but instead she cradled him as he once again crumpled into heavy sobs.

24

Sally had been in a filthy mood for a fortnight and her staff was walking on egg shells. It was a massive blow to the magazine that the wedding had to be postponed but they were still surprised she was taking it quite so personally.

Today the editor had called a brainstorming meeting and attendance was compulsory. The mood was sombre and eye contact minimal.

'Right, tell me what's happening with Wayne and Coleen? Come on somebody. Well? Cat got your tongue, all of you?'

Sally was glaring at her staff but everyone was looking steadfastly down at their notebooks. They knew the first one to look up would be toast. Never had so many BlackBerrys been checked in the same room at the same time. Long-suffering Maria knew it was down to her to break the silence.

'Well Sally, Wayne and Coleen are certainly still the best alternative but *OK!* also want the picture exclusive. I'm expecting to hear back from their agent today but I do think we should perhaps be considering other options unless we want to get into a bidding war.'

168

'Really Maria, is that what you think? Do I look like I want to get into a bloody bidding war? Do I look like I want to throw away the magazine's bloody money? Do I? That is an absolutely ridiculous idea, you stupid cow.'

Sally banged her hand on the table. No one flinched. Everyone continued to look down at the desk.

'Anyone else got a better idea for the cover? What about Adrian Chiles, he's the new thinking woman's crumpet? Simon Cowell? David Beckham? If we want to go glamour, how about Cheryl?'

Again no one spoke.

'No ladies, I didn't think so. It has to be Wayne and Coleen, doesn't it? Obviously. Now get off your backsides and sort it.'

Sally was interrupted by the sound of a depth charge exploding – Sean's attempt at a joke when he had re-programmed her text message alert. She wasn't amused and looked at her BlackBerry.

Hello my love, long time no speak. I miss you terribly. Please call when free. JJ x

She hadn't heard from him since Monty's accident and had begun to fear that Valerie had him back in her clutches. But no, it wasn't the case, he had wriggled free and he wanted her. Sally was instantly joyous.

'OK everyone, as I was saying, I appreciate how hard you have all been working on this deal. If we could press on with trying to secure it, I would be grateful. Anyway, time for lunch, let's reconvene tomorrow.'

Sally floated out of the room at 10.30 am and her team stared disbelievingly at each other. Maria merely shrugged her shoulders and took over detailing who should do what to try and secure the impossible.

Sally found herself almost running back to her office in far too high Prada heels before quickly closing the door. She took a few deep breaths to try and calm herself before speed dialling 'John', as he was labelled on her phone. Julian was delighted she had responded so quickly.

'My love, I've missed you so much. What are you wearing?'

He was feeling most frustrated. Valerie was away in Lancashire and Isla on assignment, though he was starting to doubt he would ever enjoy the sensual pleasure of her touch. Sally was his chosen *amour du jour*, perhaps for longer.

'Hello darling, I've missed you too. I haven't heard from you forever. How's Monty?'

'Thank you for asking. How thoughtful of you. Well, he's been released from hospital and is as well as can be expected. Though there seems to be another problem and Valerie dashed up there to try to sort things out for the family. Anyway, that's not important. What is important is that I am absolutely desperate to see you.

'I haven't paid you anywhere near enough attention, my love, and I was hoping we could perhaps rectify that this evening. I have spoken to our friend and he has arranged for a little dinner party *a deux*, usual venue. Hungry?'

'8.30, can't wait.'

Ending the call, Sally squealed with pleasure before grabbing her Bulgari handbag and heading for Rigby and Peller where she'd seen a pearl, Italian broidered basque, perfect for just such an occasion.

25

Downing Street flat

'Mummy won't wake up. I've tried everything. What am I going to do?'

The pleading voice of 13 year-old Jessica Jenson was more of an irritation than of any real concern to Ben Watson. Julian had warned him Valerie was back on the gin again. She'd probably forgotten to add the tonic. Who could blame her given everything that had been dumped on her shoulders of late? She just needed to sleep it off thought Ben who was most frustrated at having been woken from his forbidden dream.

'There are two empty bottles and I don't know what to do. Daddy's not here Ben, I keep ringing and ringing but I can't reach him on his mobile.'

Ben was now wide-awake and remembering Julian's heart to heart in the garden he interrupted the sobbing teenager. 'What sort of bottles Jessica, pills or alcohol?'

'Little brown pill bottles. The tops are off and they are completely empty. Should I call an ambulance? Mummy really, really needs help.'

The Jenson offspring had been drilled into checking with Ben if their parents were uncontactable.

'NO, NO, NO.'

Ben roared the instruction before softening his tone to the frightened child. Leaping out of bed he was keen not to wake Gayle and frantically fumbled around in the dark for a T-shirt, jogging bottoms and keys before forcing on his lace up trainers, discarded after a run last night.

'OK, listen darling girl, Mummy has been prescribed extra medication by the doctor. I am coming over right now and I'll call your father on the way. He'll probably be back home even before I get there. There's certainly no need to call the emergency services. Sweet tea and a biscuit, isn't that what Granny Sheila always suggests? Be right there, everything will be absolutely fine, I promise.'

Jessica was totally unconvinced. The Cheltenham Ladies' College student was completely overwhelmed by the drama unfolding in front of her. She'd woken up in the middle of the night and was heading to the kitchen for a glass of water when she'd noticed a sliver of light from under the door of her parents' room. Jessica who was on weekend break from her boarding school knew her mother had gone to bed hours ago. Her father was detained on government business at the House of Commons but should have been home well before now. Why was the light still on? Gently tapping on the door, then venturing inside, she saw no sign of her father. Her mother lay fully dressed and slumped on the bed. Despite several pleading attempts she had been unable to wake her. Panicking, Jessica had tried to call her father from the bedside phone but his mobile continually diverted to voicemail. Where was he? Eventually she had phoned Ben Watson.

He was still on the line as he dashed out of his front door and leaped into his Aston Martin DB9 Volante, a recent boys and their toys purchase after receiving a significant family inheritance. He slammed the door of the convertible just a little too hard, almost certainly waking one or two of the neighbours. Couldn't be helped, he was in a hurry.

'Jessica, can you still hear me? I am already in the car. I'll be there in just a few minutes. Put the phone down and go back to Mummy.'

There was a moment's silence and then, this time with massive relief in her brittle voice, Jessica spoke again.

'Oh Ben, Daddy's here.

'Daddy, Daddy, Mummy won't wake up.'

As Ben hurtled well over the speed limit towards Number 10 he could hear the frightened youngster trying to explain to Julian what had happened. Julian, clearly shocked, eventually came to the phone.

'I think she's dead, Ben. There's no pulse, her lips are starting to turn blue. I'm calling an ambulance.'

'Don't be so fucking stupid. Listen to me Julian, take her to hospital and there'll be photographers swinging from every tree before the ambulance has backed up to Accident and Emergency. I'm two minutes away, just passing Big Ben, stay calm, Julian.'

But Julian was not to be dissuaded.

'Ben, my wife is unconscious, maybe dead, and my daughter is totally traumatised.'

'Yeah, I know. I've been on the phone to her for the last 10 minutes and where were you, boss? Shagging that old bird no doubt. Perhaps that's why the Mrs is in the unfortunate position she is at the moment.'

Ben knew he had overstepped the mark but hoped his words would shock some sense into Julian. An ambulance in Downing Street was a ridiculous notion.

'I beg your pardon. Who on earth do you think you are talking to?'

Julian was furious. It was no concern of Ben's who he had

spent the evening with and the audacity to suggest that it had any connection with Valerie's predicament was simply preposterous. In that moment Julian could finally see why Sally had always been so keen for him to release Ben from the payroll. He was certainly behaving abominably tonight and it was totally unacceptable.

He would be fired . . . but not until after the election campaign. Barely able to contain his fury, Julian spoke again.

'Ben, for the benefit of any doubt that you may have, let me say again that my wife is at the very least critically ill and I am now putting down the telephone in order to call the emergency services.'

The phone went dead.

'Stupid tosser,' snarled Ben as he hurled his BlackBerry onto the passenger seat and within 90 seconds spun his car into the back entrance of Downing Street. He could already hear the wail of the ambulance siren crossing over Westminster Bridge from nearby St Thomas' Hospital.

'Blues and Twos heading to Downing Street slap bang in the middle of a general election campaign, just bloody perfect. Nothing to see, no story here, eh?'

Abandoning the car, sprinting upstairs and bolting through the open flat door he headed for the bedroom only moments ahead of the paramedics. Even he was shocked by Valerie's condition. Julian had dragged her limp body onto the bedroom floor and was administering a useless attempt at CPR. Jessica was slumped, sobbing on the floor in a corner of the room, unable to comprehend what was happening to her mother. Julian's close protection officers had heard the sirens and arrived a split second after Ben, giving him just enough time to grab the empty pill bottles from where they lay on the bed and stuff them into his pocket.

'Not a word,' he whispered to Jessica and Julian as Carl appeared and dashed across to Valerie on the floor.

'Sir, why didn't you call?'

'She wouldn't have wanted you to see her like this, Carl, you know that.'

A moment later a doctor arrived and immediately took over. Touching Valerie's neck and feeling for a pulse he spoke calmly and reassuringly to his patient.

'Mrs Jenson, can you hear me? Hello Valerie, I'm Dr Lloyd, can you hear me?

'Has she taken anything?'

It was a general question to the room as he began his work. Jessica was about to speak but Ben put his finger to his lips and the Jensons said nothing. Carl had no clue.

'Nothing at all?'

Dr Lloyd raised a disbelieving eyebrow as he examined Valerie's bluish coloured lips and fingernails.

'Perhaps Valium, maybe alcohol too?'

Jessica was not prepared to remain silent any longer, but not knowing what the pills were, she was attempting to take them out of Ben's pocket when the ambulance crew arrived to help provide care.

Ben took the cue to gently steer Julian and Jessica out of the room, holding on to the teenager's arm to prevent her from reaching the bottles in his jogging bottoms.

'That's not going to help her at the moment, darling. Let the doctor do his work,' he whispered reassuringly.

By now the police had also arrived. An ambulance and paramedic rushing to Downing Street triggered urgent Met attention. Ben was incandescent. The story would be in the public domain before they'd even put Valerie in the ambulance.

'Fucking brilliant, I'll unwrap a couple of boxes of Mr Kipling's and run round with a pot of tea as well, should I boss?'

Julian wasn't listening, much more concerned about

175

settling Jessica on the sofa in the enormous sitting room. The room was now filling up quicker than a Harrods sale and Ben took control, ushering the confused masses outside of the flat while the family gathered their thoughts.

'Daddy, Mummy was so unhappy earlier, she arrived back from visiting Uncle Monty and didn't know where you were. She kept trying to call you, but you didn't answer. She said you had been very angry with her before she went to Lancashire and she didn't know what to do to make everything better anymore. Then she started to cry.'

Jessica hesitated and drew her knees up close to her chest. Julian couldn't help but notice how her reaction reminded him of her mother when she cried.

'After that she sat with me for a very long time talking about Uncle Monty and how sad he was that Julia didn't want to marry him anymore. She kept telling me how much she loved me and Dominic. Then she kissed me goodnight and went to bed.'

Julian moved nearer to his daughter on the sofa and held her tight. Her pyjamas were soaked with a mixture of sweat and tears. He hugged her tightly, desperate to offer what reassurance he could with her mother clinging to life in the room next door. Comforting his children hadn't come naturally to Julian. His parents had never been there to show him affection. He'd been brought down by nanny every evening at 6 pm to spend 30 minutes with his mother before bed. As soon as was acceptable he was dispatched away to school. Julian well remembered sobbing himself to sleep night after night in the dorm at the tender age of five. When he was 11, he ran away from school and took a train back to Herefordshire where he hoped his mother would be there to meet him at the station. Instead, alerted by the headmaster, his parents had asked the police to collect him from the train and take him back to school.

It was Valerie who had finally taught him the importance of family affection. Julian tried to banish from his mind the thought that she could now very well be lying dead in the bedroom. He rested his chin on Jessica's forehead, stroking her shoulder and holding her close to him, rocking her gently as he tried his best to soothe her. Comforted by her father's presence, Jessica relaxed into his arms and closed her eyes.

As his child rested for a while, Julian's earlier decisiveness suddenly deserted him and he turned to his spin doctor for guidance. Ben had known that Julian would need him, but perhaps not quite so quickly.

'What should we do?' mouthed Julian, not wanting Jessica to hear any desperation in his voice.

He looked completely devastated, but Ben found it hard to feel any sympathy for his philandering boss.

Ben shrugged and looked away. Eventually, the bedroom door opened wide. A semi-conscious first lady covered in a red woollen NHS issue blanket was being pushed in a wheelchair towards the front door. An intravenous drip had been attached to her limp arm.

'Oh, my love, thank goodness.'

Jessica leaped from the sofa and rushed towards her mother. Ben though didn't like what he saw. Where were they taking her?

'Surely hospital treatment won't be necessary, doctor. Our wonderful National Health Service is pushed to its very limit, especially on busy nights like tonight. We are of course doing what we can to further increase funding for you. We can absolutely assure you of extra help should we win the election. It will be our number one priority.'

Ben paused, realising he was turning the scene into a party political broadcast. But he had to stop Valerie being taken to a public hospital.

'We can organise immediate and comprehensive care right

here doctor, leaving you and this fabulous ambulance crew to carry on with your sterling work.'

Dr Lloyd ignored the spin doctor's pathetic attempt at manipulation and looked directly at the Prime Minister before speaking calmly, trying to keep out any contempt from his tone.

'Despite repeated questioning and as there appears to be no evidence to the contrary I am treating Mrs Jenson as having suffered a Valium overdose. I believe alcohol has also been a factor in her condition.

'She needs hospital care, possibly dialysis, but I am hopeful that with the right treatment she will make a full recovery. Now, if you have no objection, I plan to escort her to hospital.'

The question was rhetorical and the doctor was gone. Jessica ran back into her father's arms. He in turn looked pleadingly at Ben waiting for him to make everything better, totally dependent on the king of spin. Silence descended on the room, punctuated only by relieved teenage sobs and the buzzing of Ben's vibrating BlackBerry as text messages and emails dropped into his inbox.

Ben's brain was working overtime as he contemplated and then rejected myriad solutions. Valerie being stretchered into A&E would be almost impossible to square away without repercussions for the Prime Minister. Eventually, it was Jessica who was the first to face up to the elephant in the room.

'What on earth is the press going to say, Daddy?'

Julian's children had been brought up in the full glare of publicity. Their father was always happy to wheel them out for an appropriate or sometimes very inappropriate photo opportunity. As a result, they had become extremely publicity savvy. Even in such a tense moment Jessica knew that her mother's condition would make front-page news. The penetrating question was the spur Ben needed and looking at his watch he made deadline calculations.

178

Most of the newspapers would already be printed, so no concern there until much later in the day. But print deadlines were not a problem for the 24-hour news channels. It wouldn't be long before they'd be tipped off about the drama at Number 10 and Ben's fog of inertia cleared fast.

'Julian, you go to the hospital now. Take Jessica. If the snappers do get a picture with both of you in it, they won't use it without our permission. I'll be half an hour.'

Julian accepted the instruction without question and Jessica rushed to the bathroom to wash her face and get dressed. Ben disappeared into the kitchen with his phone already clasped to his ear.

'Isla? Hi, it's Ben. Yes, it is early, isn't it? The little hand is on 4 on my watch. Get a crew to St Thomas' Hospital quick as you can.' He paused and rolled his eyes in disbelief.

'Yeah, that's the one. The big building opposite the House of Commons. It has St Thomas' written in very big letters on the outside. Ambulances, doctors, everything you need in an emergency, you can't miss it!

'Listen Isla, Valerie Jenson has collapsed. Exhaustion. The strain of her brother's accident and the challenges of the campaign trail have proved just too much. Family are with her. She'll be fine.

'The Prime Minister will not be continuing on with his campaign. Not until his wife is well again. For the present, he will be leaving matters in the capable hands of the Deputy Prime Minister, Daisy. He is hopeful the wonderful British public will fully understand and support him as his family once again face up to the challenges of ill health.

'Yup, first Monty, now Valerie, that's exactly what I meant.'

Cutting off that call, he repeated the 'exclusive' to the political editor of Sky News, the BBC news channel and Reuters. That done, he recounted the same version of events to the ever increasing group of police, security and concerned staff gathered around the Downing Street flat.

Jumping back into his car, Ben's phone buzzed constantly as he headed across Westminster Bridge and towards a back entrance of St Thomas' Hospital. It was a secure route that the family had first become aware of when Dominic had been clobbered by a golf club at school. Apparently by accident, but knowing Dominic's reputation that was highly unlikely.

26

St Thomas' Hospital

In her egg-shell white hospital room, Valerie was feeling groggy and confused. Slowly returning to consciousness she became acutely aware of her senses, the texture of the thin cotton sheet covering her, the dazzling brightness of the overhead light and an overpowering smell of disinfectant. The room felt cold, her throat hurt from the tube that had been used to pump her stomach and the needle for the drip pinched her arm painfully. Still she had an overwhelming feeling of relief that she was alive. She wondered what on earth she had done and then she began to remember.

Arriving back from Lancashire where she had been the rock for the family, Valerie was drained and in desperate need of comfort from Julian. But where was he? Once again he was becoming increasingly distant from her and now tonight of all nights, his mobile was switched off. She really needed him right now, where on earth could he be? Valerie remembered feeling the most intense emotional pain as she contemplated what her husband might be doing and walked over to the drinks cabinet to pour herself a very large gin.

Lifting the bottle by the neck she was irritated to see it was empty and replacing it settled for vodka instead with the merest splash of tonic.

The shock of Monty's accident had been a huge strain and Valerie's reliance on alcohol had begun to increase once more. Happy pills helped a little and at the end of every stressful day Valium induced much needed sleep. She knew it was a concoction that had almost cost her her marriage once already, but she reassured herself it was just for a short time until the stress of Monty's accident had passed.

Wandering over to the sitting room sofa she had tried to flick through a pile of magazines, *Vanity Fair, Harper's Bazaar, Celeb*. But despite her best efforts she was finding it difficult to concentrate on any of them and, draining her glass, headed over to the drinks cabinet again. Valerie wished she had a faith to fall back on instead.

Pouring a significant tumbler of the spirit that helped her she tried Julian again without success, just as Jessica arrived back for the weekend. Valerie knew her daughter was coming home but the alcohol had made her lose track of time. The youngster wandering into the sitting room had focused her mind and Valerie was relieved to be drinking odourless vodka. She didn't want her daughter to know she was back on the booze.

Valerie vaguely remembered making her younger child something to eat and them chatting in the kitchen for a while. The alcohol had loosened her tongue and she told Jessica more than a 13-year-old needed to know about a mother's pain. Finally kissing her daughter goodnight and with still no contact from Julian, Valerie headed for bed. She was exhausted and desperate for sleep but a wrenching anxiety about where her husband could be prevented it. She tried his mobile. No answer.

Valerie lay down on top of the duvet, completely

overwhelmed. Her unreliable husband, her poor tortured brother, her devastated parents. She needed comfort, she wanted to sleep, be released from her pain. Valium was the answer and she took two.

Crawling back onto her bed, still fully clothed, she waited impatiently for the medication to take her to a happier place, but nothing happened. She needed to sleep right now and became increasingly agitated and desperate for the drugs to work quicker before she succumbed to total despair. As she lay there, staring wide-eyed at the ceiling, Valerie had no strength left and was losing all hope. For the first time suicidal thoughts stalked into her conscious mind. She felt powerless to resist. A blessed release from the interminable pain, a perfect solution.

The last thing Valerie remembered was stretching across to the bedside table and retrieving two small plastic bottles. Slowly unscrewing the child proof caps she poured all the contents into the palm of her hand. She began to count the capsules, but why? Instead she opened her mouth and swallowed, washing all of them down with the help of several large gulps of vodka. Lying back onto the pillow she closed her eyes and waited for freedom.

Now gazing up at the ceiling in the hospital room Valerie wondered what could possibly have made her act so selfishly. How could she have felt so self-absorbed that she cared only about herself and release from her pain. She may have problems to face but no one's life is perfect. What had she been thinking? What about the children? Slowly turning her head she was greeted by two thankful faces smiling back at her.

'Mummy, I love you so very, very, very much. Truly, madly, deeply, I really, really do. Honestly, with all my heart, I do.'

Looking at her daughter's face crumple into tears, Valerie also began to cry. Hers were tears of embarrassment and relief. Julian reached forward to wipe away her distress.

'Darling, nothing can be this bad. We'll get this campaign out of the way then take a lovely holiday, all the family together. Everything will be alright, I promise.'

Valerie looked at her husband and wondered if there really was still hope. She struggled to speak despite the pain in her throat.

'I am sorry, I am so sorry.'

'Don't be silly, my love. Don't try to speak. The doctors say you need some rest now. Get some sleep. I will speak to Dominic and to your mother and father. All will be fine. Just try to rest darling. We'll see you in the morning.'

Julian leaned down to his broken wife and Jessica attempted an awkward embrace. The youngster was trying extra hard not to dislodge the spaghetti of tubes connecting her mother to medical equipment monitoring her condition. Valerie began to cry again.

'Good night my love, sleep peacefully. We'll see you in the morning.'

Father and daughter blew kisses and walked backwards towards the door of the hospital room as Ben arrived.

'Can I see her?'

'She's very tired,' whispered Julian. He was most reluctant for his spin doctor to be left alone with his fragile wife.

'I'll only be a second. I've brought her a little present.'

Julian looked sceptical but with an exhausted and clearly still very emotional daughter leaning against him, he succumbed. Ben closed the door and was alone with Valerie. He looked over at his paymaster's spouse and felt nothing but contempt. Any compassion had gone.

'This ridiculousness could well have cost us the election. You do know that, don't you?'

Valerie looked away. She didn't expect sympathy from Ben, but she wasn't anticipating an onslaught quite so soon. Ben though had no intention of drawing in his talons.

His reputation for caustic sadism was legendary and it was about to be front and centre in spades. Walking closer to the bed he stared directly at Valerie until she returned his gaze.

'You could quite easily have killed yourself, leaving your teenage child to discover the lifeless body of her mother. An image, a guilt that would have stayed with that child forever. She would have always wondered what she could have done, should have done to save her pathetic mother's life.

'Then of course there is another child away at school. A child who loves his mother probably more than anyone else in the world. I can only start to imagine how devastated he would have been to realise she didn't love him enough to stay alive and guide him through the challenges of university life.

'Oh and let's not forget elderly parents. Pensioners who thought their daughter was happy. Old people who thought she appreciated everything they had spent their entire lives striving to achieve for her. Only to be rewarded by finding themselves huddled together over her grave while photographers with long lenses grappled for the "perfect" grieving parent shot.

'A brother who. . . .'

Valerie tried to raise her arm and whispered: 'Alright Ben.'

She was already racked with remorse without his gilt edged guilt trip.

'Oh no, Valerie, not finished yet. Listen up princess.

'As I was saying, a brother who almost lost his life through no selfish action of his own. Who could spend the rest of his life in a wheelchair, but would still prefer to live than die.

'A husband who has worked his entire political life with one aim, to serve his country. A man who has already spent four successful years leading us through conflict, economic crisis and challenges that would have broken others. But not

Julian. No, he is offering himself up to take on the mantle for a further term. Some say he must be certifiable. Tony Blair would no doubt call him, quite simply, the people's prince.

'However, however Valerie, smack bang in the middle of this right royal challenge he finds himself moments away from tragedy. This evening he could quite easily have found himself addressing a stunned nation, a nation that would be at a loss to comprehend why his loving wife had taken a fatal overdose.

'In fact, come to think of it, that's a question I'd also like the answer to. Why did the Prime Minister's loving wife attempt to take a fatal overdose?

'Tell me this Mrs Jenson, are you out of your fucking tiny mind?'

Valerie tried to speak but Ben raised his hand. He was in no mood to hear whatever she wanted to say. Opening the 'little present' in his hand he dropped a handful of marbles onto her bed covers.

'Here, you've obviously lost yours.'

With that, Ben turned and left.

October

27

Michael Grifton and Carole Smith were holding the final general election planning meeting before polling day on Thursday. Julian Jenson's wobble in the polls following his wife's mysterious illness meant everything was up for grabs. No one had believed the exhaustion line being spun by Downing Street and it had led to some penetrating questions in the papers.

'Right then, listen up. The network has agreed to extend the programme by half an hour on Friday morning so this is what we're planning. I'm going to block through our coverage and then Carole will pick up with what she's expecting from you. She'll talk about not only the on air talent but also the electoral counts we might still be waiting for that morning. Carole also has the list of who we want with which party leaders.'

There were just two days to go until the general election and tension was high. Tuesday's show had just ended and the conference room was full to bursting. Bacon butties were piled up on paper plates in the centre of the table with ketchup on the side, brown sauce for Sid. Sid and Suzie walked into the room together and sat side by side exactly as they did on the studio sofa. As Sid reached for a sandwich, Michael continued.

189

'Up until a couple of weeks ago, it was a one horse race but as most of you know the PM is doing badly in the polls. His performance on the Sky News Leaders' Debate was abysmal. He looked like a man with plenty on his mind. God only knows what happened with his Mrs.'

Michael accepted a bacon buttie from Carole before continuing.

'The papers have been crucifying him over that. Anyway, the opposition is increasingly hopeful of victory or at the very least a hung parliament.'

Michael knew he was preaching to the converted. After all, those gathered in the room included the political editor, Stephen James, his correspondents and producers, several general news correspondents who had been seconded to help with *HND*'s coverage and Sid. But he felt he needed to spell it out for Suzie and Isla.

'A hung parliament, I don't understand, Michael. Aren't we against hanging in this country?'

Suzie tilted her head coquettishly, considering her question most incisive. The presence of Carole meant disbelieving laughter was suitably stifled. She refused to have her presenters ridiculed in any way by the rest of the team, though she did sometimes despair of Suzie.

'Now as you know, any filmed reports that we still have on the shelf will have to run in the morning. We can't cover anything more about the campaign on Thursday, election day, until after the polls have closed. That means Isla's "Day in the Life of the PM" piece will be broadcast twice in the morning, once at 7.10 and again at 8.10.'

Isla smiled her acknowledgement at the high profile placing of her pieces. Stephen leaned over to his senior producer and whispered something inaudible behind his hand. Michael ignored them both and continued with his Election Day A-Z for Dummies.

'We'll balance Isla's report with similar coverage for the other main party leaders. Remember people, it is a criminal offence to report how the individual electorate has voted during the day on Thursday. Be careful with what you say. Like Lord Archer, I'm not that keen on prison food.'

Michael was certainly spelling it out and Stephen James rolled his eyes in disbelief at the ridiculous minutiae. All those in the room should already know this stuff. Why was Michael being so helpful to these two silly little girls? He could understand Suzie with her links to their paymaster, but Isla? Michael wasn't on the pull again surely?

With Michael's explanation becoming just a little too kindergarten, Carole stepped in with the information that everyone in the room was waiting to hear. The decision on who would be where on Thursday night/Friday morning. Whichever team was chosen to be with the PM's camp was top of the tree. Then followed a sliding scale down to the correspondent seconded to the UK Liberation Party. That posting was a political wilderness with absolutely no chance whatsoever of being on the TV at any stage during the four-hour post-election programme.

'As you all know, whoever is with the Liberation Party has just as important a job to do as the correspondent with Julian Jenson's camp.'

Carole was interrupted by howls of laughter around the table.

'I mean it guys, it is equally important to our viewers.'

She moved quickly on to the list of runners and riders and the room fell silent.

'Stephen, we will be counting on your brilliant and incisive analysis throughout the programme. This year we would like you to be based outside Downing Street from 6 am. We would hope you could update viewers every few minutes with your take on the next Prime Minister. His victory, his prospective new cabinet and the challenges that lie ahead for the next government.'

Stephen nodded regally. In his view this was even better than being with the PM and if Stephen was happy then life would be much easier for everyone else involved in Friday's coverage.

'Sid, we thought we would take the show on the road this year. We want you to be in a purpose-built studio outside the House of Commons. Whatever happens in the polls we feel it will be a very big story. Either a triumphant second term for the PM or a disastrous victim of "exhaustion-gate". Suzie, we would like you to be with Sid. There will be a floor manager, autocue and make-up so absolutely nothing to worry about, honey.'

Sid could see the merits of the plan and nodded at Carole. Suzie took Sid's cue and smiled happily at her programme editor.

'Tommy, we want you to be with the opposition. Gerard, you with the Socialists please. Kirsty, you with the Nationalists if you would?'

All nodded eagerly in agreement.

The list was growing ever longer but Isla still hadn't yet heard her name mentioned. The young reporter became increasingly anxious and the political editor more and more smug. Finally, after what felt like an eternity she heard Carole call her name.

'Isla, we would very much like you to be with the Liberation Party.'

Gasps of shock greeted the decision. Stephen James was delirious. He waved his notebook like a backbench MP offering his Order Paper approval to a dispatch box speech from the Prime Minister. How could Isla have slipped so monumentally from grace? What did Stephen care? It was a magnificent result all round. He was ringmaster outside Downing Street and that silly little madam Isla McGovern was in nowhere land.

Carole remained deadpan though privately she was absolutely furious at the decision. She'd been trying to change Michael's mind right up to the moment they'd walked into the room. Her contacts had proved priceless throughout the campaign, yet she was being relegated to the Vauxhall Conference League. He had given her no reason for this slap in the face but had resolutely refused to budge despite Carole's incredulity.

Isla was reeling and tried very hard not to cry but the tears still came. Desperate for an explanation she glanced across at Michael Grifton. He immediately looked away. Carole caught the exchange and wanted to know more.

'OK everyone, take your butties with you and start making those calls. Good luck on Friday, let's cream the opposition.

'Isla, can I grab five minutes before you head off please, need to run through your report before transmission tomorrow. See you in my office in a second.'

Carole was determined to find out what was going on and she certainly wouldn't discover it from Michael. He'd scurried away down the corridor as soon as class was dismissed.

Grabbing a loo roll from the ladies as she walked past, Carole headed back to her office where Isla was already waiting. Closing the door she offered Isla a seat on the faux leather sofa. Wandering over to her famous 'magic fridge' she selected a Godiva bar and a Toblerone before taking a seat next to Isla. Nonchalantly, Carole placed her own version of Bob the cameraman's first aid kit between them. Looking at the fragile reporter Carole registered how inappropriately dressed she was. Today's ensemble included a lemon shift dress with a bright orange rosette and blue shoes she recognised from Dune. *HND* really needed Jane, the stylist, to go shopping with Isla.

Carole hadn't particularly liked the young reporter when she'd first joined *HND*. She'd considered her over-confident and under talented, but Bob had counselled against rash decisions and he was a very good judge. He thought she was a bit flighty and certainly naive but had proved to be a quick learner. As usual he was right. The youngster had brought in some top political exclusives throughout the election campaign. She wasn't afraid of hard work either, staying late into the night to make sure her pieces were well edited. Carole had no idea what could have gone so wrong that she'd found herself covering the Liberation Party result without a prayer of being on the telly.

Isla who had been sitting uneasily on the very edge of the sofa started to tremble. Carole surreptitiously glanced at her wall clock, correct to the second. Moments mattered in telly. She had a meeting with the chief exec about the election coverage in 10 minutes but this conversation was probably going to take significantly longer. He'd just have to wait and anyway she'd seen Suzie nonchalantly heading in the general direction of Fritz's office so he would be in no hurry to see Carole. This situation needed sorting, she couldn't have reporters so distressed. Unwrapping the Toblerone, Carole offered Isla a triangle.

'So, why not tell me what's up? Take your time.'

Isla stared wide-eyed at this wonderful, wonderful boss who was fast becoming her mentor and confidante. She didn't know what to say, where to start. As confusion and emotion overwhelmed her she reached for the Toblerone and the tissue and the tears began to flow.

'I'm so sorry, Carole. I always seem to cry when I am talking to you. I don't know why I am so upset.'

Carole looked pityingly at Isla who was trying hard to stifle her tears. The ambitious reporter's struggle was no different to so many others who had succumbed to the pressures of TV journalism. But she needed to develop a much tougher shell if she wanted to make it further up the ladder.

'Have you ever seen *Broadcast News*?'

Isla who had just put a piece of Toblerone into her mouth shook her head.

'You should watch it on DVD. Holly Hunter is a powerful

194

no-nonsense newsroom producer who doesn't suffer fools gladly. She is brilliant but flawed.

'Even she needed a good cry every now and again. It's nothing to be embarrassed about, you know. We all do it. Even me, if you can believe that?'

Isla laughed at Carole's self-deprecation, if that's what it was, though she didn't believe for a second that anyone or anything could ever make Carole cry.

'If I was to offer you one priceless piece of advice it is never, ever let the boys see you're upset. Never, ever, ever. Getting upset in the meeting room earlier didn't do your cause any good at all. I know you couldn't help it but it's a really big mistake to fall into the stereotypical image some of our male colleagues have of how we make our way in telly.

'Weak and over-dependent on their male counterparts is what they'll think. You don't want anyone to have that impression of you, do you?'

Isla shook her head and blew her nose again before reaching for more chocolate.

'Next time you are distressed and believe me there will be plenty more next times, pop in here or have a wander round the car park until you feel better. I know it's easy to say that but afterwards you'll be glad you did. You'll soon be back in control and no one will be any the wiser.

'Now tell me why you're so upset?'

Isla attempted a half smile and settled further back into her seat. She began with the call from Ben a week ago offering an exclusive day in the life with the PM. It had followed the aborted trip to Liverpool after Monty's injury. This time she and Bob were to travel to Manchester by train with the PM and his entourage. Carole didn't know the details because Michael had taken charge of that assignment. Obviously something had gone wrong. Carole sat back to listen.

28

Inter-city to Manchester

'Don't fuck about babe, be at Euston by 7.45 am. The PM will arrive by 8 am and the train leaves as soon as both his size 10s are onboard. We'll organise a meet-and-greet hand-shake on the platform, then you can have a 15 minute-chat with him in the carriage at some stage during the journey. Don't bring too many lights and just you and one cameraman, none of this "+2 bollocks". Travel light or it doesn't happen.'

Ben had never worked in TV but accepted that production was more complicated than a newspaper journalist's basic staples of a notebook, pen and a Dictaphone. Nevertheless, too often during the campaign the PM had been slowed down by more TV crews and equipment than Ben thought strictly necessary. Broadcasting companies were keen for extra angles and other shots and always wanted two cameras to every reporter for 'reverses', whatever the fuck that meant. He'd stipulated it wasn't happening on this gig. Of course *HND* had readily agreed. Michael wasn't missing out a second time on an exclusive day with the PM.

Sitting opposite the Prime Minister across a Virgin Trains

cooked breakfast, Isla rearranged the crockery to make room for her spiral bound notebook. Inside it she had duly listed all the appropriate questions for an interview with Julian Jenson on the campaign trail. She knew it would have been pointless asking Stephen James for help but thankfully Michael Grifton had come to the rescue when she'd worn her shortest dress, highest heels and popped into his office to seek guidance and advice. As she'd stood to leave, Michael had walked her to the door. Draping his arm around her shoulders, he'd accidentally brushed his fingers against her right breast allowing them to linger a moment too long. His mistake was quickly rectified as Isla opened the door to the full view of the busy newsroom.

Now sitting on the train Isla looked up at the PM from below her newly coiffed fringe and instantly re-ignited the spark. As she began her interview neither was really listening to either question or response. Isla was captivated by Julian's smiling face, totally mesmerised as he effortlessly flirted with her, a constant twinkle in his eye. He was just so warm and friendly, not only to her but everyone around them. The way he naturally engaged with the train conductor, asking how long he had worked for the company, and how old his children were, was charming. At the same time he seemed mysterious and enigmatic. Not aloof but just beyond her grasp, an unusual sensation for Isla. What was he really thinking? She really wanted to find out. All that and impossibly handsome too. Isla was smitten.

Julian was finding it almost impossible to concentrate. He had appreciated Isla's curves ever since they had first met but the pencil skirt and silk blouse she was wearing today was temptation beyond endurance. Her soft, gentle voice was sending shivers dancing along his spine and her full sensuous mouth was perfectly kissable. How could it possibly have taken so long for him to finally be in her company for more than 60 seconds? He was certainly going to make the most of it and switched effortlessly into full seduction mode. Ben caught the gaze and shook his head in disbelief. Here we go again, brains in his trousers.

Keen to keep the situation under control, Ben pointed to his watch indicating an end to the interview for now. Wandering up the carriage for some privacy with Julian, they stood together talking through expectations, meet and greets and speeches lined up for the day. As policy discussion paused Ben was keen to quell Julian's overt flirting with Isla, but how to begin?

'Anyway, how are you holding up boss? What with talk of divorce and the er, exhaustion problem you've had a lot on your plate. Don't worry about the impact of the Leaders' Debate though. You were crap, get over it, it'll all come good.'

He paused for a reaction from Julian. A love-struck teenage grin was all that was forthcoming. Ben couldn't believe it. A suicidal wife and a pernicious lover would be more than enough for most men but not Julian Jenson. He could do what he liked after the election but a Twiggy look-alike strutting her stilettos onto the scene was a distraction too far right now.

'They do say, boss, that the best way to get over a woman is get under another, but you do have Sally for that and you can't be eating too many cupcakes, bad for your wealth. Sally would have your balls on toast if she knew you were showing an interest in model missy there. Anyway, I wouldn't mind betting that you're older than her father. Seriously, what would you find to talk about?'

'Oh come on Ben, a little of what you really fancy always does you good. I want to jump her bones, not discuss fiscal policy with the pretty little thing. Can you imagine how nubile and athletic she is? Do try to fix something up, my number one spin doctor, for whom all things are possible. I would be eternally grateful.'

Julian licked his forefinger before making a ridiculous sizzling sound in an attempt to illustrate how hot he thought the young TV reporter was. Ben tried very hard not to cringe with embarrassment. Dog tired versus puppy power. Sally would have to learn some new tricks. He was about to respond when he was interrupted by his mobile.

Further down the carriage, Isla thought the day in the life strand was going well and chattered happily to Bob as he filmed general or 'wallpaper' shots, giving her plenty of pictures to edit her piece. They planned some more filming and another interview in Manchester before returning to Euston by early evening. Isla had an edit booked for 9 pm and the report should be broadcast in the morning. That was the plan until Ben wandered across.

'Bit of a change of plan, peeps. As soon as we alight from this rather swish first class carriage we will immediately be on our way to Dublin, not Manchester. Do not pass go, do not collect £200.

'You do know where Dublin is don't you, sweet cheeks?'

Bob's hand signals warned Ben that he should back off from picking on Isla today.

'There's a small issue with Emerald Isle Bank. Put simply PM needs to fly out to save it from collapsing. Details tiny bit complicated for you, Isla, but as they say in *Chitty Chitty Bang Bang* we need to be there toot sweet. Want to come?'

Bob immediately intervened before Isla could give Ben an excuse to tease her further.

'Emerald Isle Bank has millions in investments from British companies. There've been concerns that the bank wasn't faring well as a result of the sub-prime market collapse. The bigger investors are contemplating withdrawing their cash for safer investments elsewhere. The implications for the bank and the Irish economy are potentially catastrophic. That's according to what I read in the *FT* anyway, pet.'

199

Most of what Bob had just said went over Isla's head but she was desperate not to lose face.

'Yeah, I think I heard that too. But why would the PM get involved with the Irish economy in the middle of a UK general election? Isn't he a bit busy trying to win votes that matter to him in the UK?'

'Well pet, the Irish community in the UK is massive. If they can see the PM is doing what he can to help the folks back home, then they're more likely to put their cross next to his name come polling day.'

Ben was impressed with Bob's 60-second synopsis.

'Yup and apart from that, we get an overnight at the British ambassador's Residence in Dublin. Not to mention a top-notch dinner at Ivy House. So that's definitely me in. The Taoiseach is meeting us at Government Buildings and we don't want to keep him waiting, do we?'

With the inter-city pulling into Manchester Piccadilly, the question was completely rhetorical. Within moments, Bob and Isla found themselves being whisked along in the re-directed prime-ministerial convoy, travelling towards the airport and an RAF helicopter hop across the Irish Sea.

Michael Grifton had insisted Isla call as soon as filming was completed on the train and she had obediently tried several times during the journey but the signal had been poor. Assuming he wanted a quick update on how the shoot had gone she tried again in the convoy but he was in a meeting. Isla had no idea Michael who was very aware of Julian's reputation was more interested in asserting his authority and keeping her on a tight leash. He had first dibs on any totty action. Isla had inadvertently found herself smack in the middle of a lust triangle with the Prime Minister and the head of news at her channel.

Arriving at the airport and with the helicopter ready to go,

200

it was apparent that once again there wasn't enough room for the whole entourage on board. Julian looked over at his spin doctor.

'She's coming, sort it.'

With that he strode across the tarmac and clambered on board the chopper. Bob knew what was coming even before Ben shrugged his shoulders and made a cut-throat gesture towards him. The cameraman thought Isla should stay too. She would be foolish to go without either his equipment or his support. As the rotors slowly started to turn, Bob spoke directly to the young girl.

'I think you should check with the office first. Michael's expecting your package for the morning. He won't be happy if you don't deliver because you've headed off on a jolly with the PM. Think carefully Isla, there'll be other opportunities. You're in danger of making the wrong decision here, pet.'

But Isla wasn't listening to his wise words, what was Bob thinking? She was about to be whisked away in an RAF helicopter with the Prime Minister who had been flirting outrageously with her all morning. On top of that she'd be staying at the British ambassador's residence in Dublin. Compare that with an overnight in a *HND* edit suite cutting a report for the next day's programme. It was a no-brainer. Bob must be mad to think otherwise. She didn't for a moment consider the consequences of Michael being unhappy with her actions.

'Make your mind up, babe. Don't keep my boss waiting. He's a very busy man, as indeed am I. Now or never, you decide?'

Without a moment's hesitation Isla nodded her eager acceptance and waving goodbye to Bob she rushed across the tarmac and clambered onboard to join the PM. Within a minute the helicopter had taken off, destination Baldonnel Air Base, south west of Dublin.

Bob paused for a moment as he dug out his Rizlas from the pocket of his new lightweight, seal-grey suit. His charming lady wife had bought it for him from the Marks and Spencer's autumn sale. Lighting his cigarette, he shrugged his shoulders and leaned against the tripod.

'Interesting decision, sadly not the right one.'

Bob finished his cigarette, picked up his equipment and headed back to London alone.

29

Dublin

Arriving at Government Buildings, Isla found herself unceremoniously dumped in an anteroom. Meanwhile, Julian Jenson, warmly greeted by his Irish counterpart, was ushered into bilateral talks in the Department of the Taoiseach.

Waiting for what seemed like forever, boredom finally overwhelmed her and she began wandering aimlessly around the magnificent building. Eventually Isla found a friendly member of staff happy to tell her a little more detail about where she was. As she meandered through the expansive corridors her impromptu tour was interrupted by her mobile vibrating. Noticing from the screen that it was her head of news, Isla apologised to her guide. She was just about to take the call when the door to the Taoiseach's office opened and she was immediately swept up by the official party on the move again.

'Right babe, it's nearly dinnertime. The Prime Minister needs to make a quick joint statement then some top Irish posh nosh. What've you been up to?'

'Well, I had an excellent guided tour with Enda. I learned

that this building was originally the Royal College of Science. It was designed by Aston Webb, who also redesigned the front of Buckingham Palace.'

'Fascinating, get yer coat, you've pulled.'

Ben didn't want any nosey journos asking awkward questions about who she was and guided Isla away from the press conference and towards the Prime Minister's convoy. As a rule, the Irish press was generally forgiving of their politicians' proclivities. One well-known government minister fondly known as 'the jockey', though he couldn't tell a saddle from a bridle, never found himself embarrassed in print. However, the same rules may well not apply for a British politician, whatever his popularity with the Irish people.

Isla made her way back to the car without speaking to Julian who was led directly into the news conference. He was desperate to rejoin his date but also wanted to offer what support he could to his friend and Irish counterpart. Determined to conclude the briefing in double quick time, he rattled through responses to stock questions. Yes, he was prepared to guarantee all of the British deposits in Emerald Isle Bank. No, he didn't anticipate any issue with complex EU fiscal regulation. No, he didn't expect any long-term financial unrest in Ireland. Yes, of course he very much hoped to return again as soon as possible after the election. Yes, he certainly was planning on a pint of Guinness that evening. With warm thanks to his host, he offered a winning smile and a cheery wave before heading as quickly as courtesy would allow back to the car. Easing his athletic frame into the back seat his gaze immediately locked on to Isla. She looked even more stunning than the last time he had seen her, if that were possible.

'Let's go straight to the Residence. I have no appetite for dinner this evening.'

Ben knew exactly what the instruction meant. No Ivy

House, no five courses at the Foreign Affairs Ministry on St Stephen's Green. No temptation from the extremely impressive wine cellar. No opportunity for a nightcap at the Horseshoe Bar at the Shelbourne Hotel at St Stephen's Green. No chance to gossip with his peers about how much Tony Blair was loved and Margaret Thatcher hated by the Irish people, though that wasn't in any way the view of their Government of course. Not in public anyway.

Folding his arms huffily, Ben gave Isla his best Paddington Stare. It was a look that was a complete waste of vitriol as she was concentrating on Julian's hand resting nonchalantly on her knee.

Arriving at the Residence, Julian shook hands and made small talk with government staff who'd gathered to greet him, either remembering their names himself or being discreetly prompted by Ben. He enquired how their families were and how life was treating them, before asking for light refreshment to be sent to his room in approximately 30 minutes. He would ring down.

'I need to brief Isla on what I expect from her report, Ben. Not sure how long I'll be. Probably best if you make your own arrangements for dinner. I think there's a Pizza Express within walking distance, old boy.'

'Bite me,' hissed Ben but Julian was oblivious, already walking up the staircase next to Isla.

Her phone was vibrating in her pocket again but this time she chose to ignore it. She couldn't take a call in front of the Prime Minister, now could she?

As they reached the private quarters hastily prepared earlier in the day, Julian obligingly opened the door for Isla and she walked rather apprehensively inside. It was an enormous, opulent office that smelled of ancient books and old leather furniture. Gazing in awe at the magnificent surroundings she slowly turned around and was slightly startled to find Julian standing very close behind her, an impish grin on his handsome face. He said nothing but instead looked admiringly at her for what seemed an eternity until Isla became anxious, unsure of what she should do next. Sensing her tension, Julian offered a disarming smile before loosening his Hermès tie and unbuttoning his collar. Continuing to look intently into her eyes he raised his left hand to his broad muscular chest. Stretching out his right arm, he spoke softly to her.

'Dance with me, my love?'

Blushing at his familiarity, Isla nodded and eased into his powerful embrace. As Julian began to sway Isla fell easily into his rhythm and they glided effortlessly together around the vast room, Julian gently humming 'Save the Last Dance for Me'. Completely intoxicated by the moment Isla felt she was floating and swayed more and more gracefully in her seducer's arms whispering along to the lyrics of his chosen tune. She leaned her head against his chest and closed her eyes, lost in the moment. Isla was in heaven.

'Don't forget who's taking you home and in whose arms you're gonna be . . .'

As they waltzed past the antique low-level table and reached the imposing writing desk, Julian leaned down and kissed Isla lightly on the tip of her nose. His touch was electrifying and she smiled nervously, still very unsure of what was expected. Julian though was in control, an accomplished lothario he knew exactly what to do next.

Easing slightly away he stroked Isla's cheek with the outside of his cupped fingers. Unbuttoning her coat he allowed it to fall to the floor before moving towards her again and brushing her lips with his. Isla's heart was pounding so hard she was sure he would be able to hear it but nevertheless responded to his tender enquiry. Julian again teased her by moving away just a little. Leaning on the edge of the enormous walnut and leather in-lay desk he now slowly began to unbutton her silk blouse revealing a pert cleavage restrained inside a pretty satin La Senza bra. Isla was mightily relieved she had always heeded her mother's guidance of wearing good underwear, though that advice had no doubt been for other reasons. There was nothing accidental about Julian's intentions and Isla was now completely ready to succumb to her seducer.

Starting to take the initiative, she reached behind her and slowly released the zip of her pencil skirt allowing it to fall to the wooden floor. Stepping out of it she mischievously snaked her hands above her head while continuing to sway gently to his Drifters' solo. Looking directly into his sexy seductive eyes she suddenly felt a moment of fear. Here she was standing in front of the British Prime Minister in her underwear. What on earth was she thinking?

Sensing her anxiety, Julian immediately leaned towards her. Tracing his finger from her chin down to her cleavage, he kissed her again, a little more urgently this time before taking her into his arms once more.

'While we're apart don't give your heart to anyone, so darling save the last dance for me.'

Pausing from his serenade, he slowly and meticulously began to unbutton his own shirt. Isla knew now was the moment. Any anxiety had left her. She felt completely at ease and nodded her eager acceptance to Julian's enquiring glance.

He instantly turned and swept away every bit of clutter from his leather-topped desk, knocking over a Waterford Crystal water jug in his urgency, which smashed into tiny shards as it crashed to the ground. The sound made Isla jump but Julian had already spun back around and was lifting her from her feet. She eagerly wrapped her long legs expectantly around him and they kissed even more passionately. Lying back onto the desk, Isla's four-inch heels scratched deep crevices into the desktop as she writhed with heightened anticipation. Julian finally moved over her almost naked body and she gasped with pleasure. He put a finger to his lips and she tried very hard to remain quiet but as his movement became more determined and her expectation more urgent, she had no alternative but to cry out in climax.

Julian was now also completely beyond caring what others might hear as his own sexual desire that had built up since the first time he saw the beautiful young blonde in the half-light of Downing Street was finally satisfied.

30

Celeb magazine

Sally hadn't seen Julian since Valerie had taken her overdose. Sitting disconsolately in her corner office she struggled to wrestle away the fear of rejection that was closing in. Sally tried to buoy herself by remembering how Julian had cheered her up the last time she'd been upset in the days after Monty's injury. He was all over her like a cheap dress, whisking her up to the safe house and showering her with gifts. She had been sure he was going to propose. But then his ridiculous present wife had tried to top herself and suddenly his attitude had changed once more. She understood he needed to play the role of doting concerned husband at first but now he was travelling all the time and only ever called for phone sex while he was on the road. Why hadn't he rung at all during his trip to Dublin? She tried very hard to quell any rising panic and instead convinced herself to remain confident that everything would be fine again after the election on Thursday. Until then she needed to be patient.

Sally had attempted to keep busy by working longer hours and developing even more ways to destroy Valerie's reputation.

She was furious at how Ben had spun her overdose as exhaustion, a woman who'd buckled under intolerable pressure. Something had to give and it was the poor first lady's health that had unfortunately succumbed.

Today's papers were no different. A photograph of Valerie pushing her brother's wheelchair through the grounds of a Lancashire stately home, concern etched on both their faces. It was the front-page picture of every newspaper. The *Independent* noted that the location was a 250-acre estate gifted to the nation by the Earl of Crawford and Balcarres. The *Sun*'s headline: *Knocked For Six*.

Some of the more sceptical newspaper commentators had wondered whether there was more to why her health had failed. Was Julian being supportive enough to a wife who had to cope with so much family heartache?

Sally wanted to vomit. If only they knew what that obscene woman had really done. Trying to kill herself while her daughter was sleeping in the room next door. What sort of mother would do that? She neglected to acknowledge that Julian was having unprotected sex with her as his wife reached her lowest ebb.

Sally flicked through the other newspapers on her desk. Reaching page 7 of the *Star* she stopped abruptly, shocked by the headline: *Rambo Stalker Bid For Freedom*.

She reached for her Prada spectacles and with growing anxiety held the page closer, focusing on every syllable. Surely he couldn't get out yet? There must be some sort of mistake.

Richard Head was an ex-boyfriend who had been arrested in her garden while wearing a red bandana and carrying a knife, hence the Rambo reference. Sally hadn't allowed herself to ponder what his intentions might have been. Instead she'd been content that he was convicted and safely resting at Her Majesty's pleasure. He had written the odd letter, very odd letters, threatening revenge when he was released but the police had soothed her concerns. That had pushed any anxiety to the back of her mind and she reassured herself again now. An appeal didn't mean anything. There was no chance of early release. She shoved the pile of print onto the floor.

A tap at the door and Maria entered the editor's office dressed in this season's runway Prada bought by her new beau. Sally had tried to elicit more info about the obviously loaded suitor, but her deputy gave away nothing more than a mischievous smile. From the pile of papers on the floor Maria realised that it was obviously shaping up to be quite a challenging day for Sally. It wasn't about to improve any time soon. Maria was the bearer of even worse news. She decided it would be best to build up her editor before knocking her off her perch.

'Figures are up again this week, Sally. The political feature on Jenson's Gems was a great success. I really don't know how you manage to come up with such brilliant twists on what is essentially a rather dry story. I'm really surprised our readers are interested in boring politicians, especially Julian Jenson, he's incredibly handsome but oh so dull.'

Sally involuntarily shook her head at what she considered to be not only Maria's ignorance but also a massive slight to Julian.

'If you could try to leave the lack of knowledge at home, Maria, it would be very much appreciated.

'Honestly, I despair. You can lead a whore to culture but you can't make her think.'

'I beg your pardon?'

'It's what Dorothy Parker said when asked to come up with a sentence containing the word *horticulture*. Don't you know anything Maria, for goodness' sake?'

Maria was incandescent and not about to be placated by the Algonquin round table explanation offered by her boss. She surreptitiously scribbled the comment on her notebook to be filed later. Maria was tiring of Sally's superior attitude towards her and other members of the team and was collecting ammunition. Unpleasant emails, grumbly meetings and Sally's overbearing personality meant that several staff were on the brink of resigning. Sally however was oblivious to her deputy's fury and embarked on a lecture about the importance of female MPs to any new government.

'Blair had his Babes in the '97 election. 101 of them to be precise. Cameron guaranteed a good sprinkling of his Cuties with all-women constituency shortlists. Julian will do the same with his Jenson's Gems. They'll break the strangle-hold that those pin-stripe suited men have on the corridors of power.'

Maria's pout remained firmly in place as she girded her loins for a killer punch. *Condescending cow, let's see how she takes this news.*

'Well, that is really very interesting, Sally. I would absolutely love to learn lots more about politics but I'm afraid I must interject with rather bad news. Monty Mitchell's agent has been on the phone. He says the wedding is now being postponed indefinitely. I know we had been hopeful it would happen in December, making a perfect Christmas edition for our readers. Sadly, Monty's injuries are much worse than first feared. He will be in a wheelchair for some time. As you know he is determined to walk with his bride, unaided, up the aisle. As a result, it is with great regret that the deal is off, is what he said.'

Sally couldn't believe it. The Mitchell wedding deal lapsed at the end of the year. She knew that *OK!* and *Hello!* magazines were already circling with their big cheque books and superfluous exclamation marks! Once the couple were out of contract with *Celeb* the bidding war could begin for a spring wedding.

Neither editor nor deputy was aware of the real reason

for the decision, that Julia had ditched Monty for Charlie. The promised Sunday newspaper spread had been injuncted and Valerie had not yet told her husband about her brother's heartache, not least because she had hardly seen him despite his promise to ease up on the campaigning. Anyway Monty needed private time to grieve his fiancée's infidelity. It would be a source of great relief to Sally but for now she was frustratingly ignorant of the facts.

Sensing a moment of weakness in her editor, Maria took the opportunity to pile on the pain.

'I'm afraid that isn't all, Sally. The publisher feels that the divorce cake idea is unnecessarily savage at what could be a most vulnerable time for readers going through a separation. He doesn't feel it should appear in the magazine. You may or may not be aware that his third wife, Pippa, filed papers via Vanessa Lewis, the high profile divorce lawyer, last month. She has subsequently set up home with her personal trainer. I did tell him that it was very much your idea. I underlined that you were particularly keen that it should run quite soon and high up in the magazine, definitely before the fold, but he was insistent it should be dropped.

'Rather surprisingly, he seemed a little annoyed and said he would very much like to speak to you about it personally. I'll find a slot in your diary, should we say this afternoon?

'Oh, one other thing. Despite the team's very best efforts Wayne and Coleen have passed on the holiday feature. They've signed with *OK!* instead. As we speak we have no cover for next week's edition.'

Maria offered her best acid smile and without another word turned on her Jimmy Choo couture heels and headed for the door. 'Take that, bitch,' she thought as she rather too forcefully closed the toughened opaque glass door behind her.

31

Election night

'I declare Julian, Horatio, Fredrick, Montagu Jenson-Fitzsimmons duly elected to serve in parliament as a member for this constituency.'

As the returning officer concluded and the champagne corks began to pop, party workers who were gathered in the Herefordshire sports hall, still slightly wiffy from stale teenage sweat, went wild with exhausted delight.

'Flippin' 'eck, with a name like that it's a good job he's not an MP in Wigan. He'd get lynched before he was off the stage.'

Ben was joking with Dominic and Jessica who had both been given special permission from their respective schools to attend the electoral count. In fact Dominic's dispensation had been extended to two weeks and coincided with yet another unfortunate incident with a new boy. Valerie had despaired. Ben's thinly veiled innuendo about the unhelpful publicity that would undoubtedly follow the news of the exclusion of the PM's son hadn't persuaded the headmaster to be more lenient. He'd tried a line about the frail health of the boy's mother, but that had no impact either. Jessica had been hastily sprung from college to give the impression the children's presence had always been part of the plan.

The polls had closed promptly at 10 pm and the ballot papers were already being counted in the hall when the family arrived. They worked the room, pressing the flesh and thanking party workers for their indefatigable efforts. The news Julian had been re-elected came soon afterwards. Despite the negative press in the last few days of the campaign and a shockingly badly received party political broadcast he had nevertheless been returned with an increased majority.

No thanks to his bloody Mrs who had almost ruined everything, thought Ben. Valerie was standing next to the podium and Ben scrutinised every tiny move she made just as journalists and photographers would also be doing. She looked thin and exhausted and he was keen to whisk the family away as quickly as possible but there was just one more bit of business to fulfil. Julian moved towards the microphone.

'Thank you. Thank you every single one of you who have voted for me to continue with my work to help bring true equality to this country. I will treat this overwhelming mandate with the respect it deserves. Rest assured, as a party we are never complacent. I hope that the rest of the British people will also want us to continue to serve them as a party of conscience. If we are re-elected then ask me my three words for government, and I tell you: Law And Order. If we are successful at the polls then that work will begin from tomorrow.

'For now, thank you again. Let us see what the rest of the night brings.'

The crowd went wild at his humble and impromptu speech, unaware that Ben was lip-syncing the words with his boss, just as they had rehearsed them in the car on the way to the sports hall. Loving the attention, Julian pressed on, this time with an ad lib addition.

'Where there is discord, may we bring harmony. Where there is error, may we bring truth . . .'

What was he doing? Ben couldn't believe it. He was only quoting from Thatcher's '79 victory speech on the steps of Downing Street. The adulation must be going to his head.

'Where there is doubt, may we bring faith. And where there is despair, may we bring hope.'

At first Ben tried discreetly to move his hand above his head to catch Julian's attention and shut him up but with no success, he resorted to an urgent cut-throat gesture. Finally, Julian stopped and Ben sighed with relief. Tony Blair's 'hand of history on his shoulder' speech could've been next.

Waving appreciatively to the audience, Julian finally left the stage and took the arm of his fragile wife as the family was swamped by the party faithful. Politely and resolutely they managed to slowly make their way to the waiting people carrier before clambering inside. Both children, aware of their mother's frailty, snuggled in close to her. Jessica gripped her pale, clammy hand and Dominic gently put his arm around her.

As they drove away from the count, leaving party activists to celebrate well into the night, an uneasy silence fell on the vehicle. They were travelling at speed as was always the case with the PM's convoy, police outriders making sure the road was clear for some distance ahead. The group were on their way towards their constituency home for a traditional curry and a beer while watching the result of the election unfold on television. The exit polls issued immediately after the ballot boxes were sealed at 10 pm were promising. Julian and Ben were confident they would be heading to the Hammersmith Apollo for a victory rally by the early hours.

For now Dominic was keen to lift the mood in the vehicle and was the first to speak.

'I think we should take Mother on holiday as soon as you've chosen the new cabinet. What say you, pater?'

Jessica squeezed her mother's limp hand.

'What would you say to that then, Mummy? That's a cool idea Daddy, don't you think?'

Ben who was sitting up front next to the chauffeur, aka close protection officer, snatched a quick glance towards Julian. He began to gently hum 'There may be trouble ahead . . .'

Julian ignored him. He wanted the children back at school and Valerie safely ensconced at Chequers or back up in 'dreary flat cap and whippet country' as quickly as possible. He had no interest in holidaying with the family. The offer in the hospital had been a knee-jerk response to a challenging situation. Shock at Valerie's cry for help had soon given way to anger and contempt at what he considered her selfishness. He had hastily returned to the campaign trail and now the election was over he needed to shower some serious attention on Isla and Sally too.

'Children, a holiday would be fabulous but I don't think your wonderful mother is well enough to take a trip just at the moment, do you?'

Valerie was furious. Ben's stinging criticism in the hospital had shocked her into realising how much her family needed her, loved her. Her emotional journey back to full recovery would be long and challenging but it was one she had embarked on with determination and resolve. Looking at the expectant faces of her children, she wasn't allowing Julian off the hook quite so easily. He had promised Jessica a holiday, he had blatantly promised her. It would undoubtedly be their last trip all together and he wasn't wriggling out of it.

'Actually darling, I think it would be lovely for us to take the children away. This interminable campaign has taken its toll on all of us. Let's go as soon as possible.'

217

Julian was momentarily panicked by Valerie's contribution to the family discussion. Comments from her had been few and far between of late. Now she had said something, it was most unhelpful. There was absolutely no chance he was holidaying with Valerie after what she had done. Her selfish actions could have cost him the election for goodness' sake, but how to get out of it in front of the children? His brain was racing for a response and unsure of what to say, he said nothing. Instead he gazed through the window and into the darkness as Valerie relaxed into her children's embrace and silence descended on the car. As it started to rain, Julian sighed with frustration at his dilemma. How could he possibly get out of this blasted promise?

As he wondered what to do, Julian aimlessly traced with his finger the rivulets of rain trickling down the outside of the car window. He was instantly whisked back to Isla's side, Dom Perignon meandering down her naked body closely followed by his inquisitive forefinger. He closed his eyes and relaxed into the memory of her exquisite curves and china doll features with not a blemish or a line anywhere.

He smiled at the memory of her slowly pouring champagne into a Waterford Crystal flute in his bedroom at the Residence before stalking cat-like towards him. She'd mischievously dribbled the contents of the glass onto the most eager parts of his anatomy. Leaning forward she had taken him to the very edge of control before lying back again and allowing herself to succumb to his meticulous attention.

'Daddy, what do you think of Mummy's plan?'

Julian was shocked back into the present, banging his head on the window as he crossed his legs to hide any embarrassment from the children.

'Well, I think Mummy is very thoughtful and I think it really is a jolly good idea for us all to head off on holiday. Perhaps we could go back to South Africa again on safari?

We'll have to wait until early next year though after Ben and I have bedded down the new cabinet. Parliament should still be in Christmas holidays then too which means I won't have to take any time away when I really should be at the House of Commons on parliamentary business.'

Julian calculated that his divorce papers would be public by January. Valerie's suicide attempt, while distressing for everyone, had not changed his mind about future plans for separation. While he and his estranged wife may well take the children on holiday it would most certainly be separately.

'Isn't that right Ben, we're just too busy at the moment, aren't we?'

Ben scowled. Julian was doing it again. He'd already told the boss about dragging him into the middle of family matters. Pulling down the sun visor he caught Julian's attention through the vanity mirror and mouthed, 'Fuck right off.'

Dominic's mobile rang. Appropriately 'Mercy' by Duffy was the chosen tune *du jour*.

'Hey grandpops, how are you? How's Monty and Granny Sheila?'

Frank Mitchell was calling to congratulate his son-in-law after watching him being successfully returned to parliament for another five years.

'No worries grandpops, Mummy doesn't have her phone with her and pater is on yet another new number. I'll put you on speakerphone. Then you can talk to all of us at once. Just a tick.'

Scrolling down and activating the loud speaker on his BlackBerry, Dominic waited for his grandfather to speak again.

'Hello lad, can you hear me now? I can't hear you properly, sounds like you're laughing?'

Jessica and Dominic were sniggering as Frank shouted, assuming that speakerphone meant he must talk louder.

Valerie immediately jumped to her father's defence. Narrowing her eyes at the children she summoned more energy than Ben had seen since she'd clambered into the car.

'Sorry Dad, Julian was just telling us a funny joke. We can all hear you now. How are you Dad? How're Mum and Monty?'

The children, suitably chastised, leaned forward to hear their grandfather more clearly. Julian feigned interest.

'We're all fine, our Valerie.' Frank continued to shout but Valerie put her finger to her lips, warning the youngsters against any further ridicule.

'Me and Valerie's mother just want you to know, lad, that we are very, very proud indeed to say that you are our son-in-law.'

Valerie was almost moved to tears by her father's warm words. He had always been a man with a great sense of honour. His support for Julian, who he had initially thought was a 'bit of a show-off', was appreciated by everyone in the vehicle. Even Julian smiled acknowledgement.

'Anyway, we'll stay up as long as we can to watch the election results come in. After about 2ish we'll have to Sky+ it and watch what we've missed in the morning. That lovely Suzie lass is presenting from outside the House of Commons tomorrow. Say hello if ya see her. She's my favourite.'

Frank was just about to hang up when Jessica spoke.

'Grandpops, just before you go, can I ask you a very quick question please? Daddy wants to take Mummy, Dominic and me away on safari next month. Ben says he'll be too busy. What do you think?'

Ben almost laughed out loud at Jessica's blatant teenage manipulation of her elders. Frank had never allowed work to get in the way of family holidays and he was undoubtedly worried about his daughter's health. Jessica knew her grandfather's view was a foregone conclusion. On top of that Ben had copped the blame for any holiday delay. Bloody typical.

'Well our Jessica, I think that's up to your Dad to decide and you are very naughty for putting him in a difficult position on the phone.'

Frank paused before continuing.

'But I do think your Mum does deserve a nice holiday. She was lookin' very pale when we saw her on the telly at the count. If it's money your Dad's worried about then me and your grandma will have a look at cashin' in some of our premium bonds. Anyway, night, night.'

Ben turned from the front seat to face a pole-axed Julian.

'Prime Minister, it would appear we are on our way to South Africa.'

32

Number 10

Downing Street was heaving with journalists, party supporters and tourists, all keen to see the Jensons return victorious. The family could easily have been driven straight back from the Hammersmith Apollo victory rally in the early hours while it was still dark, but Ben was having none of it. Tony and Cherie Blair's triumphant walk through the black wrought iron gates at the Whitehall end of the street after his landslide remained an iconic image. Julian's runaway success in this election deserved similar grandstanding though the security services were less content. The public right of way through Downing Street had been prevented as far back as 1989 as a direct result of the IRA threat to the British government. Opening up the gates was a headache they could do without.

'I pay my fucking taxes so PC plod can get double bubble for just such an occasion. He wants the money to buy his Chelsea season ticket. I want my PM to walk hand-in-hand with his Mrs waving at the great unwashed, crammed four deep down that road. Sort it.'

Ben's persuasive approach with the Metropolitan Police

Commissioner had worked. Alighting from the people carrier at the junction of Whitehall it took the Jenson family at least half an hour to make their way from the open gates to the steps of Number 10. Waving, shaking hands, posing for photographs and signing paper Union Flags along the way they eventually reached the famous front door, home for another five years. Julian was elated at his government's 199 seat majority, an overwhelming mandate from the British people and a slap for the pollsters who even last week had been predicting a hung parliament. He waved happily from the doorstep to the throng of faces across the street.

'Prime Minister, you're live on *Have a Nice Day UK*. Do you have a word for our viewers?'

It was Stephen James shouting his question from the other side of the barriers. Julian immediately looked across, shocked that it wasn't Isla there to congratulate him. Where was she? Dublin had been sensational. Surely she would want to be in his presence at every available moment, even if there were several hundred others there too.

'I am humbled at the British people's continuing support. I will do my very best to repay their faith in my government. Earlier, I received a telephone call from the leader of the opposition wishing me every good fortune and I thank him for his grace. As I have said throughout the campaign, three words outline my plans for the next five years. Law And Order. There is much to be done and it begins now.'

With a final wave to the crowd, he kissed Valerie on her forehead and once again took her hand in his before ushering Dominic and Jessica inside. As the door closed behind them and the children scurried up the corridor to the lift, Number 10 staff who'd temporarily left their desks to 'clap in' the PM, returned to their duties. Julian immediately withdrew his affection from his wife and strode determinedly away. Valerie bit her lip and tried very hard not to cry in front of the staff.

33

Ritz Club

Jimmy Phillips was looking great and feeling even better as he enjoyed the last shared spoonful of a buttermilk panacotta with Charles in the luxurious dining room of the Ritz Club on London's Piccadilly. His bestest agent had just signed off on a two-year exclusive TV deal. It included not only four series of *Where There's Muck* but also 'other projects' attracting a seven-figure payday. He was staggered by the numbers but Tommy Gold reassured him that he was worth every penny. The channel was lucky to get him for that price.

Tommy was also negotiating with several sponsors, including Christie's. It was certainly cause to celebrate and the Ritz Club was Charles' favourite place in the world. Once the hotel's cellar it was now a magnificent dining experience with its soaring vaulted ceiling and desperately expensive sumptuousness. The club also had an exclusive casino where Tommy had discreetly arranged membership for the evening.

Charles was beside himself with excitement as he looked around at the immaculately set dining tables. Crisp white cotton covers decorated with the finest Lalique crystal stemware and Arthur Price silver cutlery.

'Darling, this is so magical, who would have believed we would ever be able to dine in such luxurious surroundings?'

Ordering a brandy for himself and another glass of Bollinger for his Charles, Jimmy sat back against his Georgian dining chair and admired his partner who was wearing a flatteringly cut dinner suit this evening. He smiled his approval and half considered skipping the casino and heading back home for their own game of roulette, but the call of the tables was as ever just a little too strong.

Charles was in no mood to leave yet either. He loved to people watch and where better than here. Enjoying a stolen glance across the room at a high roller half-hidden by a magnificent floral display he squeezed Jimmy's arm.

'Oooh look darling, over there, is that Kerry Packer? I think it is, you know.'

Jimmy smiled warmly at Charles before leaning lovingly towards him.

'Sweetheart, Kerry Packer died on Boxing Day 2005, so unlikely, but you are right he was very much a gambler while alive. Should I entertain you with a story about him?'

Jimmy was always keen to brush over his partner's mistakes and make him feel loved rather than ridiculed. He reached across the tablecloth and touched the tips of Charles' manicured fingers with his own.

'Oooh, yes please.' Jimmy was such a great storyteller and Charles waited eagerly for him to begin.

'As you may know darling, Mr Packer was well known for being quite a high roller on both sides of the Atlantic. Once, so legend has it, he lost $7m playing baccarat in a Las Vegas casino. Can you imagine frittering away so much money in just one night?'

Charles was wide eyed at the prospect and desperate to learn more.

'But he wasn't just famous for splashing the cash. He also had the reputation for being a most generous man. Apparently, he was once so appalled that a cocktail waitress had to work nights to support her children and keep a roof over their heads that he immediately wrote out a cheque to pay off her mortgage. How wonderful was that?'

Charles gasped at the story. Not for a second doubting its authenticity.

'And I'll tell you something else, a little bit like you Charles darling, he wasn't particularly keen on brash show-offs. Apparently he was once playing at the same table as a rather pompous Texan gentleman. Mr Packer eventually asked him to pipe down but the Texan chappy was jolly rude in response. He started showing off about how much he was worth. Rumour has it that he said to Mr Packer, "$60 million is what I'm worth, pardner." Do you know what Mr Packer said to him in response?'

'Ohh, I don't know darling. What would you say to someone who said they were worth $60 million?'

'Well it's said that Mr Packer looked him up and down in that dismissive way that only Aussies can and then sneered, "$60 million, I'll flip you for it."'

Charles laughed appreciatively, his appetite whetted for a spot of gambling.

'Let's go through and play some roulette ourselves, but please just ignore any silly show-offs, we can't afford it!'

As the two men strolled through into the Main Gaming Salon Jimmy immediately felt a sense of exhilaration. He was first bitten by the gambling bug when he'd come across a book on how to play roulette during a house clearance in Birmingham. That was in his much younger days and until now he had been in no financial position to risk more than a few pounds here and there. Increasing disposable income meant that he was going to have some fun tonight.

Wandering between the blue baize covered tables Jimmy was in heaven. Not only an elegant casino but in such glorious surroundings too. Whispering to Charles, he recounted a little of the history of the Club.

'Originally darling, the Gaming Room, the room we are in now, was the Ballroom of the Ritz. Before those American Roulette, Blackjack, Baccarat and Three Card Poker tables were here you could have witnessed some of London's finest waltzing around the room. Right in the very centre you might have seen the actress Lily Langtry with none other than King Edward VII. What a wonderful sight that would have been.'

As Charles fantasised about a bygone era, Jimmy was dancing on air, his only concern in the world deciding on which of the tables to place his chips.

34

Chelsea, London

'Your Excellency, if I might introduce you to Sally Simpson, a rather special lady in my life.'

Sally was unsure whether to curtsy or bow so opted to offer her hand to the ambassador who brushed the top of her fingers with his lips. 'Enchanted, my dear.'

Julian nodded his head politely as he was in turn introduced to the ambassador's partner who may perhaps have been his daughter but was most certainly not his wife. Sally looked sublime in a Ralph and Russo silk crepe creation that had obviously cost significantly more than the average monthly wage. No questions were asked or explanations needed about her accompanying the Prime Minister among the select group who had been invited to dinner at the home of Julian's sister, the Honourable Emma Jenson-Fitzsimmons.

Emma, who had been aware of Julian's fondness for Sally for some time had considered this the perfect time for a little dinner party. An ideal opportunity for the newly re-elected PM to mingle within a trusted group of friends while contemplating the next steps in his personal life.

The couple had arrived rather later than the other guests after a security scare. A routine sweep was always part of pre-dinner preparations at Emma Jenson-Fitzsimmons' Chelsea home whenever the PM was likely to call. Today, a gun had been discovered too close for comfort to the property and the PM's close protection was on red alert. They had been keen for him not to attend the event but Julian was insistent and Sally was delighted.

Meandering through to the elegant dining room set for an informal supper, Sally was enthralled by her surroundings. The Cheyne Walk property had all the understated trappings of old money, from original artwork to the most glorious antique furniture. Sally laughed as she remembered snobby Lord Jopling's ultimate putdown to Conservative grandee Michael Heseltine: 'The trouble with Michael is that he had to buy his own furniture.'

No danger of that with the Jensons whose furniture had been in the family for centuries. Sally couldn't wait to become part of the clan. There had been some tense and uncertain times before the election but now Julian was safely ensconced back in Number 10, she was quietly confident their romance was firmly on track.

Stroking the small of her back, Julian guided Sally to her seat at the end of the English oak table before returning to sit far too far away from her and next to the ambassador's partner for the evening. Disappointed at the distance between them Sally was considering how to ease her way further up the table when she was suddenly aware of someone talking to her.

'Allow me to introduce myself.'

Sally stared vacantly at the dinner guest, a little miffed to have been interrupted from her scheming.

'I'm Jimmy Phillips.'

Of course. Sally immediately offered up her most charming

smile to the unimpressed guest who was used to fawning attention and was most irked at her initial lack of interest in him. Before she could introduce herself Sally was interrupted by Emma clinking her Riedel glass with a silver spoon and bringing the room to order.

'Your Excellency, my lord, ladies, gentlemen, a toast to my brother, your Prime Minister. Where there is discord, may he bring harmony. Where there is error, may he bring truth . . .'

Those gathered laughed appreciatively at Emma's playful reference to her brother's over the top victory speech on election night. One or two recognised it as St Francis of Assisi, most as the plagiaristic use of Margaret Thatcher's words on the steps of Downing Street.

'Where there is doubt, may he bring faith. And where there is despair, may Sally bring my brother hope for a happier future.'

Sally swelled with pride as fellow dinner guests banged the table in approval before eagerly turning to their starters. She took the opportunity to try to make amends with a rather huffy TV star who was quite clearly smarting at not being instantly feted. But Jimmy was already deep in animated conversation to his left. Instead Sally found herself making small talk with Chris Columbine, a hedge fund manager.

Finance was absolutely not Sally's cup of tea and she soon bored of inane City talk. She looked to the ambassador for salvation. He was sitting directly opposite but was in conversation with Mrs Hedge Fund. Looking up the table towards Julian he was as usual charming everyone around him, recounting anecdotes about life at the dispatch box and offering titillating titbits from the campaign trail, Chatham House Rules in play of course. He was in full flow and despite bobbing around a little on her chair she failed to attract his attention. Sally turned in desperation to Jimmy.

But being offered little more than the back of his Prada lounge suit she accepted her fate and as the main course arrived she returned to desperately dull Hedge Fundery.

With the party reaching a slightly inebriated close and the guests preparing to leave the table, Jimmy finally turned judgmentally to Sally. He'd been sorry to read about Valerie Jenson and was mortified to think there could be anything to the rumours of self-harm. Now meeting this, what he could only describe as a harlot, tonight everything had fallen into place. How could Julian Jenson possibly think this woman could ever hold a candle to his wonderful wife? Good job he had better judgment as Prime Minister. That's it, he would forbid Charles from ever buying *Celeb* again. Looking Sally up and down he offered her the tightest of smiles before nodding curtly and turning to find Charles. They had been very lucky on the tables recently and a spin or two before bed was in order.

At the other end of the dining room Julian smiled warmly at his sister, delighted with the evening's events.

'Em, you're tops.'

He had been unsure when Emma originally suggested a coming out dinner for Sally and was uncharacteristically nervous when he first walked into the dining room to meet the other 20 guests. But he needn't have worried. Emma had chosen wisely and a light-hearted mix of humour and political banter had made for a delightful evening.

'You really like this woman, don't you, Jules? Is she really the one, do you think?'

'I think so, Em, I hope so. I don't know.'

'She seems utterly charming. The ambassador was most taken with her. He wondered if it would be appropriate to invite you both over to the embassy in the next couple of weeks or so? I told him I would speak to your diary secretary.'

Emma squeezed her brother's arm, the biggest outward sign

of affection that could be expected between the buttoned-up siblings. Gazing at the gathering as they offered goodbyes, she hesitated for a moment and clearly had more to say.

'You know Jules, there's no need to rush into anything. Mother and Father were able to make their marriage work perfectly satisfactorily. Divorce from Valerie doesn't have to be the answer. Sally can still be "one" without necessarily being the special one.'

How astute his sister could be. He was about to respond when Roger, one of his trusted close protection officers, strode over. Offering polite apologies to Emma he whispered calmly but decisively to his principal.

'Sir, we need to leave right now. Follow me.'

Unfolding events within the last few minutes illustrated why the earlier security sweep was needed.

Julian looked across to where Sally was saying her good-byes. She had also been interrupted. Carl, another member of the security team, had eased Sally away from the group and she was now anxiously looking back at him. Julian, who had been drilled in compliancy when instructed by Roger, Carl or any of the other security boys, nodded to Sally to do exactly as she was told. It was time to go. Julian blew a kiss to his slightly alarmed sister and promised he would call later as the couple allowed themselves to be guided discreetly out of the dining room. Once in the corridor there was less need for discretion and they were hurried along through the expansive house by Roger and Carl who were in no mood for dawdling. The group was heading towards a previously sussed exit. Carl rushed through the tradesmen's door ahead of Julian and Sally or 'principal+1' as he had referred to them on his radio and bundled them into the back of a blacked-out Range Rover.

Julian took a long deep breath to calm his nerves and wait for the adrenaline to subside as they sped away from his sister's house. Relieved to be in such expert hands but aware that Sally would be anxious and upset, he decided humour was required.

'Oh, come on, I don't think Emma's cooking was that bad, boys.

'Anyone want to tell me what's happening?'

Carl began to brief the PM on a significant security breach that had put his life at risk.

35

Islington, North London

Isla and her flatmate Camilla were squeezed into one of the two tiny bedrooms in their bijoux apartment in trendy Islington pondering the appropriate nail colour choice for a hot date.

'Would you prefer Siberian Nights or Cha Ching Cherry?'

Camilla had painted the red on her fingers and the Siberian Nights black on her toes while wiggling them along to Queen's greatest hits playing from their iPod docking station.

Isla had been particularly miserable over the last few days and her flatmate had set aside girlfriend time to cheer her up. Earlier in the day they'd wandered down Old Bond Street trying on a whole range of outfits they quite obviously couldn't afford in Ralph Lauren and Nicole Farhi. Then they'd loitered around the Chantecaille cosmetics counter in Fenwick's before settling on a kohl pencil from Mac and heading for the tube home.

This evening Camilla had organised a bells and whistles girls' night in. Both were already in their favourite, most comfortable Winnie The Pooh pyjamas, bought for each other at college to chime with their nicknames, Tigger and Kanga. They were in full free spirit mode and had almost finished the first bottle of champagne. There was another one in the fridge nestling next to a four seasons pizza and chocolate éclairs. An emergency pint tub of Häagen Dazs Macadamia Nut Brittle was in the freezer on standby for later, if needed. Tomorrow may be shrouded by cellulite and wobbly bits, but tonight they'd party.

The girls clicked their fingers in unison as 'Killer Queen' started to play. They were up on their feet singing along to 'let them eat cake she says, just like Marie Antoinette' within the first few bars. Bouncing around to the beat, both were having a ball.

Isla had met Camilla on the first day at college in Yorkshire where they were both bursting with blind optimism about their future careers. Camilla had shown a more natural aptitude throughout the year-long course. She was a high achiever in the obligatory subjects of Public Administration, English, Shorthand and received a distinction in Law. Isla had winged it and scraped through after a re-sit in English.

Course over, they had been unwilling to part but Isla had adopted a glass half full positivity and set her face towards television. She was delighted to be offered a job as a junior reporter in the North East. Camilla accepted a position with the BBC in Liverpool and with a heavy heart they headed for opposite coasts. Though seeing each other only occasionally they still easily picked up where they'd left off without even a pause for breath.

It hadn't taken long for Camilla to be discovered by broadcasting bosses in London and she was whisked away to the capital to work in the national radio pool. Isla was making a big impression in Newcastle, not least on Steve Simms, her former boss at *Northumbria Tonight*. Their little dalliance seemed to mean much more to the married father of four than it did to the young TV reporter. In fact he had rather uncomfortably become a little love struck and sent daily text messages. They'd varied from how much he enjoyed their sex to asking her to delete her name from her voicemail message. His wife had found the number in his mobile and was threatening to call. Six months on, all messages were still safely stored as a suitable insurance policy should she need to return to the North East. Probably unnecessary, given her new love interest at Downing Street.

'Come on then Tigger, spill. Who is he?'

Camilla knew Isla inside out and was more than a little concerned about the impact Mystery Man was having on her.

'Oh Kanga, he's so wonderful, I don't know where to start. He's just the best thing that's ever happened to me.'

As Freddie Mercury finished with a flurry, Isla flopped back onto the bed and squeezed a separator between her toes before choosing the bright red polish and shaking the bottle.

'He's so charming and handsome and he texts me all the time. The sex is unbelievable. He's very, erm inventive. It's still very new but we have the most wonderful time when we're together, but then I don't see him forever. He's always so busy. I never realised you could go from ecstasy to agony quite so quickly until I met him.'

Isla paused to lip-sync the end of 'Don't Stop Me Now' playing on the iPod while applying her first coat of polish. She looked dreamily at her reflection in the bedside mirror before taking a lingering sip of champagne from their new Habitat glasses. It immediately reminded her of her wonderful trip to Dublin.

'I know it's silly Kanga, but think I might be falling in love with him.'

Camilla had clambered onto the bed next to Isla and was unwrapping a family bar of Cadbury's Dairy Milk. Freddie started to sing 'It's A Kind Of Magic'.

'Does he love you?'

'Oh I don't know. I hope so but I'm not sure. What if it all goes wrong? I don't want to have to close down all those wonderful emotions that I'm feeling. It would be so painful if he didn't feel what I do. I hope he does, Kanga. I really, really hope so.'

Camilla took control of the nail polish brush to help Isla with the tricky edges on her little toes.

'Great sex isn't necessarily love, you know! Don't start down that road unless you know where you're going. One wrong turn can easily lead to a dead end of tearful, lonely nights wondering where it all went wrong. We've both been there before.'

Isla nodded. She knew her best friend was right. Her support had always been honest and heartfelt and they'd relied on each other when boyfriends betrayed them. Lost in thought for a moment she hovered on the very precipice of champagne-induced tears and just managed to check herself before she said too much. Isla knew that if she wanted to continue her relationship with Julian then discretion was critical, even with her best friend.

'I can't tell you any more than that, honestly, I just can't Kanga. I really want to but I just can't say anything else. It could spoil everything.'

Camilla scoffed. She had always prided herself on being a no pressure pal but they had told each other their most intimate secrets ever since college. That was certainly not going to change now. Narrowing her eyes she glared at Isla who immediately looked away and leaned across to change the music.

'George Michael or The Drifters. How about "Save the Last Dance for Me?"'

But her friend was not to be deflected. Squeezing the tip of Isla's big toe, careful not to smudge her polish, she recited their journalism college mantra that always provided the core facts to any story.

'I kept six honest serving men. They taught me all I knew. Their names are What and Why and When and How and Where and Who.'

The girls had the Kipling quote mounted in an Ikea frame above the kettle.

'OK, OK, let me put the pizza in the oven first, then I'll tell you everything.'

Isla eased herself off the John Lewis duvet. Struggling to walk with foam toe separators wedged under each foot, she shuffled the few feet to the shoebox kitchen with no intention whatsoever of accommodating Camilla's curiosity.

36

Celebrity lunch at Chequers

Jimmy and Charles sat completely still as solid metal pillars suddenly rose up blocking the road. Heavily-armed police surrounded their chauffeur driven vehicle. An officer gestured for the window to be lowered and Jimmy nervously quipped: 'I have nothing to declare except my genius.' The policeman who had heard it all before ignored the Oscar Wilde one-liner. He politely asked their names and address as a colleague sauntered slowly around the car. He was using what appeared to be a giant dentist's mirror to check under the vehicle. A few moments later and the officer appeared at the window again: 'Enjoy your lunch, gentlemen.'

Jimmy and Charles smiled their appreciation. It was the first time they had been to Chequers. An off the record celebrity lunch, no journalists allowed, had been Tommy's take when the invite first arrived for the Sunday celebration. Jimmy and Charles were both delirious with excitement and had accepted immediately. They'd taken forever to decide what to wear. Charles had finally chosen grey Prada with a Patel Philippe tie. It had been a value added with a watch that Jimmy

239

bought him as an early Christmas gift. Jimmy was in Ozwald Boateng, having become a convert to the British designer after admiring his wares in the latest 007 movie. They were two of 24 guests invited to celebrate the PM's re-election success. Others making their way through the security checks with their partners were Lord Alan Sugar, Lord 'Dickie Darling' Attenborough, the razor-sharp, irreverent author Kathy Lette and the ubiquitous Piers Morgan. Peter Kay was also there, much to the delight of the PM's son, Dominic. Charles was absolutely thrilled and didn't know which way to look as he stood glass in hand in the Great Hall.

'Oh look darling, it's Brucie. He's my favourite.'

Julian had been keen that today's lunch would be a star-studded event and was delighted by the turn out. Ben had initially suggested it would make more sense to host a gathering for members of the press whose invaluable support had eased them through one or two wobbles during the campaign. Julian, flushed with success, had high-handedly dismissed the suggestion. He decided a Christmas buffet lunch for political and newspaper editors would be much more in order. Today was to be an informal get together for those who were more likely to appear on the front pages rather than write them.

As guests were guided through to the Dining Room they were greeted warmly by Julian and Valerie, this time positioned either side of the vast table. Broad smiles belied the screaming row they had endured just half an hour earlier. Julian had once again tried to wriggle out of the family holiday to South Africa. Valerie was not prepared to succumb and the discussion had quickly deteriorated into a loud argument. Dominic, due back at school tomorrow, had stepped in to quieten his mother's furious tears. Finally, Julian had reluctantly agreed to the trip but was finding it difficult to even acknowledge his wife's presence over lunch. Valerie no longer cared and turned her attention to her guests.

'Do have a quick glance at the seating plan on the sideboard everyone and then feel free to take your places for lunch. Jimmy, I think we've put you here next to me. I want to know all about the Christmas special and Charles, you're sitting next to Ben. Yes, just there.'

Julian took up the mantle and was soon back in full bonhomie mode.

'Brucie, you're here next to me and Lady Sugar, I'd be honoured if you sat here.'

Jimmy pulled back Valerie's chair so she could sit, noticing as he did so that she looked painfully thin in her Ralph Lauren two-piece. Much older too than recent photographs he had seen of the first lady in the newspapers. He had never met Valerie in person before despite being due to attend her brother's wedding. The invite had been for the sole purpose of increasing the celebrity head count in magazine photos. More celebs, more money, Tommy had told him when Jimmy queried why he and Charles had been asked.

Looking at Valerie now, Jimmy picked up on her pain and felt desperately sad for her. He found himself furious with that damned Sally Simpson woman. How could she, with everything Valerie was going through? She ought to be ashamed of herself frankly.

'I do hope that I am not speaking out of turn, Mrs Jenson, but I do want to offer my sincere sympathies over Monty's injury. I can't begin to imagine how you all must be feeling at the moment. First the accident and then the engagement split, your poor brother.'

Despite the best efforts of Monty's lawyers, Julia and Charlie's kiss-and-tell had finally appeared in that morning's paper. Valerie was livid and had been keen to head up to Lancashire to be with her humiliated brother. When she'd spoken to her mother on the phone Sheila had insisted Monty was OK and that duty keep her at Chequers. She finally agreed but still anguished over whether there was much more her baby brother could take.

'Please call me Valerie. Thank you for your concern Jimmy, it's very much appreciated. Monty is struggling a bit at the moment, but he is strong and is surrounded by a loving family. I am sure he will get through this latest challenge.'

On top of her concerns for Monty, her screaming row with Julian had unsettled Valerie further and she was desperate for a drink. Sitting at this bloody table was the very last place in the world she wanted to be right now, but having followed her mother's guidance of 'get up, dress up, show up' here she was.

'Now Jimmy I want to know all about the show. We watch it every week at Downing Street. Have you started filming the Christmas special yet? We can't wait to see it.'

Jimmy took the subtle hint that Valerie had no intention of speaking further about her brother, but looking beyond her groomed exterior, Jimmy could see the desperate sadness in her eyes. She obviously needed a friend. He wanted to wrap his arms around her and tell her everything would be alright, but it wasn't his place. They had only just met and she had already made it clear that stoicism was her coping mechanism. Instead, Jimmy embarked on tales from the *Where There's Muck* Christmas Day show.

As the lamb was being served, Ben quickly glanced around the room. Everyone seemed to be happily chatting with their fellow diners. A couple of political discussions had started at the far end near the fireplace. Julian was wittily defending his election promise on the return of free school milk for the under 10s.

'Thatcher the milk snatcher now replaced by Jenson on the Dairy Button.'

Ben had a quick check on Valerie's mood. He'd heard the blazing row earlier and as usual needed to keep a close eye on her. She was extremely fragile and any public weakness over lunch could quite easily find its way into the press. He was running out of excuses to cover for her.

Catching a glimpse of Jimmy sitting to Valerie's right, Ben thought he half recognised the TV presenter. He had been in plenty of TV studios before, not least during the election run-up. Furious with opposition claims about Julian's education policy, he'd stormed in to Millbank, next to the House of Commons, where TV channels had based their Westminster teams. Thankfully his old mate Adam Boulton had managed to talk him down before he did anything stupid and they'd headed for lunch instead. But, despite his vast experience of news, Ben had never been in a shiny floor studio before and knew little about light entertainment television. He didn't recognise the name Jimmy Phillips either. No, he couldn't possibly know the rather handsome chap talking to Valerie. He must be mistaken. Ben turned to nice-but-dim Charles sitting next to him. What was he going to talk to him about?

'I'm sure I'm familiar with your other half, but I don't think we've actually met before. It must be from reading all about him in the newspapers. He does seem to be everywhere at the moment. Tell me, what's it like being married to such a superstar?'

As Charles began to regale Ben with anecdotes about life married to a celebrity, at the other end of the table Jimmy continued to entertain Valerie with stories of tat and treasure and was delighted when she sniggered at a risqué tale of what he'd once discovered in a pensioner's attic. Jimmy was really enjoying himself. He couldn't believe he was sitting next to the first lady eating Sunday lunch at Chequers while the Prime Minister sat opposite chatting to Brucie. It was a long way from house clearances in Birmingham. Wait till he told Tommy.

As he soaked up the atmosphere Jimmy scanned the

chattering diners, all of whom would have a tale to tell of their day at the PM's country retreat. He looked down the table in Charles' direction to make sure he was comfortable and noticed Ben looking back at him. Smiling politely, Jimmy wondered if the spin doctor remembered their little dalliance all those years ago.

Even back then Jimmy had been keen to raise his media profile. The young jack the lad had jumped at the opportunity to help with a newspaper photo shoot advising readers what treasures might be loitering in their attic.

Ben couldn't have cared less about 'Loot In The Loft' but it was the silly season. With news stories few and far between his editor had tasked him to come up with 800 words for a spread in next week's paper.

By the time he arrived rather irritably at the photo studio Jimmy had already deftly created a different world. What initially looked like a dilapidated old warehouse had been converted in one corner into an Aladdin's cave of colour and curios. Different-sized boxes were draped with rich coloured silks and velvets to better showcase everything from a piece of pottery to a miniature watercolour. None of it looked like it was worth very much but Ben was surprisingly impressed with the overall affect. In the middle, fussing over a deep red velvet throw stood Jimmy. Drainpipe trousers, tight waistcoat buttoned over a plain white frilly fop shirt and Dr Martens completed his New Romantic look. Ben had thought he looked . . . he couldn't quite think of the words or emotions he was feeling.

As the day progressed and Ben tried hard to show an interest in how readers could tell if they were sitting on a masterpiece, the two young men realised they had much in common. They both loved football, hated clubbing and worshipped New Romantic music, especially Adam and the Ants. Dorian, the photographer, noticed the spark between the two of them and put 'Prince Charming' on the cassette player.

Later, as the shoot drew to a close, and fancying himself a bit of a matchmaker, Dorian dispatched Ben to the off licence at the pub next door with enough cash to buy six packs while he finished off the last few shots.

'You're in there mate. Honestly give it a go, he won't say no.'

Dorian was confident but Jimmy was unsure of Ben's interest.

'C'mon Dor, I don't think he's gay. Do you?'

As Dorian clicked away he nonchalantly highlighted half a dozen reasons why his prediction was a racing certainty. The conversation was cut short as Ben returned with two plastic carrier bags full of booze and snacks. With the shoot over, the three men grabbed themselves a cold beer and sat around chatting about football. Ben was also keen to learn more about the camera Dorian was using.

'It's a Canon mate, means precision in Latin apparently. Sit on the sofa, I'll take your picture with Jimmy. I'll send you both a copy. Smile. There you go.'

Observing how well the two men were getting on, Dorian suddenly remembered a subsequent engagement. Making his excuses he picked up his rucksack and headed for the door.

'Don't forget to lock up, will you boys. See ya.'

Now was Jimmy's chance. He grabbed more beers from the plastic bags and sat a little closer to Ben on the old sofa, racking his brains about what they could talk about until he made his move. They'd done football, what else, what else?

'What sort of influence do you think David Bowie had on the New Romantic movement? I mean how would you compare him to say Spandau Ballet, Duran Duran or Culture Club?'

Ben was delighted to talk about his musical passion and

unlacing his Dr Martens made himself more comfortable on the sofa. As time passed and the conversation moved on to the London Blitz Club Jimmy took the opportunity to rest his hand on Ben's knee. Both laughed at the memory of Mick Jagger being refused entry to the club in Covent Garden.

With still no resistance Jimmy moved in a little closer.

'Another beer?'

'Wow, are you trying to get me drunk? Oh, OK then.'

Dorian had been extremely reluctant to return to the studio. In his haste to leave he had stupidly forgotten a lens he needed for a location shoot the next day. He'd already rung a couple of photographer friends but no one else could loan him what he needed. It was a shoot for a national newspaper who he'd been trying to get work with forever and this was his first freelance assignment for them. He needed to make it a good one, so he had no choice but to return. He'd left it as late as he could in the hope they might have already gone home but the door was still unlocked and he knew the two youngsters would be enjoying each other's company inside. Walking in, he tried to make as much noise as possible to announce his unexpected return. Expletives and clothes rustling greeted his arrival but as he eventually turned on the lights both were still only wearing little more than their underwear.

Jimmy could still picture Ben's poor confused face. Even all these years later, he still wasn't sure whether it was embarrassment or sexual frustration. Looking over at Ben now, in his sharp suit and confident demeanour, he once again felt the stirrings of lust.

As the guests made their way back through to the Great Hall for coffee, Jimmy wandered over to chat to Brucie and his wife. They were joined by Charles who had to dig his nails into his palms to stop himself from asking for the veteran entertainer's autograph.

Finally and most unwillingly the guests began to leave. With no sign of Valerie, Ben hastily stood alongside Julian offering thanks and goodbyes. Charles and Jimmy took their turn and Ben politely shook their hands.

'You know, I was saying to Charles earlier, I'm sure we've met before Jimmy, but I just can't remember when. Obviously I recognise your name from TV and the papers but I can't think if our paths might have crossed otherwise.'

Helping Charles with his coat, Jimmy smiled mischievously.

'It's my stage name that's confusing you, I think, Mr Watson. Jimmy Meade is my real name.'

Ben gasped, his shocked face giving away far too much to anyone standing nearby, including Julian.

'Meade, no, no I still don't remember, sorry. Anyway, thanks for coming. We're all really looking forward to the Christmas special. Your car should be waiting for you just outside.'

'What was all that about?' whispered Charles as they headed towards the door.

'I'll tell you in the car, darling.'

As the last of the guests' chauffeur-driven vehicles made their way back down the long driveway, Julian also wanted to know more.

'What was that with Jimmy Phillips? You looked at him like he'd stolen an old girlfriend. What's the story?'

But Ben had no intention of discussing his distant dalliance in the Little League, with his employer or anyone else, ever. He decided attack was the best form of defence.

'Where's the Mrs then? Not very helpful of her disappearing when guests want to say goodbye, is it Prime Minister?'

Julian took his cue and went in search of Valerie. It didn't take long for him to find her slumped semi-conscious over a tumbler of gin in one of the anterooms. Dominic was sitting next to her, unsure of what to do. Reassuring his son, he dispatched him to set up the PS3 so they could get

247

in a quick game of Formula 1, before the Arsenal game started on Sky.

Julian stared down at his crumpled wife and felt nothing but contempt. She was a drunk and an embarrassment. Picking her up with no degree of concern, he made the familiar climb up the staircase to their bedroom. Dropping her gaunt frame roughly onto the bed he stared at her for a long time before speaking through gritted teeth.

'The holiday and then that's it, Valerie. It's over, we're over. I want nothing more to do with you, ever. Do you hear me? You're a disgrace, an absolute disgrace. This time it really is over, Valerie.'

Valerie turned her tear-stained face to look up at her husband. A man she no longer knew, a man who either ignored or abused her, a man with so much stinging contempt for her in his voice.

The room was spinning and she felt sick. She struggled to offer a slurred response to his venom.

'Oh, I know it's finally over, Julian. I really know that, love. Why do you think I'm like this?'

November

37

PM's motorcade

'He can do whatever he fucking wants, you jumped up little shit, he's the Prime Minister. You, you're just a two bit snotty-nosed little git who was still in short trousers when our glorious leader started in politics. Now get off this fucking line before I have to tell your sweet little squeeze all about the goings on with Natalie at the Midland Hotel in Manchester during Tory party conference. Just because I didn't see it doesn't mean I don't know about it. My spies are everywhere. By the way, little piece of advice, that moustache you've grown looks ridiculous, better just to have "I am a dickhead" tattooed on your top lip instead.

'Oh, one other thing, Robert mate, just before you go, tell your fucking editor that she looked an absolute sight in that ludicrous frock at the lobby journalists' drinks reception at Downing Street on Thursday. She needs to lose some weight or get a bigger size. I'm sure they must do it in an 18.'

Ben was sitting next to the PM in the back of a blacked-out armour-plated Jaguar speeding towards Heathrow Airport and heading for an overnight flight to South Africa. Julian's family, including his mother and father-in-law, and injured cricketing hero Monty were in the people carrier behind. The wheelchair folded away with the rest of the luggage. The family part of the trip was being paid for by the PM. The taxpayer would foot the bill for Julian and his official visit to the South African parliament where he planned to make a landmark speech promising more aid for the developing world. A contingent of lobby journalists was travelling with them and was already waiting at the VIP terminal for the Jensons to arrive.

Up until this evening Ben had been able to spin to the public via Her Majesty's press that the 10-day trip was in the best interests not only of Britain but also Julian's loyal and exhausted wife. His trump card the hero brother-in-law who had struggled so courageously over the autumn and was desperate for some much needed sun, to be provided courtesy of the generous PM.

But, the best laid plans of mice and men had gone to 'rat shit' in one phone call. Ben had just learned that a Sunday paper was about to print a story that could play very badly for the PM. Indeed, on the face of it, there was no upside. One of his newly elected MPs had been taped recounting a racist joke during an election victory dinner. The recording was now sitting on the newsdesk. *Race Disgrace of PM New Boy* was the headline.

The newspaper had also planned an editorial questioning how appropriate it was for the PM to be travelling to a country like South Africa while showing such stark disregard for race issues back home. The phone call from the political correspondent was the first Ben had heard of the story. Julian was enraged. Shouldn't Ben have seen this coming? What was the point of a spin doctor if he didn't know what the bloody Sunday papers were running?

'Are we going to have to cancel the trip?' he asked, exasperated.

'Ben, you really should have been across this sort of story before now. Isn't that what I pay you for? Finding out on the way to the airport is quite frankly second rate.'

In fact, the real reason for Julian's ire was very much more personal. He didn't want the splash to affect meticulous plans that had taken him forever to organise.

Not only did he have a van full of family travelling behind him but there was also the little matter of Sally already waiting for him in a Cape Town hotel suite overlooking Table Mountain. In addition, he had managed to arrange some fun in the sun with Isla exploring the African bush. Nevertheless, such was his personal abhorrence of racism that he was fully prepared to cancel his trysts and return to Downing Street, but only if absolutely necessary.

'I knew James Jackson was trouble, Ben. He should never have found his name on the constituency shortlist in the first place. What's he said?'

Ben was only half listening to his boss's rant as he contemplated instant solutions to the despicable behaviour of the new boy. 'He made a racist slur as part of an after dinner speech. Then defended himself by saying the "joke" was originally told by a black comedian. So that's alright then innit Jamey sunshine? What a complete tosser.

'Happy to sack him?'

Julian most certainly was and offered his immediate consent.

'He's toast. I'm not having that sort of disgusting behaviour in my party.'

Ben nodded and scrolled through the contact list on his new iPhone. He was finding it hard to get to grips with the modern technology despite his eldest boy's best efforts to drag him kicking and screaming into the 21st century. He eventually figured out how to disguise his number, jabbed at the touch screen and the call went through.

'James, Jamey mate, mi' old mucker, just when you thought

it was safe to switch your phone back on. It's your worst fucking nightmare. Evening son. Here's Benny.'

Julian stifled a snigger at the reference to *The Shining*. He could only imagine how James must have felt when he realised who was at the other end of the phone. Ben paused for a second, taking a guiltless delight in James' nervous splutterings before interrupting.

'I don't care, really I don't. You're history, toast, finito benito, gonesky and don't call me Shirley.'

'No, now just stop it. Seriously, I mean it, just stop right there young man, there's no point in telling me porkies, I've heard the tape. You're banged to rights, buddy.'

Ben paused again and held the phone away from his ear for a moment before continuing.

'Now then, come on sweetheart, big boys don't cry, do they? Dry those crocodile tears, your Uncle Ben has a little plan. Listen very carefully. I will say this only once.'

Julian couldn't help but laugh out loud this time. Ben was having a ball going through a host of one-liners from his DVD back catalogue. He half felt sorry for James.

'Now Jamey, remember the roof collapse at that dodgy diamond mine in Botswana last August?

'Are you sure? You're not telling me porkies again are you, you naughty boy?'

This time Ben had heard enough and hardened his tone.

'OK, well let me jog your memory. 125 local workers killed, not enough roof supports in place, appalling lack of safety measures by the owners, so said the accident report. Ring any bells?

'Yeah that diamond mine, old son. The same one you have a rather significant share interest in but were very keen to keep quiet during the election campaign. A campaign that was taking place in a former coal-mining constituency, if my memory serves me right.

'Anyway buddy, one of the papers seems to have got hold of the story. Fuck knows how. I'm afraid that has left me with no option but to call your local party chairman, fill him in on the details. Not sure if you knew but Cyril used to work down the pit?

'Anyway, obviously he's gonna wonder if you cared more about profit than miners' lives. Don't know what to say about that to be honest. Can't imagine he's going to take it too well whatever I say. What with you risking the lives of his African brothers and then trying to cover it up as part of a callous attempt to win votes in a tight knit North West mining community. That'll be a bugger to get off your emphysema chest.'

Ben paused, but only for a beat, before continuing.

'Oh, hold on, hold on Jamey. Wipe your tears, old son. I've had an epiphany. Here it comes. Brace yourself.

'You resign and I don't tell Cyril.'

Ben became completely matter of fact, adopting a no-nonsense professionalism.

'The Prime Minister knows you are profoundly embarrassed about the outrage you have caused with your unacceptable racist remark. Your constituents and the party deserve better. Under the circumstances you are left with no option but to resign.

'Boo hoo, big tears. The end. There, I even wrote it for you.

'No, no. No need to thank me. It's the least I could do. Bye.'

Killing that call, Ben ignored Julian's round of applause and moved swiftly on. He needed a TV spoiler broadcast with a couple of coats of Ben Watson whitewash on it before the paper's first edition hit the news-stands that night. Who to talk to? Certainly not a story he felt he could entrust to Isla. Ben was straight on the phone to the BBC. It was their turn for an exclusive.

'Nick, you already at the airport? Excellent, see you in the lounge in 15 minutes mi' old mucker. Got a good one

255

for you. Embargoed till the plane takes off though, scouts' honour?'

As the convoy swept down the M4 and left at the Heathrow exit Ben returned his attention to print journalists. Within moments he was on the phone to the political editor of a rival Sunday newspaper.

'Hey David. No, no delay, we're almost there. We should be taking off within half an hour or so.

'Anyway, spoiler for you. That wanker Robert apparently has some line about new boy James Jackson. Apparently he says he'd been embarrassing the party and damaging the boss with a racist slur at some toff's dinner.

'Well, Robert can fuck right off cos we're not embarrassed, we're fucking furious is what we are. Trump him with this one mate.

'Exclusive quote for you from the PM: "James Jackson is an embarrassment to himself, his constituency and the party. I will simply not tolerate this sort of disgusting and reprehensible behaviour. We are a party of all the people for all the people. I have received his shamed resignation this evening. A by-election will take place at the earliest possible opportunity. I apologise to the voters of Chorley for the inconvenience this will undoubtedly cause. However, I am sure they would rather another visit to the polls than a racist bigot representing them in the Mother of All Parliaments." Close quotes.

'File it now mate but hold it until just before the first editions. Under no circumstances go to press until we've taken off. The family needs some well-earned rest and as you know you won't like me when I'm angry.

'Oh and David, Julian says he'd be delighted if you could come up to first class for a drink once we're in the air.'

38

BA flight

Isla had never been in business class on an aircraft before and she really rather liked it. She accepted a glass of chilled champagne from Al, a charming British Airways steward, and settled back into her fully reclining aisle seat. She was starting to think that on balance having slobbery sex with Michael Grifton had probably been worth it after all. His fumbling desperation to take her clothes off had made her shudder, but not as much as his subsequent delirium at the sight of her standing seductively in front of him in a black satin bra and panties. Using her manicured forefinger to trace the outline of her over-glossed lips meant that the whole sexual encounter had been little more than 'wham bam thank you ma'am' and the 10 o'clock bus home.

Isla tried to push away the memory of Michael's contorted orgasm face. It had made him look less like a man at the height of sexual pleasure and more like a constipated version of Mickey Mouse's dog Pluto. She shuddered again.

'You cold, pet? That charming steward will bring you an

extra blanket if you ask him and don't forget another pillow too. It's a 10-hour flight so best to get comfortable early on.'

Bob had travelled around the globe on assignment many times and knew the ropes. Nab the pillows and the extra blankets early on before fellow passengers felt the air-con chill and there were none left.

'No, I'm fine thanks, Bobbie. I think I just need something to eat.

'Oooh look, it says here on the dinner menu I can choose anything from four course dining to light salads and snacks, all complemented with fine wines and champagnes.'

Isla paused to peruse the choices.

'They do Caesar Salad. I'm having that and chocolate torte.'

Bob smiled at Isla as he settled into the window seat. He'd offered her 62A, what he considered the plum seat on the whole aircraft, but obviously new to this business class lark she said she preferred the aisle. She'd learn.

Two pillows, two duvets, shoes off and tucked away in the slide out drawer, DVT socks on and Bob turned his attention to the duty free catalogue and a suitable eau de cologne for his Mrs. A fine woman who had been the love of his life for every single day of their 35 years together. After a quick flick through he chose something unpronounceable from Chanel, a Bobbi Brown eye shadow palette for his daughter Janice and a cuddly toy dog with magnetic paws for his new grandson Gavin.

Setting aside the duty free catalogue, he began to peruse the entertainment programme for the journey. Bob chuckled at his misjudgment of Isla. He had foolishly thought her days at *HND* were numbered after the Dublin disaster. Now here she was, sitting next to him, living the high life on an all-expenses paid trip and had yet another interview with the PM lined up. This girl should never be underestimated.

Bob initially thought it might have been down to Carole's intervention but realised it was more likely she had seen the error of her ways with Michael and had made her peace with the head of news. He hoped she hadn't chosen a third way and gone the route of Tracey part-legs. In all honesty Bob feared that was probably the case. Still it was none of his business. He was on a jolly to South Africa, had a couple of shoots to do with Isla and then a few days by the hotel pool while the youngster headed off to meet a girlfriend up country.

'Another glass of champagne for me, Al? Well, I don't mind if I do, sir. Lovely jubbly.'

As Al obliged, the prime ministerial party, who'd been delayed by a last minute TV interview, finally boarded the flight and turned left heading for first class.

39

Cape Town

Julian helped lift Monty into the light aircraft that would take his family on a three-hour flight to the pristine shores of the Maputaland coast in Northern KwaZulu-Natal. As he did so he found himself feeling unexpectedly melancholy. His brother-in-law had been a great sportsman and was still a very fine human being. Fate had cruelly humbled him into complete dependence on those who loved him most. As he lowered Monty gently into his seat and reached for the belt to secure the precious Mitchell cargo, he was unexpectedly furious with Julia. How could she so heartlessly have left him when he needed her so much? Shaken at the thought, it made him consider his own callous actions of late. As his increasingly brittle wife's world fell apart, she had needed him to be her strength and instead he'd rejected her.

Julian dismissed the unwanted guilt from his mind and instead embraced his brother-in-law warmly.

'Just relax and let the sun work its magic on you. I'll be there as soon as I can. Take good care my man.'

Julian grudgingly glanced back at Valerie who was chattering away to her father and their daughter in the rear of the plane and either didn't notice or didn't care to notice him. He had to acknowledge that when it came to family she was the life and soul. Always the glue that held everyone together. Even when she was emotionally broken she showed no weakness in front of her parents or brother. They all loved each other and shared a deep family bond, a bond that Julian had never known with his own family. Sheila and Frank had worked hard all their lives and were now completely content spending quality time with their children and grandchildren. A valuable lesson Julian had learned from them over the years. A lesson he had recently forgotten.

As the pilot carried out her pre-flight checks and the Mitchells all gossiped cheerfully together, Julian felt like a complete outsider. Unwillingly closing the aircraft door, he waved airily in the general direction of everyone onboard and the plane taxied for take-off. As the passengers waved frantically back through the porthole windows, he became aware of exasperated tears. His painful exclusion from such loving contentment was wholly of his own making and he wasn't sure if it was what he really wanted.

Striding purposefully across the tarmac he clambered back into the waiting car and the driver headed for the Table Bay Hotel. Ben noticed his boss's demeanour and considered business the best antidote. The visit to Union Buildings to speak to the South African government representatives in Pretoria was scheduled for the day after tomorrow. That should keep his mind off family matters. Ben began his brief by advising on delivery. A cross between Tony Blair's 'Africa is close to my heart' and Harold Macmillan's 'Winds of Change' should pitch it about right.

Before the big speech in Pretoria, he was due to visit Robben Island, off Cape Town, with the magnificent Nelson Mandela, a man whose moral integrity Julian had admired

261

for decades. The 14,000-acre island had been Mandela's hell for 18 years. Now a World Heritage Site, the great man had offered a hand of friendship by inviting the British Prime Minister to join him on his 15th return visit since his long walk to freedom. Julian had been honoured to accept.

'So winds of change, boss. Remember that one? With this racist nonsense back home we need to be cautious of any slip-ups. Another quick run through for you. Here goes.

'Harold Macmillan; delivered to the South African parliament back in 1960; watershed moment for black nationalism in Africa; Macmillan suggested British government would support setting up societies where individuals were treated equally whatever the colour of their skin. Got it?'

Julian believed that wholeheartedly. He would use his speech to underline his own views on racism, both for the consumption of the South African people and the TV audience back home. He looked out of the window of the chauffeured limousine at the shanty-towns lining the route and not for the first time thanked God for his privileged life.

On the fourth floor of the Table Bay hotel, Sally had tuned in to Sky News while she waited impatiently for her lover to make his way from the lobby up to their suite. She could see that from the scenes downstairs her wait would be extended. Julian had just arrived in the foyer and was being mobbed. The PM's exclusive interview with Nick Robinson meant all the UK media travelling with him now needed a quote to satisfy their furious news editors. Sally unenthusiastically prepared herself for a long wait.

Pottering around the suite she checked her face in the mirror. Her 50th birthday was already so far over her shoulder she could no longer even see it in the rear view mirror. Surprisingly, Sally was still completely relaxed about Mother Nature, the old bird hadn't managed to mug her yet. She had, of course, made some concessions to her maturing years, including a silk anti-wrinkle pillow case just like the one Nigella said she had. That and regular Sculptra injections meant Sally could still easily pass for a woman 10 years younger. Applying a little lipstick she was reminded of an article she'd read in *She* magazine while lying by the hotel pool. It suggested that fuller, firmer lips made a woman look younger. It certainly worked for her. She had her mother's genes to thank for her sexy pout.

Smiling at what she saw, Sally smoothed down her satin, button-fronted Nicole Farhi dress. It was one of her new purchases and she entertained herself for a few minutes by flirtatiously easing the hemline up her tanned legs checking just how much she should provocatively dare to bare before Julian realised she wasn't wearing underwear. Turning to check her reflection from the back Sally admired her pert derrière.

She was briefly transported back to her early newspaper days when her ample backside had opened her up to ridicule among the group she was so desperate to be a part of. Jumping up in the pub to buy more than her fair share of alcohol in an effort to be popular had merely resulted in disparaging catcalls about her appearance as she waited disconsolately at the bar.

After decades of diet and exercise plus a little light lipo-suction, not that she would ever admit to it, all that had now changed.

'No sagging there Sally,' she said out loud, very pleased with what she saw and oblivious to the fact that Julian was sleeping with a love rival whose tush was so pert it could touch the sky.

Sally wandered out onto the exquisite balcony of her mari-time themed corner suite with an uninterrupted view of both the mountain and the ocean. She'd arrived in South Africa two days ahead of JJ so as not to rouse any suspicions among the travelling press pack. They were almost ready to make their intentions public and a nosey journo sniffing around now could ruin everything. But 48 hours alone in a foreign country was far too long for Sally. The magazine editor had soon bored of spotting Hollywood A-listers in the hotel lobby or wandering around the Waterfront shops and bars. Even worse, now the British press was in town, she was confined to barracks and had eaten an unhappy lunch alone on the balcony. Even the world famous stunning backdrop, no hardship at all for the hundreds of thousands of tourists who flocked to Table Mountain every year, couldn't hold Sally's attention for long. She was restless and desperate to see her man.

Looking back through the terrace doors into the sitting room she could see Julian's face on the telly. He was still being interviewed live. He was, quite obviously, enjoying all the attention.

'What are you most looking forward to during your time in South Africa, Prime Minister?'

Sally recognised the British accent and walked briskly back into the room. Julian was smiling his response to that blonde girl from *HND*. Sally frowned. She really didn't like that young girl. Frankly she was surprised that Iris, or whatever her silly name, was in South Africa at all. Hadn't she spoken to her old mate Michael Grifton about how unimpressive the reporter was on TV? Hadn't he agreed and said he had given her a good chance but she hadn't lived up to expect-ations? How then could she be in South Africa and getting in the way of what Sally saw as a pre-honeymoon? On top of all that she could see that the little minx was quite clearly flirting.

'Silly bitch, back off from my man, or I will crush you till the pips squeak. Do you hear me?'

Sally snarled the furious warning at the set before switching it off and hurling the remote across the room.

'Who are you talking to, darling?'

Julian was standing behind Sally with a quizzical look on his handsome, already tanning face. She was shocked and perplexed to see him.

'Er, you're downstairs being interviewed live in the lobby.'

Julian was stunned at the outburst. Ben's barbed references to her hot temper were perhaps closer to the mark than he had believed until now. He had heard Sally shouting at someone as he walked into the suite but hadn't quite caught what she'd said. He hoped she wasn't being rude to room service, but there was no one else there.

'It was a pre-recorded interview darling, just being played out now. Who were you talking to? Were you on the phone?'

Sensing her lover's displeasure Sally rallied instantly.

'Oh, don't be silly darling. I wasn't talking to anyone. I'm so embarrassed you caught me. I was acting out a scene from one of the in-flight movies on the way over. It was with Angelina Jolie. I saw her down in the lobby earlier and it just reminded me of the movie. I really think we should get her for the Christmas cover of the magazine. She's a superb actress, don't you think?'

Sally scrutinised her lover's face for any flicker of disbelief at her spontaneous explanation but she needn't have worried. After the briefest of contemplation Julian had already moved on, only one thing on his mind.

Slowly loosening his tie he gave her a look that suggested an afternoon of uninterrupted sexual pleasure. Relieved, Sally smiled and eased her hemline a little higher, waiting for Julian's next move.

His eyes widened approvingly but resisting the knee-jerk temptation to rip open Sally's dress he began to unbutton his shirt instead. Julian was soon revealing a taut physique that was a tribute to personal training by the swimming coach of the British Olympic team. Sally's breathing became a little shallower as she watched and waited, resting gently against the back of a sofa. Julian slowly put his left hand next to his bare chest, raised his right arm and spoke softly to her.

'Dance with me, my love.'

40

Cliveden, Buckinghamshire

Jimmy Phillips's day had been quite a challenge. Filming on location in Buckinghamshire had not gone well and he was unhappy with much of what had been recorded. He didn't like his cameraman and on top of all that the director was a dreadful woman. He of course had no issue with women in the workplace, but it was a known fact that they made terrible directors. Jimmy had worked in television for almost 18 months now and he was very aware of how to make excellent programming. Just because Belinda had been on secondment from top rated *HND* and in the business for 15 years didn't mean she had a Scooby Doo about the right shots for his Christmas special. Frankly she had to go.

They had just finished shooting a segment with a charming elderly lady who had found what looked for all the world like a Van Gogh in her attic, but had actually been painted by her mother. Belinda had quite simply ruined it. He had stormed out of the country house hotel and was pacing up and down the gravel driveway while on the phone to his agent.

'Tommy, this director is bloody crap. She couldn't direct traffic. She wouldn't know the difference between a Vincent Van Gogh and a David Van Day. I want her off the show and replaced with someone who knows what they're doing, otherwise I quit and that's all there is to it. I mean it Tommy, I simply can't work under these conditions.'

Tommy had seen this talent transition so many times before. Start of career equates to a wide-eyed eagerness to learn from anyone and everyone. One sniff of a successful series and the client becomes a TV diva. Luckily, experience had taught him exactly how to deal with such scenarios. He had been in the business forever and was hugely respected. A tough but fair negotiator, he'd pulled off some of the most lucrative deals in the industry. His biggest regret was having passed on Ant and Dec when they were in *Byker Grove*.

'Darling, darling, Belinda is top telly talent. I had to shed blood, sweat and tears to get Barry Fritzenburg to release her from *HND*. She is their very best director. Barry didn't want to darling, believe me he didn't want to, even for as big a star as you. But I suggested if he could do this one little thing for us, then maybe, just maybe, you might consider stepping in to present *Have a Nice Day UK* with Suzie next time Sid is on leave.'

Tommy knew that not until hell froze over would that ever happen, but he also knew that this tiny, little white lie would do the trick with his tempestuous talent. It did. Jimmy was delighted at the prospect.

'OK, OK, but she'll have to buck her ideas up.'

Tommy rolled his eyes at his lunch guest sitting patiently opposite him at the Ivy Club. Signalling two more minutes to his companion, he continued to make further reassuring noises until his prima donna client felt vindicated and victorious, unaware he had conceded to the status quo.

That had been earlier in the day and Jimmy had decided a

quick spin of the wheel at the Ritz Club on the way back from Cliveden was now in order as a little reward for his continued patience with Belinda. He may as well as his driver Craig had to take him straight past the door on the way to Chelsea embankment anyway. Well almost, so it would be rude not to.

Asking Craig to wait for an hour or so, Jimmy strolled into the club like the regular he was. After being greeted warmly by the doormen, he gathered his favourite coloured sunshine-yellow chips and headed for the roulette table.

'Hello James, my darling namesake. You look stunning, new hair cut? It suits you. I'm feeling rather lucky this evening, should we play?'

Other clients already gathered at the table eased round a little to make gambling room for the famous TV star. Jimmy had chosen a busy table as always. A seasoned punter, he knew that would reduce the number of spins per hour to around 30 and so lessen the house edge. It would also increase his chances of winning, but only slightly.

James, the croupier, smiled his welcome to the star and keeping the American wheel gently turning waited for his clients to place their bets. Jimmy studied the numbers on the blue baize table before placing his copious chips where he always did.

'No more bets,' instructed James. Jimmy waited with eager anticipation as the surrogate ivory ball ricocheted in search of a temporary home.

'17 Black,' announced James and without a flicker of emotion placed the brass win marker on top of a pile of chips including four of Jimmy's. As 144 sunshine-yellow counters were pushed towards him, Jimmy smiled his appreciation and tossed back a two-chip tip.

Jimmy concentrated for a moment before reaching again to place bets in his preferred locations. Stopping a passing hostess he ordered a glass of champagne and eased onto a newly vacant plush leather stool. As the ball found another new home, Jimmy was once again successful and he winked playfully at the croupier. It was going to be his lucky night.

It was another five hours before Jimmy finally returned home to a frantic Charles who rushed to meet him as he walked through the door.

'Where on earth have you been? You're never this late home from the Club. I thought you were dead in a ditch somewhere. I rang all the hospitals. Tommy was frantic.'

Charles was about to continue with his relieved tirade when he noticed Jimmy's shocked face and waited for an explanation. Jimmy said nothing as he dropped his keys on the hall table and walked over to the drinks trolley in a trance. Pouring himself a Remy Martin brandy big enough to down an elephant he walked over to the silk cushioned sofa and slumped down, his face ashen.

Charles was desperate to know what had happened. The filming had finished early evening, he should have been home hours ago, had he been attacked? Was he having an affair? Did he just not want to come home? He had a million questions for his partner.

'What on earth has happened, my darling? Tell me, you look dreadful. What can have happened?'

Jimmy didn't seem to hear and draining the glass in one gulp he stood to pour another but Charles had seen enough and grabbed his arm. Guiding him back to the sofa he sat him down and holding Jimmy very close he waited. Jimmy started to shake and looked up into his partner's concerned face. Still he said nothing, unable to find the words. Finally he began to speak in sobs rather than syllables.

'I've lost it all. It's all gone, all gone.'

Charles had no idea what he was talking about. Perhaps he had been mugged?

'Shhh darling, I'm here. Everything will be alright, I promise.

270

You're home safe now, take your time and tell me what's happened. Are you hurt?'

Rocking Jimmy gently in his arms, Charles waited patiently to hear what was causing his partner so much distress.

By daylight Charles had learned the full extent of Jimmy's despair. They were financially wiped out and would be for years to come. Their fairytale future lay in financial ruins on an American Roulette table.

41

Ulusaba Game Reserve

'I knew you'd enjoy some time in the bush, now can we see some lions please, Prime Minister.'

Isla was strolling naked around the magnificent deck of the Makwela Suite at Rock Lodge in the Sabi Sand Game Reserve. Julian watched, admiring the view having just enjoyed the best sex he could ever remember. Until now Sally had been his most satisfying bedfellow, but this girl, this girl knew exactly which buttons to press.

'It's so lovely here er, Julian.'

For some reason Isla still felt slightly awkward calling the Prime Minister by his first name and hoped it would become easier very soon.

Looking out from their superb vantage point, perched high on the summit of a koppie, her eye was carried over miles of Savannah and on to the Drakensberg Mountain range on the horizon. In the near distance she was sure she could see a giraffe being stalked by three lionesses. No, surely not.

'It's so peaceful here. I wish we could stay forever.'

Isla wandered back across the deck and looked again at her powerful, charming, accomplished lover and sighed contentedly. She wanted to be with him forever and wrestled away unexpected feelings of frustration.

'Even here though you're just so busy. It must be so frustrating, everyone wanting a piece of you all the time. I saw your speech at the South African Parliament. You seemed to have a very good reception. What was it like in Cape Town beforehand? Were you really bored in that lonely hotel room? Did you think about me?'

Julian slowly rose from the sun lounger and dropped contentedly into the infinity pool, startling an inquisitive warthog foraging on the hillside in front of the lodge. Isla knew nothing of Sally or his tryst in Cape Town and that was exactly how it should remain for as long as possible. Julian had always been a firm believer that a man is only as good as he has to be. A woman can be as bad as she dares, but only if she thinks she is the only one. He had every hope that Isla would be very bad indeed for some time to come.

'Of course I did my love, every moment of every day I thought of you. Now tell me, what would you like to do this afternoon?

'I spoke to Duard, our ranger, and he told me that a baby elephant was born a few days ago near our lodge. Apparently it's an impossibly cute female with one floppy ear. Would you like to try and find her? Apparently the herd is very relaxed so we should be able to get up quite close.'

Julian splashed playfully in the pool and beckoned for Isla to join him.

'No rush though.'

It was an inviting idea, but she knew better than to always submit. Slipping back into her swimsuit and picking up a towel Isla sauntered inside the magnificent suite. Her destination: a glorious free-standing marble bath in the centre of a lavish bathroom, luxury she could only have dreamed about just a few months ago.

'I'll meet you by the game vehicle.'

'No need, I'll join you in the bath.'

Half an hour later and they were clambering on board the diesel, long wheel base, open-topped Land Rover. Isla had meticulously researched what to wear on safari. She was spot on with her khaki combat trousers, a neutral coloured shirt and fleece. Only the flip-flops and pink framed Oakleys let her down. As the couple settled into their bench seats, Duard quickly went through a check list of do's and don'ts designed to prevent them from being eaten by a hungry lion.

Housekeeping over, Julian and his overexcited lover were soon heading out on their afternoon game drive. Anton, the tracker, was riding up front, on the look-out for one or preferably all of the Big 5. Isla also had her eyes peeled but wasn't quite sure what she was looking for.

'What are the Big 5?'

'Well my love, the Big 5 are lion, leopard, buffalo, elephant and rhino although hippo often gets a mention as the Big 5+1.'

Julian was no stranger to safari and was already relaxing into the game drive. He was confident Isla would also love the spiritual experience of being at one with Africa's finest. As they reached the bottom of the koppie and Duard switched from low range, Isla began a volley of questions.

'OK, so that's what they are but why are they called the Big 5, who called them that and when?'

'Well, they're considered the five most difficult animals to hunt on foot. It's a name they were given by cowardly hunters hiding behind a big shotgun while hoping to decorate their wall with the head of one of the majestic animals.'

'Had they not heard of Osborne and Little?'

Julian wasn't sure if Isla was joking with her wallpaper

reference, but hugged her tight anyway. They drove on, catching glimpses of Kudu, Impala, Duiker and a Klipspringer before Duard stopped the vehicle right in the middle of a buffalo herd.

'Cows with horns is how some people describe them,' he offered. 'But don't be fooled Isla, they're scary, unpredictable beasts, especially a lone male. If we see one while we're tracking on foot, we're straight back to the vehicle.'

Isla looked again at the herd. They seemed so calm and nonchalant here in their natural habitat but she wasn't about to test Duard's words.

'Hemingway said a buffalo bull looks at you like you owe him a lot of money.'

Julian offered the literary observation up for general consumption. Even though he knew they were safe in the vehicle, he could see what the American author meant.

'Who's Hemingway? Is he another ranger, Duard?'

Julian turned his head away to hide a smile. She was a young girl and her experience would grow, hopefully with him as her clandestine tutor. As they moved on and the sun finally began to set, Isla voiced her disappointment at the lack of animal sightings.

'Don't worry. You have to be patient, my love. It's not a Ferrari Safari. We're here for a glorious 48 hours and there'll be lots of wild beasts on offer.'

Julian narrowed his eyes suggestively as the close protection officer in the back of the vehicle tried hard not to listen.

'Sundowner, PM?'

'Excellent thought, Duard.'

During his time in the bush, the head ranger had grown accustomed to hosting high-profile clients, from politicians to world famous celebrities, and catering appropriately to their needs. His knowledge and experience were second to none. His discretion guaranteed.

A few moments later Isla was in heaven as she found herself sipping chilled champagne by lantern light with a selection of barbecued Kudu skewers on offer. She chattered happily to Duard and Julian as Anton, the spotter, busied himself mixing Julian a G&T at a miraculously erected makeshift bar. Duard suddenly stopped speaking and slowly pointed over Isla's shoulder. Almost within touching distance a giraffe was moving weightlessly through the Lowveld. Isla was mesmerised by its stately grace as it strode silently by.

Eventually, as darkness finally overwhelmed them the couple clambered contentedly back onto the vehicle to return to the lodge. Isla felt colder now the sun had gone but Duard had thought of everything with ponchos and hot water bottles to hand. Warmly wrapped up she relaxed into Julian's shoulder, looking forward to the evening ahead. He held her closer and kissed her gently. Duard allowed the couple some privacy as he drove silently back to Rock Lodge. Anton was up front shining a search light in the slim hope of a night-time sighting.

With no sign of any other game the group was almost back at the lodge when Julian noticed Duard almost imperceptibly grip the steering wheel tighter and sit up a little straighter. He was immediately aware of danger. He glanced at Carl in the back seat and at the same time wrapped his arms more tightly around Isla.

As they rounded a corner on a narrow winding path in the densest part of the bush, there was an elephant blocking the road. They'd found the herd but it was dark and that could spell trouble.

'OK darling, I need you to be really calm, this may get a bit hairy but we're in the very best hands. Duard is Sir Richard Branson's favourite ranger. He'll have us home safe before you know it.'

Isla peered out into the darkness, and saw not one elephant, but a whole herd surrounding them. Even Carl was anxious.

276

He knew how to deal with the bad guys but dozens of angry elephants and only a limited number of bullets. That was a new one for him.

Julian glanced behind them. The gravel road hugging the edge of the ravine they had just negotiated would be almost impassable in the Land Rover in reverse, especially in the pitch dark. They had no choice but to continue cautiously on. As Duard inched the vehicle forward an inquisitive, over confident young male directly at Isla's eye level moved closer. Nothing between her and the wild animal, she could have reached out and touched its trunk.

'Don't move,' whispered the ranger, ever respectful of the wildlife around him.

The animal seemed agitated and moved in closer still. Duard had seen enough and roared the Land Rover engine in an attempt to warn off the adolescent male. Isla was suddenly terrified and began breathing far too quickly.

'Be calm, be calm darling, we'll be home before you know it but try to breathe more slowly.'

Julian was continuing to whisper reassurance to Isla while looking around the vehicle to check on the proximity of other angry elephants. With a new calf in the herd he knew the females would protect it at all costs.

Then what he had feared the most, happened. He couldn't see her but he could hear the deafening cacophony of the matriarch trumpeting and crashing through the undergrowth towards them. Isla began to cry. Carl wished it was only a bad guy with a gun that was careering towards them.

'Darling, darling, listen to me. Sit still. Are you listening to me, darling? Just sit completely still. We're almost home.'

The agitated herd was surrounding them in ever increasing numbers. Where was the matriarch? Julian knew that Duard had to get them out of there fast. From his precarious position above the bonnet, Anton clambered quickly into the body of the vehicle and with him safely inside, Duard could drive faster and accelerated along the sandy road trying to hold a driving line while still managing to expertly dodge calves.

The matriarch continued to trumpet her fury at their intrusion and Julian knew she would be flapping her gigantic ears in warning at their unwelcome presence, wherever she was. Involuntarily he also started to panic and began to consider his mortality. The noise around the vehicle was totally deafening, the occupants inside it completely quiet save for the sobbing of the young girl.

Julian kissed the top of Isla's head, stroking her shaking shoulders and holding her firmly next to his chest, focusing on her fear to try and combat his own.

Suddenly the ground started to shake as the matriarch made her appearance and charged. Instantly Duard put his foot right down. He knew she could travel at 25 miles an hour and would kill to protect the new calf. He was driving a heavy open-topped truck through sand with the British Prime Minister on board. The elephant kept stampeding towards them. Julian could feel the vehicle sliding on the sandy road but Duard kept focused, totally aware of the impending danger. If she caught them she could force her tusks into the vehicle and toss it into the air, terrified occupants still in situ, crushing the vehicle with ease. Julian held his breath, then as quickly as the danger had come, it passed. The protective matriarch, content she had seen off the human interlopers, gave up the chase and returned to her herd.

Duard and Anton laughed in unison.

'You all OK back there? Ready for a drink at the bar?'

A few minutes later, arriving back at Rock Lodge, Julian lifted a trembling Isla from the vehicle. Nodding his thanks and goodnight to Duard, he carried her into the suite. Adrenaline pumping from their brush with danger, they began to make passionate love almost before Julian had even closed the lodge door.

42

'Morning boss, good night?

'Don't answer that. Here's what's happening in good old Blighty today.'

Ben had returned to Cape Town for a bit of R&R after the trip to Pretoria. He was checking in daily with Julian to update him on the latest news back home. In their absence Daisy, the Deputy PM, was due to take Prime Minister's Questions in the House of Commons that afternoon.

'I've told her no showing off this time or she'll get savaged by the opposition again and not to wear that ridiculous zebra print jump suit. I'm fed up of seeing it and it makes her look like a horse in pyjamas.

'Anyway, told her to start with an explanation as to why you can't sadly be there in person. Then to underline to the House that the holiday part of the trip is to care for Valerie and Monty and is entirely at your own expense, obviously. That little oik from the Liberation Party is already sniffing round to see if you'd tried to fund it from the public purse. Honestly, if they'd won more than one bloody seat he'd have someone else to play with and stay out of other people's business. I'll get him put on the

Queen's Garden Party list, that should keep him bloody quiet for a bit.

'Daisy knows to underline to the Chamber that you're being kept up-to-date with day-to-day issues of Government and will be back by next week.

'Apart from that boss, the chancellor is making a statement on his pre-budget report. The foreign secretary has a speech lined up at Chatham House on our Afghanistan strategy. He'll talk about supplying more helicopters, meaning fewer troop movements on the ground, and hopefully reducing the risk from roadside bombs. He knows to mention the defence secretary's son potentially joining the army and er, that's about it.

'What about your end?'

Julian was relaxing on his terrace enjoying a freshly baked croissant as he watched the butler rush by with a catapult and dried peas trying in vain to frighten away cheeky monkeys stealing muffins from the breakfast tray. Several zebra meandered through the greenery on the koppie below where he sat, cautiously working in tandem. Turning this way and that in their efforts to stay one hoof ahead of a stalking predator before they became lunch. It reminded Julian of the daily risks of high political office. Isla was still sleeping after the events of last night.

'All fine this end, thank you Ben. We're having a truly magical time. I'm heading off to the beach tomorrow to meet up with the family but this has been a very welcome respite, I must say.

'What are you doing today?'

Ben still had a few days to kill before he was due to meet up with Julian again in Johannesburg and then head home to London. Having learned his lesson from the Erica episode in Thailand he had decided to steer well clear of the gay scene in Cape Town.

'Well, boss I'm heading to Gansbaai today. It's about two

280

hours' drive from here, then onwards by boat to Dyer Island and Shark Alley. Apparently it has one of the largest concentrations of Great Whites in the world. I'm planning to climb very bravely into a cage and then in a rather manly fashion dive straight in with the magnificent creatures. What do you think about that then?'

Julian sat up, alarmed by what he considered to be a rather needless risk in search of thrills.

'That all seems unnecessarily hazardous. Aren't you afraid of being eaten, Ben?'

Ben laughed, delighted he could use the gag he'd been honing all morning.

'Don't be silly, Prime Minister. Great white sharks wouldn't dream of eating political spin doctors. Professional courtesy.'

'Truly terrible joke, Ben.'

'Thank you Prime Minister, I've been practising. See you in Jo'burg.'

43

Johannesburg Airport

As Julian and Ben were enjoying their downtime, Sally was in the BA lounge ready to board her flight back to London. She had rung Maria several times from her mobile, but her deputy was uncontactable for some absurd reason or other. Out of vexed curiosity Sally decided to remove the caller ID and tried again. Maria picked up the call before the second ring.

'Hello, this is Maria.'

'Bloody hell Maria, I've tried you half a dozen times without success and as soon as I disguise my number you answer. Care to tell me why?'

Maria realised she had been rumbled but wasn't unduly concerned at her editor's ire. She was hoping to hand in her resignation when Sally was back in London. She'd been short-listed for the editorship of *Company* and if successful would be leaving *Celeb* as soon as good manners allowed.

'Oh, I'm so sorry Sally. My phone has been on my desk while I was in a meeting with the publisher. I've just this second returned to the office and saw that you had been trying to call. I was about to call back but you beat me to it. How's Cape Town? How did the profile piece go with the PM, happy?'

Sally knew she had been outfoxed by her cunning deputy and let it pass.

'All good, Maria. I'm thinking four pages with file pix, including the Number 10 doorstep wave. Can you ask the subs to make sure they crop that picture not to include the wife. I'm thinking a headline along the lines of "*PM Uncovered*" or "*Just Julian*". Something like that. Ask the team to lay it out for me and I'll be back in the office first thing in the morning.

'They're just calling my flight, have to go. Bye.'

Ending the call, Sally sauntered across to the lounge bar pouring herself a large Bombay Sapphire and slim-line tonic. She was attracting more than a little attention in her Ralph Lauren Blue Label khaki-coloured jodhpurs and a lace vest top with signature Prada heels. Not for Sally track bottoms and trainers, even if it was an overnight flight. To pass the time until her flight was called, she picked up a copy of *Hello!* magazine and returned to her seat before cattily dissecting the high quality glossy pages.

As the steward in the lounge announced the flight was ready for departure Sally felt a moment of panic. She was keen to see Sean. He'd been left with the housekeeper and neither really liked each other. There would be fall-out from that when she arrived home, but Sally didn't want to go back to London and leave Julian here. It wasn't just the sure knowledge she would miss him terribly but also the fear that Valerie may have another trick up her sleeve. A woman who could attempt suicide would stop at nothing to keep her man. Sally had no concern whatsoever about Valerie's mental state, she just wanted that damned woman out of the way as soon as possible.

But what options did she have right now? She could hardly storm onto the beach and demand Valerie give Julian the divorce he so desperately craved, could she?

No, for now there was nothing she could do, so Sally reluctantly gathered up her Louis Vuitton carry-on and dragged herself dejectedly towards the aircraft and home.

44

Thonga Beach Resort

Sheltering under a huge wide-brimmed hat protecting her from the South African sun, Valerie looked up from her Trollope and cast a maternal eye over her holidaying family. Her mother and daughter were strolling along the shimmering shoreline of the magnificent private beach. Her father, brother and son were playing boules in a sandy square in front of one of the hotel lodges. Dominic was obligingly dragging and manoeuvring Monty's wheelchair whenever he requested a better angle at the jack. Despite his disability, Monty still had excellent hand-to-eye coordination and as he hurled yet another winning boule, Frank felt as deflated as any Aussie batsman who'd faced his bowling at the crease.

'Good shot, again, son.'

Valerie smiled contentedly at the happy family scene. While anxious about what would happen when they all returned to England, she was determined to enjoy the break. Watching for a while as Monty won yet another game, precision placing his boules to prevent his opponents from any hope of seeing, let alone hitting the jack, Valerie grieved for her brother.

His mental and physical burden would have been too much for most men. Monty, the athlete, should have been on honeymoon now and returning to the UK just in time to prepare for his role as captain of the England cricket team's tour of South Africa. Instead, his loyalty had cost him his future. Reaching out to young Phil and pushing him into the car first with no concern for his own safety had been brave and noble but had left him in a wheelchair. The doctors couldn't or wouldn't offer a long-term prognosis at this stage. The waiting, the not knowing whether he would be able to walk again, let alone return to the sport he loved was taking its toll on the whole family.

Thoughts of Julia, or that damned deceitful, no good little minx, as her mother referred to her, fleetingly entered her mind. Valerie knew she'd been right not to trust that girl and now she had left her baby brother not only broken-hearted but also broke. They had spent well when money and sponsorship were plentiful. Calling off the engagement, Julia had also taken the opportunity to clear most of their joint account and Monty was presently being supported emotionally and financially by their parents.

Valerie noticed her father looking over to her and she smiled back at him. Ever since she had been a little girl, her father had taught her right from wrong, respect for others and a sense of social justice. 'Remember, you meet the same people on the way down again,' had been one of his favourite phrases.

Looking at the beach and watching her mother search for shells with Jessica, Valerie felt blessed. Whatever happened in the months to come, she knew that her parents' unconditional love would keep her away from that dark place she'd briefly toppled into. They had never mentioned what happened and her desperation for alcohol was not as intense when she was with them.

Her love for her children and Dominic's despair at her

sorry drunken behaviour after lunch at Chequers had steeled her to try to stay off the booze. It was an addiction and she was determined to tackle it. One day at a time.

Valerie slightly rearranged her chic shift dress and returned to her novel *Orley Farm*, the story of property grabbing skulduggery by a second wife. She tried to push away thoughts about whether Julian had an interest in other women. Perhaps that's why he wanted a divorce? No, whatever else his faults, Valerie couldn't believe her husband would ever consider adultery. In that way, he was an honourable man.

'Hi Mum, is it time for lunch yet, I'm starving?'

Dominic was wheeling Monty towards her on the beach terrace as his grandfather collected up the remnants of their game and returned the box to reception. Valerie nodded and waved to try to attract her mother's attention, but Sheila and Jessica were completely focused on what they were doing. Dominic shrugged and jogged barefoot along the beach to fetch them, leaving Monty with Valerie.

'Julian's coming today, isn't he?'

Valerie nodded dejectedly. She had hoped Julian would be there with her through the best and worst of times. That no longer seemed possible.

'I'm looking forward to seeing him, but I get the impression it's not going well at the moment, is it sis? I can feel how tense and upset you are.'

Monty put his hand on top of his sister's and stroked her fingers.

'He's a good man though sis. Just try to give him a bit of time and I'm sure it'll all come good again.'

Valerie said nothing. Not knowing what else to say, Monty looked over to the beach where his nephew was now splashing in the sea and soaking his quite obviously furious sister's brand new Fat Face beach outfit, much to the amusement of their grandmother. When he looked back, Valerie was crying.

'Don't cry our Valerie. I'm here and I'll always be here for you. You know that. Everything'll be alright, I promise.'

Valerie wiped away a tear rolling down her cheek. She was cross with herself for being upset in front of her brother. She was supposed to be the one who was staying strong for him, not the other way around.

'You know sis, we've both been in the wars this year, but what doesn't kill you makes you stronger. We might still be in the dark at the moment but trust me we will come out the other end and into the light soon enough.

'Er, that was a bit awkward, wasn't it? I made it sound like a journey through the Mersey tunnel!'

Both collapsed in giggles at his amateur attempt at philosophy.

45

As the Mitchells prepared for lunch, Julian was flying high above the scorched African bush in a plush eight-seater aircraft. He looked through the window at the ramshackle homes of locals who scratched a meagre living tending the parched land. Corrugated sheets balanced on top of misshapen branches offered limited protection from the elements. Again he considered the lives of those less fortunate who coped without proper sanitation or electricity. Gordon Brown had been right in his attempts to help developing countries.

Julian leaned back in his leather seat and closed his eyes. He had very much enjoyed every moment of his sojourn into Kruger National Park but was surprised at how eager he was to see his family. He was uncertain if that desire still included Valerie. She was so different now to when they'd first met.

From the moment his future wife had rather uncere-moniously knocked him from his bicycle, Julian had been completely smitten. They were, on the surface, completely mismatched, with backgrounds that couldn't have been more different. Status and privilege had guaranteed Julian a charmed life whatever path he chose. Valerie was working class and proud of it. She had vowels flatter than the Epsom Derby and encountered many hurdles as a result. Her northern accent was even more pronounced when provoked, which happened often during heated debate at the Oxford Union.

'I'll buy you a bag to keep all your vowels in my love. You do seem to drop them everywhere when you're angry,' he'd often joked. That had only made Valerie even more furious and northern. Many of Julian's friends hadn't taken to Valerie but with his love and support she had learned to ignore the snooty jibes and in turn had proved her mettle with a double first from Corpus Christi. Julian's academic prowess was less impressive but his lineage meant it didn't need to be and he chose a political course. Practically gifted a safe seat with the help of his father's influence, he soon became an MP. Valerie struggled to clamber onto the first rung of the publishing ladder, working longer hours than any of her colleagues in her determination to succeed.

A white wedding in the chapel on the Jenson-Fitzsimmons family estate saw an unconventional coming together of two very different classes. Julian's parents had tried hard to be pleasant and not treat their son's new in-laws as they would 'the help'. Always polite but only ever superficially nice.

Star-crossed lovers had been his mother's view who predicted early failure for their romance. But, she had been proved wrong. Julian and his new bride were the perfect couple and children soon followed. Julian still remembered his elation at the gift-wrapped pregnancy predictor with the blue line announcing imminent parenthood. His father was delighted at the arrival of a boy and with him continuation of the family line. Two challenging miscarriages followed but the joyous arrival of Jessica completed their family unit. Valerie had been keen to continue as a working mother and relied on loving family support and a series of unpredictable nannies as she and Julian edged towards their ultimate goals.

Julian soon made his mark in the House of Commons as private secretary to a succession of government ministers while Valerie became a commissioning editor and then deputy publisher of non-fiction at First Stop. Julian's father had been keen for him to step down from the Commons and take his rightful seat on the red leather benches of the House of Lords but he had his sights very firmly on the role of Prime Minister. Successful briefs for transport, foreign affairs and then chancellor had finally seen him reach the definitive prize.

Throughout the journey, Julian often acknowledged that he couldn't have done it without the love and support of his beautiful, elegant, intelligent, impish, loyal wife. Her common sense, kindness and sizzling passion had soothed him on many occasions when he had considered defeat. All the while she had quietly continued in her career finally becoming the MD of non-fiction. Who knows what the next move would have been? Then, without fuss or favour she had stepped down, sacrificing her own career, at least in the short term, for her husband's success.

At first they travelled together whenever possible, but demands on her time from the children and her charities meant Valerie was increasingly tied to London. With no wife present, the lip-glossed vultures already circling could move in for the kill. It hadn't taken long for him to yield. Initially, he was riddled with guilt and paralysed with fear at his infidelity becoming public. Look at how the papers had devoured every detail of John Major and even John Prescott's proclivities. He knew any sexual dalliances would not be tolerated by the party or the country and his must remain private. He couldn't risk any of them bleating to the press. There had been many, so many it was difficult to remember all of their names but he chose his conquests carefully and his betrayal had gone completely undetected. Then he had stupidly fallen in love.

Julian opened his eyes. If that's what it was with Sally. He wasn't sure.

Due to land soon, he was looking forward to a relaxing dinner. There'd be healthy political debate over a brandy with Sheila and Frank and lively sport chat with Monty while Dominic and Jessica bickered over who was cheating at the hotel supplied Monopoly.

Touching down at the private landing strip, he waved his thanks to the pilot before climbing into the open sided Land Rover for the hour-long bone grind to the beach resort. During the journey Julian exchanged little more than pleasantries with Carl, lost in thought as he considered the emotional challenges the next few months would bring. So far, it had been much easier to blame Valerie for their marital failings, but if he was being brutally honest, was it really all her fault?

As he eventually arrived at the Robinson Crusoe style hideaway, Julian had an overpowering desire to walk barefoot along the boardwalk of the coastal dune resort to his suite. Strolling out onto the balcony of the delightful room he breathed in the relaxing sea air. A sense of ease and contentment overwhelmed him and he took several more deep breaths. Holding on to the terrace rail he leaned out and, casting his eye along the beach, caught sight of his family. Frank and Dominic were playing beach touch rugby, Monty was in his wheelchair, both arms raised, acting as the goalpost for drop kicks.

The girls were splashing in the water. Jessica was wearing the new cut-offs that her mother had insisted on buying her from Jack Wills. They were soaked but she seemed unperturbed. He could hear his daughter's excited squeals from the balcony where he was. Pleased everyone seemed to be enjoying themselves, Julian flopped into a wicker chair. Relaxing in the late afternoon sun, he allowed its restorative powers to soothe him as he questioned, not for the first time, what it was he was searching for.

He had the promise of an exciting life with Sally. As sharp as a razor, she was always thrilled to see him and was a perfect addition to any well-heeled gathering. Alternatively, the puppy-like adoration from Isla was presently running a very close second. On the surface, either option was infinitely more enticing than the tedium of domesticity and the heavy burden of being a father and husband.

There was Dominic's troubled schooling. When would that boy ever learn to toe the line? He was charm personified at home but became an ogre when he returned to school. Perhaps Valerie had been right after all and underneath he was just a sensitive child who'd felt rejected at being sent away to board.

Then there was the cavernous depression of his brother-in-law as he struggled to come to terms with a life in ruins. His sporting career was almost certainly over and finding a woman while he was in a wheelchair would be tough. Monty tried to remain chipper but Julian knew that he was a broken man.

It didn't stop there. At home, Valerie's pendulum mood swings and her inability to cope without turning to the gin bottle was too much of a challenge for him. Why had she become a shadow of the woman he'd fallen in love with?

Julian shook his head, none of his debilitating family responsibilities could ever compare with the eager anticipation of stolen time with either Sally or Isla. But, as he watched them all now, released from their daily burdens and relaxing happily with each other, Julian felt his heart lift. He was unexpectedly energised by the prospect of spending time with all of them and was surprised to realise that included Valerie.

Leaning back in his chair, Julian stretched his legs up onto the circular wicker table and looked out across the ocean, relaxing into his memories and dreams. Feeling the warmth of the sun on the soles of his feet, he closed his eyes and rolled his head gently from side to side loosening any tension in his neck.

Casting his mind back to university life, Julian remembered how enjoyment had been purely testosterone centred until Valerie arrived. In an instant all that had changed. He no longer wanted to head down to the pub or away for the weekend on a rugby trip to Twickenham with the boys. He found it impossible to concentrate in lectures. All he could think about was spending time with Valerie. Absolutely sure she was the love of his life, Valerie had been his rock for 20 years until she began to crumble. Julian swung his feet from the table and unbuttoning his shirt he wandered back into the suite to retrieve a cold beer from the minibar. Changing into polo shirt and board shorts he headed back out on to the balcony, very happy to watch from a distance his family enjoying their holiday.

There was so still much he had to get clear in his head. Did he really want to throw everything away to spend the rest of his life with Sally? He was reasonably confident that after a flurry of interest, the British public would soon come around, especially with Ben's help. Valerie would be heart-broken, his parents-in-law furious, and Monty, keen to protect his sister, would probably never speak to him again. He hoped though that the children wouldn't take sides. Then there was Isla. He couldn't imagine that she would be keen to hang around if he publicly pledged himself to another and would he really want her to? Probably, but Sally would be watching him like a hawk and travel everywhere with him. For the last few months she had seemed the perfect solution to his unhappy life, but was he being too hasty?

Perhaps it wasn't about Sally or Isla or even Valerie. For a moment the desperately disturbing memory of a policeman rather than his mother standing on the platform at Paddington Station waiting to take him back to school forced its unwelcome way into his thoughts. Julian pushed it back into the deepest recesses of his mind and drained his beer. Gazing again towards the group he noticed Valerie looking in his direction from beneath an over-sized sunhat. Jumping to his feet Julian waved both arms in a desperate bid to attract his wife's attention.

She seemed to hesitate and looked around, unsure whether he was waving at her or other members of the group. Julian was horrified. What had he done to this woman? What had he reduced her to? Not sure whether to wave at her husband of 20 years. Stretching far out over the balcony he blew her a kiss. Tentatively she waved back. Beneath her hat he could see that she was smiling. Overwhelmed with relief, Julian waved again. What was he thinking of? How on earth could he possibly consider leaving this wonderful woman? Had he lost his mind?

Valerie immediately alerted the children to their father's presence. He heard their daughter squeal with pleasure as she waded excitedly from the water and began to run towards him. Julian took his cue and dashed from the balcony, sprinting along the boardwalk towards the beach. Reaching Jessica, he eagerly wrapped both arms around her before happily relinquishing one arm to include Dominic who had also dashed to join them. As the giggling trio strolled back, the rest of the family greeted him with warm, happy smiles, all delighted to see him. Not because he was Prime Minister, not because they wanted either sex, power or money from him, but simply because they loved him unconditionally. Julian tried very hard not to cry.

'Oh, our Julian, I can't tell you how lovely it is to see you lad. We thought you'd never get here. I can't wait to hear all about your travels. I don't half fancy a nice cuppa. I bet you do too, love?

'Do you think you can help Frank and our Dominic carry our Monty up to the terrace?'

Julian looked at his mother-in-law's open face. He felt just for a moment that she could see into his soul, knew about his deceit and had forgiven him. But how could she possibly know? It was just his guilty conscience.

Taking Sheila's arm he led her up the beach towards Monty and the others.

'Absolutely, darling mother-in-law. What about a bit of cake as well? I specifically asked for chef to bake angel cake. I know it's your favourite.'

46

The family had a wonderful afternoon together in the sunshine and were eagerly preparing for dinner when Ben called. More than a foot of snow had fallen over the last 24 hours, blanketing most of the UK. A shortage of salt meant major roads weren't being gritted. It was proving impossible for millions of people to get to work. Schools were closed, mainline train links were blocked and quite obviously it was all the Prime Minister's fault according to the papers. *Wish You Were Here, PM* was the headline in the *Sun*.

'Can you Adam and Eve it, it's only fucking snowing. Fluffy stuff everywhere. You're in South Africa sunning yourself putting on your Factor 25 while the nation wraps up in winter gear. What's wrong with this picture PM? Go on, I'll give you three guesses.

'Well make the most of tonight, 'cos tomorrow we're on a flight home.'

Julian couldn't believe what he was hearing. There was no way he was going back to London tomorrow.

'But Ben, I have literally only just arrived here with the family. I'm not leaving yet and that's that.'

'Nope, wrong, guess again.

'Honestly, you're rubbish at guessing games. OK, I'll tell you. Light plane picking you up first thing, boss. Flight out of Jo'Burg 6 pm, back in Downing Street and then on to COBRA by breakfast time the next day. That's if we can make it from Heathrow to Number 10 through the snowdrifts which are as high as Big Ben if the *Daily Mail* online is to be believed.'

'I don't think the British public will care that you've had less than 24 hours with your family. In fact they might be mildly interested in where you've been for the last few days if it wasn't with the family. Taking time off to shag your mistresses, brackets two, while they freeze their bits off is not a vote winner, trust me, I know these things.

'Especially as the reason you're supposed to be here is to spend as much time as possible with Valerie and Monty.'

'Shhhhh.'

Julian pressed the phone closer to his ear, concerned Ben would be overheard by Valerie who was applying her make-up nearby.

'It's a bugger for me too, boss. I'd booked some more diving with the Great Whites and now I'll have to swim with the sharks circling Downing Street instead.'

Ben adored every moment of his shark diving experience and had been keen to spend another couple of days enjoying the freedom and exhilaration of Shark Alley. He'd loved the thrill of being lowered in a steel cage into the waters known locally as the McDonalds drive-thru for the Great White. Even when he was up on the boat waiting for his turn, the shark viewing deck had offered brilliant photo opportunities of the surface feeders.

He'd also very much enjoyed spending time with Sean, a native South African adrenaline junkie. His expert diving experience had enhanced the pleasure for the whole group and Ben had found his company liberating. Sean was a strapping hunk with a shock of sun-bleached blond hair and a six pack that rippled underneath his wet suit. Men looked so much better in diving gear than women, who always seemed too squashed with bits bulging in all the wrong places.

Sean had offered to take Ben out on a solo dive tomorrow. Sadly that was now no longer an option.

'I've asked Cynthia at Number 10 to send one of the runners to meet us on the plane with winter clothes. When you get out of the car at Downing Street we don't want you pictured in fetching Hawaiian shirt and kiss-me-quick hat, now do we? That's not quite the image we'd like on the front page alongside Doris the pensioner huddled over her two-bar electric fire wearing gloves with the fingers cut out.

'Anyway, I won't keep you from your last supper, PM. See you at the airport tomorrow. Don't be late.'

Desperately disappointed at the news Julian turned to his wife. He was about to speak when interrupted by a text message:

Thinking about you JJ. Do you miss me?

Irritated, Julian quickly deleted the message from Sally and again turned to Valerie who was sitting on the bed searching for the room key in her purse. She looked relaxed, calm and beautiful, if a little too thin. He moved towards her and kneeling down took both her hands in his.

'I know this holiday meant so much to you my love. I had no idea until we came out here just how much we all needed time to relax and take stock. I am embarrassed at the way I've allowed our home life to deteriorate to the extent where we barely speak to each other in a civil tongue.

'I know I have offered you very little support when you felt you needed it most and I can see now why you turned to the bottle when you needed a friend.'

Valerie remained silent and allowed her husband to continue.

'I have to be honest my love and say I don't know what pressures await us when we return to London, but I do want you to know that I love you very much. Will you allow me to try to make amends and offer the support that has been so sadly lacking from me and which you so richly deserve?'

Valerie was shocked by her husband's mea culpa. The holiday had been as much for the children, her brother and parents to get away as any hope of reconciliation with Julian. She had sensed a thaw from his increasingly ice-cold behaviour but he had been similarly conciliatory earlier in the year and that had ended in even further heartache. This time, Valerie had shielded herself against any hope of reunion. Now this. Looking at Julian pleading in front of her, she wondered if he was finally being earnest. She really wanted to believe there was still hope.

Julian could feel his wife start to yield. Getting to his feet he put his left hand next to his chest, raised his right arm and spoke softly to her.

'Dance with me, my love.'

47

Frank wondered where his daughter had got to. They had been waiting in the large thatched rondavel dining room for more than half an hour and the children were becoming restless for their tea. Monty was playing backgammon with his mother, but still hadn't managed to win even one game.

'Don't know where they are, love. I think I might just pop down and knock, should I?' suggested Frank getting to his feet.

'NO,' shouted Sheila and Monty in unison, only too aware of what was undoubtedly delaying the couple.

'I think Valerie needed a bit of private time with Julian. She said they would be half an hour or so late. Did I not tell you? Sorry love. Come and help Monty try to beat his mum at backgammon.'

As Frank walked across to the board, Valerie and Julian strolled hand-in-hand onto the expansive wooden deck, the chemistry between them tangible. Jessica clapped her hands with delight.

'Mummy, you look lovely. I love that dress. Your hair's a bit messy though. Do you want to borrow one of my scrunchies?'

Sheila looked sideways at Jessica, unsure if her comment was innocent or mischievous. Catching her husband's eye

Sheila winked playfully at Frank who was embarrassed at his naivety.

'Right, everyone, I have organised for us to head down to the beach right this minute. There we will find a wonderful candlelit table for seven with our names on it. This evening, ladies and gentlemen, we will be dining on the shores of the Indian Ocean.'

Everyone cheered and Jessica jumped to her feet.

'That's fabulous, Daddy.

'And Daddy when we get back home can we have a dog? I don't want a Portuguese Water Dog like Malia and Sasha Obama though. They told me it's too bouncy and naughty all the time. Can we have an Irish Setter instead and can we call it Bruce?'

Julian laughed at his daughter's opportunism and ushered his family down to their table.

Dinner was sublime. As the family chattered away about sport, pop music and politics, Julian gently patted the top of Sheila's hand. It was easy to see where Valerie and Monty had inherited their charm and grace from.

His complimentary view may have been rather different, however, if he'd been aware of what Sheila knew. That she was aware of every single one of his dalliances, his long list of indiscretions and where he had spent the last few days. More than that, if he had known who his mother-in-law's mole was, then he would never be able to trust anyone again.

But he didn't know and Sheila was content not to tell him. Despite countless threats Julian hadn't yet jumped ship. While there was still hope that Valerie could live happily ever after with this two-faced, deceitful, snivelling, little toff who wasn't fit to clean her daughter's shoes, Sheila was content to play the game too. But woe betide him if he ever carried through his threat of leaving her daughter devastated and alone.

'Oh, our Julian, you really are a smasher. I was only sayin' the same to our Frank before you came down for your tea.

I can't tell you how much we're all enjoying our lovely holiday. Monty really appreciates it and as for our Valerie, doesn't she look lovely? See what a bit of sun can do?'

Julian was flattered by his mother-in-law's kind words. As he readjusted the cashmere sweater tied loosely around his shoulders Julian felt the soft, warm sand pressing up between his bare toes and wanted to stay there forever. He looked across the dinner table to his wife who was reassuringly stroking her brother's shoulder while chatting contentedly to their father. Julian decided there and then that life with Valerie was the one he would choose.

48

Ben was waiting in the BA VIP lounge at Johannesburg's O.R. Tambo International Airport as Julian sauntered through with his close protection team. He waved cheerful acknowledgement to foreigners keen to catch his eye, the Brits far too buttoned-up to admit recognition of their own leader.

'Much exercise, PM?'

'Sarcasm not required thank you, Mr Watson. I had a fabulous time on all levels and my exercise regime was appropriate for the circumstances. What's the big deal with the weather at home?'

Ben laughed at Julian's newly discovered discretion on bedroom matters and began briefing the PM on what he could expect when they returned to the UK.

'It's a massive issue and becoming more so with each settling snowflake. There's been a foot of the fluffy stuff in some parts of the Home Counties overnight and parts of Scotland are completely cut off. Not even the snow ploughs can get through. For whatever reason, boss, we haven't enough salt for the roads. How could that have happened? How many meetings did we have about this after the weather issues earlier in the year? We should have had more grit than bloody John Wayne.'

'Wasn't Daisy in charge of that?'

'Yup, I've told her she's right in the poop and she needs to be at the COBRA meeting. Biggest problem is that the Met Office is predicting more snow overnight. We might not even be able to land at Heathrow which would be a bleedin' nightmare, unlikely though. Who listens to the Met Office? Barbecue summer, mild winter is what they predicted this year. My pac-a-mac has never seen so much action in August.

'Come hell or high snowdrifts we need you back at the helm with a shovel and a donkey jacket soonest. I want you digging your way through to a little old lady's front door delivering her meals on wheels and waving a cold weather payment cheque by the weekend.

'You'll be pleased to know I've organised a trip to the rather appropriately named Christmas Common in Buckinghamshire by close of play on Friday. *HND*, Sky News, the *Sun*, *Mail* and *Times* and that solid bloke Andrew Porter from the *Daily Telegraph* are all on standby. Should make great weekend pictures and copy. Didn't like what the *Express* have been saying while you've been away though, so they're fucked.'

Julian laughed at his spin doctor's open vindictiveness. He'd always rather liked the *Express*. He'd make sure they were invited too.

'I had no idea the weather was so bad. Still, it's taken the heat off us over James Jackson.'

'You after my job, boss,' joked Ben.

'Yeah, we're certainly in the clear as far as that numpty is concerned. One of the Sundays printed a photograph of him in a rather provocative pose minus any kit. Something along the lines of the shaming of "*MP Beef Cake*". Could have been worse, could have been "*MP Little Bollocks*".'

'Where did they get the picture from?'

Julian's question was rhetorical. He knew Ben would have sourced and sent the incriminating print.

Within a few minutes their flight was ready and Julian stood to make his way to the 747 400 that would take him, as Jessica had described it, 'a sleep away' from his family. He felt reluctant to leave them behind but had insisted that just because he had to be back in harness, didn't mean their holiday should be ruined. He had kissed Valerie fondly and reassured her that everything would once again be fine when she returned at the end of the week. He wasn't sure if it would, but he was sure that he wanted it to be.

As they were escorted to the aircraft, Ben picked up on Julian's mood and tried to cheer him up.

'Oh I forgot to mention. The BBC wants you to be involved with Red Nose Day. What do you think?'

'Er, no bloody way Benjamin. Let me state clearly for the record I will not be donning a red nose or allowing Catherine Tate to make a complete idiot of me at Downing Street. For further clarification, I will not be sitting at my desk and saying, "*Am I bovvered though*" like Tony Blair did, even if it is for charity.'

Ben had anticipated his response, but was pleased it had cheered up his boss and so continued with the theme.

'Oh PM, I would implore you to reconsider. Given everything that's happening at the moment you may decide to run away to the circus. In which case, Prime Minister, red nose wearing ability would look pretty impressive on your CV.'

Julian put a friendly arm around Ben's shoulder as they walked the last few steps to the aircraft together. He was a good man, just a little misunderstood by everyone else on the planet.

Settling in to his first class seat, Julian always enjoyed being fussed over by eager crew. He was also pleased and relieved to see that he, Carl and Ben were the only three passengers in the cabin. An obligatory chat with the captain who had reassured Julian that she had voted for him and they were soon reaching V1 and taking off for home.

Julian was immediately bored. He had always found it impossible to sleep on planes. What to do to pass the time? He disinterestedly flicked through the in-flight entertainment magazine trying to find the movie with Angelina Jolie that Sally had been acting out back in Cape Town. Surprisingly he couldn't see it listed. Perhaps they had changed movie choices since Sally flew out? That must be it.

Ben and Carl were watching *Slumdog Millionaire*, but Julian had already seen it, having attended the London premiere as a guest of the director, Danny Boyle. Valerie had been delighted when Danny subsequently collected the Oscar for Best Director and took the award to his dad's Catholic social club in the North West. She'd considered him a true man of the people and had quite rightly insisted he be invited to Chequers for lunch.

Julian tried to entertain himself by choosing a few trinkets from duty free for the Downing Street staff. Shopping complete, he looked at his watch. There were still nine hours left. He decided to stretch his legs with a stroll down through business class. The lights in the cabins had been dimmed and most passengers would be asleep so he needn't worry about being harassed. Carl wasn't keen but conceded that even if the PM was accosted then shooting a potential terrorist in a pressurised metal tube hurtling through the sky at 500 mph was probably not a good option. Both agreed Julian would be back within five minutes or Carl would wander after him.

Julian was glad of the stretch. Nodding politely at cabin crew he avoided eye contact with any of the passengers. Most were either contentedly tucked under their duvet watching a movie or seeking privacy behind eye shades. Reaching the end of the business class cabin, Julian turned to walk back to first class and smiled at the humour of a female passenger with 'Go Away' embroidered on her eye shade. He strolled on for several more seconds before stopping abruptly and walking back for a closer look.

Peering across the dividing screen he noticed Bob, he didn't know his second name, the *HND* cameraman, sound asleep. An almost empty glass of brandy was about to fall from his hand, a nightcap that would almost certainly guarantee eight hours of uninterrupted sleep. How serendipitous. Pausing for a moment to gather his thoughts Julian leaned down and whispered into the female passenger's ear.

'Dance with me, my love.'

Isla almost jumped from her seat. She was momentarily confused about where she was and struggled to remove her eye cover. As she did she found herself staring directly into Julian's handsome face and gasped her surprise at seeing him.

'I thought you weren't coming back until the end of the week?' she whispered.

'Change of plan, never mind about that, follow me.'

Julian couldn't disguise his delight at the chance meeting with his young squeeze. The recent promise he'd made to himself about future relations with his wife dissolved into giddy lust as he contemplated some mile high activity.

Checking Bob was sound asleep, Isla gently removed the brandy glass from his hand. She smoothed down her hair and dug in her bag for an extra strong mint. A few moments after Julian and as nonchalantly as possible she strolled up to first class where he was waiting. As they walked through the curtain Carl turned to check on the PM but immediately averted his eyes when he saw his companion. Ben offered a comedy tut but was soon distracted by the *Slumdog* question about who invented the first commercially successful revolver. Julian ignored him as he took Isla's hand and headed for the bathroom. Quickly locking the concertina door he shuffled around in the tight space to face Isla.

With a look that only sexual gratification could satisfy, he lifted Isla around her waist and plonked her on the edge of the stainless steel washbasin. For Isla joining the mile high club suddenly seemed less exciting. It was nothing more than sex in a public toilet. Julian though had no such qualms and within a few moments it was all over. Zipping up his chinos, Julian looked at himself in the mirror. Brushing away a couple of stray hairs from his forehead he kissed Isla on the cheek, suggested she wait a few minutes and slid open the door before returning to his seat.

Isla relocked the bathroom door and remained perfectly still, unsure of what to do next. He was just like all the rest. He didn't care about her after all. He didn't love her, he loved the sex. There was no future in their relationship. How could she have been so stupid? What would the cabin crew think?

Clambering off the basin and washing her face, she looked up at her reflection. Her flushed cheeks were more from embarrassment than mile high madness. It was the last time she would be indulging in that and the last time she ever wanted to see Julian.

Sliding open the bathroom door, the cabin was in darkness and peering over at Julian's seat she was relieved to see he was already sleeping. Unable to prevent herself looking over to Ben she was mortified to see him staring straight back at her. He offered a cheeky wink before returning to the taxing *Slumdog* question of which cricketer had recorded the most first-class centuries.

Isla made her way quickly back to her seat, looking down at the floor to avoid eye contact with cabin crew or anyone else. Sitting down, she pulled her duvet right over her head. She had thought it would be different this time, but it wasn't.

Despite her best efforts Isla began to cry. At the other side of the dividing screen Bob shook his head in sympathy. She was learning the hard way that if you lie down with dogs you wake up with fleas.

December

December

49

Cromwell Hospital

'Details are sketchy at the moment, but the latest we are hearing is that TV presenter Jimmy Phillips has been rushed to hospital with serious head injuries. He was apparently attacked in the early hours of this morning as he walked towards his central London home. Eyewitnesses say he was assaulted by two masked men brandishing baseball bats. The motive at this stage is unknown. Let's get the latest from our crime correspondent Martin Brunt . . .'

Charles muted the sound on the portable TV in Jimmy's hospital room. Gently stroking his partner's hand he tried to hide his shock at Jimmy's battered face and arms. His nose was broken and doctors feared a fracture to his skull.

'Who could possibly have done this to you, my darling? Why on earth would anyone want to hurt you?'

Jimmy tried to speak but the dried blood at the back of his throat was making him feel nauseous. Gesturing to Charles he managed to sip a little water through a straw from a hospital beaker. Falteringly, Jimmy tried again.

'All such a blur. Don't know,' he said before resting his head back onto the pillow.

But Jimmy did know. He was very aware of exactly who was responsible for the sustained and vicious beating that had left him bloodied and unconscious in a quiet London street.

'Oh my darling, don't try to speak, just rest. The doctors say you should try to sleep as much as possible. The police want to have a word with you but I have told the nurse that you are not to be disturbed. You are not well enough to talk to anyone at the moment.'

Jimmy nodded weakly and closed his eyes. He was already planning his revenge.

There was a tap at the door of Jimmy's private hospital room and it was opened gently by Tommy Gold who peered hesitantly inside. Charles beckoned him and opening his eyes again Jimmy tried to smile at his agent but the extensive bruising on his face made him wince in pain. Tommy was shaken by Jimmy's appearance and rushed to his bedside, unsure of what to say. Hadn't Jimmy suffered enough over the last few weeks without this?

'Don't you worry about a thing. We'll sort everything out just as soon as you are well again. Rest as much as you can for now and I'll take care of everything.'

Jimmy again attempted a half smile before once more closing his bloodied and swollen eyes. Charles and Tommy sat either side of him and turned to watch the latest reports on TV.

50

Carole had also been watching the breaking news from her office at *HND* and during an ad break walked across the newsroom to speak to Michael Grifton. This was going to be an enormous story for them and one they needed to 'monster' in the morning. She was already considering who should be sent to report from where in order to best cover events for *HND* viewers. Jimmy was a massive, flamboyant star, the sort of TV celebrity that her viewers absolutely loved. They'd be devastated at the news of his assault. Jimmy's show rated extremely well and his Christmas special was being promoted everywhere. Even on her way in to work that morning, she had seen a gigantic hoarding on the A4 which replicated one of Jimmy's TV sets. He was portrayed in the centre of the 3D hoarding surrounded by antiques. At the time, Carole had smiled at the rise and rise of this unlikely TV star.

Now he was lying pole-axed in a hospital bed having been beaten to within an inch of his life. But why and by whom? Those were the sort of questions her reporters needed to find the answers to by the morning.

315

Carole wandered into the head of news' office as he was flicking through the other channels. He was scribbling notes with his gnarled Bic pen, gleaning as much information as he could on Jimmy's condition. The terrestrial channels were offering a mish mash of programming including how to spruce up your house, or *Phil and Holly*. Their news bulletins wouldn't catch up until lunchtime. The BBC news channel had about the same detail as Sky. Some copper must have made a few bob flogging the story to his contacts thought Carole. Why hadn't they been tipped off earlier? She knew that was the question Michael would be asking and she could tell he wasn't happy.

'Today's show went well, happy with it?'

'Of course I'm not. Why didn't we have this bloody story Carole? This is massive for us.'

Michael was furious that the attack on Jimmy had happened hours before *HND* went to air and yet they had known nothing about it until it was too late to broadcast. He had a point thought Carole but as always she would protect her staff.

'Come on Michael, we can't break every story. OK, it ducked under the radar and now we're playing catch up. On the positive, it gives us more time to monster it properly for the morning rather than throwing it away at the end of today's show.'

'Yeah right, either that or we look like we're playing bleedin' catch up, 24 hours too bloody late.'

As Michael chewed on the end of his plastic pen while scratching his groin with grubby fingernails, Carole had to again acknowledge that he had a point.

'Look Michael, I know everyone else will have all day to cover this and you can bet it'll be the lead story on every channel. But I think Jimmy Phillips being beaten senseless by bad guys is what our viewers very much want to know about and it will still play big in the morning. We were originally planning to lead on Stephen's interview with the PM tomorrow. He's still fighting off criticism about sunning himself in South Africa while we all froze, but I think Jimmy Phillips will be a bigger story even tomorrow.'

'It bloody better be. Get that crime correspondent in here right now. He needs to have a good excuse for missing this one. I only signed off his extortionate expenses yesterday. He claimed to be lunching with what seemed like every police officer in the Met. How could he possibly have not been tipped off about this?'

Carole had seen that one coming and had already dispatched Mark Cunliffe to the hospital where Jimmy was being treated. She was keen to protect him from Michael's ire and to save Michael from an HR dressing down afterwards. Carole knew that with the march of 24-hour news channels however much her journalists wined and dined the powers that be, her programme was only on air for three hours a day which offered a limited window to air exclusives.

'Mark is already on the case. He's sniffing around at the moment and says that Jimmy will be in hospital for a few days at least. His contacts say the police are working on several leads and will be issuing a description a little later in the day.'

None of the facts she was outlining had been passed on by Mark but having been in the business too long Carole knew exactly how events would play out. The report of Jimmy's injuries meant he certainly wouldn't be leaving hospital today. The police would want to be seen to be taking charge as soon as possible, especially with such a high-profile case and make a statement as soon as they could. Everything she had just outlined to Michael would undoubtedly unfold later.

'Mark is trying to persuade the police to do a live condition check on Jimmy and also the latest update on their inquiries at 6 am. He'll be live from outside the hospital tomorrow morning with that.'

Michael nodded brusquely. It would take more than a few placating words from Carole to calm his frustration at missing such a big story that he was now having to wait another 24 hours to get his teeth into it.

'OK, so Mark will be at the hospital live. Before that though, I want him to put a background piece together that can run all morning. Any blood left on the ground, eye-witnesses, neighbours, everything our viewers will want to know about.

'I also want a piece about the rise and rise of Jimmy Phillips, the TV star. Who's on showbiz this week?'

'I believe you've rota-ed Tracey Partington . . .'

'Shit.'

Both of them knew Tracey couldn't put together a film report on her own.

'OK, tell Ruth to help her cut a piece to run after break one. I want as much footage of Jimmy on the telly as possible. I want to see him in action over the last series and see if there might be any new footage of the Christmas special we can use, but I'm not paying for it. Tell his channel that we'll fair deal it and give them a big plug on screen, but I'm not paying for it. OK?'

Carole nodded at Michael as he kicked into top gear. She knew all of this stuff but it was good to have confirmation.

'What else?'

The room fell silent for a moment. With obvious stuff out of the way both were contemplating unique angles to make their reporting fresh in the morning. Carole spoke first.

'Got it. I read somewhere that the PM's wife is a big fan of Jimmy. Apparently he and his partner went to Chequers for lunch recently. His agent did a piece in one of the papers about Valerie saying he is must watch viewing in Downing Street. Let's try for an interview with her for the morning. Perhaps either Stephen or Isla could put a call in?'

'Good idea. I'll ask Isla.'

Michael's change of heart towards the young reporter was a little too obvious for Carole, but she let it pass. She had been persona non grata only a couple of months ago and Carole had feared the reporter's contract would not be renewed. Now Michael was all over her like a cheap dress and had even allowed her a jolly to South Africa. It didn't take Einstein to figure out why. Michael would never change his philandering ways and Isla had obviously taken the horizontal option.

Still, how the reporter chose to live her life was none of Carole's business. For now she was more concerned about securing an exclusive with Valerie Jenson. Michael may have decided to entrust matters to Isla but wandering back into her own office Carole also put a call in to Stephen James just to make sure.

51

Downing Street

'Fucking hell, look what's happened to Jimmy Phillips. Gay bashin' on the South Bank, there should be a law against it, Prime Minister.'

Ben had walked into Julian's office and sitting on the edge of his desk turned up the sound on the TV. Julian who was quite obviously in the middle of a sensitive telephone conversation scowled at his spin doctor before continuing with the call.

'Yes, yes, I totally understand Mrs Jenkins. I can absolutely see why you felt you needed to speak to the *Independent* about your heating not working while I was away on a sunshine holiday with my family.

'Yes, I understand that you were very cold indeed and that your pension doesn't go anywhere near far enough.

'No, I don't know how much your last gas bill was. How much was it?

'Goodness that is a lot of money for a pensioner, isn't it?

'No! Really Mrs Jenkins, I'm so sorry to hear that about Tiddles. Is he feeling any better now?'

Julian shrugged at his spin doctor as he continued to try and placate the irate pensioner.

'Tell her to cozy up with the old man and wait till summer. Give me the phone, I'll tell her.'

Ben reached over to take the receiver. Julian moved away, no intention of handing over the distressed Mrs Jenkins to his loose cannon. He had been known to reduce hard-nosed political correspondents to tears let alone frail old ladies.

'That noise Mrs Jenkins. Oh I'm just listening to the TV reports about Jimmy Phillips. He's in hospital and not very well.

'Yes, we are big fans at Downing Street, are you?

'Yes, we're very much looking forward to the Christmas special as well.

'Yes, I will send your regards to Valerie. Yes, yes and Monty too. That's very kind of you to think of them, I'm sure they'll be very touched by your good wishes.

'Aw, Mrs Jenkins, that is very understanding of you under the circumstances and of course I promise I won't go on holiday in November again. It was most remiss of me.

'Anyway, you take care. Bye, bye Mrs Jenkins.'

Julian replaced the receiver and flopped into his leather desk chair. Ben was almost crying with laughter at the PM's predicament.

'Mrs Jenkins, is she the old bird who was the splash and two inside pages of today's *Indy*? No heating, cuddling up with her pussy to keep warm, while yours truly was sunning himself in Cape Town.'

Julian nodded. 'The very same.'

'How the fuck did she get through? Who's on the switchboard?'

Julian paused, avoiding eye contact and reluctant to answer before finally admitting: 'Erm, I called her.'

Ben was mystified and a little irritated that Julian had made the call without guidance.

'You're kidding. I told you I already spoke to the journo about that story. There wasn't much in it and there's no follow up planned. Even the headline was pretty tame. Why bother talking to her?'

'Well Sally rang about the piece she was doing on me for *Celeb* this week and mentioned she thought I should give Mrs Jenkins a call.'

At first Julian had been keen to distance himself from Sally only just back from but with Valerie, South Africa and Isla for some reason not answering her phone, choice for dessert had been limited. Sally had offered her words of PR wisdom moments after coital pleasure at the Hamspstead house. Ben was furious at the very mention of his nemesis.

'Are you going out of your mind? The whole bloody conversation with the old bird would have been taped by a neighbour.'

'Yes, we did consider that but both Sally and I thought I could still come across as caring and compassionate, as indeed I did. Don't you think?'

'Both Sally and I. . . .' Ben mimicked Julian in a comic nasal tone.

'What does she know about handling tricky issues like this? Surprised she didn't prep you to say "Crisis? What crisis?" to the frail, infirm Mrs Jenkins. That would have been a good line, don't you think, Sunny Jim?'

The spin doctor's reference hit bull's eye. Julian well remembered the Winter of Discontent. The then Prime Minister James Callaghan always denied the 'Crisis? What crisis?' quote despite it being widely credited to him. He lost the '79 election.

'Ha, ha Ben, that's not funny. I thought speaking to Mrs Jenkins was a good idea and the right thing to do. This is not a crisis.'

'See, there you go. Thank fuck you didn't just say that on the phone. That would have been the splash everywhere tomorrow.'

Ben was about to continue when his BlackBerry alerted him to an incoming text.

Does Val want to speak on Jimmy? SJ.

Ben took a second to digest the request. Was it a good idea? Jimmy Phillips was big news and would most certainly knock any negative press about Julian from tomorrow's front pages. He turned up the TV to listen to the latest news.

'Jimmy is likely to stay in hospital for the next few days at least. His partner, Charles, and his agent, Tommy Gold, are by his bedside. Police are likely to hold a news conference later in the day when it's expected they will release more details about the attack. Let's hear more from our correspondent outside the hospital . . .'

'Boss, what do you think of this? *HND* want an interview with Valerie about the attack on Jimmy. Stephen James wants to do it. They could knock it off this afternoon and hold it as an exclusive for tomorrow morning. Gives the story fresh legs for them.

'I think it's a good idea but not sure what Sally would think. Should we ask her first?'

Julian narrowed his eyes at his spin doctor who was in danger of overstepping the mark. He'd taken the point, he didn't need to turn it into a crisis. Er, not a crisis, obviously not a crisis, but something similar.

'Don't they want me to comment?'

'It would appear not, Prime Minister. It would seem that your lovely wife's views are more valuable than yours on this particular subject.'

Julian stood from behind his desk, peeved at the slight.

'I'm happy if Valerie is, but please make sure it's not Isla who does the interview.'

Julian was cross Isla wasn't answering her phone. If she wasn't prepared to play the game, she could forget her access to Number 10.

Ben nodded and as Julian left the room he made the call to Stephen James.

'Hello, mate. Good news and bad news. Yeah, Valerie is delighted and says thank you for thinking of her. We can do it in the White Room. Should we say around 4 pm? That will give us time to gather more info on the story.

'Yeah, of course it's an exclusive to you guys.

'Now here comes the bad news, mate. I've tried my best and believe me I really went in to bat for you on this one buddy but I'm afraid the PM insists that Isla must do the sit down chat with Valerie. Bummer I know, sorry about that. Anyway, can you make sure she's here by 3 pm to set up.'

Ben ended the call before the political editor could offer comment. He allowed himself a cunning smile. That'll teach Julian to take advice from Sally. Slumping into Julian's chair he put his feet up on the desk and tuned in to the latest news on the Jimmy Phillips attack.

52

The next morning Valerie chatted on the phone to her mum from the bedroom of Number 10 as they both watched her *HND* interview with Isla.

'I know Mum, I just can't believe it either. Who would do that to such a lovely man?

'Yes she is pretty, isn't she? Yes, I suppose she does look a bit like Twiggy. Anyway, I'm just out of the shower and I'm sitting here in a towel. I need to get dressed, Julian is already out and about and I have a million things to do. Love to our Monty and to Dad. I'll speak to you later.'

Valerie felt peeved as she put down the phone but wasn't quite sure why. Her mother was right. Isla was pretty but for some reason she hadn't taken to the young girl at all. Perhaps it was because she reminded her of Julia. That play-suit she'd arrived in didn't help. They may be a fashion statement but she had even refused to buy Jessica one and it was certainly inappropriate for a TV reporter to turn up at Downing Street wearing one. Never mind, she would of course still send her a note to thank her for the interview.

Valerie slid off the bed and headed towards the basin to clean her teeth. Squeezing out the toothpaste she stopped for a moment to take a long look at herself in the unforgiving mirror. The antiquated lighting was particularly harsh in the old bathroom. It probably hadn't been updated since Winston Churchill brushed his molars there. Taking a closer look at her reflection Valerie was still sporting a South Africa tan and felt happier with what she saw. She was once again starting to get her life back under control and it was slowly beginning to show in a healthier looking glow.

After lengthy discussion she had chosen not to take the advice of the charming young doctor at St Thomas' who had cared for her after the unfortunate accident in September. The pills he had prescribed were staying in the bottle for now, as was the gin.

The holiday had proved a turning point for the whole family. Julian had finally come to his senses after six long months of oscillation and indecision. They were now once again heading cautiously in the right direction.

Stroking her cheek, Valerie considered herself still presentable but definitely more careworn after the year she'd endured. Months of hard drinking had taken their toll. Gaunt features with protruding cheekbones belied her once sound health. She shook her head with frustration. It would take some time yet before she could recover fully.

Valerie rinsed her mouth and headed towards her wardrobe to contemplate her sartorial options for the day while also considering what to cook for dinner. She settled on capri pants and shepherd's pie. It had been Julian and Valerie's favourite dish since their first date at university and she knew her husband would love it. She worked through the ingredients for the online Waitrose order in her mind as she slipped in to a Marc Jacobs cashmere sweater.

A dress was always the order of the day whenever she was likely to be photographed, but frying off mince and onions in the Number 10 kitchen didn't demand such formality.

Valerie checked out her outfit in the full-length mirror on the back of the wardrobe door. She had found a style that suited her long ago and was confident enough to have stuck with it, whatever catty magazine articles suggested.

She laughed as she remembered how just a couple of months ago she would have been more likely to spend her day in pyjamas rather than in tailored trousers. Again, she found herself considering the holiday that almost never happened. Quality time with the family had made her realise just how lucky she was.

As she sat at her dressing table, Valerie thought about the morning she had woken up early, and seeing her father sitting on his balcony opposite, had suggested a walk along the beach. They crept down to the shore without waking anyone else and strolled contentedly together as the waves tried to catch them unawares. Frank was worried sick about her. She was his little girl and he wanted to protect her. He wasn't sure what to say, how to broach a conversation he had wanted to have with her for months now. They walked and walked and walked in silence lost in their own thoughts. He could feel her sadness and he wanted to help. But how? As they walked still further along the shore, eventually it was Valerie who broke the silence.

'Dad, you do know that you don't need to wear black tie-up leather shoes on the beach, don't you. Flip flops work just as well.'

Looking down at his feet, Frank realised she had a point.

'I wasn't really thinking about my shoes to be honest, love. I was thinking about my precious little girl and why she is so sad. Your mother and I have always been so proud of you as we watched you grow and find your own place in the world.

'You know, I've learnt enough over the years to realise that whatever is taking such a toll on you our Valerie, it will pass. It's a cliché love, but time really is a great healer.

'Whatever it is will be only a memory soon enough. I am your Dad and I will do anything in the world I can to try to make things better.'

Valerie smiled and looked down again at her father's inappropriate grey socks and shoes now ruined by the incoming tide and crumpled into his arms.

Standing ankle deep in the Indian Ocean, Frank hugged his daughter tight offering her the safety net she needed to release her inner stress.

Eventually he whispered to his broken child.

'You don't need to cry love, yer mother's packed me another pair.'

Reaching for her solitaire diamond from the dressing table Valerie struggled with the tricky clasp.

'Let me help you with that, my love.'

Julian had been standing at the door watching his wife dress. Although she was far too thin, he felt that after the challenges of the election, she was finally returning to him. Being overwhelmed by the black dog to the extent that she self-harmed was not something he could have prevented. He was just relieved she was back.

As Valerie walked towards her husband and lifted her hair so he could fasten the necklace she was slightly surprised by a gentle kiss on the back of her neck.

'Oh darling, that's lovely. I thought I might make shepherd's pie for dinner, would you like that?'

Closing the clasp and positioning the diamond, Julian stroked his finger slowly down Valerie's chest bone before allowing it to rest at the top of her V-neck sweater, tugging the cashmere playfully with his index finger.

'That sounds lovely,' he whispered, nibbling gently on Valerie's earlobe.

'I do have a lunch with Judith this afternoon,' he said as

he slipped the sweater from his wife's right shoulder and kissed her bare flesh before gently replacing it.

'I must say though, I do suddenly feel very hungry right now.'

Valerie looked affectionately at the man she had always loved. She stroked his dark hair now speckled with just a few flecks of grey at the temples. It only made him look even more distinguished.

'I love you.'

Julian gently kissed her in response and lifting Valerie in his arms he walked towards their marital bed.

'Ever since I first saw you outside Corpus Christi all those years ago, I knew you were the one.'

'The only one my darling.'

Lying next to her, Julian slid a little closer resting his hand on Valerie's stomach.

'Do you remember that tiny little room where you were expected to eat, sleep and study? We were both so nervous. We wanted it to be perfect.'

'I remember you brought me roses and champagne and I cooked shepherd's pie. You looked so handsome. I couldn't believe the most gorgeous boy at college was interested in me.'

Julian smiled and kissed his wife passionately.

'I couldn't eat my food quickly enough. I was desperate to make love with you. The champagne gave me courage but when it came to it, I didn't know what to say, I wasn't sure if you were ready. I didn't know how to ask. I was completely tongue-tied. Do you remember?

'You were nervous and unsure and said I was the first.'

They both laughed at their fond memories.

'I know darling and I didn't know what words to use to tell you it was what I wanted too. Do you remember what I said in the end?'

329

Valerie stroked her husband's chest. Julian knew only too well but wanted to hear his wife's invitation again.

'Remind me.'

'Dance with me, my love.'

Julian could contain himself no longer.

53

Celeb magazine

Shining like a beacon of inappropriateness Sally exited the lift ignoring the lower orders and shimmied towards her office. Ever since her 'honeymoon' in Cape Town she had adopted a much younger style which she was confident made her look sexy. Others in the office thought she was more mutton dressed as lamb. Today she was wearing a micro miniskirt with six-inch heels and a plunge top sweater accompanied by the most enormous Conran costume jewellery. She completed her look with an Hermès double strap wrist watch, a gift from a grateful advertiser.

'Get me a skinny latte Maria, quick as you can chop, chop.'

Sally had been unhappy with her deputy for several weeks now and was planning to replace her as soon as possible. Surprisingly the applicants were sparse so she would just have to do for now.

Maria had eventually been unsuccessful in her recent job search with *Company*. So while she waited for other opportunities she had to continue to indulge her ungrateful boss. The deputy chuckled as she reached for the full fat rather

331

than skimmed milk in the fridge. The extra calories were already showing on her unwitting editor's rhino hide behind.

'Wow, this tastes good. Are you sure it's skimmed milk?'

Maria nodded dishonestly.

'OK, I've just been at the Ivy having lunch with Julia and Charlie. I'm staggered by the scruffy ordinaries they're letting in these days. Where have all the showbiz people gone? Probably upstairs to the Club, make sure you sort out that membership please, Maria. Anyway, you'll never guess who was in there.

'OK, I'll tell you. It was one of those former international rugby players, can't for the life of me remember his name. He was talking about those secret millionaires on TV who help the underprivileged on council estates. He was speaking much too loudly and I overhead him suggesting that if they were truly philanthropic then why couldn't they help without the need for television cameras there? I almost laughed out loud at his naivety. Is he mad?

'Anyway Julia and Charlie are keen to do an at home piece. Look how in love we are. How we're sorry we've broken Monty's heart, but true love must find a way. Isn't our dining table posh? All that bollocks. I've also done a beauty deal with her. How to apply foundation. 10 ways to wear blue eye shadow. I don't care, whatever she wants.

'I've spoken to Monty's agent as well and made a donation to his wheelchair charity. Told him we want to do a "how I nearly died" spread, then a road-to-recovery piece, rehab, walking back to happiness etc etc.

'I'm pleased to say, Maria, that both sides have gone for it. So, I need to go through the roll out plan with you. Whichever gets the better pick up we'll drop the other like a hot brick.'

Maria had to admire her boss's Machiavellian approach to editing.

'Get Brian Aris to do both photo shoots. He's brilliant and discreet. Don't want a second on him, no pencilling. Just confirm it, don't care if it costs more. I want him. Tell what's his face, the business manager, I'll sign off the expense.'

Sally had never bothered with pleasantries like names of her staff and tottering to her feet she dismissed Maria with a wave of her hand. She wasn't sure which of the two former sweethearts would sell better but was secretly hoping it would be Julia. Dropping Monty would allow her to indirectly stiff Valerie by this time crushing her brother within the pages of *Celeb*. It was a shame as Sean was a big fan of Monty's. She'd taken Sean to Lord's a couple of times to watch his idol play, but business is business. She hated Valerie more than she cared what happened to the former cricketing hero.

Flicking through the proofs for the coming week's magazine Sally was pleased with the Jenson's Gems piece. '*10 ways to wear tracky bottoms whatever your size*', was spread over four pages. Sally was delighted the journalist had managed to slip in political profiles on the women as well as their exercise routines and fashion label choices. Julian would be very pleased with her.

Or at least she hoped so. He was being a little elusive again but he had explained that was down to the weather crisis. He was hosting COBRA meetings sometimes twice a day. Still, come the New Year, everything would be absolutely back on track. Valerie would be history.

Sally pushed any anxiety to the back of her mind as the art director, the ad manager and the deputy chief sub filed into her office for the planning meeting. She already had very definite thoughts about the pre-Christmas editions of the magazine and they were about to hear them.

'OK, so here are my thoughts for next week. Christmas is a stressful time for families and early January has the highest record for couples filing for divorce. Let's be ahead of the curve. I want a piece on how maintenance payouts encourage gold-diggers. Positive discrimination in favour of the woman has gone just too far and they should no longer be able to have it all.'

Sally had already been carpeted by the publisher for her previous divorce idea. Given that he was being taken to the cleaners by his estranged Mrs she was sure he would be much more happy with her new take on separation. It was of course also another way to have a pop at that Downing Street hussy. She wasn't leaving the marriage with a penny more than was necessary. Sally seemed oblivious to the raised eyebrows and she pressed on.

'Do the shoot in the studio downstairs. I want a model carrying lots of shopping bags with "*I'm in the Money*", "*All for Me*", "*Hands Off*", that sort of thing written on them. The headline should be something like: *No Ladies, You Can't Have It All*.'

As her team sat aghast it was left to Maria who had just wandered back into the room with another freshly made latte for Sally to voice everyone else's concerns.

'That's a really interesting idea, Sally. Given that our readership is mostly female what would be the best way to sell that to them, do you think? I mean, they'll probably be quite stressed anyway leading up to Christmas.'

'Nonsense. Women shouldn't expect to be kept by men if their relationship ends. Maintenance in high-value divorces teaches young women to be gold-diggers. They should be marrying for love not money. If it doesn't work out they should stand tall in their L.K. Bennetts and not look for their husband to support them. We cater for the 21st century woman at *Celeb* who can earn her own money.

'I want the model to be a young girl, smiling. She might be surrounded by the trappings of marriage but I want our readers to know they can throw it all away. They don't

334

need inappropriate maintenance payments. It's the way forward.'

Maria despaired. Did this stupid woman have any idea of what she was saying or who read the magazine? But Sally hadn't finished. Going through her pile of article cuttings, she spewed more venom.

'So, if we're all agreed? Good. Now I see from *Elle* magazine's best dressed list that Michelle Obama is more stylish than Carla Bruni when it comes to political chic. Well, I'm looking for something on our first lady's ludicrous dress sense. Something about Valerie Jenson's ridiculous Burberry meets Armani provincial wardrobe nonsense and how she just can't pull it off. Maria, do a ring round the agencies and ask if they have any Not For Us snaps we could use.'

'But, didn't we do something similar with our Valeriek spread?'

'Yes, Maria we did, just goes to show we're always ahead of the curve, doesn't it? Anyway, can't let *Elle* take all the praise can we? Now's the time for a follow up.

'Everyone happy? Good, have to dash to John Frieda. Lester's doing a little deep root conditioning for me.'

54

Less than twenty minutes later and Sally was sitting in her foils at the hairdresser sipping Earl Grey tea. Their latte just didn't taste as good as Maria's for some reason. Sally was a woman in love and ignorant to almost everything else around her. She was oblivious that her miniskirt was so embarrassingly short that every client in the salon was aware she shopped at Agent Provocateur.

Flicking disinterestedly through the salon's impressive array of magazines Sally found herself starting to wonder if Julian being so elusive was something more than just pressure of office. She instantly dismissed the very idea. South Africa had been so wonderful and he had whispered everything she wanted to hear at the height of his sexual pleasure. As Sally sipped her tea she did wonder for a moment why it seemed that ever since they'd returned to England it had been her initiating the phone calls and texts. OK, he'd called when there was that issue with the Buckinghamshire pensioner and they'd met up briefly at the safe house. But surely that wasn't enough. Could he be cooling again? Could Valerie have stuck her talons in during the beach holiday?

Sally pushed the rising panic from her mind. Don't be silly, it was just a little wobble before he was hers forever.

Taking another sip of Earl Grey she returned to her magazine but stopped abruptly at a colour photograph of a man she feared greatly. Staring back at her was the image of her ex-boyfriend, Richard Head, who was looking pleadingly at the camera lens.

'Fuck.'

Sally was unaware she had uttered the expletive out loud until Lester looked disparagingly over his glasses at her from the other side of the salon as he tended the tresses of middle ranking royalty.

Sally speed-read the article. Richard had been released after all. How on earth could that be? What were the courts thinking? She well recalled how the high-flying City banker hadn't been used to people saying no and had found their break-up impossible to accept. The tearful late night phone calls were soon replaced by trailing Sally home from the office and turning up at her door unannounced when she had other gentlemen callers. His work suffered and he was eventually let go giving him even more time to concentrate on his obsession. Sally's son, Sean, had done his best to be the man of the house and protect his mother from Richard's increasingly unwanted attention. The two had once grappled on the front step until Sally came between them and threatened him with a heavy-duty torch. Being a journalist she knew better than to wield a baseball bat, or even worse, a knife.

Sally shuddered as she remembered how nothing had deterred her love-struck ex. His passion became obsession and eventually a desire for revenge. He was arrested in her garden with paraphernalia that suggested now was the time for the courts to intervene and he had been put away for a long stretch. How could he be free and giving a magazine interview now? All those anxieties she'd long since pushed to the back of her mind were very much front and centre now as she continued to read the story. Richard had told the reporter how he still loved Sally and was confident that she still loved him too. He had plans for a candlelit reunion dinner and had already bought a beautiful solitaire diamond. He was hoping to propose and he was confident she would accept.

Throwing the magazine on the floor Sally fumbled for her phone before leaping from the chair and dashing outside the salon, ignoring the waiting paparazzi. Sally had seen Harriet Harman inside the salon but assumed they were there to snap Sienna Miller who was having a quick blow-dry.

Sally didn't care that they had decided to amuse themselves by taking pictures of her tint foils while they waited for the actress. She was confident none would appear in print if the paps wanted to sell her magazine any pictures in the future.

Dialling Julian's number, Sally noticed her hands were shaking and tried a couple of yoga breaths to calm herself before pressing connect. Julian answered after the second ring. He had a romantic evening with Valerie planned for later and he didn't need Sally ringing all night. Placate her now and she wouldn't get obsessive.

'Hello my love, what are you wearing?'

But Sally was in no mood for nonsense and starting to cry she turned her back to the photographers as they continued to snap away. If only they had known who she was talking to.

'Richard is out. You said he would lose his appeal and he hasn't. He's done an interview, have you seen it?'

Julian was alone in his office preparing for an early evening squabble with the Lib Dem leader about the Single Transferable Vote. A distressed mistress was the last thing he needed. He took off his glasses and spoke soothingly.

'Sally my love, I don't know where you are, but I can hear a lot of traffic noise in the background. Listen to me, I am very aware of what is happening with Richard and there is absolutely nothing to worry about.'

Sally was in no way comforted by Julian's words. Panic was rising in her. She couldn't cope with Richard's obsessive behaviour all over again. It had been almost too much last time. She just couldn't allow him to take over her life again.

'But he says he's in love with me and I'm in love with him and he's going to propose and . . .'

'Sally, stop. Just stop and listen to me right now. There is absolutely nothing to worry about. Trust me. He did lose his appeal but was nevertheless released early because of prison overcrowding. That was more than a month ago. That interview was done shortly after that.'

But Sally was beyond reason and in danger of becoming hysterical.

'I am standing in the street surrounded by photographers. I have stuff in my hair and Richard could come and get me at any moment and you tell me not to worry, Julian.'

Despite her panic, Sally was immediately aware that she had used her lover's name and spun around to make sure none of the photographers was within ear shot, only to be met by another barrage of camera clicks. She quickly turned away again. Julian was becoming increasingly alarmed, especially with her reference to photographers present. Once again he used his soothing, trust me I'm the Prime Minister voice, but with just a little more urgency.

'Sally, that interview was done more than a month ago as I said. Richard is no longer in a position to harm you. I will tell you everything when I see you darling. I'm busy this evening but we could meet in Hampstead tomorrow.'

'No, not tomorrow, now. Tell me now Ju . . .'

Sally managed to stop herself using her lover's name again.

'How on earth can you know that?'

Julian started to pace around his oak panelled office. He

couldn't allow her to spiral any further out of control. She was on the edge of meltdown on a city centre street surrounded by photographers. He had to take charge.

'OK my love, get in a cab as soon as you can and I will see you in Hampstead, say in an hour?'

Ending the call, Julian buzzed through to his assistant asking for his next meeting to be cancelled and then rang Ben.

'Big probs with Sally, I have to see her in Hampstead. Could you do me a favour and tell Valerie that I have an urgent meeting at the House and I won't be back for supper.'

Ben had been up in the Downing Street flat earlier in the day and knew that Valerie was planning a romantic supper for the two of them, alcohol free. He was certainly not offering cover while Julian headed for rumpy pumpy with that bitch instead.

'Nope. No can do, nicht, nein, non, not happening.'

But Julian was in no mood for his spin doctor's flippancy.

'Sally's found out about Dick Head. I need to tell her what we've done about it.'

'Understood, on my way to the flat now, boss. Must admit, I did quite fancy a bit of your good lady's shepherd's pie.'

55

Sally arrived in Hampstead a few minutes after Julian, looking flustered and concerned. He couldn't help noticing her rather inappropriate attire and wondered what the photographers must have made of it. It certainly wasn't an enticing look. He was relieved that they were here to talk rather than for a romantic liaison.

Dropping her oversized Mulberry bag and Tiffany key ring on the hall table, Sally pushed her Linda Farrow vintage sunglasses up into her newly coiffed hair.

'Tell me.'

Julian took Sally's hand and guided her to the sofa. As she sat down and crossed her legs, he was shocked to see her underwear on full show.

'Darling, first of all I want you to know that you are completely safe. Richard Head cannot hurt either you or Sean.'

'But how do you know? Did you not read the fucking article, for fuck's sake?'

Sally was spitting out the words. He had never seen this side of her before. Ben had often hinted at her sharp side, but Julian had dismissed his comments as sour grapes. Her reputation was of a tough no-nonsense leader who got things done, a quality he had always admired in her. When they were alone she had always been calm, witty, composed, completely charming and of course a little raunchy in the bedroom when requested. The character on show now was a complete shock.

'Fucking tell me.'

Julian jumped with surprise at Sally's contorted fury. Waving her arms angrily she knocked over a Lalique Crystal Lamp from a side table, which shattered into small pieces.

Julian was horrified. Could this wild-eyed woman spitting venom be the same person he had wanted to spend the rest of his life with? What had happened to her? Suddenly keen to leave, he began to quickly explain what he knew about Richard.

'OK darling, OK, calm down and I'll explain.

'Remember when we went to Emma's for dinner a few weeks ago and we had to rather rudely leave before the ambassador?

'Well, you may also remember that we were somewhat tardy in our arrival too? That was all because of Richard. During a routine sweep, a gun was found near Emma's home. Security had been keen that we didn't attend the supper party at all but after consultation we agreed that the risk was contained.

'Sadly, towards the end of the evening an intruder was spotted in the garden and it was thought best that we leave promptly. The intruder was later detained. It was Richard.

'He was arrested and had with him some inappropriate bits and pieces. After being assessed by a psychiatrist the decision was taken that he would be sectioned under the Mental Health Act. He is now resting in a high security psychiatric hospital. He is likely to be there for the foreseeable future. You don't need to be aware of its location.

'Those are the only details I can offer you my love, but

be safe in the knowledge that he will not cause either you or Sean any further concern.'

Sally gasped with relief. Her face relaxed and she offered her warmest smile. The blind panic for her own safety and more importantly her son had passed. Sean was her raison d'être. She had sacrificed so much for him, even her relationship with her parents. The fear that he could be in danger from a lovesick madman had created an emotional maelstrom she had no control over. Now Julian had made everything alright again. In that moment she loved him more than ever.

'My darling, that is such a blessed relief. I love you so much. Thank you, thank you, thank you. Dance with me.'

But Julian was in no mood to spend a second longer in her company. Stunned by the outburst, he hated what he saw behind the veil. Her panic had fractured a carefully constructed facade of calmness and malleability. He realised she was a woman he hardly knew. He needed time to think.

'I would love to, my darling, but I have an incredibly important meeting at the House. Have delayed it as long as I could but really must dash. Take care and I will call you tomorrow.'

Getting to his feet, Julian headed for the front door.

'No darling, please don't go. Let's dance.' But Sally's words were muted by the slam of the heavy oak door. As Julian strode smartly down the pathway and into the waiting Jaguar XJ with its engine already running, he paused for a moment and leaned back against the leather headrest trying to gather his thoughts. His security officer looked watchfully through the rear view mirror. His principal looked shocked and pale.

'OK, let's go back to Downing Street please, Carl.'

Julian sat silently as the car made its way down Rosslyn Hill, towards Camden and through Regent's Park. It wasn't until they had reached Piccadilly Circus and Julian looked up at Eros overseeing the theatregoers heading up Shaftesbury Avenue that he reached for his phone.

'Kenton, hello, just leaving the house now. Bit of bad news old boy, I'm afraid. The Lalique lamp in the drawing room, I broke it. Massive apologies, unforgivable of me. I'll send someone down to Old Bond Street first thing. All sorted before your good lady is back at the weekend. Acutely embarrassed, I have to say. Tell you all when I see you, perhaps at the Reform Club next Thursday?'

Arriving back at the Downing Street flat Julian headed straight to the kitchen. Valerie looked delighted to see her husband and walked over to greet him warmly. He was surprised to see Ben still sitting at the table eating shepherd's pie. He'd thought the spin doctor had been joking about a desire to tuck into his dinner.

'Any left for me?'

'Of course. What happened to your Commons meeting, darling?' asked Valerie as she retrieved another plate from the old cupboards.

'Crashing bore. Very keen to dine with my beautiful wife instead.' Julian kissed Valerie and he took the Wedgwood dinner plate from her. He had insisted that just because the public purse demanded they lived in antiquated squalor didn't mean they couldn't eat from decent plates.

'With that in mind, leaving so soon, Ben? Never mind, see you tomorrow, buddy.'

Ben reluctantly took his cue and genuinely thanked Valerie for supper. He had forgotten how interesting and intelligent she could be, when she was sober. As Julian walked him to the door, he seemed rather agitated.

'What's up, boss?'

'Get rid of Sally. Don't care how, but ditch her.'

Ben was surprised and delighted. Was this the same man who had vacillated between his wife and Sally Simpson since the summer? He could hardly contain his joy at the news of her impending demise and was keen to know much, much more.

'Whoa, this is all a bit sudden. What happened, boss?'

'I can't go into it now but I want her gone. She's a basket case Ben, why didn't you warn me?'

Ben raised an eyebrow in disbelief at Julian's selective memory.

'Seriously, she completely lost the plot tonight. Cancel that Christmas *Celeb* interview we had in the diary, that's not happening and I definitely don't want her at the Chequers lunch either. She'd be a bloody liability.'

Ben was trying hard not to dance a little jig. Whatever had happened, he didn't care. He could tell from Julian's tone that Sally was finally finished. It had taken two years but revenge was always a dish best eaten cold. However, Ben was a pragmatist and realised to ditch the bitch would take some careful choreography. Stopping at the door, he leaned on the frame.

'Well boss, I heartily concur with your insightful perspective if I may say so. However, there are one or two challenges ahead. For instance the Chequers lunch, that might be a bit tricky. The invites have already gone out. I told you at the time not to invite either her or Isla, but you insisted, boss.

'Do you remember the conversation? It went a little bit like this . . . I said, "Don't invite them," and you said, "No, I insist." Do you remember that, boss? Do you, do you?'

Julian slapped his head against his hand in frustration.

'Dinner's ready, darling.' Valerie had appeared at the kitchen door and Julian realised time was running out to make decisions this evening.

345

'Just coming my love, Ben's running through a couple of issues ahead of PMQs tomorrow. Will just be a tic.'

'My advice, boss, is not to cancel. Ease yourself out of this one gently. If you don't, the repercussions could be significant. Hell hath no fury like a woman scorned. OK, if she did decide to go public we would manage it. Let's face it, the opposition leader is not likely to kick off given the stuff about his sister and the Archbishop. Still, I'd rather not have to deal with her shooting her mouth off this side of Christmas if it's all the same to you. Take it slowly and whatever you do try not to piss her off. As Lord Byron said, sweet is revenge, especially to women. If you mess with her, she'll get ya.'

'Spoken by one who knows,' acknowledged Julian.

'Yup. Night, night boss, enjoy the shepherd's pie.'

56

Islington, North London

Opening the front door to her tiny flat Isla bent down to pick up the mail. Flicking through the pile of circulars she noticed a stiff white envelope. Dropping her keys in the basket next to the door she headed for the kettle and opened the post as she waited for it to boil. It was an invite to a lunch at Chequers. Isla caught her breath. She knew it was the Prime Minister's weekend retreat, was somewhere along the M40 and was an invite that media types would kill for. Its arrival was completely out of the blue but totally gelled with what she'd just been told.

Isla had returned from a visit to a fortune teller in Fulham. All the girls at the studio had been raving about him. Claire, in accounts, said he'd predicted she would split up from her boyfriend and Emily said he'd foreseen a dark handsome stranger walking into her life.

Undeterred by the obvious vagueness of the comments Isla couldn't wait to see what the fortune teller had to say about her love life.

Crossing his palm with silver to the tune of £100, he had

promised her a surprise invitation and a couple of hours later here it was. Isla immediately starting rifling through her copious notes to see what else had been predicted by the expensive oracle. *'Wear red to attract a dark, handsome man. Expect fireworks under a famous painting.'*

Not waiting for the kettle, Isla grabbed her keys and purse and ran to the door before hailing a black cab and heading for Oxford Street and the women's floor at House of Fraser. She'd seen the most gorgeous red prom frock in Coast. Dune probably had some shoes to match. If not she would splash out her parents' Christmas money on a matching handbag and frock from Karen Millen. This was big.

Fastening the bow on the crimson dress and turning to admire her reflection in the changing room mirror it was all she'd hoped for. He would love it. Isla suddenly realised why she was so excited about the invite. Of course it was wonderful to be asked to lunch at Chequers, wherever it was, but it was the prospect of seeing Julian again that had lifted her spirits.

At first she had been furious at the way he'd behaved on the plane. He had tried to call many times since but she was determined not to have anything more to do with him. How dare he treat her like a piece of meat? Who did he think he was? He may be the Prime Minister but his behaviour was completely unacceptable.

Time had passed and her anger subsided but by then he had stopped trying to call. She was far too cussed to pick up the phone to him and had accepted their relationship was over and she needed to move on. Hence the visit to the fortune teller. As Isla replayed the predictions in her mind she was frustrated to be interrupted by her mobile. Delving into her bag to retrieve it and glimpsing at the screen she was shocked to see it was Julian. Taking a deep breath and anxious not to appear too keen she answered on the sixth ring.

'Hello, Isla speaking.'

A few moments later she dropped the phone back into her bag and flopped disbelievingly onto the hard wooden bench. Julian had invited her on a date, in the UK, just the two of them. It was to be at a private address in Hampstead and he was cooking. She would be collected from her home at 7 pm and driven to the location. The unpleasantness on the plane was fading from her memory and instead Isla chose to remember the soothsayer's words. She wondered if there was a famous painting somewhere in the Hampstead house.

57

Manchester

Monty was panicking so much he started to hyperventilate but carried on anyway, determined to destroy his former best friend.

'I can let you have the pictures for £50,000. They're dynamite, definitely worth it. Your readers will be gobsmacked and it will totally destroy his public image. Fifty grand, it's a snip. What do you think?'

The journalist and photographer sitting in a Manchester hotel room couldn't believe the images they were being shown. They were crystal clear photographs of Charlie Jones taking Class A drugs, cocaine to be precise. He was snorting the tell-tale white powder through a £50 note.

'Yeah, they are dynamite, Monty. How did you get them?'

The freelance journo was keen to gather as many facts as possible before he hawked the gold dust to the highest bidder. But Monty was giving away nothing more. He was now out of his wheelchair and walking with the aid of crutches though his long-term prognosis was still unclear. The England Cricket Board was superficially sympathetic but had decided not to renew his central contract for the following year while his health issues continued. Monty was short of cash and desperate for the £50,000.

But his motivation wasn't just the money. He wanted revenge. How could his best mate, who was to be his best man, steal his girl? Charlie knew how much Julia had meant to him. He'd confided in the premiership footballer on a number of occasions about his hopes for the future with the only woman he'd ever loved. How could Charlie have wooed her away while he was on life support? Disbelief and despair had given way to anger and hatred and eventually Monty had hit on a plan for retribution.

Charlie had been sceptical when he first received the call from Monty to meet up and try and put the past behind them. Julia had counselled against it, but Charlie wanted closure on the unhappy period and agreed to Monty's request. He wanted them to be mates again, just like they had been since school.

He'd agreed to a meeting in the front room at Monty's parents' home. Sheila and Frank had been a little stiff with him when he arrived and had quickly left for a Tesco shop while the two boys tried to sort out their differences.

'The only way to have a friend, Charlie, is to be one,' had been Sheila's parting shot as she followed Frank to the door. Charlie bowed his head, suitably chastised by Mrs Mitchell who had been an integral part of his life throughout his childhood.

Desperate to improve the tense atmosphere, Charlie chattered incessantly and the talk had soon turned to the former cricket idol's time in hospital. Charlie was keen to steer well clear of any emotional suffering and asked instead about the physical pain his friend was quite obviously still suffering. He sat with his legs apart, elbows on his knees supporting the weight of his Audemars Piguets wristwatch.

'What you taking, mate?'

Looking at Charlie sitting on his mum's couch, it was the

first time Monty had noticed how much his former friend dripped wealth.

'Was on diamorphine for a long time but I'm trying to cope with just codeine now. Doesn't always work, but am giving it my best shot. Don't want to get hooked on anything too strong. Must admit though, I've been feeling pretty down, could do with something to give me a bit of a lift.'

Monty was taking it slowly, trying to reel in his ex-buddy without being too obvious about his motives.

'You know what mate, you should think about maybe taking a bit of coke, does the trick for me every time. The only thing is you need to watch the drug tests after training, but er, anyway, that's not really a problem for you just at the moment is it, sorry.'

Monty let the embarrassing gaffe pass. His plan was not going to be derailed by crass, insensitive comments from Charlie. He leaned forward in his wheelchair, trying to keep his tone level and calm.

'Really, never taken it before, not sure what it does or even how to do it to be honest.'

He leaned back again wincing a little with the effort. Charlie took the bait. Before Monty could say game of two halves, he'd whipped out a £50 note and a credit card from his bulging Smythson wallet.

Producing a wrap of white powder from his hand tailored jeans, he laid the gear onto Sheila's glass coffee table and began expertly preparing lines of cocaine. Monty remained completely motionless, anxious that any movement may obscure the pin-head camera he had concealed just above the fireplace. It was hidden in the frame of a Van Gogh *Poppies* that his mum had painted in oils at night school.

Monty had known for ages that Charlie had a habit, but had always stayed well away from the Bolivian marching powder. Seeing it for the first time was a shock. Charlie confused the wide-eyed look for excitement and pleased with his work offered the rolled up note to Monty.

'Want some, mate?'

The cricket legend was momentarily stumped. He certainly wasn't going to indulge but it was imperative that Charlie did.

'Er, sure do. Give us a clue though.'

Charlie was relieved that the reconciliation was going well and was keen to sustain the jovial atmosphere.

'It's easy, just watch.'

He happily leaned forward and snorted a line, in full view of the camera lens.

58

Celeb magazine

Looking through the photographs spread out on her desk, Sally knew they were dynamite. They would guarantee a massive hike in sales and certainly damage, perhaps irrevocably, Charlie's career. At the very least he would lose the captaincy of his club. Look at what had happened to John Terry and that was just his private life, nothing to do with illegal drugs.

But, as always, Sally's main motivation was Julian. Ever since the little incident with the Lalique lamp he was once again being Mr Elusive. Honestly, he was starting to make her work far too hard for his attention. How would he react to the man who stole Monty's girl being brought crumbling to his knees in such a public way in her magazine? She was sure he would be very pleased indeed.

Sally put the photographs into the office safe before locking it and signing the cheque. £100,000 for exclusive worldwide rights on all platforms. Picking up her mobile she was about to call Julian, but acknowledging that he was not always able to answer she decided to text first.

What would be the best choice of words to spark his interest?

Monty caught in sting. Have pictures. Will call.

Sally waited a couple of minutes for him to digest the text before dialling his number. Reassuringly it took him just a couple of rings to answer. Thank goodness he had finally forgiven her for the little outburst the other night. He must have realised the strain she was under after learning about Richard's antics.

Sally had no idea that Julian was implementing a damage limitation strategy, with Ben's help. Easing himself out of a potentially turbulent situation without a nuclear fall-out. He had hoped not to have to speak to Sally on the phone ever again but mention of Monty being in trouble had changed all that. His plan was to stay chatty, find out what the problem was with Monty and be off the phone again as quickly as possible.

'Hello, how are you? Everything OK?'

Julian was clipped with his greeting. Looking at his Cartier he calculated a maximum of five minutes to work his charm. Sally noted there was no reference to 'my love' or 'darling'. She immediately felt anxious.

'Hello JJ, I'm so sorry about the other night. I hope you have forgiven me, darling. I was beastly but I was really concerned about Sean with the whole Richard situation. That sort of outburst has never ever happened to me before.'

Most of which was true, thought Sally, except the 'never happened to me before.' She had given herself a good talking to and it wouldn't happen again.

Julian wasn't interested in her explanation. All he was concerned about was making sure Monty was OK and getting off the phone.

'No problem. Pleased you are feeling a little calmer today. What's happening with Monty?'

Sally picked up on her lover's coolness and wasn't sure how to play her hand. She decided on white knight.

'Oh, little misunderstanding with Charlie, don't worry though darling, I have it all under control. He'll come out of it absolutely smelling of roses.'

Relieved that Monty was fine, Julian wasn't interested in the details or indeed any other syllable that Sally might want to utter. He was very keen to end the call.

'That's brilliant. Thanks. Really sorry but I have a meeting in the House and it'll take me 10 minutes to walk even if I leave this second. Gotta go, sorry.'

Sally could feel her anxiety rising. Still no 'darling'. What about all the plans they had? Why was he being so cold? All over a silly lamp. She pressed on.

'Absolutely, I know you're madly busy, darling but I also just wanted to check we're still OK for our trip to Babington House this weekend? I'm so excited about swapping all sorts of rather special early Christmas gifts with you.'

Julian leaned forward and banged his head on his leather-topped walnut desk. He'd completely forgotten the roll-out strategy that Ben had initially worked out to gently introduce Sally into the public arena as his new beau. Julian ran the plan quickly through his mind, desperately scrabbling to remember the details. Election over. Rumours of rift with Valerie. Attempts at a reconciliation in South Africa. Sadly that fails. Valerie spends more and more time alone at Chequers. Separation regretfully announced soon after. Acceptable time passes before Sally is gently eased into friendly newspaper coverage, starting with photographs of her consoling a disconsolate Julian as they walk through the grounds of the uber trendy Somerset hotel. Just friends who in the fullness of time become more than that. Julian and

Ben had recently decided on a complete change of script but hadn't told all the players.

Julian's brain was racing. With absolutely no intention whatsoever of honouring the liaison, he quickly tried to think of a good reason for cancelling the tryst.

'Darling, didn't Ben call? Why on earth I pay that man I have no idea.

'He should have told you that we have a hush, hush mission to Afghanistan, darling. We're going tomorrow morning first thing and won't be back until Sunday morning. I'm absolutely devastated my love, tried everything to move it but the security services have insisted we keep to that timetable.'

Sally immediately smelled a rat. Suddenly he was calling her 'darling' and 'my love' again. What was going on? She'd spent a fortune on couture, cologne and cashmere. Not to mention child cover for Sean. He may be 16 but he couldn't be trusted to be left alone for the whole weekend. Now Julian was trying to back out of their tryst. How could he? It was all part of the plan for them to eventually be together forever. The thought of their long weekend away had kept her sane over the last fortnight as she tried increasingly desperately to contact Julian. Why was he saying this now? Was he taking the coward's way out?

Sally's instinct told her to end the call immediately, but instead she found herself starting to plead.

'No, no, I beg of you JJ, please don't say that. Everything has been organised. This was to be our early Christmas weekend away, just the two of us. Remember, the photo of us strolling together that we'd organised. We were going to have lots of lovely time talking about our future, our hopes, our dreams. Please don't cancel it darling, please don't.'

Sally began to cry just as Ben walked breezily through the door and tapped his watch, tutting theatrically. Julian had to think quickly and glancing down at the newspapers spread out on his desk he came up with a solution.

'Don't cry. I'm devastated I can't be there but there is really nothing I can do to get out of this trip.

'I have to present Treo the Labrador with the canine equivalent of the Victoria Cross. Surely you must have read about him, my love? He's quite a little character, let me tell you. He's spent five years sniffing out bombs planted by the Taliban. Of course I would much rather be with you than pin a medal on a dog's collar, but what can I do? It's Ben's fault.'

Ben cursed his cowardly leader for trying to use an army bomb dog as an excuse.

'That's a bit wuff, boss. Tell the old bag the truth. She's being traded in for a smoother ride.'

Julian tried to shush him but Ben was in a playful mood and began to bark before panting excitedly and lifting limp wrists up to his shoulders. Finally dropping to the floor, he invited his boss to rub his tummy.

'Not funny,' mouthed Julian as he turned his back, trying not to laugh and continuing with his lies.

'Of course I'm not putting a silly mutt before you but I do need to see the troops before Christmas and this is an excellent peg for optimum coverage in the papers. A photo of me pinning an honour to Treo's collar moments after he's searched out yet another daisy chain Taliban bomb is gold dust and absolutely front-page stuff.

'Listen, I'll be back soon and anyway we'll see each other at Chequers. You're still coming to lunch, aren't you my love?

'There we are then, I'll see you there. Now, I really must go. Ben has just walked in.'

59

Cromwell Hospital

Jimmy was healing quicker than any of the doctors had anticipated and they were confident he would be able to leave hospital by the end of the week. Charles who had totally refused to leave his partner's hospital bedside was starting to look tired and drawn. Tommy had made sure he popped in every day and had cancelled several scheduled trips to LA until Jimmy was better. Everyone, especially the police, was keen to learn more about who'd tried to destroy the face of terrestrial TV. Despite gentle and then firmer coaxing by officers Jimmy insisted he still couldn't remember anything about the attack.

He had lain at first motionless but increasingly restless between the crisp cotton sheets of his state of the art hospital bed, becoming progressively more irritated by cheery nurses and the smell of sanitised hand gel. While he didn't know the exact names of the assailants, he did know who was responsible for the attack and as his body repaired Jimmy used the time to hatch revenge. He knew that Charles and Tommy would eventually have to leave him alone for more than just a few moments and that would be the moment to act. That moment had come.

Reaching in to his bedside locker and retrieving his mobile, Jimmy disguised his number as he dialled. The call was answered almost immediately.

'Yeah, who is it, I'm busy.'

'Hi Ben, I suppose you have been expecting my call. I think it would be sensible for us to meet.'

Ben recognised the TV presenter's voice immediately but said nothing. He looked across at Julian who was poring over paperwork ahead of tomorrow's Prime Minister's Questions. It was always difficult to know what MPs from other parties might ask. There was nothing more embarrassing than being caught off guard by an unexpected question from left field. He would be engrossed for a good half hour yet.

Mouthing to Julian, 'It's Gayle,' before rolling his eyes, Ben pressed the phone to his ear and walked out of the office. Heading towards the walled garden, it was a journey of a minute or so in which Ben didn't say a word. Jimmy was content to wait. Finally Ben spoke.

'Seriously, who is this?'

Ben was surprised the TV presenter had his number and was playing for time while he judged Jimmy's tone.

'This is someone with three fractured ribs, a broken nose and puffed up eyelids the colour of the rainbow. I have been flat on my back in hospital for the last week. If you don't agree to talk to me Ben Watson, I will talk to the papers and the police instead.'

Jimmy knew aggression would get him nowhere and correcting himself, softened his tone. He still needed Ben's money but now he had the whip hand. If Ben didn't offer cash he would tell the police everything.

'Listen, I regret asking for your help but I didn't know who else to turn to. I told you I have gambling debts that I can't pay and I know you have money. I thought with our past you would help me.'

Jimmy was struggling to breathe with the strapping on his ribcage and broke off to cough painfully. It was agony and he lost his cool.

'Instead you had me beaten to a pulp by a couple of East European thugs.'

Ben had heard enough.

'Needed my help, don't make me laugh. You were trying to blackmail me with that photograph and that got you a good hiding. Now go away and never call me again.'

Realising he was saying too much Ben dropped the call. It was too late. Jimmy had already recorded every syllable.

60

Chequers

Dominic and Jessica Jenson were not at all enthusiastic about being wheeled out for a press lunch in that stuffy Chequers Dining Room. OK, so Carole Thatcher might have loved it, but it was just SO not cool. Both were prepared to put up a monumental sulk to try to get out of the unutterable tediousness of being semi-polite to people they didn't know or care about. Their ace card was that both knew their mother would be just as reluctant to attend the event organised by 'Uncle Ben.'

'Why do we have to go? I know you don't want to go either Mummy, so let's just not. Why don't we head out for a day in the country instead and leave pater to his boring party.'

'Don't try isolating me, young man. You're in enough trouble for that at school.'

Julian was exasperated by his son's nonsense. He had only returned last night from a gruelling trip to Afghanistan to honour Treo or 'pin a medal on a mutt' as Ben had put it. He was exhausted and with another busy day ahead was not prepared to tolerate this sort of dissent. The lunch was a big deal, a huge thank you to those journalists who had supported him during the campaign. It had already been delayed twice and had eventually become a Christmas lunch too. The children simply had to be there.

Dominic scowled at his father, stopped twiddling with his leather bracelet and began to root his way through the giant American fridge, searching for a suitable breakfast. Jessica had only just woken up and having made her way down to the kitchen for the same reason as her brother, went to join him by the fridge.

'Yeah, Dominic's right. Anyway, you can't make us. Kathryn Blair never had to go. Neither did Euan or the other two. Why should we? It's so unfair.'

Julian was about to erupt when Valerie took over. She was much more used to handling teenage tantrums. Patting the top of her increasingly irate husband's hand, she simply ignored the youngster's outburst and waited for the next move in this game of three-dimensional family chess.

'Seriously Mummy, I mean it, we're not going, neither of us.'

Jessica closed the fridge and stood closer to her brother who immediately draped his arm around her shoulder in a show of sibling solidarity. Valerie continued to ignore them both and concentrated on the Sunday papers.

'Darling have you seen this feature in the *Mail on Sunday* travel section, six things you must do in Oxford? It mentions the Lamb and Flag in St Giles. Remember that's where we went on our first double date, with Rupert and Jenny?'

The couple smiled at each other as they were whisked back to their university days and sat closer together to read the rest of the article. At the other side of the kitchen their children became more and more enraged.

'Are you listening to me, Mummy?'

Jessica was now hopping up and down in her pristine Ugg boots, their first outing since Ben had bought them for her as a Christmas gift.

'Yeah Mummy, are you listening to Jessica?'

The children had hoped their divide-and-rule policy may pay off if they picked solely on their mother. Valerie was aware of every scowl but continued to ignore the teenagers' tantrum.

'Oh look darling, it talks about the Pitts River Museum. Remember those *objets d'arts* from Captain Cook's voyage?'

'Hmm, I can't quite place that.'

'It's just next to the Museum of Natural History with the dodo collection. Remember?'

Jessica was incandescent with rage. She shrugged off her brother's arm and stomped towards the kitchen door followed closely by Dominic. Both foolishly assumed that stomping would bring victory, but as they reached the doorway, hesitated for a moment too long.

'Ready by 12:30 children, if you wouldn't mind please, guests arriving at 1 pm sharp. And don't forget to wash behind your ears, especially you son.'

Furiously accepting defeat Jessica and Dominic stormed out leaving their mother to clear away the breakfast debris. Laughing, Julian offered his wife a well deserved round of applause. Kissing her warmly he headed to his office to prepare for a telephone conference with the US president about troop deployment in Afghanistan.

61

Dressed in appropriate Sunday lunch attire, Jessica and Dominic made their way down the imposing carpeted staircase. Their mother was waiting to greet them at the bottom. Jessica looked pretty in a Ralph Lauren dress that Granny Sheila had bought for her. It had been far more expensive than her grandfather had thought necessary but Sheila always spoiled her grandchildren at Christmas. Monty had bought her a beautiful hair clip to match the outfit and Jessica had applied a little Bobbi Brown make-up. Her father wouldn't have approved but he was still on the phone to the US president so didn't have a say. Valerie thought her daughter looked lovely. Dominic had decided to go just the right side of rebel with his Hollister shirt un-tucked.

'You'll do your father proud, children. Remember, be charming, be polite and offer our guests a tour of the Long Room. Nelson's diary is always a winner and one or two might have done their homework and might want to see some of the Oliver Cromwell memorabilia. Do you know where that is, Jessica? Good. Smile, be friendly but remember most of them are journalists and not to be trusted. No personal or family conversation. As your granddad always says: "*If in doubt, say nowt.*"'

The children nodded their acquiescence.

'Excellent. It's chicken for lunch Jessica, your favourite and chef is making bread and butter pudding especially for you Dominic. Surely that must be worth tucking your shirt in for!'

The teenage boy grinned at his mother. If only his masters were as gently persuasive as she was, life would be so much easier for everyone.

Valerie's request hadn't even raised an eyebrow in the Chequers kitchen. Chicken followed by bread and butter pudding the week before Christmas, rather than a traditional lunch with all the trimmings was certainly unusual but she knew it was what the children would want. As usual, the staff had been more than happy to oblige. The rule of thumb with the team was what the PM and his family wanted was what they would be given. Staff drawn from the army, navy and air force made Chequers a home from home for the Jensons and the family was suitably appreciative of the attention. If only they hadn't needed to entertain there, life at Chequers would have been perfect, thought Valerie.

Inspection over and with only a few minutes before the first guests were due to arrive, the children headed straight for the kitchen. Ostensibly to check on lunch but in reality to hide away from dull, dull, dull guests. Valerie shrugged acceptance. She wasn't looking forward to lunch either, but many of those present today had been hugely helpful during the campaign and she knew their continuing support was essential. However, having to be charming to those responsible for the negative column inches about her husband during the campaign would be tough.

There was no doubt Julian had performed badly during the Leaders' Debates. Some newspapers had taken the opportunity to rip into her husband both professionally and personally. Most she could ignore, but some had crossed the line. A furious Valerie had been keen to challenge them, but Ben had counselled against confrontation. He knew from poacher turned game-keeper experience that it would only lead to further negative comment.

However, Valerie was still determined to speak to the one columnist who had been consistently rude about her personally. OK, it was in a rag whose circulation was falling off a cliff but his bile had finally gone too far and upset her mother. If he wasn't here, which Ben had probably rather wisely ensured, then she would talk to his editor instead.

Feeling her irritation build Valerie wandered over to the drinks cabinet to pour herself a soda water and lime juice. The booze was usually put in a cupboard away from temptation but with guests expected there was an enticing array of spirits on display. Hesitating for a moment and with no sign of Julian, Ben or the children, Valerie felt her resolve weaken. Hovering over the gin bottle, she remembered Ben's previous warning and reached for the vodka instead.

Pouring a large measure and adding copious amounts of ice and tonic water Valerie stirred the drink very slowly. Replacing the cocktail spoon on the silver tray she hesitated again for what seemed like an eternity, wrestling with temptation. She hadn't had a drink for more than two months, surely she didn't need to start now? But the desire to stay dry was not as strong as the need to dull the edge on the day.

Taking her first sip Valerie sighed as the tonic bubbles burst around her nose. The chilled nectar slipped down easily and Valerie waited for a moment as the alcohol began to work its magic. Within a few seconds she felt calmer and more sociable. Not having had any booze for so many long weeks meant the vodka was quickly taking hold and she was soon feeling a little light-headed. Aware of increasing self-confidence and courage Valerie was eager for a second sip and keenly raised the glass back up to her lips. 'Hi Mummy, the guests will be here soon. Can I have a Coke please?'

Dominic had been returning with his sister from the kitchen a few moments earlier when they had stood in shocked bewilderment watching their mother mix her drink. Panicking, they were unsure what to do. As she took her first sip and with their father still on the phone to Washington, Jessica ran to find Ben while Dominic wandered over to her as nonchalantly as he could. Now over six feet tall and a keen sportsman, he lovingly wrapped his arm around her delicate frame.

'Sorry about earlier in the kitchen, Mummy. It was Jesse's fault.'

Both laughed at the inaccurate slight against his sister and Dominic tightened his grip around his mother's shoulder.

'Anyway, just wanted you to know that we love you Mummy. Remind me what we need to do today again?'

The unspoken message from her son was clear and as Jessica dashed in with Ben, Valerie patted Dominic's broad chest. The effect of the alcohol was exquisite but not as wonderful as the love of her supportive family.

Ben winked at the children, their quick thinking had undoubtedly saved the day.

'Right guys, let me tell you who we're expecting. The editors of the *News of the World*, *Sunday Times*, *Indy*, *Guardian*, *FT*, *Sun*, *Telegraph*, *Mail*, *Express* and *Star* along with their political editors. One or two magazine editors and the heads of news from the major broadcasters. It's going to be busy which is why we've set up the overspill table in the Great Hall.'

Ben was hoping for continuing positive press coverage the week before Christmas. It had started well, with the photograph of Julian pinning the Canine Victoria Cross on Treo, which had made the front page of every newspaper, even the *Financial Times*. Ben also had plans for an off guard image of Jessica, hiding behind a sofa in her father's office, as he sat at his desk, hard at work in Downing Street. Corny, but it had worked for President Obama, who'd been photographed in the Oval Office with Sasha sneaking up on him. Luckily, the official White House photographer had been right there to catch the super cute moment and thankfully her father hadn't been startled or even alerted by the camera flash.

Perhaps he could also organise a photograph of Julian and Dominic bonding while taking down the tree on Twelfth Night – that would be another winner. But for today he was determined the children didn't find themselves cornered.

'Careful with the family chat, kids. For guidance you can certainly say Dad helped decorate the tree, you're looking forward to spending time with him on Christmas Day, you've been playing in the snow, Uncle Monty is getting better all the time, that sort of stuff, but if in doubt . . .'

'Say nowt,' the children chimed in unison, prompting laughter all around.

It was the perfect scene to greet the first guests who had just arrived and were being handed a glass of champagne. Ben had suggested his boss serve reasonably priced Cava so as not to prompt *PM Spending Our Cash On Champagne Party* headlines, but Julian was having none of it. After some debate they'd settled on Julian funding the champagne from his own pocket. It was also a good diary story for the papers, underlining the fact that the PM was keeping an eye on the public purse, while also guaranteeing Julian didn't have to drink rubbish plonk.

Guests were usually greeted in the Hawtrey Room but with so many expected today Valerie had decided the Great Hall would be a better place to welcome them especially as the Christmas tree looked so magnificent. With more and more people arriving, Ben soon peeled away to speak to a Fleet Street editor and his family who had just walked in. The children decided to stick together so that they could execute a teenage pincer movement on any unsuspecting enemies and so Valerie strolled among her guests alone. She was feeling a little tipsy but in control and nursed her glass for the odd heavily watered down sip, which would undoubtedly be required a little later. She noticed Ben trying desperately to catch her eye. He wanted to introduce her to a terrestrial TV broadcaster but Valerie was far enough away to feign not having seen his wave. She may be being superficially gracious, but it would take more than a couple of warm words from the odious little man for her to forgive him previous hostilities. Instead, she headed towards the editor of the *Times Literary Supplement* who was an old friend from her publishing days.

Unsuccessful at beckoning Valerie over and finding himself alone with the channel head, Ben took the opportunity to have a confidential conversation with the woman who rather usefully was also Jimmy Phillips' ultimate boss.

'Terrible news about Jimmy. How is he? Will the Christmas special still happen?'

Padi Freith didn't much like Ben Watson but she was cornered. Valerie had quite obviously ignored him and with no sign of anyone else joining the conversation she accepted her fate for the next few minutes at least.

'Yes, we were all massively shocked by what happened to him. But he is making an extraordinary recovery and we're still hopeful that he'll be well enough to complete the Christmas special. If we can have it in post-production by Tuesday that should still give us time to broadcast on Christmas Day, fingers crossed.

'Jimmy is an integral part of our festive line up. Wouldn't be the same without him.'

'Wow Padi, you really are a sensational boss. Can I come and work for you? I can't believe you're so understanding, especially given that little bit of naughtiness he was up to.'

Ben was on a fishing trip and despite her better judgment Padi immediately took the bait.

'Sorry, "little bit of naughtiness", what on earth are you talking about?'

Candy off a baby, thought Ben as he moved in for the kill.

'Oh, no, don't tell me you didn't know. Goodness I've said too much. Ignore me.'

'Ben, what is it that I should know? If it's something to do with my TV talent then you'd better tell me about it, please.'

Ben looked from side to side like some comedy Inspector Clouseau before taking Padi's elbow and pulling her a little closer to him.

'I know one of the papers is sniffing around and I assumed your press office would have been on it. I think there's a story planned for Christmas Eve.'

Padi wasn't sure whether to believe him but she needed to know what he was hinting at.

'What's the story say? What's Jimmy supposedly done?'

Ben adopted his most sincere 'trust me I'm a spin doctor' tone and continued.

'Apparently, he's been selling tours of the studios, Padi, for two grand a pop, throwing in a make-over for the ladies too. Made about 100 grand or so already, so the story goes.'

Padi was sure it couldn't be true. Jimmy was paid a fortune by the channel. Why would he lower himself to be a tour guide? But after the phone line furore when TV channels had been fined and forced to pay back millions to disgruntled viewers, she couldn't afford to risk another scandal. She needed to know more.

'I can't believe it. How on earth would you know this Ben, even if it were true?'

Ben tapped the side of his nose. He knew he had her and moved a little closer while trying very hard not to smile.

'Listen Padi, I'll tell you what I know, but you must promise that it didn't come from me. OK?'

Padi nodded wary acceptance.

'Well, Jimmy was caught up in a newspaper sting when a journo handed over two grand for one of the tours. It's all on camera apparently. Once the newspaper fronted him up he tried to wriggle out of it. Apparently he said he had your permission but that you'd be in deep doo doo with the chairman if he found out. The journo I spoke to said Jimmy had suggested you were getting a kickback too. Not sure how they're planning to portray that in the paper.

'The only reason I know about it, Padi, is because Jimmy stupidly tried to rope me in, asking if I could organise some unofficial visits to Downing St. Er, don't think so. Told him he was a fool and to back off.'

Padi was aghast.

'I'm so sorry to be the one to have to tell you. I honestly thought you knew.'

Job done, Ben patted her arm soothingly before moving on, leaving the executive desperately digging out her iPhone from her bag and heading for the door, in her anger and confusion not yet hesitating to wonder why a newspaper, if it had such a bombshell story, hadn't already printed it.

Valerie could see Ben grinning as a smartly dressed woman walked quickly away from him. Keen not to be led around like a prize pig at the Gloucester Show she executed a swift heel turn that even Len Goodman would have been impressed by and headed in the direction of two mismatched women standing admiring *The Lion and the Mouse* by the magnificent fireplace. She half-recognised both of them, especially the younger one. Wasn't that the *HND* reporter who had come to Downing Street to interview her when Jimmy Phillips was attacked? Valerie groaned inwardly as she noticed the girl's outfit. She was wearing a crimson red off the shoulder prom dress with sparkly red high heels that reminded Valerie of Dorothy's shoes in *The Wizard of Oz*. A fuchsia-coloured clutch bag completed the ensemble. Poor girl, she had probably taken forever to choose what she thought was just the right outfit for lunch with the PM. Instead she looked like an extra from *Grease*.

Mind you, thought Valerie, the older woman looked more ridiculous. Who was she anyway? Although Valerie recognised the signature Prada she'd never seen it worn quite so short before. Her Colour Me Beautiful guru had always warned 'Doesn't matter how good your legs are, never go mini after 40.' It was sound advice that this woman would do well to heed.

Valerie couldn't fathom why the women were standing away from the gathering throng, unaware that one knew no one and the other liked no one. Feeling some sympathy for what she interpreted as social awkwardness, Valerie made her way towards them.

Sally took another large swig of red wine. She was livid. For the last 10 minutes she had found herself stuck with this ridiculous little minx off the telly. The last thing she wanted to do was make small talk with an imbecile. She needed to see Julian. She needed to talk to him about why he was avoiding her. She wanted some answers. But with no alternative and to pass the time until he made his appearance Sally had held court.

'It's a fascinating painting, isn't it? It's an Aesop fable and originally by Rubens but Churchill left his mark on it.

'It was hung rather high up on the wall and Churchill felt the mouse looked too small. Allegedly, late one night he called for his paints and despite being in his cups he clambered up a stepladder and made the mouse bigger.'

Isla wasn't remotely interested in the story. She was desperate to see Julian. Their dinner at a very impressive house in Hampstead had been just wonderful. He hadn't cooked himself, but had someone called Lady Sieff in the kitchen. It must have been one of his posh friends. Isla hadn't seen her but she certainly cooked well. He'd been warm, attentive and approachable and apologised profusely for his behaviour on the plane. He was much more gentle and passionate this time. Isla had left feeling confident that everything was back on track.

On her way to lunch today she had received a text from him apologising in advance as he may still be on the phone to the president. He also said he hoped she was wearing the La Perla underwear he'd presented to her. A saucy text from the Prime Minister while he was talking to the president of the United States of America. That was certainly one for her computer files. Maybe this time it was love but there was nothing wrong with a little insurance to be on the safe side.

As the old bird droned on Isla looked around her. She wondered if she might be standing in exactly the same spot as Victoria Beckham had when she came to Chequers. Lorraine Kelly had been here too. How cool was that? She couldn't wait to tell her mum all about it on the way home. Still, the novelty was starting to wear a little thin and she really didn't like this haughty woman. Who was she anyway? Oh well, better ask a question.

'What do you do?'

Isla couldn't care less really. She could see the woman's lips were moving in response but had no real interest in what she was saying.

'. . . the biggest selling weekly glossy in the country. Surely you must have heard of it?'

'Yes, yes of course, *Celeb*. What is it that you do there again?'

'I just told you sweetie, I'm the editor. Weren't you listening?'

Isla thought the magazine editor, she still hadn't caught her name, was being rather grand. So what if she was an editor, obviously everyone was only here to see the Prime Minister.

Sally was also hating every moment of the conversation, mind numbingly bored by this frivolous ill-educated little madam. What on earth was she doing at such a prestigious event? First, Michael Grifton had said he was about to bin her and the next minute she was in South Africa on the official tour. Now she was a guest at the hottest ticket in town. Who did she know? She must be shagging somebody with power. It was probably Ben.

Sally took another large sip from her wine glass and looked over Isla's shoulder towards the entrance. She was desperate to move away, but with no other guests close enough to include in the conversation, there was little choice but to stay. Allowing a waiter to top up her Rioja, she thought she would show off with more facts about the house.

'I believe that during the Falklands War, Margaret Thatcher used to convene War Cabinets here to help pull everyone together.'

'That was a long time ago. I wasn't even born then.'

That was it. Sally had had enough. She wasn't even pretty with that silly blonde bob and ludicrous dress sense. If Ben was sleeping with her then he needed glasses. Offering Isla her most withering stare she was about to leave the young girl high and dry when her worst nightmare came true.

'Hello ladies. So sorry but my husband has been unavoidably delayed. He shouldn't be long. So, tell me ladies, when have you met the Prime Minister before?'

Oh no, not her as well? Sally had been determined to avoid Valerie at all costs and here she was standing next to her and blocking the escape route. Sally was getting herself

375

into quite a lather waiting for Julian to make an appearance and feeling a little tipsy she needed to get some fresh air. She had been just about to head out for a stroll around the lawn where she'd seen John and Fraser Brown play football while she'd interviewed their mother. Sally was vexed she hadn't seen Valerie coming. Another sip was called for.

Reduced to making ridiculous small talk with a woman who was still fulfilling a role that was rightfully hers, Sally went straight for the jugular.

'Well, I first met Julian two years ago at the Saatchi Gallery. We've got on famously ever since. Really very, very well indeed. I think it is fair to say that he treats me as a confidante.'

Who on earth did Valerie think she was, wandering around like the lady of the manor chatting with her peers? Well she had a rude awakening coming any day now when JJ walked out and into her arms instead. That would take the smug swagger out of her step.

Isla picked up the hostile tone in Sally's voice but assumed it was left over from their prickly exchange. She was a little nervous speaking to the first lady socially and terrified that her guilty secret would show on her face.

'Hello Mrs Jenson, how lovely to meet you again. Thank you for agreeing to the interview about Jimmy Phillips. Well, I first met the Prime Minister just before the general election. I was working an overnight shift at Downing Street when he came out to announce the date.'

'Oh yes, Isla, I remember. It caused quite a stir at the time. Your editor must have been most impressed by your exclusive. What did it do for the ratings?'

Valerie's socials skills meant she knew a little about a lot of things. She was confident that TV talk about audience figures was all important to on air talent. Isla sighed with relief that *I AM SLEEPING WITH YOUR HUSBAND* wasn't obviously tattooed on her forehead. She started to feel more relaxed, increasingly confident she wouldn't give away any secrets about the incredible sex she had had with Julian just a few days earlier. She was about to respond to Valerie's follow up question about ratings when Sally interrupted petulantly.

'Actually, I think my magazine's support for the Prime Minister during the election campaign was far more impressive than revealing the date. The first tip on a story is all well and good but it's staying power that's required, young lady. I have worked very hard with the Prime Minister over many long hours to polish his image. Finding out the date was frankly the easy bit, sweetie.'

Sally was continuing to spiral. She wasn't having this silly little ignoramus being praised by this equally stupid woman. Didn't they know she was the one who would soon be calling the shots around these parts? They both had a big shock coming.

Isla flushed the colour of her dress. Why was this old bird being so antsy? Her boss had been delighted at the exclusive. OK, not as delighted as when she had entertained him in her best La Senza lingerie, but nevertheless. And anyway, that first meeting with the PM and the subsequent exclusive had given her mother massive bragging rights at Toni and Guy.

Valerie was also somewhat taken aback by the magazine editor's aggression. Noticing Isla's embarrassment she was keen to intervene.

'Oh I don't know, I think Isla being the first to reveal the date of the election shows rather impressive access to the Prime Minister.'

Sally scoffed, spilling some of the crimson contents of her glass onto her dress. This conversation was absolute nonsense. It was no good. She could contain her rage no longer.

'Oh really, do you really think so Mrs Jenson, because frankly I don't. I think you will find that no one has better access to your husband than me. Not you, not Ben, or Gollum as I prefer to call him, not anyone. Let me tell you that absolutely no one has more impressive access to your husband than I do.'

Her raised voice was starting to attract attention from other guests. Ben was glued to the spot at the other side of the room having seemingly lost the use of his legs. When he had first seen the women gathering he wasn't sure if his presence would help or hinder, so he had stupidly waited. Now it was too late.

Startled by the aggression and the scene it was causing, Valerie was keen to control the editor's tantrum. She was even more eager to know just what was meant by no one having more impressive access to her husband than this mutton dressed as lamb trollop.

'I think you might need to calm down just a little erm, I'm sorry I didn't quite catch your first name . . .'

Sally was apoplectic at the slight. Intended or otherwise, she didn't care. Any attempt to control her voice was lost and gesticulating furiously her wine sloshed freely as she began to shout at the top of her voice. The intonation a little more slurred than she would perhaps have wanted.

'Sally, my name is Sally Simpson. Soon to be Mrs Sally Jenson, I think you will find. JJ is divorcing you and marrying me. We have been inseparable almost since we met. He doesn't love you, he loves me and there's nothing you can do about it. He's leaving you and your ridiculous children straight after Christmas. Make the most of your little hostess duties today because from now on it will be my role. Do you hear that everyone? My role from now on. Next time you all come here I will be the hostess so you all better be fucking nice to me, or else.'

Valerie steadied herself against the fireplace, so shocked by what she was hearing that she didn't notice the colour draining from Isla's previously flushed face. Everyone else in the room gawped open-mouthed and began to shuffle a little closer to the three women, inadvertently forming a semi-circle. Acutely aware of the enthralled audience Valerie stared directly at Sally, and lowered her voice to a whisper.

'I do not know what you are hoping to achieve from this outburst, but I must ask you to refrain from swearing and stop right now. You are making yourself look ridiculous. I do not believe your wild accusations and I'm afraid I must ask you to leave immediately.'

Valerie paused for a moment before moving forward to take Sally's elbow in an attempt to steer her towards the door without any further outburst. Sally though was spiralling and no longer in control of her emotions. Julian could hear the commotion from the first floor and sprinted towards the balcony of the Great Hall, reaching it just in time for the finale.

Roughly pulling her arm free, Sally splashed red wine from her glass all over Isla who was trying very hard not to cry. Sally downed what was left of the wine and smashed the glass against the piano.

'Don't believe me, really? Well, where to start? I know, remember when you were sunning yourself on that South African beach pining for your husband unavoidably detained on government business in Cape Town? Let me tell you Mrs Jenson that while you were waiting with hope in your heart, he was in fact pleasuring me in an exquisite suite overlooking Table Mountain.'

Incredulous gasps filled the room, interrupted only by Isla's screams.

'No, he wasn't. No, he wasn't. That's a complete lie. He was with me on safari. He said it was the best sex he'd ever had.'

Slowly and systematically, Valerie looked around at the semi-circle of disbelieving faces, and then up at the balcony where she saw her husband standing pathetically rooted to the spot, a mixture of desperation and terror on his face. She offered no emotion in response, but instead looked around for Dominic and Jessica only to see them being rushed upstairs by Mrs Hubble, the housekeeper. Good.

Taking a moment to dispense with her glass Valerie glared first at a hard-nosed Sally and then a sobbing Isla. She had a captive audience hanging on every word. Slowly, she cleared her throat.

'Ladies, there is no place for either of you at my table. I must ask you to leave without further incident. I do not expect to have to ask you again.'

Isla was about to head for the door but Sally, who had caught sight of an ashen-faced Julian, shouted up to him.

'Oh my love, don't let her speak to me like this. Tell her it's me that you love. Tell her and this silly little floozy about all the plans we've made. Please darling, tell them.'

As the shocked guests turned to stare up at at him and Sally descended into begging Julian realised he had to act and dashed for the staircase. Arriving in the Great Hall a moment later, overjoyed journalists parted for just long enough to allow him to rush across to the fireplace.

'Ms Simpson, as my wife says, we really must ask you to leave and you too Ms McGovern if you please. I have no idea how much either of you have had to drink but quite clearly too much. You are embarrassing yourselves with this fanciful nonsense and it will cut no truck with either Valerie or I.

'Now if I could escort you both to the door?'

Isla was now sobbing uncontrollably and wanted to flee but her exit was blocked by a putrid purple Sally.

'But, my love . . .'

'Ms Simpson, desist from any further nonsense and leave immediately.'

As Julian reached out to take Sally's arm, he was caught square on the right cheek by a knockout blow from the magazine editor. A moment later, Sally turned and shoved Isla roughly against the ornate fireguard.

Moving on to Valerie, Sally was momentarily shocked into inaction by the first lady's continuing composure.

'Your actions are completely inappropriate, madam. I will not ask you a third time. Now go.'

As security, personal protection and other staff finally swung into action, Valerie calmly raised her voice above the melee.

'Ladies and gentlemen, with apologies for the interruption, if you would like to follow me into the Dining Room, lunch is served.'

62

The Morning After The Fight Before

Ben was flicking through the morning papers while he waited at his favourite table in his local greasy spoon café. He'd ordered double fried egg, sausage, bacon and a mushroom as his one of five a day. It was fair to say the front pages didn't make very happy reading.

Devil Wears Prada, *Cat Fight At Chequers*, *PM Punched By Lover At His Country Home*, *Yes, Yes, Yes Prime Minister*, *PMTension*.

Each headline was more salacious than the next. Looking at the Twitter trend from last night didn't help either. Everyone was talking about the showdown at the Chequers Corral. Ben shook his head, what would an exasperated public, already reeling from the expenses scandal, make of this? They must be wondering whether there was anything left to be fiddled with. It was too early to say how much damage had been done to the PM but it would certainly be significant. It would take all his best rotational physician skills to try and dig the boss out of this one. He didn't know whether to laugh or cry.

Laughing won as he replayed events from yesterday in his mind. He would have to talk to the boss about his agility around the ring. Catching that right hook from Sally was just schoolboy and would leave him with a shiner for at least a week.

But Ben's mirth turned to a frown as he considered his own lack of awareness. He'd recalled the conversation with Jimmy Phillips in his head again and again but frustratingly still couldn't quite remember exactly what he'd said. Had he incriminated himself? Was there anything that could trace Jimmy's good hiding back to him?

When he had initially planned the 'incident' Ben had chosen carefully. The boys had done a good job for him in the past. The brief this time was simple: give Jimmy a smack, a tenner tucked in his top pocket, no obvious clues that would lead back to him. That way gay boy would know not to come asking for money ever again. The timing dovetailed with the South Africa trip so Ben wouldn't even be in the country. All that and it would only cost a grand for each of them. Excellent value for money.

Everything it seemed had gone according to plan. He was sure the good hiding would've taught the little shit not to try to threaten him in future with old photographs from way back when. How dare Jimmy Phillips think he could use a grainy picture to blackmail him out of hard earned cash just because he lost a fortune at the casino. Little fucker deserved a beating.

Ben again tried to recall what he'd said on the phone. Would that bitchy queen have even thought to record the call? Nah, surely not. Ben tried to push the worry to the back of his mind, though he knew it would plague him a dozen times again by the end of the day.

Breakfast over, he headed towards the front entrance of Downing Street, dropping off the newspapers with the boys in the security screening hutch on the way through. The latest scandal would offer half an hour of titillation for them and he really couldn't be seen walking through the front door with those headlines under his arm. What a photo that would be. An already unusually busy road was quickly filling with more and more voracious hacks. Ben was pleased. He'd made a conscious decision to be high profile this morning and had banked on lots of media interest. As he reached the shiny black door he wasn't disappointed, bombarded with questions shouted from the other side of the street.

'Ben, Ben, is the Prime Minister going to resign? Tell us about the catfight, who started it?'

Without breaking his stride, the spin doctor half turned towards the frenzied pack and raised his right hand. He mimicked holding a glass to his mouth before staggering a little. Without saying a word he headed inside and the big black door closed firmly behind him. That would give them something to think about. He didn't care which one of the three women the press speculated was the piss-head as long as it cast doubt on the credibility of the philanderer claims and took the heat off the boss. Round One of the fight back to the PM.

63

Sally was furious at the innuendo. Watching live pictures of Ben walking in to Downing Street she knew exactly what he was doing and switched off the TV. Looking out over the river Sally surprised herself by starting to cry. Not in the office. NEVER show weakness in the office. But as she contemplated how everything had fallen apart so colossally, she couldn't stop the tears from flowing freely.

Two months ago she was in line to be the next first lady and spend the rest of her life with the only man she had truly loved. Yesterday she was swinging a right hook at him in front of her peers.

Even worse than that, some little slut who wasn't even any good at her job had suggested that JJ had been sleeping with her at the same time. Lying little bitch. Leaning her elbows on the table and putting her head in her hands Sally remembered the look on JJ's face as he instructed her 'to leave immediately'. She was roughly shown the door to where her chauffeured car was waiting. Once inside, her driver Tom had handed over a box of Kleenex and Sally had sobbed uncontrollably all the way back to London. The dream was over.

As she crumpled just inside the front door, Sean had once again stepped up as man of the house and, helping her up to her room, tried to comfort her. Laying with his mother he gently held her hand until she gave way to exhausted sleep. The following morning he'd made a teenager's effort at breakfast, but still nothing could console her. Sally had hoped coming to work might have helped but stifled sniggers in the lift had stung. As she walked through the open plan office she'd seen her staff rush to turn the page away from the Chequers story in the morning papers. She had to accept that everyone was avidly reading every sordid detail. She didn't really care about their inane gossip but each glimpse she caught of the headlines underlined that her future plans now lay in pieces.

Revenge, that's what she wanted, revenge. If her dreams were shattered then everyone else would have to suffer too and that would start right now. Sitting up and blowing her nose she applied a little Clinique base to take the redness away from around her eyes and buzzed through to Maria who seemed unusually cheerful today. Sally wasn't yet aware that her deputy had accepted a job at *Harper's Bazaar* magazine. As she walked into her monstrous employer's office, Maria couldn't think of a better day to tell her.

'Hi Sally, so sorry to hear about what happened yesterday. It must be so terribly embarrassing for you. The *Daily Mail* is suggesting you might be sued. I do hope that doesn't happen. The *Sun* is referring to what happened as Slappergate. I'm sure you hope they don't mean you personally.

'Anyway, not a great day to bury bad news so I will just have to come right out and tell you. I'm resigning. My month's notice period starts today so I will sadly be leaving you from the middle of next month.'

Sally detected an air of self-satisfaction in her deputy's tone. That certainly wouldn't do.

'With apologies to Dorothy Parker sweetie, I'll excuse your dust. Off you go, clear your desk now.'

Picking up her desk phone, Sally called security who were at her office door within moments. As Maria was marched past the desks of her former colleagues, she tried to smile through her tears. This was the start of a new, happier chapter in her life without the constant bullying of her tyrannical ex-boss. It was just a moment in time. Smile.

Even before Maria had reached the lift, Sally had already moved on. There was no time for sentiment. There was a job to be done.

'Kate, in you come, chop, chop.

'Right darling, you're the new Maria, congratulations well done. We'll talk about terms and conditions after Christmas but I have a little rush job for you sweetie, and I want it in this week's edition.'

Kate was reeling, unsure if she really wanted the promotion. Looking at Sally's face, now wasn't the time for a career discussion. Sitting uneasily on the editor's sofa Kate immediately realised she'd left her notebook and pen on her desk at the other side of the firmly closed door. Pushing up the sleeves on her M&S V-neck sweater she tried to give the impression she was ready for business. Writing materials were for lesser mortals.

'Rightio then Kate, here we go. The Monty Mitchell pictures, did he cash the cheque?'

Until sixty seconds ago, Kate had been Maria's deputy, and she was relieved to have been asked something she could easily answer. She was up to speed on the Monty case.

'Yes, we paid the third party £100,000. I believe £50,000 cleared into Monty's account on Friday morning. The photographs are in the safe, never to be seen again. Charlie's reputation is safe and we have the engagement shoot planned for him and Julia the week after next in the Maldives.'

'No. Change of plan. I want every single frame in this week's edition and I want you to write the words, Kate. The story needs to be about Charlie turning to his oldest buddy in his hour of need and how Monty Mitchell, that so-called friend, betrayed him. It's most important that we highlight Mitchell's treachery. How he realised his friend had an addiction, a weakness, a flaw in his character. How he sought that out, manipulated, duped and then framed him. Make it clear that Monty's motives were to cause maximum embarrassment and hurt to Charlie and of course to make money out of it.'

Kate was staggered. Had Sally finally gone mad?

'But the photos will destroy both Charlie and Monty. That would be madness, Sally. Our readers love them both. Monty's fight back to fitness against all the odds and Charlie finally finding love. We never sell more copies than when either one of them is on the cover.'

'Indeed so, my dear. Imagine sales in this the week before Christmas with the cover shared between them. One is a desperate addict with a £50 note up his hooter. He needs our help to turn his life around. The other is a duplicitous, lying, underhand, disloyal, not to be trusted snake in the grass.'

It was justice. The fallen cricketer would have to pay for the sins of his brother-in-law.

64

TV centre

Waiting outside Padi Freith's office on the sixth floor of TV centre was a strangely unnerving moment for Jimmy Phillips. They usually met for coffee or lunch at the Ivy Club. The piano bar was their particular favourite. He couldn't comprehend why he was being expected to wait outside her office today. What did she want?

Filming was due to continue for the Christmas special that afternoon and a car was waiting to take him out to Blenheim Palace. They really needed those crucial shots, even Belinda agreed. Jimmy was still in a great deal of discomfort. He was relying on industrial strength painkillers to get him through the day and copious amounts of brandy to help him at night. Doctors had been reluctant for him to return to work so early and had encouraged him to rest until at least the New Year, but Jimmy had other ideas. He wasn't about to allow that bastard spin doctor to humble him, the most popular TV presenter in the country. Besides, if he was honest, he really needed the money. His gambling debt was slowly being eaten into, but was still colossal.

As Jimmy saw it, if only Ben had seen it in his heart to help him with a short loan, life could have been a whole lot easier by now. He'd read in the paper how Ben's mother had left him a significant inheritance. Ben could easily have afforded the few hundred thousand he needed. Now he still had the photograph and a grievance to go with it.

Eventually, Padi's door opened and Jimmy leaped to his feet to dash across and air kiss the chief executive. Walking in to her newly refurbished office he could see why the executive floor had now been nicknamed 'Mahogany Row'.

No expense had been spared with the face-lift, rather like his own. Luxurious Italian leather sofas framed a solid oak 18th century Indian ox cart, converted into a low level table. Jimmy was impressed. Gazing around the room he noticed the *Water Lily Pond* on the far wall and considered it an original Monet, but surely not. His appreciative eye was abruptly halted by the sight of Tommy Gold. What was he doing here? By the look on his face, Padi had been imparting bad news. Jimmy had warned him that idea for a new game show was a stinker and the chief exec wouldn't like it, but he just wouldn't listen.

Padi was as immaculately presented as her office. Stella McCartney, her designer of choice.

'Jimmy, take a seat, would you like some tea? How's the recovery going? Tommy says you've been very brave.'

Jimmy started to speak but he could see Padi wasn't listening as she took a seat at the ox cart table opposite the two men.

'I can't begin to tell you how concerned we were. It's great to see you up and about again so quickly. It's certainly a testament to your grit and determination. What a trooper.'

Jimmy smiled his appreciation but Tommy didn't move. He knew what was coming.

'But I have to be honest, Jimmy. We're worried that you might be trying to do too much too soon.'

Jimmy wasn't sure where the conversation was heading and vainly tried to interject. Tommy avoided his client's exasperated stare.

'With that in mind Jimmy, we have decided to relieve you of some of the pressure that the deadline for the Christmas special is undoubtedly causing. It is with great reluctance that we have been left with little option but to ease the show into next year's line-up.'

Jimmy gasped, unable to believe what he was hearing.

'I know, I know, but believe me, no one is more disappointed than I am, darling.

'Still, we have managed to secure a brilliant *Two Ronnies* show that absolutely deserves another airing. In fact, you may remember it. It's the one where Ronnie Barker goes into the shop and asks for fork handles. Ronnie Corbett is behind the counter and mistakes his request for four candles. It's hilarious.'

Tommy and Padi laughed in unison at the memory of the famous scene but Jimmy was in no mood for levity.

'That was 35 years ago. My show is new, happening and now. What on earth are you saying, Padi? Are you telling me I'm being quietly dropped from the schedule? Is that what you are saying because if it is, believe me I won't go quietly. I won't smile and make bloody tea for journalists clogging up my driveway. I'll tell them everything. I'll tell them what a cruel heartless organisation you are. How you dumped me the week before Christmas. How do you think that would play out in the papers?'

Jimmy was on his feet and jabbing his finger towards the still composed TV executive.

'Jimmy, please don't be so aggressive. It really isn't necessary. I have already spoken to Tommy about renewing your rather lucrative contract. It's up to you whether to accept the very reasonable offer we have made. As far as the Christmas

391

special is concerned, as you know it is still not completed. With less than a week to go until it is due to be aired and with schedules not yet finalised we are left with no choice. We have had to take the extremely reluctant decision to pull it. We couldn't be left with dead air time on Christmas Day, now could we?'

Jimmy turned in disbelief to Tommy, who said nothing.

'We have compiled a press statement to that effect. It explains how your terrible injuries meant you simply couldn't fulfil your commitment. Of course the channel completely understood and wished you a speedy recovery. It goes on to say that contract negotiations for next year are ongoing.'

Padi looked at her Rolex. 'It was released 10 minutes ago.'

She stood and offered Jimmy her hand.

'How very dare you. I'm the biggest celebrity this channel has ever had and you are replacing me with a repeat of the *Two Ronnies*. Well you can just fork off.'

Jimmy strode furiously towards the door. Tommy shrugged at Padi and gestured he would phone her as he followed his client out of the office.

Exiting TV centre, Jimmy looked around for his chauffeur driven car. Where on earth was Craig when he really needed him? Tommy waved down a black cab. He had seen this sort of meteoric fall enough times before to realise the car was the first thing to be taken away. As they clambered into the back of the cab Jimmy slumped into his seat and Tommy switched off the intercom. He didn't want the driver overhearing this conversation.

'I already have calls in, everything will be fine. Get Christmas over, go away somewhere hot and start afresh in the New Year.'

'What about the new contract? Should I sign it?'

'I'm afraid the contract offered by Padi is derisory. It's for 6 months with 80% less funds.'

Could Jimmy's day get any worse?

'Not to worry darling, everything will come good, trust me. I'm sure she'll be regretting her decision when you're a big star on one of the other channels.'

Tommy loosened the button on his Jermyn Street suit jacket, the pre-Christmas festivities already taking a toll on his waistline. As the taxi rounded Trafalgar Square and headed down the Mall towards Buckingham Palace, Jimmy turned from looking sulkily out of the window. For the first time he looked directly into his agent's eyes.

'I thought I had a two year contract. How can they get out of that?'

Tommy had already tried to negotiate a way through without success.

'There was a break clause for no delivery on the Christmas special. If we push it, they'll go for gross misconduct.'

Gross misconduct. What on earth was Tommy talking about? What was he supposed to have done?

'Please tell me what I'm supposed to have done, Tommy?'

'Ben Watson. He told her you'd been caught in a newspaper sting flogging tours around the studios. The station couldn't afford to be caught up in that sort of scandal. Just lay low and it will all blow over, I promise.'

Jimmy nodded and turned again to look out of the window. He'd been monumentally screwed by Ben Watson and hadn't even seen it coming. That vicious little oik. Not content with having him bashed up, he had taken his job away too. As the cab reached Hyde Park Corner and turned towards Park Lane, Jimmy hatched the perfect plot for revenge.

65

Downing Street

Julian was still only semi-conscious when Ben opened the door to the bedroom in the upstairs flat. While journalists were thronging the road outside, all the disgraced PM could muster was a bunker mentality and no doubt a hangover from hell. An empty Laphroaig Isla malt whisky bottle was discarded on the floor. There was no sign of a glass tumbler. Who needs a glass when you're drowning your sorrows, thought Ben.

Hadn't he warned Julian of the potential repercussions should all three women find themselves in the same room together? But would he listen? Like all powerful men, Julian had thought he was invincible. He had been unable to resist the temptation of having all of his conquests in the same place. Ben chose levity as his first approach.

'Wakey, wakey, boss. Wait till you see the morning papers. You'll never guess what they're leading on? Nope, not Posh and Becks. Guess again. OK, I'll tell you. It's you. You're not the son of God. You're a very naughty boy. Frankly you're looking like a bit of a tosser.'

Ben was surprised to find himself pinned against the

wardrobe door. He was only momentarily impressed by his boss's agility before becoming slightly alarmed. A wild-eyed Julian was holding on to his lapels and only inches away from his face. The two had found themselves in the occasional standoff before and had hurled insults at each other but their arguments had never become physical. Ben was not happy but given that Julian was taller and broader, there would be only one winner if it came to fisticuffs. He decided talking would be preferable.

'Hey, hey, hey, I'm one of the good guys, remember. We can sort this. OK, so it looks bad now but remember Alastair Campbell's mantra? It's only a resigning matter if it's on the front page for more than five days in a row and that won't happen. I have a plan.'

Julian's anger began to subside and his contorted face soon crumpled. Releasing his grip on Ben's lapels Julian put his arms around his spin doctor and started to sob on his shoulder. Ben returned the hug and as the seconds passed found himself increasing the intensity of the embrace. Controlling himself, he reluctantly pulled away before he did anything that he would regret later. Instead, he patted Julian manfully on the shoulder.

'Have a shower, boss. I'll go and make some strong coffee. We have quite a day ahead of us.'

Flicking on the electric kettle, Ben switched on the kitchen TV to check the latest headlines. He was pleased to see his off-the-cuff suggestion that the showdown was nothing more than boozy high jinks playing well. It was a trick he'd picked up from Gordon Brown's watch. Brown's team had often dismissed verbal attacks by combative backbencher Charles Clarke as nothing more than the result of a good lunch.

But Ben knew the stalling tactic wouldn't last for long. The broadcast political heavyweights would be drafted in, probably before the kettle had boiled. Julian slunk into the room.

He was still unshaven but smelled a little sweeter than a few moments earlier.

'Right, here's the plan, boss. I suggest we go for a three-pronged attack. First up, we plant the story about the shadow health secretary and that dodgy nursing home he owns. It's been an open secret for some time in the Westminster village but no one's been able to stand it up. Anyway, I have it on good authority that he's evicted two more old dears in their 80s again this week. Apparently they'd run out of funds and could no longer afford the extortionate fees. One of them is being forced to sleep in the sitting room of her grand-daughter's flat. The other is in hospital after slipping on ice and breaking her hip.

'I've given some strong un-sourced quotes to the BBC News Channel. They will start running them from 10 am. Fingers crossed the other news programmes will see it as fresh and follow their lead. That should mean the morning papers will soon look out of date.

'Secondly, now's the time to sack the chancellor. I know he's doing a reasonably good job, but I'm sure he'll under-stand it's for the greater good of the party. We should give the job to Judith. She's polling well over Afghanistan. Her walking up to the front door this afternoon will soon throw those newshounds off the scent. Even Bradby might buy that.

'Thirdly, a huggy, feely Christmas Eve sit-down with you and Valerie at Chequers. Children round and about. You wishing the great unwashed a very Merry Christmas while an impossibly cute Irish Setter puppy licks your ear. By the time we come back in the New Year, philandering forgotten, job done.'

Julian stood and raised his arms to again hug his genius spin doctor. Ben offered a playful punch instead.

'Only one tiny question, Ben. How do we get the girls onside?'

'Ah, I was coming to that, Prime Minister.'

66

Chequers

Valerie pulled on her Driza-Bone and Hunter wellies and picking up Bruce's training lead headed with the Irish Setter puppy towards the Buckinghamshire countryside surrounding Chequers. Bruce had only just had his second injections and wasn't really big enough for a walk, but Valerie needed to get out of the house. She would carry him in her pocket when he was tired, probably by the end of the lawn.

Two desperately distressed children had been hurriedly dispatched to stay with Julian's parents at their Herefordshire estate well away from prying camera lenses. Neither had wanted to leave their mother, but Valerie had insisted. She'd reassured them they would definitely be back for Christmas but quite honestly she was rather unsure what they would be returning to.

Julian had been immediately exiled to Downing Street. He too had wanted to stay with Valerie, but the look on her face meant her wishes should be accepted without further debate. He'd left soon after the rest of the guests and would no doubt this morning be cowering inside the Downing Street flat unlikely to show his cheating face for at least the rest of the day. She'd seen Ben's jovial reference to too much alcohol being responsible for high jinks at yesterday's lunch party on TV. A typical damage limitation move by the uber spin doctor.

Valerie had opened the first bottle of her husband's specially bought party champagne as she heard his driver start up the car heading back to London last night. The second followed soon afterwards. She'd spilled most of the third. This morning she very much regretted her return to the bottle. She felt terrible even without the hangover. She couldn't guarantee it wouldn't happen again, but she would try. One day at a time. Starting again from today.

Valerie was a toxic mix of fury and remorse as she strolled through a nearby field and tried to lift her spirits by playing with the puppy. She could only just see the top of Bruce's head as he attempted to stretch up above the long grass. Smiling, Valerie bent down to pick him up and he immediately piddled with excitement.

'Good job this is waterproof,' she chastised, grateful for the distraction from her dark thoughts. She had wanted to cling on to the wonderful life she imagined she'd had with Julian and the children, but how could that possibly happen now? Her husband had betrayed her with not one but two women. Two very different women. One was hard-nosed and quite obviously brutal, the other a pretty little thing young enough to be her daughter. Valerie sought comfort in stroking the top of Bruce's soft head as she walked on dejectedly.

Her mobile phone rang, startling the tired puppy who began to whimper a little. Valerie gently tucked him inside her three quarter length coat.

'Don't wee in there,' she warned Bruce before answering the call.

'Hello love, it's your mum ringing to see how you are.'

Without waiting for a response, Sheila continued.

'Me and your dad have been watching the telly this morning. Then, I went down to get the papers and Cyril behind the counter had something to say about the front page of the *Sun*. I told him to mind his P's and Q's and to keep his nose out of things that don't concern him. Anyway love, we're on our way down in a minute. Your dad has just gone to check the tyres and fill up the windscreen washer bottle. He's gone to the Waitrose garage to do it there because he has to pay if he does it at Exxon. Our Monty is making some balm cakes for the journey so we don't have to stop off. Those motorway services are so expensive.'

Valerie smiled at her mother's thriftiness. It immediately took her back to the long, long journey from Lancashire to Oxford all those years ago. Her parents' reluctance to exchange hard earned cash for over-priced, sub-standard, roadside food meant motorway service meals had been her guilty pleasure ever since her teenage years.

'Mum, Mum don't worry, I'm absolutely fine. I'm still at Chequers, but the children have gone to Julian's parents and my husband,' Valerie almost spat the words, 'my husband is back in London. I have masses to do, there's no need for you to worry about me.'

But Sheila had no intention of leaving her daughter to deal with the disintegration of her marriage alone. She had kept quiet until now in the hope that Julian would see the error of his ways. The events of yesterday had changed the landscape.

'Everything's already packed, love. I've asked Doreen next door to cancel the milk when she sees Bert tomorrow. The postman's been round and I've given him his Christmas tip already. I've left an envelope under the dustbin for the bin men when they come on Wednesday. I've also put a few Christmas bits I bought from Marks and Spencer's food hall in a cooler bag in the back of the car. We should be with you by tea-time, love.'

Valerie knew there was no point in protesting any further. She was secretly quite relieved that her family would be with her, in what was a dark day.

'What about our Monty, is he coming Mum?'

'Oh yes love, he's very cross about what's happened, but I've told him he's to behave himself. Anyway, see ya later.'

67

Islington

A bleary-eyed Camilla was padding around her tiny linoleum-floored kitchen in her favourite Kanga pyjamas when she noticed Isla's torn dress in the recycle bin. Suddenly very awake, she ran towards her flatmate's room. Flinging open the cheap plywood bedroom door she exhaled with relief at the sight of her friend sound asleep on a mascara-smeared pillow. She was still wearing her clothes from the day before, minus the discarded dress.

'Hi Tigger, want some tea?'

Isla struggled to open her swollen eyes, puffy and sore from hours of crying. She had been desperate to speak to Camilla last night but the journey back from Buckinghamshire had taken forever. She had only just managed to open the front door and dash inside as a photographer arrived. Creeping to close her bedroom curtains without being seen, she could see him loitering across the street. Tiptoeing into the kitchen Isla saw that it was almost 11 pm. Camilla was working tomorrow, she couldn't possibly wake her now. As she put a teabag into her favourite Kath Kidston mug and reached for milk from the fridge, Isla noticed the large tear along the side of her new dress. It had become caught up in the fireguard when Sally had pushed her and had ripped as she struggled to her feet again.

As memories of the disastrous day came flooding back, Isla ignored the milk. Grabbing the Chardonnay and a Green and Black's chocolate bar instead, she headed for bed.

'Morning. What time is it, Kanga?'

'Time you told me what happened to you yesterday. Your lovely new dress is all torn. Why didn't you wake me last night when you came in?'

Camilla moved to open the curtains but was stopped in her stride by Isla's alarm.

'Don't, there's a photographer outside, probably quite a few by now.'

Camilla was deliciously intrigued. Clambering onto the bed next to Isla she tucked her cold feet under the edge of the duvet.

'OK, I have 15 minutes before I absolutely have to go to work. I'm listening.'

68

Christmas Eve

Jimmy was wandering aimlessly around his apartment as he waited impatiently for the newspaper journalist to arrive. Checking his watch, he saw that he had another half hour before the interview. He decided to spend it productively by packing up the remaining few removal boxes ahead of his move to more modest accommodation on 27th December. Charles had not wanted to leave him alone but Jimmy insisted he go that morning to spend Christmas with his ailing mother in Surrey. He had promised to join them later in the day though, to be honest, he would much rather be alone this Christmas. How could the year have ended so calamitously having begun so well?

His melancholy was cut short by the door buzzer and Jimmy was soon joined in his riverside apartment by a journalist and photographer from one of the country's biggest selling tabloids. A substantial payment less commission had been brokered by Tommy, but it was making only a modest dent in his massive debt. Tommy had initially advised against a kiss-and-tell, but on hearing who was responsible for

Jimmy's beating had immediately reconsidered. He'd played hardball with several publications before the deal was finally done.

The photographer prowled around the almost empty flat searching for a suitable portrait location as the journalist wasted no time in getting down to business.

'Where's the evidence?'

Jimmy was shocked by the abruptness of the question but now was not the time for regrets. Without another word he walked over to one of the few remaining pieces of furniture and pulled open the central drawer of his solid mahogany writing desk. Glancing at the faces smiling back up at him from the photograph he paused just for a moment before picking up the print and the tape. Handing them over to the journalist, she made no attempt to disguise her glee at the image of a young Jimmy Phillips with his hand resting on the inner thigh of a quite obviously delighted Ben Watson, his expectation most apparent. Both sat close together on a shabby sofa smiling innocently at the camera. Ben's arm was wrapped tightly around Jimmy's shoulder while holding up a plastic beaker of alcohol.

'Any without any kit on?' asked the journalist. Her question was met with a chilling glare.

'Just checking, don't worry, this is fine. Right, let's listen to the tape.'

Her editor had been burned by Ben Watson's acid tongue too many times before. The paper planned a front-page lead and at least two pages inside, maybe four, on Boxing Day. The festive season was a quiet period for news stories and so an excellent time to cause maximum damage to the government. Readers would be at home, bored by relatives, with no money for the sales, toys already broken or batteries flat and little else to do but look through the papers.

Listening to the tape and looking at the picture again, the

journalist couldn't believe her luck. Not only did macho Ben Watson bat for both sides but he was also responsible for a bit of gay bashing. Oh and his lover boy was none other than TV celebrity Jimmy Phillips.

Watching the journalist salivate at the covert recording, Jimmy felt underhand and grubby. How could it have come to this? But remembering his broken ribs and massive debts, he took a deep breath and poured himself an enormous brandy. Slowly, he walked back towards the sofa where the journalist was eagerly waiting with her spiral bound notebook and Dictaphone.

'Right then Jimmy, where do you want to start?'

69

Ben was in the back of the armoured Range Rover speeding from Downing Street to Chequers. He was trying not to listen to Julian's pleading conversation with Valerie and instead mulled over the impact of his three point plan. It was going as well as could be expected.

None of the women were talking and so the press could do little but speculate about the Prime Minister's infidelity. Ben was sure that Sally would say nothing. Having looked into Isla's eyes as he helped disentangle her from the fireguard, he was confident she would be too spooked by the whole experience to fuel the flames. So, it was just rumour and speculation. No serious blows had yet landed on his boss. Well, apart from Sally's right hook, but the swelling had almost gone.

The chancellor had been pissed to be biffed but had been suitably placated with the job as foreign secretary. *The Daily Express* had found the elderly ladies a new nursing home and the shadow health secretary was already sweating in anticipation of his meeting with the boss, scheduled for the first week of the New Year. He wouldn't be having much of a Christmas. Ho Ho Hum.

Yes, everything was under control. The final part of the plan involved Valerie agreeing to a sit down interview and playing happy families later today. Up to now she wasn't playing ball.

She had spent the earlier part of the week steadfastly refusing to even take her husband's phone calls. Her determination had caused serious embarrassment to staff who had been instructed she should not be disturbed by her husband. Julian had been hopeful that the presence of Sheila, Frank and Monty would soothe his incandescent wife but unfathomably it had only fuelled her anger further. Only the return of the children from his parents had finally seen a thawing of the Ice Age conditions and she had grudgingly taken his call as he headed back to Chequers.

'I know that, my love,' Julian paused as he tried to turn his back to Ben but was hindered by the seatbelt.

'But you are my love, my only true love, and I want to call you that. I know you are paying a heavy price for my despicable behaviour. I completely understand the concern and embarrassment I have caused to everyone, truly I do. Please, please, please believe me when I tell you that I am determined to save our marriage. I will do anything, everything I can to make that happen.'

Julian held on to the phone for a moment or two longer. He was desperately trying to save face but Ben had clearly heard Valerie scream abuse before quite obviously slamming down the phone.

'That went well then, boss. The sit down chat should be a piece of cake later. Good job I made sure *HND* weren't sending Isla, eh?'

Valerie glared into the dressing table mirror and tried to calm down. As she blew her nose and wiped away yet more tears, she was distracted by a gentle tap at the door. It was the unmistakable rat-a-tat that had woken her every day for school when she was a child.

'Come in, Mum.'

Frank and Monty were down in the Great Hall putting the finishing touches to a Treasure Trail around the house and gardens for tomorrow. Dominic was helping while Jessica held on to Bruce who was confused by a real tree indoors and had already soiled two unidentified parcels.

'Hello love. How are you? Mind if I sit with you for a bit?'

Valerie nodded and eased to the edge of her dressing table stool making room for her still trim mother to squeeze beside her. Sitting down, Sheila took hold of both her daughter's hands and began to stroke the top of Valerie's fingers. When she eventually spoke, her tone was measured and maternal.

'I have something to tell you our Valerie and I want you to be calm and say nothing until I've finished. OK?'

Valerie was alarmed by her mother's words. Fearing there was a problem with Monty she instantly forgot her own worries.

'Of course, what is it mum? Is it our Monty?'

'No love, it's about Julian. I'm afraid I've known for a while about what he's been up to. I knew about that Sally woman and I knew about that young girl off the telly. There have been lots of others before that too.'

Valerie snatched her hands away and leaped to her feet. She stared open-mouthed at her mother. What was she saying, how could she know? She began to shake and wanted to run but didn't know where to. Sheila had expected the reaction and reached out to calm her daughter. Taking her hands, she waited until Valerie sat down again before continuing.

'I never said anything before because I was sure he would come to his senses. I thought he might realise what he had with you and Dominic and our Jessica. When we were in

408

South Africa, I knew what he was doing when he wasn't with us. I knew where he was and who he was with. It was hard work keeping it to myself. It's been a heavy burden but I was praying it would be worth it in the end. Your dad knows nothing of this and neither does our Monty.

'But I can't keep my silence any longer. Not after he embarrassed you by inviting both those hussies to your house love, and them behaving the way they did. Their mothers should be ashamed.'

Valerie was spinning. She had so many questions to ask but seemed to have lost the power of speech. Rubbing the top of her thighs over her silk wrap-over dress, she began to shake with confusion. Sheila hugged her tightly and waited before reading her daughter's mind and continuing.

'I suppose you're wondering how I could possibly know what that philandering husband of yours has been up to, aren't you?

'Well, do you remember Gayle Honeyford who I used to teach geography to in 12G?'

Valerie nodded, not sure what Gayle Honeyford had to do with her husband's infidelity. Had he been sleeping with her too?

'Lovely girl. Anyway she rang me out of the blue about three or four months ago. I thought she was calling to ask about our Monty after his accident, but she wasn't. She asked if we could meet for a coffee next time I was in London. Remember when I came down to go to our Dominic's school? I went to see her after that. Anyway, I met her at that lovely hotel, just on Hyde Park Corner there, what's it called, erm The Lanesborough? We went and had afternoon tea, which was really lovely and very reasonable for London prices. I was happy with the one without the champagne but Gayle wanted one so I ordered it too and she had mine.'

Valerie was exasperated by her mother's ramblings but

was too shocked to interject. Sheila though knew that the more she talked the calmer her daughter would become. As Valerie eventually quietened and leaned against her mother's shoulder, Sheila meandered towards the conclusion.

'Anyway, it turned out that Gayle needed both glasses of champagne. Eventually she told me exactly what Julian had been up to. Who with, where and when. She said she didn't know how you would react and that's why she was telling me and not you. She's always been a decent girl that Gayle Honeyford.'

'But mother, come on, seriously. This is just nonsense. Gayle confiding in you doesn't prove that Julian was having an affair, let alone a string of them as she suggests.

'Honestly, how on earth would someone you taught Geography to in Lancashire 20-odd years ago know the dates and times of my husband's alleged infidelities?'

Valerie again leaned her head on her mother's shoulder, disbelieving and exhausted. Sheila paused and put her hand on her daughter's knee.

'Oh love, I know he never invites her anywhere and to be honest I hadn't made the connection until she rang me out of the blue. Gayle Honeyford moved down to London when she married Ben Watson.'

70

Isla shuffled nervously in her seat in a third floor suite at the media-friendly Soho Hotel. She had taken the unilateral decision to kiss-and-tell without any guidance from her employers, knowing they would certainly have warned against it. But Isla no longer cared. As she chatted to Camilla the morning after the Chequers fight, 'Slappergate' as the papers had called it, Isla knew this was the way she wanted her revenge. The way Ben had portrayed her in the press had further steeled her to reveal everything about her love affair with one of the most powerful men in the world. A man she had loved passionately and a man she had been convinced, loved her just as much.

Padi Frieth had convinced Isla that the hour long sit-down was the right thing to do to help put the record straight. She said the interview, guaranteed a massive audience, would be broadcast on Christmas Day instead of the *Two Ronnies*, whoever they were. As she looked across at Piers Morgan, Isla yielded to his charm.

'Tell us why you've decided to speak about what happened, Isla?'

'Well Piers, there were four of us in this marriage . . .'

411

71

Bruce's excited yapping and impromptu piddle announced the arrival of his master. The rest of the family were downstairs and they all rushed to the door, including Monty, who narrowly missed stepping on the dog.

The eight-page exposé in *Celeb* magazine yesterday had not been mentioned. Frankly there were bigger issues than whether Monty had behaved improperly by exposing his friend's coke habit. The media had been divided. Some felt his actions underhand and duplicitous. Others, with the help of a crisis management company employed by Monty's agent, had thought he had acted in the best interests of his buddy. Charlie had headed to the Priory Clinic for Christmas only pausing to thank his friend for helping him see the error of his ways. No one seemed to care where Julia was.

'Daddy, we've missed you. Thank goodness you're back for Christmas. I was really worried you were going to stay in London.

'Daddy what's going to happen about last . . .'

Dominic dug Jessica in the ribs. She had been meticulously briefed by both sets of grandparents not to bring up last week and there she was ploughing straight in with their father only just through the door.

Thankfully Bruce's presence offered an immediate distraction as he excitedly rooted out any attention.

'Julian, hi. Our Valerie's upstairs with Mum,' said Monty.

72

Stephen James was with the *HND* film crew at a nearby pub waiting for a call from Ben Watson. He had been keen to wait at the end of the driveway for the PM's convoy to arrive from London but the idea had been mooted by Bob, the cameraman, who had pointed out that the PM's close protection team wouldn't be too pleased to have the press hovering around. So a pint for Bob, a half for Colin, the sound recordist, and a lime and soda for Stephen had turned into a couple while they waited for the call that would confirm or deny a pre-recorded Christmas morning interview with Julian and Valerie Jenson. Carole Smith was also with them. This was a massive interview for the channel and she was taking charge.

Michael Grifton had been furious at Isla's public antics and had immediately fired her when he heard she had been interviewed by Piers Morgan. Why would she do a kiss-and-tell? If she was going to anyway, then why with another channel and not *HND*? His greatest irritation: the gaping wound to his macho pride that she had chosen Julian Jenson over him. Isla's six month contract had been due for renewal and she'd been in line for a promotion but Slappergate had put paid to all that.

For once Carole couldn't sympathise with the youngster who had played with fire once too often. Sleeping with your boss was one thing but sleeping with one of the most powerful men in the world at the same time was quite another. On top of that, going to a party at his country home where you knew his wife would be, that wasn't just playing with fire, it was stepping into a furnace.

Isla had been devastated by the decision not to renew her contract. No amount of chocolates and tissues in Carole's office yesterday had been able to console the young reporter. She had left the building sobbing, embarrassed newsroom colleagues heads down as she walked towards the exit. It was a learning curve so steep she had a nose bleed but Carole was sure Isla wouldn't be down for long. Maybe the interview with Piers would help? Certainly the cheque would.

The long awaited call eventually came from Ben and the crew headed out into the light snow to drive the short distance to Chequers. Carole sat in the back of the crew car with Stephen, talking him through the interview.

'Remember, it's not a heavy-duty political interview, Stephen. We want to know what Julian Jenson the man has to say for himself. Our viewers would like to hear an apology, not only to his wife but also to the public for his appalling behaviour. Has Valerie forgiven him? If not, then why should the public? He'll try to suggest the newspaper headlines were hyperbole. Bollocks. We know what Isla's said. We want to nail him on how he managed to hide a string of tawdry affairs. We also want to know what he plans to do next, whether he feels he's weathered the storm. He's good and will give you the run around, but you're better buddy.'

Stephen James nodded a little aloofly but was secretly relieved that Carole was with him. There was no better producer in the business and in less than thirty seconds she

415

had summed up everything that was required from one of the most important interviews of his life.

Arriving at the great oak door they were ushered through to the Hawtrey Room where Winston Churchill had broadcast many times during the Second World War. Bob was shown the exact spot where he could set up his camera. Carole was aware from her research that one of the stipulations from the Lee family who had gifted Chequers was that it was not to be used for official business. She had read about the stained glass window in the Long Gallery which bore the inscription:

This house of peace and ancient memories was given to England as a thank-offering for her deliverance in the great war of 1914–1918 as a place of rest and recreation for her Prime Ministers for ever.

In other words, Ben Watson was taking a big risk by allowing the interview to go ahead at Chequers. He must be rattled, thought Carole as she wandered over to soothe Stephen who was starting to pace. She needed him to be calm and incisive, not overwhelmed as he was threatening to become.

73

Julian had taken Monty's hint and headed straight up the stairs to see his wife. The rest of the family had been herded out on to the croquet lawn to play in the snow, which was now falling more heavily. Bruce was confused and excited by the fluffy stuff floating onto his wet nose.

'No, no, no, a thousand times no, I will not do it. I hope I am making myself clear. No.'

'But my darling, I am truly, truly sorry for what I have done, what I have put you through. You need to give me the opportunity to make amends. We just need to get this silly little interview out of the way. Then we can spend Christmas together as a family and I can show you that those women meant nothing to me. There is very little in their ridiculous claims. I admit I flirted with them, you know that I'm a flirt darling. I am sorry if they thought it was more than that, but it wasn't. I am a one-woman man. I promise, hand on heart.'

Until about an hour ago, Valerie would have believed her husband's lies, would have yielded and succumbed to his legendary silver tongue. That was before her heart to heart with her mother, a woman who did not lie, who only had Valerie and her grandchildren's happiness at the centre of

417

her world. Valerie would not betray the confession by Gayle to her mother, but neither was she prepared to sit with her husband on TV, condoning his behaviour, his lies.

Unannounced Ben marched into the room.

'If you don't mind Ben, I was in the middle of a private conversation with my wife.'

Valerie knew that Julian's artificial annoyance at the interruption was purely for her benefit and sighed her dissatisfaction at his attempt to manipulate her.

'Right people we have a very big problem. I need you both to listen very carefully.'

Ben's tone was sincere, no sign of the usual cheeky chappy delivery. It immediately focused the attention of the warring couple.

'I just had a call. That bitch from *HND* has done a kiss-and-tell. She sang like a canary and even had the audacity to quote the Diana line about "three of us in this marriage" except in this case, there were . . .'

Ben paused, embarrassed.

'But it's not true Ben, take out an injunction. I'll call Vanessa Lewis right now.' Julian was desperate to carry on the pretence.

'Prime Minister, we are past that. We need honesty. We are in the shit.'

Julian sat on the edge of the marital bed, crestfallen, his head in his hands, shoulders hunched against his bent knees, finally realising the game was up. Valerie refused to even look in her husband's direction and merely shrugged.

Looking at the embittered pair, Ben knew he had to act quickly. The crew was setting up downstairs. Damage limitation against Isla's Christmas Day broadcast was the only option now. He needed to coach them on what to say and do it quickly.

'Julian, this is career threatening. You need to apologise

418

publicly to Valerie for your infidelity. You need to say you were overwhelmed by the burden of office. You were struck by bouts of depression which caused you to act in a manner that was both out of character and self-destructive. Valerie has forgiven your . . . hmmm, indiscretions. As a family you will pull together and in time hopefully start to repair the damage.'

Julian raised his head and looked towards his stone-faced wife.

'Valerie won't do it, Ben. I have begged and pleaded but she just won't.'

Valerie glared at her pathetic husband.

'Not five minutes ago you were assuring me it was all lies, now you tell me otherwise and still you want me to appear on television as a loyal wife? It will not happen. Ben, please tell the crew to leave.'

She spat the words. Ben turned to face her.

'Now then princess, I'm not sure this holier-than-thou attitude is completely appropriate from you of all people. It's not that long ago that a pair of pyjamas and a gin bottle were your best friends. And let's not forget who tried to top themselves when their teenage daughter was in the next room.

'Julian stood by you then. Look what happened as a result with the help of a loving, mostly faithful husband. Julian supported you when you needed him most, now it's your turn Mrs Jenson. Don't let it be too late.'

Valerie showed no flicker of emotion as the stark details were underlined. Ben pressed on.

'Valerie, I know this would be the hardest thing you could ever have to do. Your husband has cheated on you and one of his lovers is about to confess every sordid detail to the nation.

'But if we don't fight back, this will be the end of Julian's career. If you don't stand by him then the British public certainly

419

won't. He'll be crucified by the press and while you probably think that's what he deserves at the moment, trust me you won't always feel that way, but by then it will be too late.'

Julian stifled a sniffle. Valerie continued to stare straight ahead.

'Valerie, we can talk again about the next steps after Christmas but please, please don't underestimate how important your role is right now.

'This interview would be broadcast tomorrow morning, before Isla McGovern's confession. It will help offset some of her stronger claims, but only if you agree to stand by your man. And if you don't want to do it for Julian, then do it for the children. After the year they've had, don't they deserve a decent Christmas without drama or distraction? What do you say?'

Ben left the question hanging and neither man said another word, both looking pleadingly in her direction. Valerie ignored them and instead sat for a long time considering the case for the defence. Ben had a point. The children did deserve a break as did the rest of the family. It had been quite a year. But how could she possibly be at the side of this man who had put her through so much, made her feel so worthless. She'd thought their marriage difficulties were all her fault and only now did she finally know the truth. How could he? A thousand thoughts washed through her mind and finally, reluctantly she faced her biggest dilemma. Despite everything that had happened, did she still love him? Valerie subconsciously fondled her wedding ring. What was the right thing to do for everyone?

Eventually, she picked up her hairbrush and tidied her appearance in the dressing table mirror before reaching for a lipstick and slowly applying a clear gloss. Her emerald-green, silk, wrap over dress looked suitably festive. Standing up and heading towards the door she spoke over her shoulder in a monotone.

'Let's do it before I change my mind.'

74

Julian settled nervously into a winged armchair by the fire in the Hawtrey Room. Valerie did as she had been told to by Ben and refusing the chair set out for her instead sat on the arm of her husband's chair, close to him, resting her hand on his muscular shoulder. The perfect forgiving wife. Mrs Hubble had made sure refreshments were available and Valerie took a sip of iced water as Colin attached personal microphones to her and Julian before concealing them under their clothing.

Bob checked the framing of his shots through his camera viewfinder as Carole chose a seat where she could watch the couple interact. Their body language was likely to say more than any words could and she didn't want to miss anything. As the crew made their last minute checks for the historic interview, Julian looked up at his wife.

'I love you my darling, thank you,' he mouthed.

Valerie's rictus smile stayed in place. Carole could feel the first lady's fury, but there was also a sense of inner calm. What could that mean?

Oblivious, Stephen James took a seat opposite the pair and waiting a moment for everyone to be ready, he began.

'Prime Minister, it's been quite a week, how do you feel?'

Julian took a deep breath and squeezed his wife's hand, which was still resting on his shoulder.

'Stephen. Where to start? I hang my head in shame. I am deeply embarrassed. My selfish, thoughtless actions have caused crippling pain to the people who loved and trusted me the most. Everyone is paying a devastating price for my appalling behaviour.

'But let me tell you this Stephen, I can hand on heart say how truly sorry I am for my infidelity.'

Pausing, Julian looked dewy-eyed up at Valerie before continuing.

'I am deeply aware of the heartache that my beautiful wife must feel. I have no right to expect her to stand by me after the injury I have caused, but here she is. Here she is.

'I have begged her forgiveness and promised that I will work tirelessly to try to repair the damage that I alone have caused to our marriage. I thank God that she has found it in her heart to give me another chance.'

Carole couldn't believe what she was hearing. Despite Isla's interview she still expected a robust denial rather than a humble confession. Stephen was in shock and seemed to be dumbstruck by the admission. He glanced across to Carole for guidance. She nodded her head towards Valerie for a reaction.

'Mrs Jenson, so many of our viewers will understand your pain. Not all of them would have been quite so forgiving. What helped you excuse your husband's behaviour?'

Valerie paused for a moment and eased her hand around the back of her husband's neck draping it onto his other shoulder. Even Ben was impressed with the image of the perfect, forgiving wife.

'Oh Stephen, make no mistake, Julian is most certainly not excused.'

Ben gasped, Carole remained focused. Here it comes.

'The last few days have been very, very tough. I have to be honest with your viewers. There've been tears, lots of them. We have shouted and we have cried but despite everything we have never hated. I love Julian. I have and will continue to be faithful to him for as long as we are married.

'As your viewers know, my husband has wonderful leadership skills and relates superbly to other people. Unfortunately, rather too well to some people of the opposite sex.'

Ben was relieved, forgiveness and humour. They were going to get away with it after all.

'After the many tears and recriminations of the last week eventually stopped, I asked my husband if he was still in love with me. He reassures me that he is.

'That love, Stephen, is a solid foundation for us to try and start to rebuild the relationship we have shared for the past 20 years. We have decided we want to honour our vows and work together with our families to make this marriage last.

'So, Stephen it is true that after sleepless nights and much soul searching, I have decided to forgive my husband his indiscretions.'

Valerie leaned forward to kiss Julian who had adopted his most persuasively contrite face and kissed his loyal wife's hand in return. She further responded with a squeeze of his shoulder.

With the job done Ben was keen to hurry the film crew away.

'OK, Stephen, the Prime Minister and his wife have much to discuss so if we could end it there.'

But with the red camera light on and Bob still rolling Valerie had one more comment to make.

'Finally, Stephen I should just add that this is not a short-term fix. We realise that it will take not just love, but also patience and a great deal of effort from both of us to save

423

our marriage. We have spoken late into the night and again this morning about the best way forward.

'After much soul searching my husband has decided that nothing is more important to him than his family. Therefore, and with great reluctance he feels he needs to take an indefinite break from politics. With that in mind he will step down as Prime Minister with immediate effect.

'To illustrate his love and regret for what has happened Julian wanted me to be the one to make the announcement to the British public.'

'Sweet is revenge, especially to women'
Lord Byron

WIN A PAIR OF DESIGNER SHOES WORTH £500

To celebrate the publication of *First Ladies*,
we're offering you the chance to win your
own pair of killer heels worth £500.*

The prize, for one person, enables you to choose a pair of designer
shoes of your choice. So, whether you fancy a pair of Christian
Louboutin peep toes, Isabel Marant court shoes or classic
Jimmy Choos, you'll find the perfect footwear for you.

Log onto **www.harpercollins.co.uk/firstladies** to enter